Nightmares of Terror

Nightmares of Terror

by
KEN R. ABELL

RESOURCE *Publications* · Eugene, Oregon

NIGHTMARES OF TERROR

Resource Publications
An Imprint of Wipf and Stock Publishers
199 W. 8th Ave., Suite 3
Eugene, OR 97401

Scripture taken from the HOLY BIBLE, KING JAMES VERSION, Public Domain.

www.wipfandstock.com

ISBN 13: 978-1-4982-1965-5

Manufactured in the USA.

For my maternal grandmother, Geraldine Naomi Major, a woman whose profound grasp of otherworldy goings-on wove its way through fascinating oral history lessons. Her supply of tales gleaned from family and friends had a serious impact on my worldview.

&

For Anita Irene, who in a once upon a time long ago, listened to the bright-eyed imaginings of a socially awkward foreigner. The razor's edge of her beauty and toughness cut away the fluff, and across the years and miles, we've dreamed our dreams together.

&

For our sons and grandchildren. May they acquire the discernment to understand that the barrier separating the natural world from the supernatural realm is ofttimes paper thin; in response to that wonder, may they have the wisdom to honor the One who is sovereign over all.

&

For my friend, Baby Lion, a courageous warrior of a man who, without ever knowing it, inspired many ideas for storylines. He fought the good fight, finished the race strong and won the prize whilst this novel was being written.

Contents

ALSO BY KEN R. ABELL

Nonfiction

An Ordinary Story of Extraordinary Hope

Fiction

Days of Purgatory
Shadows of Revenge
Echoes of Evil

Websites

www.wantedman.org
www.danceswithcorn.com

Acknowledgments

I FIRST MET Kathi Ellicott around a table littered with pizza boxes. It was an informal job interview in a whole other century—I was the applicant and she was one of the six inquisitors. All went well. We had serious discussions, but as I recall, we also engaged in a fair amount of cracking wise. I remain thankful for that meeting and the long-term consequences of it. I am extremely grateful that after all these years Kathi still freely applies her school marm gift of copyediting on my behalf. Kathi and her husband Jim, along with the other five folks at that table on a long ago evening, are prominent amongst those mentioned below.

No one ever arrives anywhere without being encouraged or influenced by fellow sojourners encountered in both bleak and cheery locales. On the trail I've traveled, the blessings of friendship has found me in uncountable numbers. I owe much to kindred souls who shared stories and snippets of life that made me laugh, cry, or quite literally, scared the hell out of me. If you glimpse a slice of yourself in any of the fictional characters or situations, I plead the fifth and blatantly steal from the onetime Robert Zimmerman: *Don't think twice, it's all right.*

chapter one

Dreams & Visions

"And it shall come to pass afterward, that I will pour out my spirit upon all flesh; and your sons and your daughters shall prophesy, your old men shall dream dreams, your young men shall see visions . . ."

~JOEL~

THE MAN WAS IN agony. His head throbbed as though in the vise-grip of a tourniquet. The noontime sun was scorching, but darkness enshrouded him. He was staked out on a rocky knoll of desert terrain, arms and legs akimbo, and stretched as taut as possible. His bones were like melted wax, his shoulder and hip joints aflame.

Pain, as constant as a mighty river, flowed through nerve endings all over his body. Vile slashes across his chest and back seeped a continuous discharge of blood. He remained stiff and still, refusing to strain against the leather thongs strapped around his wrists and ankles. The sunrays were relentless; the flayed skin of his torso was being seared to a shriveled crisp.

Death shadowed him, but a surging will to live swelled in his veins. There were crows squawking somewhere. He heard the caws go back and forth, but had no comprehension of the song being sung. The dancing foot-steps and mocking chants of his tormentors seemed to be in rhythm with the notes struck by the flock of blackbirds.

The rag of his shirt was in tatters on his oversized shoulders. His lips were blistered and bleeding. His shaggy hair and wildman beard were crusted with blood, sweat and grime. He knew not the number of those who had come against him and now held him captive, but understood the braves were commanded by a boom-voiced warrior.

He sensed that his days of being beaten and made sport of were near an end. The nattering of his captors was becoming increasingly agitated. He felt hands loosening and twisting the stick that leveraged the knot on the bandana pressuring his temples. The odor of tobacco was thick in his nostrils and gagging at the back of his throat. The blindfold came off in a rush and sunlight stabbed at him. His eyelids shuttered into a flapping squint.

"Aarg," growled the Ute towering over him. A yellowish grin parted his lips and his head tilted at a grotesque rightward angle. His left eye was sick and milky; it pulsed as it fixated on the tortured man. "I will leave you here to die and be food for my crows."

It was then that Deacon Coburn came awake, sweating and shaking. He sat up and swung his legs out from under the covers. His head ached and disorientation gripped him. The deformed eye lunged from the recesses of the dream and he recoiled; fourteen years had passed since the ordeal, but the grayish-white orb lurked in his memory to haunt him.

He grit his teeth until the ghoulish imagery retreated to its lair. He prayed by calling upon sentiments written by a king of ancient Israel. "*O God, thou art my God; early will I seek thee: my soul thirsteth for thee, my flesh longeth for thee in a dry and thirsty land, where no water is.*" He soothed the tension by massaging his forehead. "*My soul followeth hard after thee: thy right hand upholdeth me. But those that seek my soul, to destroy it, shall go into the lower parts of the earth. They shall fall by the sword: they shall be a portion for foxes.*"

It would be hours before dawn arrived. The room was as dark as a pit. He got up and adjusted his skivvies, then lit an oil lamp and placed it on the dresser. The brightness chased a wedge of night away as the flicker cavorted in the mirror. He stared at his reflection. Sadness tugged at the lines of his face and he fingered the scars that crisscrossed his chest. The intersected pattern of lumpy tissue was replicated on his back.

A chill passed over him and his skin prickled. He grabbed a blanket, wrapped it around his shoulders and padded across the room. He shoved a high-back cushioned chair close and pulled back the drapes. Fresh air eased into the second-story room. He put his rump on the seat and slouched so that he could prop his feet up on the windowsill.

He settled into what had become a favorite nighttime position. In recent days, sleep often eluded him. Three or four hours of shut-eye had become normal, but instead of being frustrated, he put the circumstances to work for him by practicing the discipline of solitude. Many fourth watches of the night found him gazing out the window and meditating.

Just now, the discomfort in his head was receding, but sorrow and a sense of loss skittered in its wake. The visitation from yesteryear had jarred loose fragments of regret that resided below the surface of his stoic bearing. His conscience spiked and he felt lonesome to the bone. The smiling face of the only woman he had ever loved came floating out of the past.

Angela Langton. He closed his eyes and remembered. What first came to him were the evenings after supper when they would play cards or board games. There was an easy warmth and connection between them; a like-minded give and take developed the foundation for a friendship that became something so profound that it stirred their souls.

Though they were both broken and vulnerable, she rescued him. Her acceptance was unconditional. She presented an opportunity that was much more than mere companionship; she offered a life and a home. On a bitter cold February night, in a longing search for meaning, she gave herself to him. Their lovemaking was delightfully tender.

Then he left forever. He discarded her, but had not forgotten what they had shared, or the possibilities of what could have been. Neither did he ever let himself off the hook for his choices or actions. Despite embracing the forgiveness of God, guilt and remorse had been woven into the fabric of who he was; grieving at some level was a natural everyday occurrence. It kept his heart set on eternity, which among other benefits, caused him to be a giver of grace to others.

He dropped his feet to the floor and leaned forward, elbows on his knees. The coolness of autumn filled his lungs and he shook free of bygone times. Today held enough for him. His room overlooked the backyard of the boarding house, but the moonlight was dull so he couldn't see his garden. At first light he would be harvesting, then a walk to the train station awaited.

A visitor was due to arrive in Dodge City who would keep him busy.

The woman had already lost one baby. She was terrified. There were pale-skinned demons crouching in the corners of the room shrieking hideously at her. She cringed on the bed, an arm pressed over her swollen abdomen and the other held up as if to ward off the fiends. The presence of evil made the air creepy; frigid goosepimples swarmed over her.

Spasms clawed at and cramped the small of her back. She clenched her fists and cried. A contraction roiled through her midsection.

"No . . . no . . . no," she stammered, tears streaking down her cheeks. "Help me, Jesus. Please . . . please, help me, Jesus."

The malignant imps screamed laughter and pranced close to her. Their sharp-toothed smiles were gory slashes with bits of flesh clinging to disfigured lips. She resisted the foul forces writhing and reaching for her, but realized that any attempt to escape was doomed to failure because the beastly creatures formed a barrier between her and the doorway.

Her labor pangs increased. The baby was kicking, and it was as though her body wanted to take control. Her stomach was tightening into a fiery little ball. A contraction came with the intensity of a punch that knocked the air out of her lungs. There was a gushing release as her water broke. She gasped. Her legs and bedding were soaked.

She got up on her knees. Upon examination, she saw that she was bleeding. She sobbed and clamped both hands over her privates in a desperate attempt to stop the issue of blood and prevent her child from being born. It was as if she was forcibly pushing the baby up inside her. She hunched over and held on, her mouth distorting in a distressed grimace. A twinge originated in her back and rapidly became a convulsive wave that radiated through her.

The demons hovered over the bed and screeched in triumph, their voices rising and falling in high-pitched ecstasy. One of the hellions bent low and blew its wretched breath on her, and prepared itself to snatch the baby. "Your newborn will die. We will devour it."

"You will not take my child!" she hollered, fierceness cracking in her voice. She squeezed her legs shut. The ghastly brutes became a crushing circle that clutched at her. A ball of horror clogged up her throat as she shrank back, but the demons were undeterred. Bony fingers scraped and scratched at her. A brilliant white light flashed and encompassed the room.

Sally Twosongs awakened and almost tumbled out of the bed. She was greeted by the barking of a dog. She caught her balance and fear instantaneously departed because of the pure iron of faith that framed her outlook. The reoccurring nightmare, though awful and dangerous whilst she was inside it, had no sway over her. She sternly hushed Hank. The tricolor collie complied and whined in a friendly manner as it rubbed against her lower legs, which dangled over the edge of the mattress. She patted its head, then nudged it away.

Her eyes adjusted to the nighttime darkness. She sat up in bed and carefully lifted the nightgown to check down below. Her bloomers were in place; there was no bloody or watery seepage. A murmur of thankfulness whispered off her lips. She shifted forward, put her feet on the hardwood floor and clasped her hands over her hugely pregnant belly.

She was alone, except for Hank. She stood and stepped into moccasin slippers. Her movements were slow and methodical. She pulled on a housecoat and looped the belt loosely, then left the bedroom. Hank followed at her heels. She slipped through the empty house and went outside to sit on a loveseat rocker swing on the front porch.

Dampness in the air caused a shiver to scrunch her shoulders. She adjusted her backside and chaffed her forearms. *WT Ranch* was quiet and magnificent, like some medieval estate enclosed by a fortress of mountains. She took deep breaths and enjoyed the majestic panorama of the bluish-black sky; traces of wispy clouds scudded past millions of twinkling stars.

Hank paced anxiously, but never took its attention away from the woman. Its soulful eyes were expressive and persuasive. She pursed her lips to suppress a grin. After a few moments, she invited the collie to join her by patting the vacant seat. The dog wagged its tail, then jumped up and turned around awkwardly before settling with its head resting on her knee.

She sighed sadly. An upheaval of emotions plunged through her. She wanted to talk to her husband, but Caleb was gone. She was grateful for her bushy-haired buddy; especially now. The kinship she had with the animal helped her to sort through and process her feelings. Being by herself was never a burden before, but lamentable news had unleashed an upset of moodiness. She was stuck in a valley of heartache and there seemed to be no end to it.

The time of her childbirth approached, which set loose anticipatory joy, but underneath the miraculous marvel of new life, emptiness gnawed at her. Death had made a close encounter visit and she was missing someone. Nagging pain emanated from a giant hole in her heart. The sorrow hurt so much that she doubted she would ever get through it and recover.

There was a gaping disconnect within that had her seeking innovative answers to questions about the misery of mourning. Life was a blink in time and she knew that in the midst of bereavement there was hope; it might be fragile and illusive, but when grasped and nurtured, hope generated strength to overcome all obstacles.

A paradox had her imagination leaping. She knew that across the great divide there was the beauteous wonder of perpetual peace, but in these moments as she slugged it out with a jangled mess of ragged feelings, that knowledge provided no comfort. She thought about her father, Daniel Twosongs, the man from whom she had learned about the power of hope. He was wise and savvy, and those attributes were tempered by realism.

For him, the universal nature of humanity and the problem of life and death were worthy of contemplation and discussion, but when philosophy was exhausted, the crux of the matter was open and shut, and truly not debatable; the gift of life was to be cherished day by day because it was a foggy mist passing through the world on its way to eternity.

She yearned to spend a few hours with him to soak up his wisdom, but that would not happen any time soon. He was in his own hard place being tested and tried. She cuddled a hand around the dog's neck and ruffled it. "Why is my heart so heavy and lonely, Hank? Why should I begrudge anyone stepping over to the other side?" she asked in a whisper. "Heaven is our pure and golden inheritance. I should be rejoicing instead of blubbering."

Hank licked her hand, compassion in its eyes. An easterly breeze wafted, and the rustle of aspen leaves made her smile. The baby kicked or elbowed her. She altered her posture in a futile effort to be comfortable and began rocking. The rough timbers of the veranda's roof, to which the swing was connected, creaked. She listened to the squeaky groans and waited expectantly for the newness of hope which would be embodied in the colorful spectacle of the sunrise.

The girl was ten years old and scared out of her wits. Overwhelming fear kept nagging at her, but she determinedly resisted it. She had bawled and begged for mercy until she was hoarse, then in a burst of defiance, she became resigned to outlasting the punishment. She had endured being locked in the box numerous times, but on this occasion, the pitch-black of her surroundings hadn't changed in more days than she could tally.

She was hungry. The lining of her stomach was puckered and she was nonstop queasy. Dysentery had her bowels in an uproar of burning diarrhea. There had been no proper meal since her confinement in the cellar closet began. Every so often the door would open and a stale hardtack biscuit or wormy bowl of gruel would be placed inside, along with a tin cup of tepid water. No words were ever spoken by the delivery person.

The musty cubbyhole stank. Decay and mildew had formed an alliance with urine and excrement to create an acidy stench that permeated every breath she took. There was no lid on the overflowing chamber pot; it had not been emptied since her initial deposit. From previous experience she knew that when released, it would be her responsibility to dump it.

She was cold; her clothes were threadbare hand-me-downs that had a dozen or more owners before her. The neglect and mistreatment would not defeat her because there were seeds of toughness buried in the soil of her heart. Her routine of survival had her on the move as much as her failing strength would allow. She ignored the noisy uneasiness in her belly, and paced so incessantly that the dirt floor had ruts from her footsteps.

The thud of heavy boot heels were on the stairs, then the clodhoppers were thumping toward her. A creeper of anxiety caused her to begin biting on her bottom lip. She stood straight and tall, her back against the cool limestone wall, in preparation to be confronted by the superintendent of the workhouse, a mean-spirited biddy in her middle years.

There was a jingle of keys, then the door nearly slammed off its hinges. The large-bodied matriarch filled the doorframe, silhouetted by dim streamers of light. She had meat-hook hands which were lodged on the ledges of her hips. "Well, missy! Have you learnt your lesson?"

"Yes, ma'am."

"*Yes, ma'am,*" she mocked in scornful glee. Her flabby mouth wrenched into a smarmy sneer. "You stink like a pig. Have you been wallowing in your own waste?"

"No, ma'am."

"Clean up this room and make it smell flowery," the woman said, taking a lumbering step forward. "Then bathe. Dinner bell is in one hour. You best be in your seat when it rings."

"Yes, ma'am."

"You polite ball of snot!" The foul-breathed matron hurriedly charged at her. "I ought to smack you around for the sake of amusement. Knock you into the middle of next week just for fun." She raised a threatening fist and bellowed profanity, and in that instant, the contorted expression of the battle-axe transformed into the face of her mother.

Avis Lahay lurched up. She was sobbing. Her heartbeat pounded in her throat. The sheet was damp with sweat, and the blankets were tangled and clinging to her like living vines. She thrashed and wrestled free, then stood and immediately began walking to and fro alongside the bed. She tasted sourness and realized that what was real in the appalling throwback memory had actually happened in her sleep; she'd bitten her lip hard enough to draw blood.

A sliver of morning sunlight snuck through a crack in the curtains. The ground-level room in the boarding house was tiny and sparsely furnished. It had a bed and tallboy chest of drawers against one wall, and opposite was a hard-backed chair and pedestal-legged desk positioned in front of a window. She went to it and had a peek outside. When she spotted her mentor hard at it in his garden, a smile climbed up her cheeks and sparkled her eyes.

She sat and opened a leather-bound notebook, which was soft and engraved with a display of butterflies. It was the fourth edition of her journal. She typically made daily entries and seldom missed doing so. As she thought through ideas to share, she prepared the pen and ink well. She pressed her tongue against the inside of her bottom lip, then started writing.

September 15, 1882

Dear Diary: Again. I had the same nasty dream again. It never ends. The details are a true enough reenactment of a long ago reality, but its conclusion cuts me and is horribly unkind. It doesn't make any sense at all. Mom and I have an excellent relationship. I miss her and am looking forward to when she'll be coming to Dodge City.

I'm sure Deacon will be pleased to see her too. I expect Mom to be here by October, then before the snow flies we'll be taking the train back to Santa Fe. I have mixed feelings. Going home is entirely natural, but I will miss Deacon, Whitey, Sam and Abbey. I'm anxious to ride the rails, though I'm not sure whether or not Pumpkin will tolerate the stable boxcar.

The sun is hardly even up and Deacon is already in the backyard gathering baskets of potatoes, carrots and melons. He puts in an enormous amount of labor, then portions out all the produce to any and every one. I am blessed to have this time with him. He treats me with respect and is my protector. He makes me feel like a princess or something.

Maybe I ought to talk to him about my nightmare. It's disturbing and deeply personal, but we've gotten real close and I know that I can trust his counsel and wisdom. He rode alone to Santa Fe in the springtime so that we could travel here together. My first time on the trail was tremendously fun and it was beneficial to learn tricks and tactics from Deacon. He taught me much. I have high hopes of having the opportunity to ride with him again.

There is a full day ahead. After doing chores at the livery and caring for Pumpkin and Gilgal, I'm planning to have lunch with Whitey and then we're supposed to go riding together, but who knows? He is always occupied and so popular. Everyone demands a piece of him. Our intentions consistently get trashed or postponed because of his schedule.

Yesterday, while I sat watching him work, he told me that he doesn't care how busy the Tonsorial Parlor is or how many customers want his services, he's blocking out the whole afternoon for me. He's so much fun—that is whenever I can get to hang around with him. I am so glad that he's my special friend. Mom is going to get a laugh out of the fact that he's got me hooked on tea. He drinks some fancy blend and makes a big production of brewing a pot.

Sometime today I have to check in at the newspaper office. It often reminds me of a beehive buzzing with gossip and information. Despite all the deadlines and excitement in her life, Abbey has been schooling me in proofreading and how to do research.

*She is involved in a large project and I'm not sure how helpful I've
been, but I try as best I can.
That's all for now. I have to skedaddle.*

She closed the book and put the lid on the glass jar of ink. She reached
across the desk and made sure that the drapes were completely shut. When
she stood, she shed the nightgown and stepped free of it. She had no hesitancy or inhibitions, but rather, moved in a self-assured gait. She went to the
chest of drawers and gazed into the looking glass above it.

Her reflection was shadowy in the grayness, but she appreciated what
she saw. She had inherited the packaging of her mother's beauty; discovering the effect it had on men sometimes alarmed her because she possessed
layers of genuine modesty. Though fully aware of her shape, she did nothing
to highlight top or bottom. Her wardrobe, mostly ranch work clothes and
such, consisted of loose-fitting apparel that obscured her curves.

She brushed her wavy auburn hair until it was shiny, then tied it back
in a floppy ponytail. As she put on underclothes, her bottom lip started to
sting. She pressed it down and leaned close to the mirror to examine the
nick. She shrugged, then dressed quickly. Five minutes later she was in the
garden assisting her friend as he dug up the last of the potatoes.

In Las Vegas, dawn had come and gone, but at the Wyanhell Roadhouse,
four gamblers were unaware of the change from night to day. The town was
up and around, beginning to bustle as businesses opened and commerce
vaulted into gear. Citizens were out and about, but a poker game that began
in the wee hours still had plenty of steam to keep it going.

Ben Slaton, distracted and impatient, surveyed the front door while
nurturing a hot streak of luck, which was about to abandon him. The last
several pots had been his because he had uncanny audacity and was an exceptional bluffer. Now, he held one of those rare unbeatable combinations.
The fact that he had dealt the sequence to himself was a coincidence of good
fortune, or at least, that's the way he would tell it.

He aimed to make a clean sweep of the table, scoop up his winnings,
grab a plate of hot grub, then visit the bathhouse. After that, he was going to
find a woman who used to love him a lot. His hat was low on his forehead
shading his darting eyes. When he wasn't ogling the cleavage of Sassy Sue, a
partially clad whore tending to the bar, or obsessively observing the batwing
doors, he considered his opponents to glean an edge from their tells.

"Are we fishing or cutting bait, Slaton?" One-eyed John asked, puffing on a cigar. "You got your mind focused on the boardwalk like you're expecting Sonnyboy Jesus to walk on in."

"That ain't so," Ben replied tersely.

"Horse crap," Slick Willy said, slapping the table. He had a ruddy complexion and spoke in a girlish sing-song voice that didn't fit his block-bodied bulk. "It ain't Sonnyboy Jesus, is it, Slaton? The only reason you're in this rathole is because you're moonstruck and on the lookout for a wench who gave you the boot years ago. She's all you ever talk about and you're hoping she's going to sashay in here to give you a sloppy wet one and take you back."

"That's straight arrow true," Clem chimed in, glib and grinning. He was ferret-faced and had a prominent upper lip. He wore a pencil thin moustache, which he habitually stroked as though checking to make sure it hadn't relocated. "You're dead as a door nail lovesick."

"You could be right, boys," Ben said, scratching his stubbly chin. "I'm man enough to acknowledge the corn. I expect I made the mistake of my life with her." He leaned back, folding his cards over his belly. "If she'll give me another chance, I'm settling down with her."

"Well, whoop-de-frigging-do," One-eyed John sniped, scowling. "Ain't a one of us here interested in your pitiful lonely hearts story. Give me two cards." He put his rejects aside.

"Two for the half blind man," Ben quipped, flicking them to him.

"Gimme one," Slick Willy said, dropping a card on the table.

"I'll take three." Clem snapped his discards down. "Deal me sweetness."

Slaton finished passing out the replacements. "I'm sticking."

"Really?" One-eyed John queried, cocking his head. "You dealt this mess and you're sticking?" He fingered the rawhide string of his eye-patch. "A dealer sitting atop a pat hand might cause a hayseed to be suspicious and sure as shooting, I ain't no hayseed."

"You calling me a crook, pal?" Slaton coolly kept his composure. His eyes tightened into snake-like slits. "If so, you must be wanting to acquire six feet of real estate."

One-eyed John held steady. "I'll put you down like a sick dog."

Slaton slowly calculated the odds, then sudden-like, the batwing doors clattered shut. The downy hair on the back of his neck tickled. His lips curled in surprise as he gawked wide-eyed at someone he had been chummy with in another time and place. His eyes became snarky and bright even as his countenance hardened. "Looky here, it's Dogface Greer."

One-eyed John swiveled his head in the direction of the notorious outlaw, then almost tipped his chair over scampering out of the way. Slick Willy simply slumped back and took a gander at his cards. Sassy Sue scooted off a barstool and did a jiggling run into the kitchen. Clem fondled his moustache so aggressively that it was in danger of being erased.

Kid Greer didn't blink or show any emotion. Neither did he say a word. A plug of tobacco put a bulge in one cheek. He slouched lazily across the room, stoop-shouldered and slack-eyed; his thumbs were hooked into the front pockets of grimy dungarees. The brim of a dusty old hat and a feral thatch of straggly whiskers masked his features.

"Been awhile," Ben drawled, shuffling his cards top to bottom; bottom to top. He casually arranged them face down on the table. "You still a pussified piss-pot?"

The temperature chilled palpably, as if an arctic blast had swooped through the barroom. Greer stopped ten yards from him, hands hanging free and feet set languidly apart. There was gaunt deadness in his eyes. His gunbelt sat at a sloping angle between his waist and groin. The holster was tied down and the handle of the pistol tilted slightly forward.

Slaton moistened his lips. Perspiration beaded on his brow. His hands were flexing and twitching. He went for his revolver. Greer rocked back on his heels, drew the Smith & Wesson in a blur and caressed the trigger. Slaton was hurled backward when the bullet struck the bridge of his nose. His head exploded, filling the air with a splatter of pinkish goo and bone fragments. His arms flailed like a broken-winged bird and he toppled to the floor.

Kid Greer pounced on him, blade in hand. He took a knee and cavalierly hacked off his left ear. He stood, closed the jackknife and pocketed it, along with the flesh souvenir. He smirked and coughed up phlegm, then swirled it around his mouth with the chaw before depositing the slop on the dead man's shirt. He spun around and calmly strolled out of the saloon.

Slick Willy took hold of Slaton's cards and turned them over one by one. "A royal flush in hearts." He puckered his mouth and exhaled a muted whistle. "He palmed those."

"A bottom of the deck dirtbag," Clem said matter-of-factly.

"Kid Greer did the west a favor." One-eyed John crouched to examine the expanding puddle of glutinous gunk spreading over the floorboards. "He rid it of a lowlife cheat."

The old Mexican cook came out of the kitchen in a filthy apron. He had a cleaver in one hand and the other clutched around Sassy Sue's keister. The two of them joined the cardsharps around the corpse and chattered. Each eyewitness had a different version of the killing. It was nearly twenty minutes before anyone was clearheaded enough to send for the undertaker.

Hans Weitzel had been splitting wood since sunup. He stacked it systematically. The cord that currently had his concentration was designated as firewood for next winter so was being stockpiled to lose its greenness. There was nothing in his makeup that would allow him not to plan or be prepared. He completed the task to his satisfaction and put the tools away.

The air had crispness in it, but there had not yet been a frost this season. He stretched and arched his back to release a kink, then began the half-mile hike to the cabin. The woods were serene. He admired the yellow feather duster look of the leaves on the aspens that appeared to be battalions of sentinels at the base of the San Juan Mountains encircling *WT Ranch*.

He and Eliza had been in Colorado for two years. Their snug and efficient one-bedroom home, built with ponderosa pines, was situated on a level clearing along a slope several hundred yards away from the laneway that ran between the two main houses. The building site was chosen by Hans after studious deliberation of significant wind patterns. His wife valued the bird's-eye view of sunsets available from their front porch.

The scent of coffee and bacon caught his nostrils. He hurried along the rock-lined path and took the two steps onto the veranda as one. The door was propped open. He quietly slipped inside and soundlessly admired the wide hips of the willowy woman at the cookstove. After virtually thirty years of marriage she still had a serious effect on his heart-rate.

He crept up behind her. She glanced over a shoulder and gave him a cheerful smile, then kept on task flipping an omelet. He put his hands firmly on her waist, but that was not the final destination. His arms went around her in a demonstrative hug that lifted her feet off the floor. He raked her longish hair out of the way and bussed her neck.

"Do you want breakfast on a plate or spilled all over the place?"

"Just saying good morning, Eliza."

"It feels more like a bedtime embrace."

"Sap rises even in an old tree."

"Far be it for me to put a damper on our affection, but there's a fatal flaw with your metaphor," she told him, wiggling free and giving his chest a playful slap. "Sap runs and is active in the springtime, so shall we only enjoy each other at that time of the year?"

"Heavens, no. I withdraw my comment."

"Good. I will be waiting for you at nightfall," she said, then earnestly shooed him. "Now if you want your belly filled it'd be good to be gone from my kitchen."

Weitzel chuckled, eyes full of gratification. He poured a mug of coffee and took a seat at the table. A crease dug deep across his forehead as he became aware of a dog eared telegram received three weeks ago from Max

Dawson. The yellow paper sat in front of Eliza's usual chair. He cast a dubious look at her, then picked up the message and read it once more.

Gray Cloud tortured and killed by Smoky Crowe. We gave him a proper burial. Charley and I are presently on the evildoer's trail.

He pushed it back to where he had found it. "You best leave all this alone, Eliza. No amount of sorrow on our part will change what happened. We can't do anything."

"I realize that, Hans." She placed a stoneware dish in front of him. It was loaded with a bacon and cheese omelet, and had a mound of fried taters on the side. She brought her much smaller portion over and sat across from him. They held hands as their heads bowed in unison and she spoke unassuming words of thanksgiving. Amen was said together.

"Then why not put the telegram away for good?" he asked flatly. "Taking it out to revisit the ugly news every other day or so is not at all helpful."

"I'm sorry, Hans. I cannot stop thinking about poor Gray Cloud."

"He was a trustworthy friend and dependable worker."

"Gray Cloud was more than that to us and you know it, Hans," she said, sternness in her tone. She had a forkful of cheesy egg halfway to her mouth and was staring sad-eyed at him. "He was family. When we sold out in New Mexico and moved here we deserted him."

"No, Eliza. I do not accept that premise. It is unfair."

"We might have been able to protect him, is all I'm saying, Hans."

"Might haves are meaningless."

"Maybe so, but I still think on them now and then," she replied straightforwardly. "That doesn't make me flighty nor reveal a lack of faith, but rather, it means I'm human. Sorting through doubts and questions impossible to answer is part and parcel of life." Her manner became lively and teasing. "We all can't grind our emotions to the bone like you, Hans."

His eyebrows raised and a sly smile nipped at his lips. He had no argument with her assessment; in fact he acknowledged the rightness of it with a miniature nod. Ofttimes he knew that she understood him better than he could ever comprehend his own complexities. Silent gratitude for her intimate friendship, and enjoyment of her culinary skills was his response.

Brenda Hawkins had shock coursing through her. The sensation was overwhelming. She felt as though she was unraveling. Her blurry vision and muddled mind wouldn't allow her to process what was happening. She ran as fast as she could in the middle of the thoroughfare, dodging wagon and horse traffic. Her heartbeat hammered against her eardrums.

Shouts and exclamations were directed at her. A square-faced teamster loudly cursed her to damnation, but her only reaction was to keep running. She wore a conservatively cut maroon dress, but had the skirt yanked up to her thighs so she could lift her knees higher and harder. Her apple-dumpling cheeks were flushed; her eyes red-rimmed and watery.

A gaggle of gawkers near her destination scattered like birds flitting from one branch to another to avoid colliding with her. She crashed through the batwing doors of the Wyanhell Roadhouse and almost banged into Sassy Sue, who was in a hurry to get outside. Brenda reeled and staggered to a shaky stop, breathing rapidly as she smoothed down her skirt.

She forcefully pushed through a knot of gathered onlookers and got on her knees beside the body of Ben Slaton. Her stomach rolled over. His boyish good looks had been smashed to smithereens by the bullet; the back of his head was outcroppings of splintered bone. She touched his whiskery chin. "Why, Benny? After all these years why'd you come back here?"

The room seemed to be spinning. Voices were spewing out words that reached her ears as meaningless banalities. She was crying. Her chest heaved and shuddered as she tamped down a hysterical outburst clawing at her skull. She wanted to bellow at him, but what emerged was a whimper. "Why, Benny? No letter, no telegram, no nothing."

She crooked her head upward. Her soaked eyes were pleading and she flinched because the bystanders' faces were distorted. Their mouths were all moving and she heard Fernando, the greasy Mexican cook say, "Once upon a time, when she was a whore, she loved him."

When she was a whore. The phrase sliced her. She ignored the disgrace and shame. She bent forward to press a kiss against his ear. "You gave me a fine son, Benny. I'm sorry you never met him," she whispered, stifling a sob. Her heart ached with a heaviness that sank to her belly. It set off a splash of nausea, which crept up her throat and burned. Her eyes pinched shut and she laid her hands on his shoulders as her lips began moving with an ever increasing urgency.

Brenda Hawkins had learned how to pray.

$$\approx \approx \approx$$

On the boardwalk across the street, Sassy Sue was occupied entertaining a four year old boy. The dishwater-blonde had scooped him up in her arms and scuttled away from the crowd of spectators, who obviously shunned her and were not impressed by her attire. Her ankle-high boots, striped stockings, cream colored petticoat and matching camisole were shabby. She had fastened all the buttons and tied the ribbons tight, but the flimsy undergarment could not conceal the enticing swell of her well-endowed topside.

Sassy Sue would've had to be blind not to see the fingers jabbed at her, or deaf not to hear the derogatory remarks. The condemnation bothered her, but for the short-term she was able to slough it all off because she was naturally protective. To guard and care for a child she could willingly endure being ostracized by those who chose to pass judgment on her.

She sat on a bench with the towhead lad on her lap. Her hands had his arms crossed and locked around his torso like a straitjacket. He was grinning and squirming as she swayed side to side, singing softly in his ear. When the song ran out of verses and her resourceful creativity failed her, she wheeled him around and lifted him so that he stood balanced on her thighs.

"Who's my Bubbly Boy?"

"Me," he yelped, jumping a bit.

"And who am I?"

"Suey . . . Suey," he lisped happily.

She laughed and rolled her eyes. "Suzy, honey. Suzy." She sat him down and enfolded him in a secure clinch. She bounced him like a bucking horse for a while, but that soon lost its appeal and he tried to break free. It was then that she captured his imagination by pointing to the sky. They had a grand time prattling about the clouds changing shape above them.

Brenda Hawkins was numb and dry-mouthed when she sallied forth from the saloon. The undertaker came along and slipped past her to go inside. She stood at the hitching rail staring at nothing in particular. Stragglers were still milling around and questions were being asked, but she had no interest in talking to anyone. Her ears pricked up; she hearkened to her name being called overlapped by the chortling squeal of her son.

She whirled around. In the commotion and with her eyes bleary from moisture, it took several seconds for her to spot them on the other side of the avenue. She raced over and lifted the youngster onto her hip. "I told you to stay at the mercantile, Stace." Her face crinkled into a worried frown. "You're going to make your mama old before my time."

Sassy Sue got up and tousled his sandy hair. "He didn't see anything," she said, voice lowered to a conspiratorial level. "I came to his rescue and caught him."

"Thank you, Suzy. You're a good friend."

"I saw him following close behind you."

Brenda slumped onto the bench. Her body sagged in defeat. "I was charting inventory. Someone came into the store and shouted that Ben Slaton had been shot . . ." She covered her mouth. "I don't know what I was thinking. My mind went blank and I took off."

"What are you going to do?"

"I suppose I'm not sure," Brenda replied, exhaling a sigh. "Now there's really nothing here for me and Stace. I think we'll be moving on and make a new start someplace."

"Where?"

"Whichever way the stagecoach is going when we get on it."

"Brenda, I've got something to tell you."

"What is it, Suzy?"

Sassy Sue hemmed and hawed, acting skittish. "I was at the bar," she said hesitantly. She perched on the edge of the bench and crossed her legs. "The joint was quiet and empty except for the card game." Her eyes tensed nervously. "I overheard the conversation. Ben told them he made a mistake and if you'd have him, he was going to settle down with you."

"Are you saying that to try and make me feel better?"

"I heard what I heard," Sassy Sue answered bluntly. "And I wasn't the only one. You can go ask One-eyed John, Slick Willy or Clem. They'll tell you the same thing."

Brenda winced and shook her head. "I don't need to, Suzy. I believe you." Her thoughts were cluttered; she was unsure of what to do or how to feel. She let her boy climb down. He skipped off the boardwalk and squatted to draw lines in the hard-packed dirt of the street.

"You and Stace will be alright," Sassy Sue said, rising.

"Would you come to church with me on Sunday?"

"What?" Sassy Sue giggled derisively. "Where'd that come from?"

"Friends invite friends."

"That wouldn't be a good idea, Brenda."

"Why not?"

Sassy Sue made a shrugging gesture to hangers-on lingering across the way. "I can do without the holier-than-thou attitudes of all the righteous do-gooders in this town."

"Pay no attention to the dear saints," Brenda said, taking hold of her hand. "You can't allow others to hurt your heart or steal your hope. Rip a page out of my book. Keep your chin up and when you learn the hymns, sing them at the top of your lungs."

"I ain't got your courage, Brenda."

"Yes, you do, Suzy."

"Nope. I'll always be just a chirpy whore."

"The Lord has something much better for you," Brenda said decisively. Her lips curled in an encouraging smile and she shifted forward. "You won't be alone, I promise. I'll be standing near the steps waiting for you. We'll sit together, with Stace between us."

"Maybe." Sassy Sue shaded her eyes. "I have to go, you know?" She turned and abruptly departed. Halfway to the Wyanhell Roadhouse, she angled sideward to give a goodbye nod.

Brenda Hawkins waved amicably. She watched her son as he continued being amused by the marks he could dig or sketch. A rush of love flooded her senses. She decided there and then that no matter what, she would make any new beginning a big adventure for him. In the quiet chapel of her heart, she renewed a vow to always do right for her little man.

At six inches over six feet and just shy of three hundred pounds, Big Bull Wallace was a tycoon rancher appearing to be a walking mountain. He wore a gray ten gallon hat that made him seem even taller and broader, which was fine with him because he had a streak of rascal, and was not above using his girth to intimidate others if it suited his purposes. And make no mistakes; he was a singularly driven man, so his objectives were always primary.

Sixty years ago, he was born to Scottish immigrants in the Smoky Mountains of Tennessee. His parents named him Angus James, but long ago that had been discarded and forgotten. From the start he was bigger and stronger than his childhood peers. He was put to work on a hardscrabble hillside farmstead and grew up fast. He received the basics of an education from his mother and displayed a voracious aptitude for learning.

Puberty came early and by the midway point of adolescence he had reached his full height. The awkward gawkiness swiftly passed and he took command of his physical attributes. As his frame widened and filled in with muscle, he performed herculean feats usually reserved for beasts of burden, which sealed his lifelong moniker.

He carried himself with a sense of authority that was made manifest with each step. His body language never revealed any secrets. He was uncompromising, with skin similar to an alligator's hide, but underneath that calloused exterior beat a heart that had a special tenderness for the fairer sex and anyone he chose as a friend. His loyalty had no boundaries.

The train chugged into the Atchison, Topeka & Santa Fe Depot. On the platform he saw a man he hadn't seen in fifteen years, and immediately decided that except for a gray-speckled moustache and some extra wrinkles, his trustworthy associate hadn't changed at all. A smile extended its branches across Wallace's ruddy-cheeked face.

He latched onto a large leather satchel on the seat beside him; it was the only piece of luggage he had brought along. He customarily traveled light—three changes of clothes were plenty on the road because laundry services were readily available wherever he went. He waited until the other passengers disembarked, then stood and moved to the exit.

He had to duck and twist his body to get through the doorway and down the stairs. The sun was making its ascent to the top of a pale blue sky dotted by a smattering of thin clouds. He went straight to the man who, for over a decade, had been serving as the end of trail agent for the *Double B Ranch*. The men shared a nod and a hearty handshake fortified with respect.

"Good to see you, Deacon."

"Good to be seen, Bull."

Wallace let out a bellyful of hoarse laughter. "I'm pleased that I've not had to hunt down your corpse and put up a tombstone with the epitaph, *Here Lies A Crazy Man*."

Coburn chuckled knowingly. "I'm kind of gratified about that myself."

"So this here is Dodge City?"

"In all its glory."

"My first visit." Wallace dropped his bag and turned around to have a gander at the scenery and storefronts. "This hellhole better treat me like a king since I helped make it *Queen of the Cowtowns*. I've been herding and selling my cattle here for years."

Coburn smiled thinly. "We're all mighty appreciative of your altruism, Bull."

"Don't crack wise with me," Bull said, jabbing him. "I only came to this dust bowl to finalize a deal and settle accounts with Morgan Fletcher. If he has his ducks lined up, I'm going to be investing in a large tract of real estate somewhere in the vicinity."

"He was last here in March for a few hours between trains. We had a brief visit. He's a bit of a dandy and difficult to nail down," Deacon reported, sharp and direct.

"He's an entrepreneur. It's all about the profit margin."

"A telegram came for you from him the day before yesterday."

"Later, Deacon. It can wait," Bull said, leaning side to side to loosen some cricks. "My arse needs some recovery time. We'll talk and catch up on business matters later. First, I'm desperate for a shave and a haircut. Then I could use some decent whiskey."

"I'll introduce you to the finest barber in the country," Deacon replied, picking up the haversack. "While you're in his chair I'll sign the register and deliver this to your room at the Great Western Hotel. We'll connect afterwards. You'll have no problems finding me."

"Finest barber in the country, you say?"

"I guarantee it, Bull."

"You still studying the Good Book?"

"Everyday."

"Then your guarantee is bankable, Deacon."

"Kind of you to say." Coburn started walking. Wallace fell in beside him. They had to pause and give way to a fully loaded freight wagon moving speedily along Front Street. The driver had control of the reins and was calmly barking orders. When the roadway was all clear, the old friends crossed and stepped onto the boardwalk, heading to the Tonsorial Parlor.

Eliza Weitzel was enjoying the picturesque autumn day. Even though the sun was not yet high enough to bask the front porch in sunshine, the warmth was plentiful. The rocker creaked as she knit a blanket for her unborn grandchild. She was using store-bought pink and blue wool; the strands were interwoven in a neat pattern. When the coverlet was completed, she had plans to make some booties, along with a sweater and bonnet in the same colors.

She heard a dog barking, but ignored it. Her fingers kept diligent. The dog persisted and was obviously getting closer. She looked up from her handiwork. A startled noise caught in her throat. Hank was running friskily around Sally Twosongs, who was scaling the incline to the cabin at a brisk pace; much too hastily for her condition.

Eliza put the needles and wool in a handbag, then jumped to her feet and ran down the slope. She placed an arm around her back for support. "What are you doing, girl?"

"Just coming for a visit."

"Sally Twosongs! What am I going to do with you?"

"It's such a lovely day."

"You have to take it easy, young lady."

Sally Twosongs smiled soberly. "I have much on my heart."

Eliza held her hand and helped her the rest of the way. She got her settled in the rocking chair beside hers, then went inside and returned with a glass of water for her. "I want to respect your privacy and wishes, but you shouldn't be alone any longer, Sally Twosongs."

"Naomi will be over this afternoon and stay until Sunday."

"Don't you dare overdo it playing with Jesse and Amanda."

Sally Twosongs emptied half the glass, then placed it on the floor. Her eyes narrowed and she stared off in the distance for a long moment, seemingly engaged in her thoughts. When she spoke, her voice was disheartened. "I won't be doing any roughhousing with them."

Eliza was concerned. "What's wrong?"

"I am frustrated by happenings whilst I sleep," the Navajo woman replied, her fingers twined together over her swollen belly. "A nightmare has awakened me several times. I am on alert to understand the meaning of dreams and though fear is not present, I am certainly watchful and wary. It very clearly came to me that this revelation might be a warning."

"You must tell me about it."

"That's why I came, Eliza."

"I shouldn't have scolded you. I apologize."

"Was that scolding?" Sally Twosongs asked, grinning. "I only heard love."

"I'm glad."

Sally Twosongs rocked at a steady rhythm. Her expression became glum. Hank pressed close, then lay down at her feet. "I could still lose this baby. I can't shake that possibility." She related the details that disturbed her and ended by saying, "The demons were clutching at me. I was holding myself and squeezing to stop the child from being born."

Eliza shivered. She had no doubts about her daughter-in-law's heightened awareness of activities in the spiritual realm, but was also cognizant of the impact of stress and grief. "That's horrible, but not necessarily prophetic. There is sadness in your heart."

"I know."

"And many questions," Eliza said, an emotional quiver in her voice. "Your mother's passing from time to eternity came so suddenly. You are aggrieved and managing a multitude of feelings. You would be wise to mourn, for in doing so, you will be encouraged."

"I want to be strong and faithful."

Eliza reached over to gently rub her forearm. "You are strong and faithful, Sally Twosongs. It's not weakness to cry or be upset. On the contrary, it is entirely natural and completely necessary. Tears of sorrow are good for our souls because we receive reassurance from above. *Blessed are they that mourn: for they shall be comforted.*"

"Of course I cannot disagree, but it's difficult because I've had no closure," Sally Twosongs said emphatically. "I have an idea, though perhaps it's silly. As soon as can be done after the baby is born I want to visit Mother's grave and play songs on my flute for her."

"That's an excellent idea. May Hans and I come with you?"

Sally Twosongs beamed. Her cheeks filled with rosy color. "Yes, that would be pleasing to me. Caleb will appreciate it too, as would Father also, if he is around."

"Consuelo was dear to my heart," Eliza said, growing misty-eyed as she leaned back and rocked. "Our friendship was forged in adversity. She and I became closer than sisters while picking up the pieces and rebuilding our homestead after it was burned down."

"I remember. Caleb and I bonded in those days of troubles."

"From the ashes of heartache your relationship blossomed."

"The Creator worked his way through all that hardship." Sally Twosongs picked up the glass and finished off the water. She altered her position and shifted weight as she turned to fix her mother-in-law with a stare, and unexpectedly asked, "What's your full name?"

Eliza frowned, intrigued and puzzled. She hunched her shoulders. "My parents named me Elizabeth Joy. Up into early adulthood I was known as Beth, which changed the day I met Hans. He immediately called me Eliza. It irritated me at first, then I saw the determined set of his character and sensed the softness and respect in his voice. I've been Eliza ever since."

"Beth? That's interesting. Does Caleb know?"

"Yes. Why do you ask?"

"No special reason. I've just been thinking about stuff."

"What are you up to, Sally Twosongs?"

"Nothing!" she insisted, eyes widening. She pushed to the edge of the chair. Hank got up, stretched and let out a growling whine. "I should be on my way."

"Let me pray first," Eliza said warmly. "Then we'll walk together." She closed her eyes and folded her hands in her lap, and boldly entered the throne-room of grace. There was no hint of doubt or hesitancy as she opened her heart to the Giver of all good gifts. Her supplications for protection and provision were intense, couched in the language of thanksgiving.

"So you be Big Bull Wallace." Whitey Fitzgerald had comb and scissors in hand. He moved around the chair as lightly as a dancer, surveying his customer. His eyes were sparking and his face was consumed by a grin. "I've heard tales about you from Abilene to Dodge City, and some were so tall that I supposed for a while that you were just a made up man."

"I'm as real as real can be, young fella. Or at least I was the last time I checked," Bull said in a snickering rumble. "I hear tell that you're the finest barber in the country."

"That be dandy, but who'd of said such a thing?" Whitey asked, punctuating it with a snappy click-click of a laugh. "I be good, but I ain't sure I be the finest."

"Well get to it. I ain't got all day."

"Now you listen here, Mr. Big Bull Wallace," Whitey said, stepping back. "I can do a chop-chop job or give you the full treatment and make you pretty. What'll it be?"

Wallace nearly hacked up a lung in laughter. His face reddened and he clapped his hands as he wheezed asthmatically and stymied his mirthful tantrum. "Have at it, young fella. If you can make this grizzled kisser pretty, you're a better man than I'll ever be." He crossed his arms under the sheet and gazed at three cowboys waiting. "You gentlemen can watch a miracle."

"Don't be sacrilegious," Whitey said, wagging a finger at him. "I gets into enough snags with the Almighty all by my lonesome and don't need much help from others."

"The dickens you say?"

"I jest aplenty, but not in regard to the man upstairs," Whitey replied, making the scissors snap and sing. "I likes to keep the ledger as clean as possible, but if these here Tonsorial Parlor walls could yak, I surely be at least bellybutton-deep in trouble."

Wallace chuckled and rolled his eyes. "If the walls wherever I've hung my hat *ever* start talking someone better throw me a lifeline because I'll be treading water."

"It'd take a stout rope," Whitey said slyly.

"Not to worry, young fella. I cut a deal years ago," Bull countered, making a gesture that indicated he required a pause in the barber's clipping. "I have an understanding with the Almighty. I enjoy the living snot out of the abundance of life and most certainly cross the line quite frequently, but since I do the decent thing whenever possible, I got it set up so God will send me notice before I die to give me time to get the books squared away."

"I be sure it ain't going to be that way, Mr. Wallace."

"The name's Bull, Whitey," the cattleman gruffly ordered. "Only lawyers and politicians call me Mr. Wallace, as a prelude to picking my pockets or attempting to fleece me."

"Well then, Bull it is," Whitey said, and got back to cutting. His eyes twinkled as his hands moved with skilled swiftness. "I don't ever want to be mistaken for a shyster or a snake in the grass. You'd be a wise man not to get me started on lawyers or politicians."

Wallace balked and took the bait. "One time a lawyer and a skunk were shot and buried outside of Fort Worth. How could anyone tell which grave was which?" He cleared his throat before delivering the punchline. "The killer erected a tombstone for the skunk."

"I wouldn't know about such things 'cause I ain't ever been to Texas," Whitey replied, putting the instruments on a shelf below the large mirror. "But I can tell you this: From coast to coast burglars never rob politicians because of professional courtesy."

Wallace grunted. "Not too shoddy, but I can outdo that one easily enough," he said, poised and confident. "The difference between a lawyer and a herd of buffalo is that the lawyer charges more." He leaned back and thrust his jaw out, readied to be lathered up. "And when looking for politicians, you can find a good one in a box at the funeral parlor."

Fitzgerald brushed the soap into foam. As he dabbed it in place, he spoke in a jolly tone. "This contemptible politician had surgery and when he awoke he be in total darkness. The nurse had drawn the curtains shut because there was a raging fire across the street and she didn't want the man to think he had died and was on his way to his eternal reward."

"Amen, young fella," Bull said, stifling laughter. He inhaled and his chest swelled like a huge balloon. "I got another one. Most folks don't understand that we can all do kindness to a lawyer and rescue him from drowning by shooting him before he hits the river."

Their three-man audience were being thoroughly entertained—their knee slaps made that fact obvious. Also, over the course of the one-up-manship, each cowhand expressed appreciation by contributing affirmative comments wrapped around snippets of merriment.

Fitzgerald click-clicked between cheek and gum. "It be best to put a kibosh on all this joshing so as I can shave you safe and proper." He began rapidly sliding a straight-razor against the thick leather strop hooked on the side of the chair. "I ain't ever defaced anyone and as sure as I was born a slave in Alabama and my hair be as white as cotton, I'd rather not have my first victim be a man known as Big Bull. I could get me stomped to dust."

"No danger of that, Whitey."

"Of what? Me making blood flow or me getting stomped?"

"Neither, I'd wager," Bull answered sincerely. "A man like you, who has the same healthy perspective on lawyers and politicians as me, also gets my respect and trust."

"Whew doggies. Ain't that topnotch?"

"Can we jawbone whilst you scrape my muzzle?"

"You keep your tongue tied. I be the one to do the talking now." Whitey got down to it, wielding the blade with the precision of a maestro conducting an orchestra. "I understands you be in Dodge City because of a big business transaction. I can't imagine such things. I be a simple man who minds his piece and enjoys the little bits of gossip that comes my way. It just makes my head spin to consider the highfalutin backroom intrigues of big shots and moguls."

"Movers and shakers . . ."

Fitzgerald shut him down with a wide-eyed glare. "I canst be telling you more than once to tie off your tongue." His hands were deft and sure, moving rapidly. "You be the boss man on your ranch and with your men, but them who sits in my chair gots to do what I says." His voice rose as he used the razor with a theatrical flourish. He finished the job by massaging in a liberal splash of bayberry-scented lotion. He click-clicked and held up a hand mirror.

"You done did it, young fella," Bull said, standing. "You got me as shiny as a strapping whippersnapper ready to go courting one of those high society ladies."

"You does look pretty, Bull."

Wallace chomped down on a chuckle. "And you're one helluva prevaricator, Whitey. Either that or an all-time great salesman." He reclaimed his hat from the rack and put it on. "I expect to be here a couple weeks. You slot me in for a daily sit in your chair." He ambled to the door. "I'll clear my bill and square things up before I leave town."

"First one be a freebie out of courtesy," Whitey replied, shaking out the sheet. "I be here bright and early every day excepting Sunday. I takes that day to rest and go to church."

Wallace cocked a finger at him as though it was a pistol, then went outside. The smallish black man tipped him a nod. He scooted onto the boardwalk to see the heavyweight make his way as his name implied, like a bull shouldering past lesser souls. The sunshine was warm, but as Whitey Fitzgerald watched the big man, he felt a centipede chill slither down his spine.

The girl was fifteen years old. She felt scared. Underneath the fear there was anger; a whirlwind of agitation spiraled through her head. She had nowhere to go to escape the confusion. Her sensibilities were out of control. She wanted to unload the questions gyrating inside; dump them on God in a spitting mad attack, but worried about committing blasphemy.

It was nighttime. She had been awake and caught in the tumult for what seemed like hour after hour. She sat perfectly still at her mother's bedside. The darkness and unrelenting disorder of thoughts kept the juices in her stomach roiling in queasy tension. She was in the grip of some kind of emotional meltdown that threatened to put her over the edge.

Her heart ached. All that was transpiring was grossly unfair. Her hands were clamped together so tight that tiny darts of pain radiated around the knuckles. She kept vigil as her mother slept fitfully. The woman was dying in horrific agony. She had a skeletal appearance; her cheekbones protruded and her eyes were sunken hollows. Her skin was yellowish and gathered in wrinkles; her once beautiful hair was stringy and frazzled.

"What am I going to do?" The teenager jammed her eyes shut. Teardrops were taking shape, but she refused to allow them to fully form. The disquiet was intensifying and her thoughts were jumping like popcorn, but she intended to remain steadfast and brave. Her fear and anger became a churning pressure that unleashed a piercing and rancid animosity. Her teeth clenched and in bitterness, she asked, "Why is God killing my mother?"

Abbey Langton twitched awake. Her eyelids fluttered. Heartburn erupted up her throat like an acidic geyser. She almost gagged, and had to press her tongue against the roof of her mouth to force a swallow. Her vision was blurry. She blinked as she looked left and right. It took several moments for her to realize her location. The words spoken in the dream echoed around some deep inner chasm, haunting her: *Why is God killing my mother?*

She wiped moisture off her cheeks, which were mottled blotches of white and crimson. Her calves were cramping; her lower back felt as though it was aflame. She removed her legs from the crate that served as a footstool and eased forward. Her ankles were retaining water all the time, regardless of how much she rested with her feet up.

The wooden swivel chair creaked and a low moan slipped off her lips as she strained to get into a comfortable position. She opened a desk drawer and rummaged around until she found her stash of peppermints, then placed one in her mouth to subdue the indigestion. According to the doctor she had another two weeks until her due date, but she was convinced that she could pop at any moment; that certainty, however, didn't slow her down at all.

Why is God killing my mother? The query whipsawed through her head. She cringed and fought back the dampness forcing its way out of her tear ducts. She pivoted the chair and leaned back. The room was dusky and smelled of ink. Late afternoon sunlight shimmied through the thick panes of the window. She glanced at the activity on Chestnut Street, then turned her attention to an overloaded file on the desktop.

She thumbed teardrops away and tried to concentrate. She was fulfilled by the practical arrangement she had with Nicholas B. Klaine, editor and publisher of the newspaper. He provided the desk in exchange for her copyediting skills and brashness in analyzing articles. He was ambitious and exacting; straitlaced and puritanical in a town famous as a hotbed for gunplay, gambling, whoring, and general all-out rowdiness.

The baby gave her a swift kick, which resulted in a puckered smile and a sigh. She sorted through the folder. It contained the product of a personal project; years of correspondence with benevolence organizations and government agencies. She reshuffled a stack of telegrams as she searched for a specific one from a high-ranking official in the Bureau of Indian Affairs.

Galloping hoofbeats caught her ears. She looked up to see a strawberry roan decelerate in the middle of the avenue and walk directly toward the *Dodge City Daily Times*, swishing its tail contentedly. Her smile increased. The rider leapt off and spoke to the horse while looping the reins over the hitching rail, then skipped into the workplace. The box-like office, with its printing apparatus and supplies on the back half, was compact and claustrophobic.

"Good day, Avis," Abbey said brightly, even before the tinny bell above the door finished tinkling. "You're more reliable than an expensive timepiece."

Avis Lahay frowned in a pouty manner as she peeled off calfskin gloves and doubled them over in the waistband of her trousers. "Why do you say that?"

"I've come to count on having you check in on me every afternoon," Abbey replied, making a slight motion for her to take a seat. "I welcome and value our visits."

"As do I," Avis said, and sat on the edge of a hard-backed chair. The ladies were separated in age by a month less than a decade. Abbey was twenty-eight, with her birthday in March—whereas the younger woman had been born in February. The common denominator in their lives was Deacon Coburn and his circles of influence.

"What's happening?" Abbey asked cheerily.

"I was just riding with Whitey," Avis replied, crossing her legs. "He can't wait until the baby is born because he's going to be an honorary grandfather. He's so excited."

"I think I used the term adopted grandfather, but honorary is fine."

"Any changes?"

"You mean, are labor pains occurring?"

Avis grinned. "I guess."

"No. My bottom hurts. A hemorrhoid the size of an apple, but don't ask," Abbey said, shrugging. "I was relaxing earlier and dozed into a deep sleep, which is good, I suppose."

"You have to get your rest when you can."

"Yes, but I had a weird dream."

Avis tented her eyebrows. "Maybe there's something in the water."

"What?" Abbey asked, scowling in bewilderment.

"I've woken up with the same nightmare the last three mornings."

"Huh."

Avis giggled. "You sound like Mr. Mackenzie."

"Oh, I do not."

Avis scrunched her brow and deepened her voice to grunt, "Huh."

Abbey laughed easily. "Stop it. Butch is such a nice man, but he's been underfoot so much lately." The chair squeaked a complaint as she leaned forward. "I have copy for him if you can deliver it to the telegraph office." She pushed through notes on the desk. "Here it is."

Avis read it, gave a short whistle and remarked, "Are you trying to cause a disturbance? That is fervent language. Inflammatory, even. You could stir up a hornet's nest."

Abbey dismissed the concerns with a flippant wave. "When one fights for justice against faceless bureaucrats, one must not mince words. If this message gets ignored, I'll string harsher sentences together, along with some phrases that'd never be heard in a church-house. If I wasn't pregnant, I'd take a train to Washington and punch someone in the nose."

"Whitey calls you a feisty lady."

Abbey's eyes gleamed proudly. "Coming from a gentleman who knows feisty, that's a high compliment. Feisty is what shakes complacency and moves obstacles out of the way."

"I'll run this to Mr. Mackenzie." Avis said, standing and sidling to the door.

"Assure Butch the coffee will be on in the morning."

"Okay. I'll be back to walk you home."

"Thank you, Avis. See you in a bit." The bell made its thin metallic noise. She collected her files and paperwork, and in an orderly fashion, placed them in the scuffed leather attaché that had served as her carryall for many years and miles. As she waited, she put her hands on her distended abdomen and caressed ever so gently. Her face flushed in a happy expression.

That evening, the Alhambra Saloon had a full house. The air in the dimly-lit room was stagnant and decorated by a haze of bluish smoke; as bodies moved about, it wafted like holey dishrags strung out on a clothesline in a confined space. The crowd was mostly mannerly and well-behaved, but raucous guffaws and loud-mouthed discussions sporadically flared up.

At a back corner table—the one commonly deemed to be his—Deacon Coburn hosted the cattle-baron boss of the *Double B Ranch*. The men were reminiscing about old times and trading exaggerated yarns of experiences since they were last together. One whopper led to another and another. And another. Wallace had a highball of bourbon, while Coburn coddled his trademark combination; a mug of black coffee near his right hand, a shot of whiskey on his left.

Whitey Fitzgerald entered the joint and stopped at the bar. He chatted with several patrons as he waited a moment to get the bartender's attention, then made his way over. There were a few wary or mistrustful eyes on him, but mostly he was greeted cordially.

When he came up behind Wallace, the big man straightened up in surprise. "Are you joining us, young fella?" he asked, almost disbelieving. "I'm feeling a swell of generosity, so before you sit down get yourself a drink and put it on my tab."

"I be a teetotaler," Whitey replied, shuffling side to side. "I keeps a supply of black Darjeeling behind the bar. It comes all the way from India and costs a pretty penny, but drinks just fine. Every barkeep takes care of me. I gots a pot brewing even as I speak."

Wallace howled brashly. "Tea? You strike me as a shot and a beer man."

"I was once," Whitey answered, click-clicking merrily. "More shots than beer, but I gots into a mess a few years back and liquor became a difficulty, so I be an abstainer now."

"You tell me where I can order some of that Darjeeling for you."

"Will do, Bull." Fitzgerald nodded, then strolled back to the bar.

Wallace leaned in close. "Good to see Whitey accepted here despite his color."

Coburn smiled. "I'd have words with anyone who caused a problem."

"Then you're a better man than me, which I've known all along," Bull said as he took a sip. "Whitey is good people. I'd have more than words for any troublemaker. A haymaker to the jaw would be my opening gambit, followed by kick in the crotch."

"You were never one to be subtle, Bull."

"Subtle is for weaklings and crybabies."

Fitzgerald returned with a bluish teapot in one hand, while balancing a flowery china cup and saucer in the other. He took a seat and asked, "I ain't interrupting business, is I?"

"We're just gabbing, Whitey," Deacon answered, taking a mouthful of coffee.

"We can chinwag business and get it out of the way," Bull said, shoulders hunching up. He absently cracked his knuckles. "Any of the *Double B* crew hanging around town?"

"Six cowpokes," Deacon replied forthrightly. "You want a sitdown with them?"

Wallace took a long pull of bourbon, then tapping a finger against the glass, he said, "No, that's not necessary. I'll bump into one of them hereabouts. They're surely not planning to leave anytime soon. I saw a poster for the Harvest Street Festival at the end of the month."

Coburn fingered his walrus-like moustache. "True enough."

"They're apt to stay for that shindig," Bull stated dryly. "My affairs should be concluded by then or shortly thereafter. If the weather turns lousy I'll put them on the train with me."

Coburn reached into the top pocket of his cotton work shirt to retrieve a telegram. He handed it over to his employer. "This came for you two days ago. It's from Fletcher."

Wallace read it aloud: "*Be in Dodge City by the 26th. All investors are lined up. We await your bank draft and signature on legal papers.*" His eyes glinted as he crumpled the message and tossed it aside. "That's it then. Four years of groundwork comes down to a face-to-face."

"What's the deal, if you don't mind me asking, Bull?"

"None of your concern, Deacon."

"I reckon not."

Wallace shrugged nonchalantly. "Almost a decade ago, Morgan Fletcher put together a consortium on land speculation in Arkansas that made a slight bulge in my bankroll. It was a low risk high reward venture. Now he has a bigger and better arrangement here in Kansas."

Coburn squinted a smile. "He strikes me as a fancy talking flannel mouth."

Wallace arched an eyebrow. "What's your opinion of the man, Whitey?"

"I ain't never met no Morgan Fletcher," the white-haired barber replied as he lifted the lid to check on the progress of his steeping tea. Satisfied, he poured a cup. "He's been in and out of town, hither and yon whilst I was here and there. There's always a flurry of chatter surrounding his whereabouts, but me and him, we have the charm of those ships that pass in the night."

"Too bad," Bull said, hunkering forward to rest his elbows on the table. "Your estimation of his character would be worth weighing against Deacon's assessment."

"No need for fleas in the ear from me. Deacon ain't likely wrong."

"Maybe so."

Fitzgerald click-clicked testily. "No maybe so about it, Bull."

Wallace polished off his drink. "I'm a businessman, Whitey. I'm always looking for an edge. I want all the angles I can get on potential partners." He flexed his hands and his lips pinched as he averted his eyes, which took on an impish gleam. "I need every insight I can get on Morgan Fletcher, since he's going to make me a rich man."

"I thought you already be rich, Bull," Whitey said, frowning.

"You can always get richer, young fella."

"Money is power and influence," Deacon opined, somewhat glibly.

"And regardless of how you come by money, it all spends the same."

"Is that the way of it, Bull?" Deacon queried, suspicion in his tone. "Are you the same man who gave me an appaloosa and refused any payment? Your attitude seems to have changed some. And not for the better." He put one hand atop the other and quoted Solomon. "*He that loveth silver shall not be satisfied with silver; nor he that loveth abundance with increase: this is also vanity. When goods increase, they are increased that eat them: and what good is there to the owners thereof, saving the beholding of them with their eyes?*"

Wallace chuckled cynically. "What good is there to the owners thereof?"

"It's Bible, Bull. You'd be wise to heed it."

"There you go getting cryptic on me, Deacon," Bull said, peevish humor rattling in his voice. "I'm a businessman. I'd be a piss poor one if I didn't make money. I value our friendship, but don't preach to me. My investment choices and portfolio are off-limits."

"What game are you running here, Bull?"

Wallace winked playfully. "Closing the books on a financial matter, is all."

Coburn eyeballed him, terse and skeptical. "I'm calling it a night." He snapped back his whiskey and washed it down with coffee, which was cold and bitter. His mouth tightened into a pucker. He gave a brusque bob of his head, then stood and departed. When he stepped outside, he stopped and allowed the nighttime coolness to calm the doubt gathering in him.

The woman was up and moving around. There were noises in the other room that had her curious and anxious. She found it strange that the creaking floorboards were cold on her bare feet. The air was heavy and her lungs hurt from storing up tension. Each stride closer to the doorway caused the glitch in her breathing to constrict even tighter.

Her hands were clasped in front of her; the downy hair on her forearms was prickly and extremely sensitive. The sounds had gotten inside her head.

It was as though the past was encroaching on the present, which made no sense. She rose onto her tiptoes and crept forward. She summoned bravery and took three quick steps. She put her hand on the doorknob.

When she pushed the door open, all her uneasiness expanded in a gasp. The room was shining as brilliantly as noonday and her four-year-old was standing there, but it wasn't exactly her son. He had the unmistakable bearing of the man from whose seed he'd sprouted. He wore a pair of one-piece thermal underwear with the arms tied around his waist like a belt.

"About time," he said in his father's voice. "Where you been?"

She froze. Her mind raced. Her mouth warped into a grimace. "I don't know."

"You just done Dogface Greer, didn't you?"

"No."

"Don't lie, Brenda."

"Those choices are behind me forever."

He hooted snidely. "Ain't you an uppity whore?"

"I'm no kind of whore anymore."

"Hellfire, Brenda," he said, skewering her with a scornful look. "You're nothing but a slut whore." His eyes practically popped out of the sockets as he berated her with a bevy of swearwords. He fisted his hands and tottered threateningly toward her, but then was gone.

She reeled and lost her balance. She was thrown backwards and thudded to a stop, which woke her up. Darkness surrounded her. Her chest was heaving up and down abnormally fast. She was on her backside, a sheet dampened by sweat matted around her. Her left hip hurt, presumably from striking the floor when she had fallen out of bed.

The ugliness in her head had staying power; she determinedly pushed it away, but remnants lingered like mites caught in cobwebs. She tamped down apprehension and steadied her breathing, then got to her feet. She was as tentative as a frightened kitten as she approached the cot where, after telling him a Bible story, she had tucked her child in.

Stace was sound asleep, for which she was grateful. She gawped as though she expected him to open his eyes and start talking to her. She moistened her lips as she crouched low to study him. His innocent expression made her weak. She touched his brow, then bent to kiss his cheek. "I love you, my little man," she whispered, holding back tears.

She eased her way to the window and drew the curtain wide enough to allow slivers of moonbeams to brighten the room. The star-speckled sky was cloudless. Her heart felt like a jagged hunk of granite, abrasive and rough as it sank through her. She pressed her forehead against the glass and tried to pray, but bad thoughts about her son tripped through her brain.

What if Stace had inherited his father's character, or more specifically; had his father's lack of character poisoned his veins? Could the inevitable be avoided, or was the dream a harbinger of the future? Was her son destined to be a bully and ne'er do well?

She shivered and shook free of the repugnant ideas. An icy lump thickened in her craw. She vaguely wondered what it had been that had put her and Ben Slaton together. It seemed so long ago when she was young and vulnerable. There was a first-sight attraction that thrilled her and a wildness allure in him that at this junction was difficult to explain.

Looking back, she realized he had always been a taker. Her efforts to foster a connection she thought was mutual were doomed to failure because he wanted only one thing from her. Fun in the sack making the bedsprings sing was what had made them a couple; she could never deny her enjoyment of their physical relationship, but she desired so much more.

She closed her eyes and quieted her heart. She considered what Suzy had overheard Ben say about being prepared to settle down with her. A piece of her wanted to believe him to have some honor—she would never lose a certain tenderness for him, but based on previous behavior, she dismissed the notion of his spoken intentions.

The coldness in her throat suddenly melted. In its wake a sense of comprehension and relief spilled over her. There and then, she concluded that the offensive dream was a symbolic communication from her subconscious, which she fully understood; to the end of his life, Ben Slaton trifled with the truth to accommodate his wants. He hadn't changed at all.

She sighed so deeply that the solemn sound of it surprised her. She placed three fingers against her lips. All her yesterdays had gone to some cosmic storage vault, while an unknown number of tomorrows waited for her to seize each one. She tugged the drapes shut and sat in a homemade rocker, which despite its pesky squeaks, she would miss.

Brenda Hawkins remained motionless in the darkness. Her thinker went to work sorting through options. There was much to do and little time, for by and by would not hold still for her to dillydally. She planned to sell off or give away most of her possessions, then move on to somewhere different as soon as possible. Her mind was set. It would be days not weeks.

≈ ≈ ≈

He came awake because his wife was sobbing. The darkness could not veil the groans and snuffles, though it was obvious she was attempting to repress the deluge of sadness. Sam Beadle listened for several seconds, alarmed and full of a need to protect her. She was on her back. He elbowed onto his side and rested a palm on the prominent knoll that was her midsection.

"I can't sleep."

"What's wrong, Abbey? Is it the baby?"

"The baby's fine." She held his hand and lifted her head so that his right arm could hook into place and as it did, she snuggled against him. "I'm just being silly."

"Crying isn't silly. What has you upset?"

"Nothing, Sam. My emotions are off-kilter."

"Perhaps, but even so, something worrisome is provoking you," he said softly. He moved her hair aside to nuzzle her neck. "I'm no slouch when it comes to listening."

She sniffled breathlessly. "I am aware of that fact."

"So let's not do this dance."

"What dance?"

His hand gently roamed over the mound of her belly. "The one where you do a series of sidesteps before I persuade you to drop your guard and allow me to give you a helpful whirl."

She giggled girlishly. "Oh, that one."

"As if you didn't know."

"What if I get lip-lock and go back to sleep?"

"I'll start a tickling war."

"You do and I'll pee my bloomers."

"We can't have that, so talk to me, Abbey Langton."

She released a sad-sounding rush of air. "As you already know, I was fifteen when my mother died. Some kind of cancer or consumption or something." She stared straight at the ceiling and spoke in a stressed monotone. "I never did hear an exact diagnosis; nor did I care to be filled in on any of the cruddy details because all I understood was that Mom was sick and in excessive pain. I was her primary nurse at her bedside constantly."

"I cannot imagine, Abbey."

"I watched a vibrant woman wither away," she said, her voice straining against the crying. "This afternoon I relived it and saw my mother dying all over again. I dozed off at the office and had a dreadful dream. It was so vivid and real that it shocked me." She gulped to try and catch her breath. "It's still clear and fresh in my head. I'm kind of scared, Sam."

"Scared of the memory?"

Her body tensed. "No."

"What then?"

"Nothing. Forget it."

"Do you want me to get up and light the oil lamps, Abbey?"

"No, Sam. We don't have to do that dance either."

"The one where I force the issue?"

"Yes."

"Then please don't slam the door shut and freeze me out." He felt rigidity course through her body. He kept rubbing all around her tummy. The silence between them became ever louder and stronger, with each second becoming another brick in the wall. He held his tongue for an inordinate stretch of time, then coughed and casually asked, "What is it, Abbey?"

Her breathing increased. Just then, the baby moved vigorously, all heels and knees. She inhaled a quavering gasp and he hugged her closer. "Did you feel that, Sam?"

"Yes, indeed."

"Our baby is going to be a fighter."

"Just like his or her mother and father."

She shuddered. "I'm afraid, Sam."

"I know, Abbey."

"No, you don't, Sam."

"Are you being deliberately secretive?"

"No. It's complicated. What if the illness that took my mother is hereditary?"

"My Lord, Abbey!"

"It's on my mind, Sam."

"That's borrowing a lot of junk and grief."

"I may never see our baby grow up."

He chuckled tactfully. "You also may live to be a grand old lady."

"And see you reach your dotage before me?"

"That's been the plan all along, hasn't it?"

"I suppose," she said, stammering. Her resolve broke down and the waterworks came in full force. Forlorn mourning wrenched from her throat. "Just as likely, I'll die young like Mom. She missed so much. She was only thirty-five years old." Her voice quivered in a shrill and shaky falsetto. "If God allows me that much time, I have only seven years . . ."

"Abbey," he cut it, severe and uncompromising. "Cry it out, but don't be deceived by those disagreeable ideas." He pushed up and over to make eye contact with her. "Think about us. You and I take each day as it comes and make the most of every hour. We're always looking ahead to the next horizon. Yes, life has no guarantees, but kindly, let's not imagine a worst case scenario when we can pool our optimism and do so much better."

She wiped her nose. "Thank you, Sam. I so need your strength."

"And I need your planning and taking charge."

She palmed wetness off her cheeks. "I tried telling you I'm an emotional ninny."

"Emotional ninny or not, I love you, Abbey Langton."

"I love you, Mr. Beadle." She cupped a hand around his chin and kissed his lips, then with much effort, turned onto her right side. He arranged the quilt over them and eased down to spoon her. She whimpered faintly as they cuddled as tight as possible. The night still had plenty of conk out time, which was good because their eyes were heavy. They placidly listened to the slowing cadence of each other's breathing for a half-hour, then fell asleep together.

Whitey Fitzgerald had been here more than once. The fringes of all that surrounded him were tainted by a drab sepia coloring. He kept moving stealthily along some uncharted avenue that had swarming throngs of strangers pressing in on him. His eyes were focused on a nattily dressed whippet of a man twenty yards ahead.

Nothing ever changed. A lunatic intensity drove him onward. He was in the middle of some bizarre carnival midway. There were barkers shouting and balloons floating or popping. And clowns; dozens of clowns were in the crushing mob, their faces masked and distorted by greasepaint. A cacophony of pump organ music pulsated in the air.

The harlequin jokers pushed and pulled at him. Fitzgerald ignored them and shed their oversized glove hands. Murder was in his heart, while hornets buzzed in his skull and rats gnawed on his innards. He had a half-empty bottle of liquor in one hand and a revolver in the other. He relentlessly stalked his quarry, never slowing or even hesitating.

He was gaining ground on the object of his rage. The man wore a felt derby hat and carried a brass-handled cane, which he occasionally used, but mostly it was a prop or affectation that he twirled like a baton, as though he was a virtuoso leading a parade. Fitzgerald sped up and brushed past orange-haired madcaps grinning crazily at him.

The dandified man turned and scooted down an alley between big tents. Fitzgerald ran faster and faster. His heartbeat drummed against his ribcage. All that was around him mutated. The sights and sounds of the circus revelry were gone. A tornado of fireworks caught him up and carried him to a ramshackle room where four walls boxed him in. The brownish tinge remained at the corners of everything like tatters of burnt paper.

All was as it ever was inside the madness. The man with the cane was on his knees begging for his life in a whiny voice. Fitzgerald had nothing but ire and violence stoking the fire in him. He pressed the pistol against the base of his enemy's neck. He swilled mouthfuls from the bottle. His eyes were wild—bloodshot and bleary.

"You pay now, Huey Butters."

"That's not my name, mister."

"No? Who you be?"

"An investment banker and real estate broker."

"A swindler and con artist, you mean.

"You got the wrong man."

"I gots the right man. You stole my life and now, you gonna die." He slowly curled his index finger on the trigger. The handgun roared and flashed like lightning. His body convulsed in a squirming spasm. He jumped out of bed and was halfway across the room before he was roused enough to comprehend that he had escaped the nightmare.

It was always the same. The barkers and balloons, a pump organ and clowns. Against a festival backdrop, he pursued and executed Huey Butters. The blood on his hands was imaginary, but the intent stuck within his heart was real. He breathed heavily and did what he could to gather his senses as he stood helpless and undone in the darkness.

Whitey Fitzgerald had a severe case of the shakes. He tried to gain control, but failed miserably. His flannel underwear seemed to be useless; he was cold and shivering as though trapped inside a snowbank. His hands had a palsy that he couldn't stop no matter how hard he held them together. He hadn't had a drop in four years, but could smell and taste whiskey.

He salivated thirstily. "My God, I needs some help." He slumped onto the edge of the bed and stared at his trembling hands. His shoulders sagged forward and he hung his head, then words rushed out of him in an unbroken monolog punctuated by periodic click-clicks.

"I ain't ever going to be free. I be ashamed because I got killing in me. It ain't ever leaving me alone. I pray and give it to God, but he ain't never taken it from me, so it be my cross to bear or my battle to fight, however one wants to say it. I be one sorry man. If I was to ever cross paths with Huey Butters I knows in my heart of hearts that my dream be true.

"I ain't me. I be happy-go-lucky on the outside, but inside, I be in turmoil. I mean, I *wants* to do murder. Nobody knows because I put on a good show. I ain't the man I used to be. I has got to get this vengeance out of my head, but canst figure how to do it. It comes to harass me when I slumber and makes the longing for liquor strong. I be scared to go to sleep."

He groaned and bent his eyes upward. "Lord, you be listening to me or am I just a poor nigger man talking to hisself in the dark?" He sat up straight as if he had heard an answer. His neck craned sideways and a teeny-weeny smile split his lips. The shakes had passed. He bunched the pillow into a ball, then slipped beneath the covers and chucked around to get cozy. A sensation of relief came over him and for the remainder of the night he slept restfully.

Smoke and booming artillery shattered the pastoral stillness of the farm. The war had come to the boy's backyard; he was big-eyed and full of fear, but he stuffed it down and toughed it out. He kept watch on all the happenings while lurking in hidden places and staying out of the way of military personnel. It was as though the nine-year-old was invisible.

His favorite spot to disappear was high up in a crook of a big maple tree between the house and barn. From his perch he saw the movement of troops and how the countryside was being scarred and torn apart. Crouched there, as he was just now, he took advantage of a camouflage of green leaves to be a silent eyewitness to bloodshed and mutilation.

Below him, his father was hard at it; never a man to linger or wait upon instructions, he was working with soldiers and other civilians loading body after body onto flatbed wagons to be carted away. There were also piles of discarded limbs that had to be disposed of—arms and legs that had been sheared off by shrapnel or a surgeon's saw.

The boy was transfixed by the gore; he had developed a morbid curiosity. He heard a piercing scream that made him cringe. He glanced around and determined the pain-racked shriek came from what had been the sitting room of their home, but was commandeered to be a surgical ward. He scampered to the ground and ran to where his mother labored as a nurse.

Chaotic pandemonium was in charge. Orders were sporadically shouted, but the sounds of suffering ofttimes was louder than any other voices. There were sick and wounded men hobbling about and wandering, blank-eyed and mindless. He hurried past stretcher-bearers and bluecoats, darting and weaving like a water bug beetle.

He was seemingly unseen as he ran into the house. The floor had bloody footprints scattered in a grotesque pattern. He gulped air. He scudded to a stop in the doorway of the operating theatre. His heart was racing; his breathing herky-jerky and constricted. He slipped into the room, pressed tight against the wall and made himself small.

The scene assaulted his senses. He wanted to run to his mother and drag her away from the bedlam, but dutifully kept those feelings at bay. She was attempting to hold a patient down on a table while a crabby-faced man cut and dug around his belly. Blood was squirting and splattering everywhere;

her arms and white apron were covered in it. The patient writhed as the doctor cursed. His mother was stone-faced and crying endlessly.

He inched away from the wall. The dying man heaved up and screeched in agony, then collapsed. An unnerving groan and reddish mist sprayed from his mouth. The physician swore or prayed, the boy was not sure whether it was reproach or supplication. He stepped closer, eyes wary and fixated on his mother. The angst in him climbed up and twined around his throat.

She was gape-eyed and appalled. Anxiety poured out of her. Their focus dovetailed; the connection that took place was murky and muddled by the carnage surrounding them, but it was real and tangible. "Lord, have mercy, Caleb," she said, gasping jaggedly.

At that instant, Caleb Weitzel sat up straight, eyes blinking as he searched the darkness. The ricochet of cannons remained in his head. He was years and thousands of miles removed from his boyhood home in Gettysburg. The horrors of the battlefield that had descended upon their household were like the righteous judgment of an Old Testament plague.

Those days of bloodletting had plowed ghastly furrows in his soul, but he came from stock that gave him the mettle and wisdom to rise above the tribulations. He took counsel from the example set by his parents and applied those lessons day-in and day-out. He grabbed hold of circumstances over which he had no control and shaped destiny into a good fit for him.

A chill of autumn was in the air. He silenced the noise and squelched the trauma from the past. He sat back against his saddle and listened intently to the night. He was in deep shadows away from the campfire. He looked up at the clear star-speckled sky and grinned at a childish notion to begin trying to count the sparkling dots.

Relaxation eased through his sturdy frame. All was quiet; the herd of horses enclosed in a rope-corral were peaceful. The animals were for delivery to a division of the U.S. Army at Fort Dodge, southeast of Dodge City. Camp had been made at dusk in eastern Colorado or western Kansas. Come sunup he would reconnoiter the area to determine a more precise location.

His thoughts drifted to Sally Twosongs and their baby. He was thankful that his mother and father were nearby to help and be with her, but that didn't take away the dense weight of concern anchored in his gut. She was constantly on his mind. He launched arrow prayers, then recalled an after supper conversation that had pushed and pulled them.

They were on the porch gently swinging the loveseat rocker. Hank was on the top step to watch and guard them. The twilight colors were blissful. She was restraining tears and trying to pretend that she had conquered her grief. It had been two days since Daniel Twosongs arrived at *WT Ranch* alone, with news that Consuelo had taken ill and died on the trip from Taos.

"I can't go now." His manner was adamant. "Fort Dodge will have to wait."

"No. The contract with the army has to be honored."

He put an arm around her shoulders and pulled her close. "I can send a telegram and cancel the contract. If that puts *WT Ranch* in bad standing with the army, so be it."

"You listen to me, Caleb Weitzel," she said, stiffening against him. "You have worked too hard and your word is too important to violate a contract on account of me."

"The situation has changed."

"That's called life, Caleb."

Grooves edged his brow. "Consuelo was to be here."

"Mother passed over to glory. The Creator called her home."

"Sally Twosongs . . ."

She cut him off by jabbing a finger in his side. "No. The passage to the hereafter world was at the root of Mother's faith. She's in the presence of Jesus. I will make her proud."

"I can't argue, but I worry on you, *lucero*."

"You are not to worry on me. *Ever*. Love and care for me as your little bright star, but have no worries." Her voice thickened with emotion. "I will miss Mother more than anyone will ever know, but I would not be the daughter of Daniel and Consuelo Twosongs if I did not bear down and put my backbone to work holding tight to the truth of eternity."

He sighed a groan. "You are always my little bright star. I know I can insist on staying put from now until the cows come home and not make a dent in your determination."

Her dark eyes, full of mystery and laughter, rested on him. "I have Eliza and Naomi for when the baby comes." She gave his thigh a squeeze. "And do you think your father is going to let me do anything around here? He'll be hovering over me more than Hank."

"The decision is final?"

"Yes. I want you to go," she replied, succinct and urgent. "Father cannot be cooped up in ranch activities, especially now. He needs to be on the trail to come across renewal in the wonder of creation. Traversing the prairie on horseback will be good medicine for him."

Weitzel returned from the memory. He leaned back to read the sky-lights. The night still had hours before the eastern horizon would be aglow. He saw his father-in-law feeding fuel into the fire. Even in the dim flickers despair was evident; it hollowed his cheeks and lined his face. Caleb Weitzel murmured a few more arrow prayers, then settled in to get some shuteye.

Sally Twosongs stirred restlessly beneath the blankets. She was sweated and irritable, having tossed and turned for more than an hour, wide awake and struggling with a hyperactive imagination which refused to be shutdown. There was also discomfort across her lower back, but compared to the troublesome mind games, those aches were manageable.

The nightmare had gotten under her skin to keep her in a state of disarray. It wasn't fear, but rather, a visceral indignation bordering on anger that had her all balled up inside. How dare the enemy of her soul plan an attack to steal her baby? Satan had no power over her; he was a defeated foe and all his tactics were smoke and mirrors designed to agitate her. His demons were imbecilic minions akin to court jesters and buffoons. She would have none of it.

After all, she was Sally Twosongs, a Navajo princess with ancestral ties and a mystic connection to the Creator which had been forged in an inferno. When she was eleven years old, she endured the repulsive ordeal of being kidnapped and terrorized by a monster-man, which had the savagery to utterly destroy her, but instead, the One who is from everlasting to everlasting provided deliverance and redeemed her sufferings according to his purpose.

The healing—physical, emotional, spiritual—came supernaturally; she received a compelling dream in which Jesus appeared to her. He told her he loved her and expressed regret for what the bad man had done to her. She saw the terrible scars from the crucifixion. He placed his hand on her heart and promised to be on her path alongside her.

That remembrance caused an impetuous escalation in her annoyance. She rolled over and sat with her feet on the floor. Her teeth clenched. Gutsy faith rose in her like a flaming tide to cauterize her resolve. The prince of darkness was a liar and the begetter of lies. How *dare* that profane mongrel taunt her! She spoke aloud in a hushed tone aquiver with conviction. "In the name of Jesus Christ, the king of glory, get thee away from me and mine."

Unbeknownst to her, tears were trickling down her cheeks. She stood and realized that Hank was huddled against her legs. The collie's tail was wagging and its eyes were angled on her. She put a hand on its head and stepped into doeskin slippers. The dog stayed pressed close as she moved across the room to pick a flute off a shelf that contained several choices.

With her selection made, she pulled a housecoat on over her flannel nightgown and also draped a woolen shawl over her shoulders. Her skin was chilled by an outbreak of goosebumps. Hank, seemingly aware of her intentions, stepped lively to lead her through the nighttime shadows and stopped at the front door. She opened it and stepped onto the porch.

It only took her a moment to get reasonably comfortable on the rocker swing. Her heart swelled as she scanned the purplish-black expanse of the starry sky. The spectacular beauty spoke comfort, uttering knowledge about the Creator's command and sovereignty. She smiled in contentment; the wisdom literature written in glimmers soothed her soul.

Hozhó. Her lips spread wider as the ageless word sprang to the forefront of her mind. A warm shiver chased over her and joyful teardrops blurred her vision. Her father had taught her much truth about the Navajo concept which meant being responsible to keep all aspects of life in proper alignment to be in balance and harmony with the Creator.

Understanding seeped through her. She knew what had to be done to deal with her loneliness and sense of loss. She moistened her lips in preparation to make music, but then, the child in her womb moved rowdily. She sighed, and in that split second, imagery of heaven overwhelmed her; she saw the baby she had lost safely cradled in her mother's arms.

Peace, as perceptible as a physical presence, enveloped her. She readied the flute and closed her eyes to hear the song hidden in her heart. The instrument she had chosen was aromatic cedar with chips of turquoise inlaid between the holes. In perfect sync with the cathedral of the cosmos, she played melodious prayers for her father and in honor of her mother.

Hank lay atop the steps attentive and listening.

The community gathered on a perfect autumn afternoon to raise a barn for a young newlywed couple. Good-natured wisecracks were accompanied by jovial laughter. Adam Engle was hard at it setting the pace for others. The job was almost completed. He was at the peak of the roof checking on details and collecting a half-bundle of left-over shingles.

His wife, a brown-eyed brunette, was adjacent to a weeping willow where several picnic tables had been set up using sawhorses with planks set across them. Baskets of fried chicken and salads were being unpacked for a communal meal. She was busy putting out place mats, but her eyes never strayed from her husband. She enjoyed everything about him.

He slipped. She straightened up. He took two shaky stutter steps in an attempt to find his balance. Gasps and shouts blistered the air. The muscles in her neck constricted tightly. His feet got entangled, but for one frozen second it appeared as though he was going to get steadied. She dropped what she was doing as trepidation encased her.

His face contorted into a twisted grimace. The armload of cedar shakes went flying. She took strides toward the barn. He clutched feebly at nothingness and pitched backwards off the edge. A shrillness tore from her lungs. He flailed and thrashed in a wildly futile attempt to get his legs under him. His countenance was unspeakably disfigured as death rushed to greet him.

She was running. He landed flat on his back, striking the ground with a gruesome thud. His head bounced thrice and came to rest in a peculiar position. She knelt beside him. Her vision was fuzzy. He was unconscious and paralyzed. She grabbed at him and pulled him close. Blood oozed from the corners of his mouth. Her eyelids palpitated and shock stabbed at her.

It wasn't Adam Engle; Pete Axler was nestled on her lap. His head on its broken neck flopped listlessly. His eyes were dead and empty. Her hands flittered over him. Scorching cries untethered from her voice box as she fiercely clung to him. Her torso throbbed with emotion. She sobbed and prayed; prayed and sobbed. Darkness engulfed her.

Naomi Axler wobbled awake, totally disoriented. Her breathing was sporadic; cramps of pain put pressure on her chest and she felt as though she was suffocating. Tremors shook her from the inside out. She gulped and urgently reached across the mattress for her husband, but discovered she was alone in a strange bed.

Everything was wrong. Where was she? Where was Pete? What was happening? Her brain bellowed the questions. Panic stampeded through her and any measure of calmness was nowhere to be found. The darkness squashed in around her. She did a crazy crab-crawl, crumpling the sheets. She was lost, lonely, scared.

The soft notes of a soothing song sliced through the near-hysteria gripping her. She folded her hands over her bosom and consciously forced herself to take even breaths. The in through the nose out the mouth process slowly had a positive effect. She wiped her face which was wet with sweat and tears. Her ears perked up and disbelief pursed her lips.

She fell back onto the pillow. It was a hymn-like melody being played by Sally Twosongs. Naomi began to relax as each rise and fall of the tune gave her more and more comfort. It took several moments for perception to filter through the confused upheaval in her head; she was in the guest bedroom of the first house built at *WT Ranch* to be a companion and helper to the pregnant woman serenading the night.

Naomi sat up against the headboard to listen and rethink the dream. She didn't want to be hoodwinked by the trickery of nocturnal imaginings, but couldn't find release from a feeling that had come over her when she was clearheaded. What spooked her was the fact that while Pete was readying to be away on ranch business, she had a premonition of bad tidings.

She now wondered if the nightmare was an affirmation of the fore-warning. Wetness formed in her eyes and she clamped her top teeth over her bottom lip. Her husband had been gone for nearly two weeks; he had departed with a string of yearlings to be taken to a rancher north of Gunnison. She expected him to arrive home in the next few days but the ominous rehash from a cavernous nadir of her past had her in an uneasy guessing mood.

She got up and pulled on a colorful patchwork housecoat and looped the belt. She padded barefoot across the room and crouched low to check on Jesse and Amanda, who were sound asleep beside each other on a pallet made up on the floor. Their cheeks were rosy, reflecting guileless purity. She secured the rumpled covers up under their chins.

The wooden flute enthused her faith. She quietly opened and closed the door, then went to the living room where she could hear the music more distinctly because it was coming from the porch. She alighted on a tall-backed oak rocker near the fireplace, got comfy and shut her eyes. Naomi Axler fell asleep praying for her hubby's safety and wellbeing.

The streets of Abilene were unchanged. The hotel clerk was at a front window in the lobby of Drovers Cottage keeping his eyes peeled. His fingers were fidgety. He kept varying his angle or popping up on the balls of his feet. His anger was in check, but wariness had him on edge. A troublemaker had been staked out across the way for an hour.

Blistery heat and oppressive humidity seemed to leach from the whitish ball of fire midway across the western sky. Pedestrians were scurrying on errands or clustered together in gossip circles. The cowtown was not at all quiet. Plenty of wagon traffic back and forth kept the noise level high as drummers and teamsters hauled freight and goods.

The stalker was on the move, slouchy and swaggering. The clerk lurched in his footsteps and his heightened vigilance soared even higher. He raced to the door as his blood got hotter and rose in an adrenaline charged burst. He heard a rusting movement and voice behind him, but ignored it because he was zoned in on happenings outside. Old Blue was standing sentinel in the doorway, but he stepped past the cattle-dog and ordered it to sit and stay.

He rushed off the broad veranda toward the man who was coming steadily forward, with his shoulders shoved back and head slanted upward in a show of determination. His Stetson was aslant high on his forehead and listing to one side. His shallow-cheeked face was dominated by a cocky smirk that was eerie and disconnected.

Liam Greer waggled his legs and stopped, cold and angry. "You best stay out of my way, mister," he said in a snarl. "I got a date with my woman." He pointed a finger toward Drovers Cottage. "Are you going to give me clearance or do I get mean and ornery?"

Sam Beadle had his hands on his hips, rigid and unbending. The men were eyeball to eyeball in the middle of the thoroughfare. Greer bopped on his toes and grinned like a deranged jack-o-lantern, as though he possessed a fantastic advantage. He hooked his thumbs in the waistband of his trousers for a casual moment, then cursed and threw a punch.

The blow caught Beadle squarely on the chin. His head slackened backward and to the side as if his neck was elastic and unhinged. He staggered and gasped for air. Greer was emboldened and euphoric. He waded in and lunged with an untamed brutality. He was a bundled flurry of flying fists. Every punch struck solidly and did damage.

Beadle attempted to react as his training demanded, but instead, every instinct failed him. He jerked around like a marionette and his head dangled witlessly; he was being schooled by a smarmy punk with a baby-face fringed by a crop of downy peach-fuzz. His opponent persistently kept coming at him, hands fisted in tight balls and held in the classic style.

Greer had no restraints on what he wanted to do. He slipped and slid, jabbing at will. He feinted in one direction and unleashed a punch that was undeniably veiled in speed. The straight right was blinding in its swift ferocity. He turned his hips and rolled his shoulders to drive the wallop through the target. The sledgehammer clout struck between the eyes.

Beadle's nose took the full brunt of it. Blood erupted and spewed from both nostrils as his head snapped back at a weird skyward angle. He was airborne, then slammed to the ground on his back, arms and legs outstretched. His nose was a rubbery flab of flattened flesh. His tongue slathered over his lips as rivulets of blood formed a mucky pool in the dirt.

Greer proceeded to stomp him repeatedly. He beat the man until he was bruised and battered, feckless and twisting in the dust. He gave him a final kick in the crotch, then spat on his vanquished foe and walked to Drovers Cottage. Abbey Langton, cheeks rouged and eyelids shadowed, was there waiting for him. She plastered an amorous kiss on his lips and pressed her body against his. He swept her up in his arms and carried her off.

Sam Beadle awakened and opened his eyes. The roof of his mouth was dry and his tongue was furry. "That's not the way it happened," he muttered, shaking his head. Pale yellow was radiant in the room. "That's not the way it happened," he repeated grimly.

"What?"

He sat up on his elbows and saw his wife sitting at a desk near the window. In the lamplight he could see the lines of her face wrinkled into a frown fixed on him. She had a tablet and pencil in hand. He exhaled a weary groan. "Nothing. How long have you been up?"

"Just a few minutes or so, I guess," she replied, viewing him with a hesitant and puzzled look. "Nothing, you say? It was your thrashing that chased me out of bed."

"Sorry. I had a loopy dream."

She laughed airily. "Perhaps Avis is correct."

He scowled, eyes narrowing. "What's that mean?"

"There seems to be a contagion of odd dreams in this town," she answered, and shifted around to brighten the room by fiddling with the wick on the oil lamp. "Her. Me. And now you. She thinks there's something in Dodge City's water supply."

"That's a nutty notion," he said, chuckling.

"Likely so. Tell me yours."

He related the highlights but omitted the particulars of her harlot appearance and the fact that she had been caught up in Greer's arms. He finished by saying, "I was a bloody pulp."

Her smile was large. "That no account Liam Greer trounced you?" she queried, a giggle woven through her words. "How in tarnation could that *ever* happen? Now methinks that what you referred to as a *nutty notion* could be an entirely accurate assessment."

He sloughed that off and lifted the quilt. "Come back to bed."

"I'm working on an idea, Sam."

"Please, Abbey. I *need* to hold you."

Her eyebrows dipped low as she squinted at him. There was quirkiness in his tone. She studied her notes for a moment, then put her writing tools down. She snuffed the lamp and it sputtered a hiss. He reached for her in the darkness. His arms knotted around her as she slipped onto the mattress and melted into him. They chatted about tender matters until sunrise.

The man was on fire. Flames gobbled at him, but his flesh was not consumed. He was in a labyrinthine canyon that was a place of perpetual desolation. Blazing bonfires streaked from the sky as nourishment for molten rivers that flowed freely and burned continuously. The stench was asphyxiating; soot and noxious gases hung in the combustible air.

He cringed and cried for relief from the torment, but the miserable agony had no end. He was not alone. Thousands upon thousands of tortured souls were writhing and bawling as carefree imps capered about and carried on. Battalions of freakish gargoyles held vigil in an enclave of encampments along a ridgeline of sulfur and brimstone.

Horrifying pain clawed at the walls of his skull. His insides were rolling lumps of seething convulsions. He wanted to make a breakout getaway from the infinite prison camp realm where time had no meaning. There was nothing to mark its passage and no way to know how long he had been squatting on his haunches, wailing and gnashing his teeth.

In an explosion of blackness, Smoky Crowe appeared from behind a jutting crag. The Ute witch was naked except for a diaper loincloth. His left eye—milky and pulsing—reflected a sinister sickness; his right eye dripped blood. He strode forward in a preening strut, a shell rattle in one hand and a stubby-stemmed pipe in the other.

"Aarg. Watch me," he demanded, looming over the crouching man. The necromancer chanted a chorus that thundered from his throat; his feet began shuffling in fluid skips and hops. He lifted his knees high and kicked up his heels, whooping louder and louder. Round and round he went, spinning into a whirling blur and as he did, a dumbfounding mutation occurred. He transfigured into the red-skinned devil brandishing a three-pronged pitchfork.

"So good of you to come, my son," the archfiend said, reptilian eyes slit-like and jaundiced. His lengthy arrowhead tail intermittently slithered around his shoulders as he spoke in a prankster's voice slimy with mockery. "Greatness and exploits are yours for the taking."

"Why am I here?" the cowering man asked squeakily.

"A foretaste of glorious evil," he answered, smiling broadly. The pointy tops of his ears inclined in such a way as to nearly touch the curved horns protruding from the peak of his hairline. "You belong to me, my son. I promise you rewards and never-ending infamy."

The man screeched. His tongue ignited. He vomited smoldering embers. A pair of imps dashed at him and he had to scramble to escape their clutches. In doing so he dropped onto his backside. He wept. Off in the distance a choir of gargoyles in the quaking throes of victory sang a maniacal refrain. He knelt and bowed his head. "I am unworthy to be in your presence."

"The netherworld favors you," the devil said, entwining the barbed whiskers of his goatee around his curled fingernails. "Inflict havoc and revel in anarchy. Savor vengeance."

"I fear I will fail."

"Failure will not be tolerated," the diabolical prince replied irately. "The riches of my kingdom await your triumphant entry, but my will must be done as dictated."

"I will try to do as I am told."

Satan erupted in fuming rage. His eyes gaped wide and shot fiery darts. Grimy smoke and orange flames gushed from his pores to become a billowy crown wreathed upon his horns. His ever moving tail cracked like a bullwhip. "Obey or be devoured," he hollered in a voice akin to a roaring lion. He hoisted the pitchfork in a threatening manner, then clip-clopped forward on cloven hooves and gnawed the air, exposing finely sharpened dagger-teeth.

Liam Greer a.k.a. Kid Greer squealed and jumped awake with the putrid odor of perdition in his nostrils. He was on his hands and knees entrapped in his bedroll, which was almost tied into knots around him. He fought against it until realization that he wasn't on fire struck his consciousness. He tipped over face down in the grass, panting and huffing.

He incrementally gained his senses. When he was liberated from the jumbled mess of blankets, he flipped onto his butt and had a look around. He was camped on the edge of a grove of cottonwoods beside a rock strewn creek. His mount, a crowbait speckled bay mare named Daisy, was picketed in a swatch of lush meadow with access to the water.

He pulled the bedding to his chest and hugged it. The campfire was burnt out ashes. He wouldn't bother to rekindle it because he had no coffee to boil and only hardtack biscuits to munch on. He got to his feet. His gear and belongings were against a shady tree; he dragged the sleep-sack with him and set it aside, then perched on the saddle.

The brilliant golden hues of daylight were spreading across the sky as the rising sun crested above the eastern horizon. He yawned noisily and rubbed his eyes with the heels of his hands. The residual horror of the all too real dream remained embroidered on his brain. He was scared. His skin felt shriveled and his mouth was parched.

He licked his lips, then backhanded dried goo off his chin. He opened his saddlebags to retrieve a pouch of tobacco and inserted a wad along the inside of his bottom lip. When he put the packet away, he saw a checkered handkerchief. His hands had tremors as he lifted it to his lap. He was reverent as he carefully unfolded it to examine the grisly left ear that not so long ago belonged to Benny Slaton, the bully who menaced his growing up years.

A shiver passed over him. One down, two to go on his retribution tour. Slaton was dead. Now, it was on to the killing of Sam Beadle and Charley Jondreau. *Obey or be devoured.* His eyes bulged, as though the threat in his head had been spoken aloud. Fear viciously gouged at him. His body shook as he sank to the ground. Liam Greer was crying like a baby.

A month ago, Daniel Twosongs had no reasons to be discouraged. All was well as he returned to camp just past dawn with a catch of trout gutted and ready for the frying pan. Squat and solid, he moved in an easygoing bow-legged amble. A flat-brimmed gray hat was worn low on his forehead. He came up a rising slope and was whistling pleasantly as he approached his wife, who was crouched low preparing a pot of coffee.

"A fish fry for breakfast, Consuelo," he announced, coal-colored eyes smiling. He came close to her and gently patted her shoulder. "How's the fire?"

"The coals are perfect," she replied, placing the coffee pot at the edge of the cinders. She stood, cast iron skillet in hand, and pecked his cheek with a soft kiss. Her roundish face was flushed and there appeared to be tension straining in her eyes. "Though I'm not too hungry."

He took the cooking utensil and got busy. He sat on his heels and lay the fillets side by side in the bottom of the pan. "Your appetite will perk up as I work my seasoning magic."

"Always possible," she said, strolling to their bedding. She knelt and pulled a hairbrush out of a handbag, then went and sat on a smooth granite boulder across from him. Her manner relaxed some as she glanced around the campground, which was situated in the midst of a copse of aspens. Their horses and a pack-mule were tethered closeby. She began grooming her hair, which was dark and wavy, with silvery strands becoming more and more prominent.

"What's on your mind, Consuelo?" he asked, crushing bits of sage and savory on the sizzling fish. The coffee mixed with the scent of the spices to perfume the bracing morning air. "You have the charming look of a lady who is lost in some faraway land."

She sighed wistfully. Her eyes crinkled at him as she kept brushing her hair. "This scenery reminds me of that site where we purposefully sojourned all those years ago."

"I was thinking that same thing myself."

"Do you remember our time there?"

"I do. It was a kind of pilgrimage. Forty days."

She raised an eyebrow. "Roughly this time of year, as I recall."

"Yes. We sought the Creator."

"We were both at a point of resignation." She stopped working on her hair and leaned back. Her expression darkened into a frown. "We wanted a family, but I was barren and age was coming up against me. I felt shame and regret." She paused and a wince deepened the crow's feet around her eyes. "My faith was frail and brittle. You were, as always, a rock."

"We prayed. We fasted. We sang songs." He poked at the trout with his knife. "We waited upon the Creator, who demonstrated his longsuffering patience for us."

"We prayed through to peace."

"Indeed. We were blessed."

"Did you ever mark the time, Daniel?"

"Of course. As we have marveled about on many occasions."

"Nine months, almost to the day we departed for home, Deacon Coburn arrived in Taos with our daughter." Her voice tensed in a hitch and she began flexing her left hand. A pang of distress flared in her eyes. "Sally Twosongs was and is God's extra special gift to us. And now our precious princess is having a baby. We are soon to be grandparents."

"But first we shall eat."

"I think I'll pass, Daniel. I have some bad indigestion."

"I have dried mint in my saddlebags. Do you want me to brew a pot of tea?"

"That might help." Her breathing quickened. Color instantly drained from her face, which became a misshapen mask of disbelief full of knowledge that her heart was malfunctioning. A gasp tore from her throat and she lurched forward off the boulder, her hands grasping at her chest like claws. She took several wobbly steps and whimpered a screeching groan. She keeled over, forcefully striking the ground with the thumping finality of a felled tree.

Her body didn't move; not even a twitch. He rushed to her side and turned her over onto her back, immediately recognizing that she wasn't breathing. Her eyeballs were rolled back in her head and the whites were glazed. He frantically attempted to massage her lungs into functioning by pumping harder and harder, but nothing happened. She stiffened beneath his touch. He slumped back and stared off in the middle distance, eyes bleak and moisture-laden.

Daniel Twosongs had the same aggrieved stamp of turmoil on his face now. The sun was on the rise. He had been awake and sitting alone at the campfire for several hours. He dredged up the memory of tidying his wife's body for burial and digging the hole. His teeth were clenched as he lowered her in it; his prayers were gut-wrenching.

After filling the hole, he spent several days collecting rocks to pile a substantial heap on top of the grave. He also took the time to carve and lash together a cross, then stayed beside her final resting place for almost a week, speculating and lamenting—he was still in that state of bewildering sorrow. Contemplation was a keen razor that had no mercy.

He hobbled forward to tend to the needs of the fire. When the flames were crackling, he surveyed the area. He surmised that his son-in-law was scouting or hunting for fresh meat. The horses in the rope-corral were quietly feeding on the lush grass. He grunted in defeat. No matter how strenuous his efforts, he could glean no motivation or meaning. Daniel Twosongs felt helpless to fend off the discouragement that currently bedeviled him.

Pete Axler had never experienced the interior of a jail cell. Until now. His hands were clasped together as he sat on the steel-framed bed that had a feather mattress so thin he could feel every knot in the web of ropes that held it suspended in place. He hadn't slept since being arrested and tossed in the hoosegow—two nights without so much as a wink.

The stonewalled lockup was twelve-by-twelve, with one iron-barred window on the backside; it faced west, so at this early juncture of his third day of incarceration the room had the dusky gray qualities of a dungeon. He heard the hammers of workmen outside; apparently they had progressed past the sawing of lumber stage.

He stood, a tall and thin man whose face was cast in the seemingly permanent lines of a puzzled frown. In his present predicament, those features were chiseled in deepset trenches that highlighted a recent addition to his face. His right eye was swollen into a puffy squint and encircled by a welted rainbow bruise.

There were other bumps and discolored contusions hidden beneath his shirt, received courtesy of a liquored up mob. He sauntered in his dawdling shuffle to have a gander at the construction project outside. One man was nailing boards on the platform, while two others were tinkering with and testing the swinging trap door. He watched them labor on the gallows for a short spell and wondered if the magistrate had declared a time for the hanging yet.

A grim smile pinched his mouth. He returned to the bunk and sat across it, his back up against the wall. His stomach was tense. He pondered on how circumstances had conspired to provide him with a jackpot of trouble. He thought about his son and daughter; how much he cared for them and wanted nothing more than to be a good provider for all their needs.

What if help didn't arrive in time? How was it possible for him to be the scapegoat waiting to reap the penalty of a criminal? What if the oddball turn of events were rigged against him? He may never see Jesse and Amanda again; they might be destined to grow up fatherless. He couldn't bear to dwell on that idea. His lips puckered even more tightly.

He let his mind drift to his wife, a woman who he held responsible for redeeming his dreams; she had, in fact, given perspective and purpose to his entire life. She believed in him in ways he couldn't comprehend. He recalled their time together the night before he had set off from *WT Ranch* on a business trip to Gunnison.

The bedroom curtains were drawn open to allow moonbeams to stream in and create shadow dances on the floor. They were snuggled beneath the covers in the tender afterglow of goodbye lovemaking. Their bodies were sweaty as relaxation tingled to their bones. Her head was on his chest; his right hand cupped over the curve of her hip.

"I'll miss you," she said softly. "I do every time you're away."

"Me, too."

"This time is different."

"How? Why?"

She hesitated. Silence, as prickly as thorns, sprouted up between them. "Naomi?"

She palmed his whiskery chin. "It's nothing."

"Really? What's different this time, Naomi?"

"I'm sorry, Pete."

"For what?"

"I wasn't going to say anything."

"Spill the beans, Naomi."

"I've got a bad feeling about Gunnison."

"A bad feeling? I ain't tracking with you."

"Misgivings. A foreboding. I don't know, Pete."

"A premonition?"

"Yes. I'm afraid something terrible is going to happen."

A shouted curse from the yard brought Axler back to the reality of his situation. Over and over again, the Lord's name was being taken in vain. He went and pressed his forehead against the bars to have a look. One of the workers was alternating between shaking his hand and sucking his thumb, having obviously hit it with a hammer.

He pondered how he had gotten into this pickle. A lump materialized in his throat. He was as uptight as his even-tempered personality would ever allow. His helpmate's voice startled him as it whispered through his head. *I'm afraid something terrible is going to happen.* Pete Axler chuckled weakly. Her foresight had correctly discerned the handwriting on the wall.

Every detail had been thoroughly vetted. There were no loose ends needing her attention, but that didn't prevent Delores Solrizo from reevaluating the plans once again as she patiently waited to board the stagecoach. As she did so, she was being distracted and entertained by an energetic schoolboy doing handsprings in the street.

She smiled thinly. It was much too early in the morning for *anyone* to be that peppy. She turned away from the acrobat and thought about the Suncurl Café; she had no concerns. She had recruited a go-getting Mexican couple into her care and for the past six months, along with room and board, she provided intensive training in all aspects of the restaurant business.

Now, for the next six months they were in charge of the Suncurl Café— her three-man breakfast crew, who did most of the heavy lifting in exchange for hot meals, would willingly pitch in whenever needed. She was fully confident that any glitches or problems that developed would be taken care of with efficient effectiveness.

When she returned to Santa Fe, as part of the bargain, she intended to make an investment in the couple's future by financing their own establishment somewhere across town. They were trustworthy and had an abiding faith which was important to her as she sought prospective candidates. She met them at an Our Lady of Guadalupe benevolence meeting.

Delores adjusted her sunbonnet. It was stylish, with a frilly blue ribbon fringed around the circular brim. She took a step toward the team of six horses harnessed and ready. Her two large suitcases were being strapped down in the luggage rack on top. A pair of teamsters made a final walk-around checkup; both men had weathered faces that had been etched and seared by innumerable hours exposed to the wind and sun.

She climbed aboard and swished her skirt as she sat on the cushioned seat. She'd been told that there would be one other passenger accompanying her, but that appeared to be wrong. Her eyes darted sidelong in time to see the tumbler do a series of cartwheels that ended with him on his feet. He scooped up a knapsack, raced over and jumped in the carriage.

"Jack, ma'am," he said, slamming the door. "Jack Whistler, at your service."

She gave his offered hand a cursory shake. "Delores Solrizo."

The coach pulled out in a rocky jolt. He stowed his bag under the seat across from her and roosted, folding his legs under his bottom. "Happy to make your acquaintance, ma'am."

She smiled and nodded agreeably. She was impressed by his demeanor. Sinewy and stocky, he projected a raw confidence that crept close to the kind of audacity which could only be forged in the furnace of age, but he was a mere youngster. His gray eyes were bright and inquiring, his complexion milky smooth. "Where are you off to, Jack?"

"Everywhere, ma'am."

"Are you a gypsy wanderer?"

He scrunched forward and locks of dark hair fell across his brow. "I've been making my way across the country." He flicked his hair with a thumb. "Started in San Francisco, where I was born and referred to as a street urchin, among some other not so nice names."

"Do you have a final destination in mind?"

"No, ma'am," he replied, swaying to the jouncing bumps of the ride. "I've been stopping long enough to earn vittles and fare money to the next station. Today I'm going to Las Vegas. I'll stick around there for a few weeks and pick up a paying job that tutors me in some way, then hit the road again. I'm aiming to get to New York and when I do, I'll put a grubstake together, then book passage to Europe. I'm going to see the world before it's all used up."

"How old are you, Jack?"

"Twelve, ma'am."

"Twelve going on thirty, I'd surmise."

He laughed, eyes twinkling. "Yes, ma'am."

"You've got gumption, I'll grant you that much."

"Thanks. What's your story, ma'am?"

Her eyes narrowed cautiously. "I beg your pardon."

"No offense intended, ma'am. Data and facts," he answered, arms outstretched as his lips curled and eyebrows crooked in a disarming smile. "Life's all about information."

"That's a curious view, Jack," she said, grabbing the handhold on the wall as the vehicle thudded over a jarring pothole. "My story is my business, but since we are going to be together for a while, I'm bound for Las Vegas for starters, then it's on to Dodge City."

"I'll get to Dodge City soon enough, but Las Vegas is the bull's-eye just now." He leaned askance to have a look out the window, then placed his feet firmly on the floor. "A cardsharp got himself shot in a saloon yesterday. And it was Kid Greer who done the killing."

"What?" she asked, voice rising sharply.

His shoulders hunched upward, evidently surprised by her reaction. "Information, ma'am. I can never get enough information so I tend to hole up at telegraph offices whenever I can. My job in Santa Fe was as a runner for Western Union. For two-bits a day and a mat in a nook to sleep on I've been just about living there for a month." He rolled his eyes excitedly. "News came in yesterday that Kid Greer shot and killed a gambler in Las Vegas."

She blanched. Her face took on an enfeebled pallor and her posture withered. She felt hotness fill her eyes. He kept chattering for a mile or more, but she passively ignored him. He finally clammed up, leaving her alone with a slew of disagreeable memories. As the stagecoach pitched and shook onward, Delores Solrizo screamed silent prayers for the soul of her son.

Charley Jondreau had finished shaving and wash-up. The campsite was on a lonesome stretch of the Pecos River. He was bare-chested at the water's edge. His timeworn red flannels were holey and tattered. He pulled them up from his waist and slid his arms in. His fingers went to fasten its front because he kept forgetting that all the buttons were missing.

He loosened his belt and adjusted the saggy britches of the underwear. He put his denim shirt on and tucked it in. As he picked up his kit, he was captivated by a lone hawk upstream. His heart did a little jump and he paid close attention to the red-tailed raptor as it flew over him in a southerly direction. He remained still until the bird became a dot, then walked up the bank.

A coffeepot was on a flat stone at one side of the fire-pit. He squatted on his heels and poured a cup. It smelled good, but tasted bitter. He sipped it and listened to padding footsteps approaching through the shrubbery. A tiny smile formed as he turned to see Max Dawson returning from a secluded cove around a bend in the river.

Her strawberry-blonde tresses were wet and her face had been scrubbed to reddish hues. She wore a checkerboard orange shirt and dungarees. Low on her right hip was a bone-handled Colt Peacemaker in an unadorned holster. She crouched beside her gear to put a washcloth and soap away. "I swear, I'd give my eyeteeth for a tub of hot water in a steamy bathhouse."

"Those can't be that expensive."

"Very funny. I saw the hawk, Charley."

"A good omen, eh."

"When will we break camp?"

"As soon as we see to the horses and pack up." He looked at the blue skies; clouds were drifting off to the west and the sun was at eight o'clock. "Two hours at the outside."

"Sounds like a plan." She stood and finger combed her hair, then slid a black Stetson in place. She went about the business of examining and positioning her weapons. A double-barreled derringer in a shoulder-sling under her left arm and its twin in a sheath inside her right boot. An Arkansas toothpick was lodged in the other boot. "We got to make ourselves some luck."

"Luck ain't nothing more than hard traveling."

"You got it, Charley." She pulled cheesecloth from her saddlebags and opened it to get two slender slabs of dried beef. "This is the last of our jerky," she said, offering him a slice.

He took it. "We need to resupply, eh."

"How long have we been partners?"

"The better part of four years, Max."

She shrugged into a dull-colored jacket. "We've never been this ragged. In our pursuit of Smoky Crowe we always have to be prepared and well provisioned. If we came upon him now it'd be nitty-gritty and we'd be hard pressed because we're both haggard and played-out."

"That miscreant's tracks are cold," Charley said, chewing slowly. "He's gone to wherever it is he vanishes to whenever we get close. I ain't quitting the chase until he's dead."

"Quitting?" She laughed throatily and went to the campfire. "Who said anything about quitting? That's never going to be an option." She jiggled the coffeepot, then filled a cup and swallowed a mouthful. "That's as black as sin and just as nasty."

"More chicory than coffee, eh."

"In all the miles have you ever heard me complain, Charley?"

"If so I have disremembered."

"Bad weather, hungry, tired, beat down, discouraged, bamboozled by Crowe again and again, and we always draw strength from each other, but now, I'm plain fagged out," she said, and had another sip. "Drinking boiled crud and calling it coffee makes me want to puke."

"I ain't fool enough to argue with you, Max."

"I need a change of scenery, is all," she told him, arching her back and stretching. "A tub and properly laundered garments are in the offing, Charley. Plus a restaurant meal or two would be nice and just one night in an honest to God bed, even if it's in a flea-trap hotel."

"We need to resupply, eh," he said again, nodding. He thrust his jaw out in its bulldog guise. "A set of new threads from the inside out would do me good. Get necessities and be ready for winter because sleet and snow will be coming whether we like it or not." The noise of horns caused him to do a slow turnabout and explore the sky. "Honkers."

"What?"

Jondreau, born and raised in the territory of the Great Lakes, had a broad grin. In a moment a flock of Canada geese breezed into view from the north and flew twenty yards above them in a perfect V, singing lyrically. "Majestic and graceful. Loyal and protective."

"You getting homesick on me?"

"An amazing gift from the Great Spirit," he said, reverence in his voice. "My Iroquois forebears use goose grease mixed with certain herbs as a poultice for sickness in the chest." He was still focused on the sky. "Humans can learn much from honkers. If a goose is injured, its mate guards it until it recovers or dies." He gave her a steely look. "The hawk and now the honkers. We go south and dog it off the trail at the first shanty shacks of civilization."

"Hope the town has some hurly-burly entertainment," she said, flipping her cup upside down so the liquid splashed and sputtered on the hot coals. "I could use an influx of drama."

He grunted dismissively. She gave him a devil-may-care gesture and sported a stunning smile, then got busy bundling her belongings. He went to where their animals were foraging on long lead lines. The dapple gray stallion and soot-gray mare greeted him in unison, but the mule was standoffish. As he fed them oats, the sunshine on his newly shaven scalp felt fine.

An hour later, the allies were mounted and riding side by side.

chapter two

Truth & Vagaries

"O Lord, how long shall I cry, and thou wilt not hear! even cry out unto thee of violence, and thou wilt not save! Why dost thou shew me iniquity, and cause me to behold grievance? for spoiling and violence are before me: and there are that raise up strife and contention."

~HABAKKUK~

DEACON COBURN WAS STUDYING in the backyard of the boarding house on Paladora Street. The morning had freshness and was laden with the seeds to become a beautiful autumn day. He was on the shady side of the toolshed sitting in one of the two slope-backed chairs he had cobbled together from hickory purchased at Zimmermann's Hardware & Lumber.

He had his Bible open on his lap, his head lowered and mind engaged. He was on his third read-through of the book of Hosea—fourteen chapters that fascinated him. Hosea, a prophet in the northern kingdom of ancient Israel, was married to an adulterous woman named Gomer, who caused him much anguish. The historical story had metaphorical overtones.

His index finger moved below each line. He stopped and tapped the page, deciding that the first verse of chapter three was key to the narrative. He read it aloud: "*Then said the Lord unto me, Go yet, love a woman beloved of her friend, yet an adulteress, according to the love of the Lord toward the children of Israel, who look to other gods, and love flagons of wine."*

A grin lifted the thick swatches of his moustache and furrowed his brow. He had the text and tale to tell. He relaxed and closed his eyes to think over essential elements of Hosea's story. When he was satisfied that he had the sequence of events clear, he looked toward the street in expectation, and riffled pages to land in the Psalms. He perused the vibrant poetry as prayers and where possible, personalized the praise or pleas for mercy.

More than ten minutes passed, then his friend and son-in-law came around the house, wearing a hangdog expression. "Running late for our weekly confab, ain't you, Sam?"

Beadle took his hands out of his pockets. "A restless night."

"That's been normal for me of late."

Beadle moved the empty chair so that its back was angled away from Coburn, then settled in and braced his right ankle on his left knee. "I suppose I should get used to sleepless nights. I'll likely have many of those ahead of me when our baby is born."

"Most certainly. How's my daughter?"

"Complicated and stubborn, to say the least."

Coburn chuckled wryly. "Partially correct, but not her full measure."

"She's working at the office, so what does that tell you?"

"At this hour? On a Saturday?"

"Yes, sir," Sam answered, frustration noticeable in his voice. "I just got the bum's rush out of there because she had an idea that required her undivided attention."

"Stubborn, she is indeed."

"And single-minded," Sam said tersely. "I don't know what to do with her, Deacon. She needs to be taking it easy. I'm worried and nervous, but she'll hear none of it."

"I have no sage advice for you, Sam."

"What was her mother like, Deacon?"

Coburn scratched at a three-day growth of scruffy chin-whiskers. He squinted, and his eyes got a murky and faraway gleam. "Complicated and stubborn, tender and kindhearted."

Beadle nodded perceptively. "So there was no windstorm when that apple fell?"

"Not even a stirring. It was a dead drop, Sam."

"Do you have any insights into what disease took Angela?"

Coburn grimaced hard. "What? How would I know? Why would you ask?" A blush of scarlet crept up and darkened his complexion. He projected a sense of transparent vulnerability and stared at the sky; he was genuinely rattled. He released a loud breath.

"I apologize. I meant no . . ."

Coburn halted him with a raised hand. Tears misted his eyes as he spoke in a tone thickened by emotion. "I was a different man, Sam. It still hurts. When I knew Angela there were factors in the mix that got screwy and confused. I was unhinged."

"You? Unhinged? That seems farfetched."

"Not really," Deacon replied sadly. "The slaughter of war lacerated my sensibilities. A part of my brain turned off. I had amnesia. Niceness was in me, but I was lost."

"Lost?"

"I make no excuses," Deacon said, thumbing moisture off his cheeks. "My transgressions against a good woman were mine alone. The circumstances of her death emphasizes my guilt and failings. You ask about the illness that took Angela." He shook his head and hiked in a shivery breath. "I didn't even know she was sick, let alone died, until Abbey showed up in Abilene."

"That's a hurtful weight to shoulder, Deacon."

"We all carry burdens of one kind or another."

"Sure enough, but you're different."

"No, I ain't, Sam."

"Others look to you for strength and comfort or something."

"And I do my best to accommodate folks."

"But you're a closed book."

Coburn smiled and cleared his throat good-naturedly. "I ain't ever been one to advertise my wrongdoings. Any vestige of righteousness in me truly is nothing more than filthy rags. All I do is wrap the hope of God's grace and mercy around my wounds and soldier on."

"I admire your faith, Deacon. It often challenges me."

"Thanks for saying so." He laid a palm across the Bible. "I've been reviewing Hosea and have been inspired anew by the love of God. No matter what we do or where we go his love ceaselessly hounds us. We commit grievous sins against God's holiness and justice, yet he seeks and pursues us. His tender love is unchangeable and always within reach.

"Then I was reading the thirty-seventh Psalm and took much encouragement from these verses: *The steps of a good man are ordered by the Lord: and he delighteth in his way. Though he fall, he shall not be utterly cast down: for the Lord upholdeth him with his hand.*"

Beadle nodded. "Reassuring words."

"Ones that have seen fulfillment in me," Deacon said candidly. "I could have been *utterly cast down* because I fell horribly in my actions with Angela, and though the consequences still come to vex me from time to time, the Lord orders my steps and upholds me."

"That's akin to a Sunday service testimonial," Sam stated, getting to his feet. "And on that fortifying note I'll be off for a shave and a haircut, along with an exchange of hearsay."

"Let Whitey know I'll be in later. Take care." Deacon waited until he was gone, then sat back and took some relaxed moments to relish the boundless blue of the sky. The glassy beauty of it reinvigorated his contemplative mood. He balanced the Good Book against his chest and flipped to Hosea. His inner clock told him he had time to read it over once more.

Butch Mackenzie was alone at the Western Union office in Dodge City. The blinds were pulled down and he sat despondently at his desk. The splendor of the day meant nothing to him. He suffered chronic miseryitis and had awaken in the grips of a flare-up. There was no rhyme or reason to the bouts which came upon him without so much as a by-your-leave.

To add to his gloom, he was the addressee of an unfortunate telegram. He squinted at it and had been doing so for the better part of an hour. In the dreary half-light of the room he couldn't actually determine the words, but ascertained the contents of the message. It came from the supervisor of the neurology department at a medical facility in St. Louis.

His sleeves were rolled up above his elbows and his bifocals rested near the bottom of his nose. The stump of a burnt out cigar was clenched at a corner of his mouth. He had an uncouth habit of smoking a cheroot halfway, then snuffing it so as to chew the butt until it was gooey and saliva soaked. When it was nothing but brownish slime he'd deposit it in the trash.

He slumped in the barrel-like swivel chair and grumbled tiredly. He appeared to be a pair of circles attached to chunky stubs for arms and legs—a rotund torso accentuated by an expanse of table muscle overhanging his beltline and a round face with flabby jowls. Above a thin grayish beard, his cheeks bore the scars of the acne that had afflicted his adolescence.

Born on a Missouri farm in the region that came to be called Buchanan County, he had grown up within spitting distance of the Missouri River. He married a nearby neighbor girl and they ran off to Kansas City to make a life, though that hadn't turned out as either of them hoped. There were difficulties from the beginning, but they persevered. After a couple false alarms, a daughter arrived and immediately became the center of their world.

He was now fifty-seven years old and had been batching it for fifteen years. Always private and somewhat eccentric, since being on his own he had become reclusive, cultivating antisocial tendencies. He was gruff and abrasive with customers and acquaintances alike, which didn't hurt business, but would often be back-fence chitchat for busybodies.

"Huh," he said, pushing to his feet. He chomped sloppily on the cigar so that it moved to the center of his mouth. He bent over and spat the sopping wet tobacco in the garbage can, then lumbered lopsidedly to the window and raised the blinds. A bright splash of sunlight caused him to wince as he read the telegram, unkempt eyebrows dipping low.

> *Patient not doing well. The staff reports a failure to thrive. Will update when there is news.*

"Huh." A clump of emotion made him quiver, but from much practice, he smothered the tender feelings. He slid the paper into his shirt pocket. He left the office and didn't hesitate for an instant on the boardwalk. His arms slugged in vehement locomotion as he went to visit the only individual in town he treated with respect and for whom he harbored compassion.

The ten year old girl was backed into a corner. All she had for a weapon to defend herself was a wooden spoon, which she handled as though it was a butcher knife. Her nose had already been bloodied and a welt was rising on her upper forehead. Her eyes were red and watery. Spittle frothed over her lips; her teeth were bared as furiously as a rabid wildcat.

An older and bigger classmate had her boxed in. She was a snarky-faced redhead with close-cropped hair and a darkish birthmark prominent on her neck, who had given herself the nickname Peaches. "You stole my pudding, Lahay. I'm gonna make you pay for it."

"You're a liar."

"Am I?" She threw a punch that missed. The tables in the lunchroom had emptied and a crowd of girls were laughing and shouting catcalls. Squealed vulgarities and noisy jeers of encouragement overwhelmingly favored the instigating aggressor. Peaches, the unchallenged bully of the workhouse, ruled by hoarding the currency of intimidation. The goads and taunts were a continuous upsurge of cheers that split her face apart in a delighted smile.

"Lahay's a thief!"

"Get her!"

"Kick her in the pussy!"

"Slap the snot out of the shitheel!"

Peaches was bug-eyed proud. She stepped closer to her target, hands held up with the fingers curled menacingly. "Don't be a hero, stupid. Just lay down and take the beating."

Lahay stood her ground. "No."

The redhead lunged at the smaller girl, who ducked and jabbed upward with the wooden spoon; it caught Peaches in the trachea. She gasped and backpedaled, then attacked again. This time she warded off any potential blow by twisting the would-be blade from her grip. It clattered to the floor, and the combatants were slamming against each other.

Fists were flying; feet were kicking and stomping. Peaches easily dominated. She was stronger and a more experienced fighter. She got her hands around Lahay's neck. She squeezed with brutal fierceness. Lahay was gurgling and turning blue. She grabbed her assailant's wrists and used the leverage; she kneed her in the crotch. The two tousled and fell together. While they were rolling and slapping, the onlookers shrieked gleeful heckles.

"Kill her, Peaches!"

"Beat her bloody!"

"Rip her guts out!"

"Gouge her eyes! Gouge her eyes!"

The last directive became a chant that the throng sang out; the swell of their voices surged louder and louder. Peaches was grinning wickedly. Intense pride shone and glistened on her face. She had complete advantage. Lahay was pinned beneath her and she wasn't squirming. Peaches had her head in her hands, thumbs digging at the eye sockets.

"Gouge her eyes! Gouge her eyes! Gouge her eyes!"

"You pay now, Lahay!" Peaches slurred, applying pressure. Her victim shrank and was docile. Peaches turned toward the swarming cheerers and removed her right hand to wave it like a maestro commanding a choir to hit the high notes. It was then that Peaches received her comeuppance. Lahay locked her teeth on her left wrist and chomped viciously.

Blood spurted and Peaches recoiled, squawking obscenities. They tumbled around. Lahay was a whirling, thrashing dynamo. She employed elbows, knees, fists with equal velocity. She got on top of her tormentor and fought fiercely; mindlessly, even. Her arms were bashing in a seesaw motion and every knuckle sandwich struck its mark.

A thunderous bellow followed by the thudding of running clodhoppers parted the yelling spectators as surely as Moses divided the waters of the Red Sea. The hulking matriarch clutched hold of Lahay by the scuff of her neck and spun her around. "You again? All you are is trouble! Back to the basement with you!" Her meat-hook hands shook her mercilessly and in a crazed fraction of a second, the shrewish hag became the crudely malformed face of her mother.

Avis Lahay wrenched from sleep and was battering the air; her hands were balled so tight that her fingernails cut deeply. "Oh, my God!" she exclaimed, panting breathlessly. Her face was wet with tears. Pressure found release in a whooshing exhale. Her cramped fists opened. She rolled onto her side and gawked at the bleeding imprints on her palms.

The fisticuffs had been real; she'd spent her childhood scrapping to defend herself against being browbeaten to death in an institution that warehoused orphans. Then, at the age of twelve, she was rescued from the prisonlike school by Pinkertons working at the behest of her mother. Peace had been brokered with the woman who bore her. All the broken fences were repaired, so the reason for the nightmare's outlandish ending eluded her comprehension.

A steady discharge from her tear ducts moistened the pillow; she turned it over, then pulled her legs up into a near fetal position. The sunbeams slanted through the windowpane at an angle that told her it was midmorning. She remained in bed for another hour, crying and sniffling as she hoped and prayed that the weeping would wash away the malicious memory.

Abbey Langton was stooped over her desk transcribing an essay. Every so often she would pause and do some on-the-fly editing, but mostly she kept the pencil moving to get the bare bones of the ideas on paper. First drafts excited her and she could not be side-railed when she was mining creativity and putting the foundational sentences together. Second drafts were for rearranging and building; she rarely, if ever, had to do a third transcript.

"That does it fine," she said aloud as she drew a squiggly line across the bottom of the final page. She slid it beneath the four previous sheets, then tapped them together. Pencil in hand, she leaned back in the chair for an initial look over. As she did so, she made occasional stars in the margins to indicate which sections required extra consideration.

The tinny bell tinkled. She glanced up and smiled happily as the short and bespectacled town grump tottered through the doorway; though he was coarse with others, he cared for her with the fondness of a kindly old uncle. "Did you get a response from my latest telegram?"

"Huh." Butch Mackenzie duck-waddled to a stool, plopped down on it, then pogoed it closer to her desk. He was wheezing and sweaty. "You'll be asking me that until the sun decides to go down in the east, Miss Abbey," he informed her in his grinding gravel voice. He palmed his brow. "You won't be hearing back from those do-nothings in Washington."

"I might surprise you, Butch. I may wear them down."

"Huh. Do you intend to work all day?"

"Just until noontime," she replied, placing the composition in a file folder. She turned her chair to face him. "I have a lunch date with Sam, then we're going for a buggy ride."

"Huh. That husband of yours should take heed of your condition."

"I'm having a baby, Butch. It's not a condition."

"It won't be all cookies and ice cream, huh."

"Really?" She giggled jauntily. "I thought it'd be a painless breeze."

He visibly stiffened. His lips twisted into a sneer. The chubs of his cheeks reddened, which made the decades old pockmarks rise like newly acquired welts. Shards of anger or fear or humiliation teemed in his eyes. "You ought not to joke about such a delicate matter."

She was startled by his conduct. "What is it, Butch? What's wrong?"

"Nothing," he replied, dismissing the inquiry with a terse backhand.

"Butch? What has you riled?"

"Huh. I'm concerned for you, Miss Abbey."

"I'm fine. Tired, but that's to be expected."

"You're going to wear down to a frazzled nub."

She pooh-poohed the notion. "I will not. I'm a tough bird."

"Your husband needs to be more conscientious."

"Sam is plenty dutiful, Butch. I've no complaints."

"Huh." His breathing had eased; he was no longer raspy and short-winded. Perspiration, however, remained in beads on his forehead and along his upper lip. He shifted and had to adjust his roly-poly belly as he leaned forward. "Did you really know Kid Greer?"

"That's an odd question," she commented, eyebrows shooting up in bewilderment. "He was just plain Liam Greer when I met him in Abilene ten years ago. And he wasn't right in the head." Wariness permeated her voice as she inquired, "Why do you ask?"

"He's forsaken his hidey-hole."

Her expression wrinkled. "What?"

"Huh. He's in the news and on the move again."

"That certainly takes the rag off the bush, doesn't it?" she said, mouth pursing in a flare of annoyance. "I thought perchance the dunderhead troublemaker had met his Maker."

"Huh. No such luck, Miss Abbey."

"How long has it been since we've heard reports of him?"

"Let me think," he answered, tapping his fingertips together. "There's been no headlines since he and Smoky Crowe butchered that woman in San Antonio in December of '77."

"Yes, that's exactly right," she said, nodding slightly. "Sam and I were in the Dakota Territory. We had taken a room in Spearfish in late November. The tales about the debauchery perpetrated by Greer and Crowe in Texas reached us in mid-January as I recall."

The disheveled clumps of hair above his eyes wiggled like little worms. "Huh. Then the pair were gone, but as of yesterday, it appears that Greer is riding alone. The murderous scumbag is all over the wires. He shot a man in Las Vegas and cut off one of his ears."

"Excuse me?" she blurted, shock-eyed.

"Huh. That's the scuttlebutt."

"Cut off an ear? That's screwball crazy."

"Quandaries and quagmires, Miss Abbey. Quandaries and quagmires, huh."

The tension in her face relaxed and drained away. Her head tilted and a good-humored chortle jostled free from her throat. "Quandaries and quagmires?"

"A dilemma awash in a miry bog of trouble," he replied, grinning. "Huh. Or another way of saying screwball crazy. It was a phrase I heard my dear grandmother use on a regular basis to cover a multitude of situations. She could zing it out in sarcasm or be solemnly serious."

"It communicates much, Butch."

"Huh. It's been collecting dust in my head forever."

"I mean to tell you that I'll be appropriating it as my own."

"Have at it, Miss Abbey."

"Whew." She sat bolt upright, hands folding over her midsection. "Wow. That was a heave-ho or an almighty kick. I think this child is practicing to be a bronc buster."

"Quandaries and quagmires, ma'am."

Their eyes connected and sparked jubilantly as a mutual chuckle became full-blown laughter. The jocularity continued until tears were sloshy and slippery. He repetitively slapped his knee, crimson-cheeked and slobbering. It was a side of Butch Mackenzie that only Abbey Langton saw because no one else could ever crack his cantankerous exterior. The hilarity passed and the friendship deepened; they conversed about possible names for the baby.

Sally Twosongs sat still on the rocker swing enjoying the blue skies morning. She was being amused by Hank as the collie diligently kept Jesse and Amanda herded together. The children were running and exploring along a far tree line, mindful of their tag-along, but having no inkling that the four-legged playmate was taking care of them.

Every so often the tri-color dog would get aligned to the house and bark three times to let Sally Twosongs know that she remained its top priority. Each time it did so her smile enlarged in amazement at the animal's intelligence and trustworthiness. She bent forward, but the immediate pressure on her abdomen caused her to incline back to find a degree of comfort.

The front door opened and Naomi Axler came outside. "The kitchen is spic and span, and a casserole is ready to be put in the oven for supper. We can have sandwiches for lunch." She took a prolonged look in the direction of her son and daughter, shook her head blithely, then sat beside the Navajo woman. "Have we decided what to prepare for gathering tomorrow?"

"No. That's usually Caleb's department," Sally Twosongs replied, hands entwined over the swell of her tummy. "He takes pleasure in preparing Sunday dinner when he's here."

"I never knew that," Naomi said, shimmying out the folds of her skirt. A frown crimped her brow as she turned sideways. "I don't think I would have ever guessed that about him."

"No one would," Sally Twosongs noted, succinct and plain-spoken. "He's a private and quiet servant who wants no fanfare or claps on the back. I miss him terribly."

Naomi agreed with a quick bob of her head. "I know," she said, undiluted melancholy in her tone. "I'm missing Pete more than ever. I'm finding it especially difficult just now."

"I hear dismay, Naomi. What is it?"

"Dismay?"

"Something has you downcast."

"Yes," Naomi admitted, clasping her hands together on her lap. "It's nothing to concern you, Sally Twosongs. You have more important matters on your plate just now."

"What's more important than being kind?"

"Nothing, of course."

"So why are you holding back, Naomi?"

"I'm trying to be kind," she replied halfheartedly.

"Are we going to get into a kindness contest?"

Naomi laughed feebly, balking at the query. "Certainly not."

"So what's the problem?"

"You're processing grief for your mother."

"Reaching out is a healing balm," Sally Twosongs countered assertively.

"You're anticipating the birth of your child."

"Your protests are lame, to say the least."

Naomi slumped her shoulders and sighed hugely. "You're missing your husband as much or more than I'm missing mine. I do not wish to take advantage of your listening ear."

"The Creator gave me ears to listen," Sally Twosongs said, "and a discerning heart where now and again bits of wisdom sprout. Please allow me to be helpful, if I can."

Naomi checked on her children, who unknown to them, were being methodically rounded up and steered toward the house. The bushy-haired collie was yelping and zigzagging to achieve its purpose. "That dog is almost human," she absently murmured under her breath, then abruptly exhaled a burst of run-on sentences that were emotionally charged. Her voice constricted in tension as she spoke of her intuition and recounted the nightmare from beginning to end.

Sally Twosongs listened. Empathy pooled in her dark eyes.

". . . but it wasn't Adam. It was Pete," Naomi concluded dourly.

"I understand your disheartened mood."

"It was definitely Pete on my lap. His neck was broken."

"You've had the dream once?"

"Once was more than enough."

"Yes." Sally Twosongs bowed her head for a moment; when she raised it, her teary eyes fixed on her friend. "An unpleasantness will disturb your sleep again. I am sorry. The meaning is unclear. There is an inexplicable aura around you. Dense and impenetrable."

"Can you *see* anything useful?" Naomi asked, startled and apprehensive.

Sally Twosongs scowled gloomily. "Much mystery and confusion. A tangled commotion in shades of obscurity. Fear is the enemy. Give in not to fear. You are to keep the faith."

"For me? Or for my children?"

"Both," Sally Twosongs answered sternly.

"Easier said than done."

"Necessity demands being a doer."

"I am frightened, Sally Twosongs. I cannot shake free of fretting."

"You are not alone, Naomi."

"I *feel* cut loose and abandoned."

"Feelings can be liars," Sally Twosongs said, adamancy in her voice. "Jesus is with you always. He will never leave or forsake you. He is good medicine."

Naomi pinched a smile. "I must buck up and put Joshua 1:9 into action." She took a hefty breath. "*Have not I commanded thee? Be strong and of a good courage; be not afraid, neither be thou dismayed: for the Lord thy God is with thee whithersoever thou goest.*"

They exchanged a glance of affirmation, which was forthwith interrupted by squeals of laughter. Hank had Jesse and Amanda near the porch, running circles around them as the kiddies made futile efforts to escape. The charming scene lightened the weight and did much to increase the encouragement and bolster a sense of confidence passing between the women.

~ ~ ~

"You shouldn't have conscripted me, Eliza."

"It's too late for complaints, Hans."

He grunted and wagged a finger at her. Husband and wife were at the table. Faded afternoon sunrays slanted through the window and danced across the room. He had the Good Book in front of him, squinting at it as he fluttered the pages and randomly skipped from cover to cover. She observed his discomfort, amusement rampant in her eyes.

"I'm no Bible man."

"Lord, have mercy!" she exclaimed, humor rising in her voice. "This isn't supposed to be a theological treatise or dissection of some controversial doctrinal opinion. You are to bring a devotional for the *WT Ranch* Sunday gathering, which means you'll be among friends."

"Well, that's a fine tidbit of news to soothe me," he said, low and grouchy. "Just the same, you shouldn't have volunteered me. I'm no Bible man. I understand little of it."

"Sometimes you think too hard, Hans."

"What?"

"Tell a Bible story," she answered easily.

"Which one?"

Her lips curled, sly and impish. "Whichever one you choose."

"That's not at all funny, Eliza."

"I know for a fact that you are familiar with at least one story from the Old Testament," she said directly. "Years ago it used to be the standard go-to in your repertoire."

He sat back and rubbed his jawline. "How could I forget? It's the only Bible I ever heard growing up in Hessia. Over and over I was enlightened in its principles by my father."

"You replicated the process in our son."

"I did no such thing, Eliza."

"Please, Hans. What's the name of Caleb's horse?"

"Shadrach."

"I was there when we sold out in Gettysburg," she said, eyes gleaming. "Your memory might be getting mushy, but it was me beside you in that Conestoga wagon."

His mouth twitched into a smile. "I'm not *that* addled yet."

She beamed at him. "I sat around the campfire every night as we traveled across country and listened to you retell the same passage from the book of Daniel. It wouldn't take much for me to recite large portions of your rendition of Shadrach, Meshach, and Abednego."

"Why do I not doubt you?"

"I can still hear the points you drilled down to bedrock time and again," she replied, determination ringing in her voice. "Staring at the penalty of the fiery furnace, those Hebrew men stood boldly against power for no other reason than it was the right thing to do. They were men of principle who refused to bow and scrape before the golden idol."

"All true, Eliza."

"Yes, but you personalized it, Hans," she said flatly. "You concluded by saying: That's the kind of man you want to be, son. Always stand firm and be willing to pay the price. Those are life lessons that took hold and shaped Caleb into a man of virtue and character."

"I now have a text to study."

"Get to it, Mr. Weitzel," she said, rising swiftly. "Whilst I pack a bag to take with me tomorrow. I am anxious and excited to stay with Sally Twosongs for a few weeks until after the baby is born. Are you going to be able to get along without me?"

He grinned boyishly. "I'll find my way over at mealtimes."

"I expect so." She was chuckling as she went into the bedroom. He waited until she was out of sight before he turned his attention to the passage. He was no longer testy or flummoxed, but rather, with inspiration and a strategy to go forward, self-assurance took hold. For the next several hours, he meticulously contemplated how best to communicate his convictions.

That evening, the Alhambra Saloon in Dodge City had a quiet crowd for a Saturday. The tavern's doors and windows were open to allow whiffs of a breeze to keep the air relatively clear of smoke. Deacon Coburn sat at a back corner table nursing a mug of coffee and shot of whiskey, while cramming more Scripture into his head and heart.

His Bible was open to Hosea. He cradled his chin in his hand and two fingers tapped absentmindedly against his cheek. He had paid a visit to the Tonsorial Parlor, where Whitey Fitzgerald worked his magic; he was slick and shiny, his shaggy hair shortened and whiskers shaved except for the moustache which was clipped evenly along his upper lip.

He blocked out the hum of conversation to concentrate. His imagination was alive. He squeezed his eyes shut and pondered Hosea's embarrassment with his wife Gomer; how she lost interest in him and chased after many paramours. Despite her serial unfaithfulness, Hosea pursued her to bring her back. Coburn felt the rawness of emotion involved.

He heard the movement of a chair. His eyelids flinched open and he saw Avis Lahay taking a seat across from him. "Howdy-do, young lady. What brings you here?"

"This arrived for you at the boarding house," she answered, handing over a letter. She removed her straw skimmer and twirled it to her lap. "I thought it might be important."

Coburn turned the envelope over, then set it aside as his eyebrows scrunched into a frown. "Postmark and return address in Abilene. It's been ten years since I was in that town and I don't recognize the hand, but I'll get to it after we visit." He gestured to the bartender.

A moment later a glass of sarsaparilla was placed in front of Avis. "Thank you." She took a sip and sighed. "I'm on my way to Bell's Livery to give Gilgal and Pumpkin rubdowns."

"As I suspected." He sensed upset in her. "What's troubling you?"

She hesitated and started fidgeting with her hands. "I've been debating whether or not I should talk to you." She shrugged in resignation. "I've been having a bad dream."

Curiosity peaked in his eyes. "That interests me. About what?"

"Mom placed me in an orphanage as soon as I was born," she replied, toying with strands of her thickish auburn hair, which was loose on her shoulders. "You knew that right?"

"She told me many years after the fact, yes."

"I ended up in a workhouse that was brutal," she said bleakly. "It was supposedly a school, but had the characteristics of a penal institution. Reading, writing and social studies were doled out along with beatings and abuse that was purely psychological torture."

"You endured and overcame, Avis." He reached over and gently squeezed her hand for just a moment. "That doesn't diminish or dismiss any of the cruelty forced upon you, but understand that no one is unscathed. We all carry the wounds of bad memories."

"I'm not making excuses or complaining, am I, Deacon?" she asked, head tilting as her brow furled darkly. "My past is what it is and I guess the recurring nightmare demonstrates that I'm still coming to terms with it, but I don't ever want to be a whiner."

"You ain't a whiner, young lady," he said sincerely. "You have processed an abundance of emotional chaos and are triumphing over atrocious circumstances that sought to destroy you. Like your mother, you are more than a conqueror." He leaned forward, eyes insistent and affixed on her. "Now tell me about the tricks the night has been playing on you."

Her voice lowered and she drew invisible circles on the table as she proceeded to tell him the vital details. She laid it bare and came to the conclusion by painting a graphic description of her mother's face being twisted into an ugly grimace. "It's been disturbing me for more than a week. The particulars change, but it always ends the same. The spiteful hag becomes Mom."

His eyes were clouded with mist. "That's all sixes and sevens," he said, scowling. The reflection dominating the mirror of his mind was that of Delores Solrizo's marred expression; he saw it, distinct and striking. He blinked rapidly, but the sight refused to dissipate; instead, the seething distortion laced itself down to become a permanent construct of his psyche.

"Any thoughts or suggestions for me?"

"Nothing particularly profound, Avis," he answered, dull and tense. "Your mother made a plethora of mistakes, but she did an about-face and lives in forgiveness. Don't doubt her love."

"I won't, Deacon. Not ever," she said inflexibly. "I can't say why I think so, but I'm convinced the raging look in the dream is directed at someone else. It's not meant for me."

"That's a conundrum, young lady."

"I don't know what else to say." She stood and flipped the golden skimmer to a jaunty angle over her wavy tresses. The hatband was an inch-wide black and red ribbon. "Thanks for giving me a listen." She picked up her glass and finished off the sarsaparilla in a long pull. "I'll go care for our horses, then I'll be knee-deep in a rummy tournament with Whitey."

"Alright. Will I see you at church in the morning?"

"Of course." She strolled across the barroom. He scraped his chair on the floor and got to his feet, which was warning enough to cause a couple cowboys to avert wandering eyes away from her backside as she departed. When she was gone, he resumed his position. He tossed down the whiskey and coffee, then tore the envelope and shook out the single sheet.

> *August, 1882*
> *Abilene, Kansas*
>
> *Dear Mr. Coburn: First off, I must apologize for the tardiness of this correspondence. Your mother was extremely kind and encouraging to me and my wife when we were disciplined by the River Brethren. It was a difficult time, for which we took responsibility. I promised her that I would try to connect with you after we got settled in Kansas.*
>
> *We boarded a train in Pennsylvania and migrated here to join fellow River Brethren from Dauphin County and Perry County, and arrived in the summer of '78, so you can see that my delay is exorbitant. My name is Abraham Mueller. I am married to your sister Martha's eldest daughter, Anna. We have twin sons, Eli and Seth, born in April '78. Anna suffered difficulties last year and we lost a baby, but she is expecting again sometime this winter.*
>
> *Shortly after we got situated on the plains, Anna initiated contact with her Aunt Naomi in Colorado. She was pleased to do so. Since then they faithfully exchange missives, which keeps the family connected with news and happenings. It seems Anna has discovered a kindred spirit in Aunt Naomi, which much encourages her.*
>
> *We had to endure hardships from weather in our early time here, but perseverance has resulted in life being mostly reliably advantageous. The land is fertile and the opportunities are tremendous. We are working an acreage somewhat north of Abilene. Growing wheat, along with tending to chickens, goats, milk cows, and a few cattle.*
>
> *Our faith is vibrant. We are involved with the River Brethren. Each Sunday we gather with others from the community for services held in barns or in the open air. Most recently the Pyke family has hosted, which is good because their home is only a few miles east of us. We are endeavoring to raise our children in the fear and admonition of the Lord.*
>
> *I pray that you are well and as your mother says, centered.*
>
> *Cordially Yours,*
> *Abraham Mueller*

He exhaled a cheery groan and pondered the enjoyable communication. He wasn't inclined to letter writing, so decided he would respond via the telegraph. His eyes winked shut and he jerked; he was mugged by Avis Lahay's nightmare. The likeness of Delores Solrizo's face knotted in a wrathful glower unleashed a stabbing stiletto of pain in his skull.

Deacon Coburn was stunned and all at once, mightily mystified.

The woman pushed through the swinging doors into a roadhouse that had sawdust scattered on the floor and a smoky haze rising to the ceiling. Fright had her so far over the edge that her legs were functioning bonelessly. She wobbled and weaved past gapers assembled to watch the melodrama of a bombastic young buck holding court.

An unseen fingerpicker was making a banjo's strings trill a jubilant tune. There was an outrageous foolishness in the music that discombobulated her. She shoved her way to the mouthy pup's table. He sat like a preening rooster, a thin cheroot dangling from his lips as he shuffled a deck of cards. She gulped, breathless and frozen inside. Her fears were realized; the shifty-eyed teen performing sleight of hand tricks and quipping one-liners was her son.

"Why hello there, woman," he said, doffing his hat in a grandly sarcastic motion. His eyes roamed over her, dismissive and obscene. "Have you all met my whore mother?"

She blanched, cringing as strangers openly ogled her. "Why?" She stepped closer to him. "Why are you being like this? What are you doing here and what, in the name of all that is right and just, are you trying to prove? Won't you just please behave yourself?"

Snide laughter whistled in his windpipe. "Hey, just 'cause you done some sweating and grunting to squeeze me out don't give you any say-so over me." He cut the cards and turned up the Ace of diamonds. "You're a good for nothing whore and always will be."

"I'm no whore. I was once, but no more."

"You ought to have kept your legs closed, woman."

"Maybe so."

"There ain't no maybe," he fired back, puffing out wisps of smoke. "Excepting the fact that whores like you can't help themselves. Whores hump like birds fly and fish swim."

"I changed and made different choices."

"Changed? Hellfire, that ain't possible."

"How would you know?" she asked, standing strong.

"Don't give it no never mind because I got plenty upstairs, woman," he replied smugly. He insistently tapped his forehead. "I've been around and seen the way of the world."

"You know nothing, son," she said, blunt and truthful. "The totality of your knowledge has gaps and is sadly lacking because you're a mere child masquerading as a man."

He shrank back, then tipped the chair over as he stood, cursing and spitting. He raised a fist and shook it at her. The crowd cheered and applauded; hoots and hollers bounced off the walls and became a heaving crescendo of vibration as their feet stomped in time to the banjo, which shrilled up and down the scale at an ever increasing tempo.

"Hush your yap, Brenda," he said, and in that moment he was no longer a teenage version of her son; he had become his father. "I was always more than man enough for you."

"Making a baby doesn't mean you're a man, Benny." Sadness and regret encompassed her face. "You pretended to be an adult, but were always just a boy in a man's body."

He blasphemed and clobbered the table with both fists. His face enflamed and he shrieked as though his gonads had been crushed by a pointy-toed boot. He aired out his lungs by expelling choice swearwords to denigrate and stigmatize her. It was during the spittle-fueled cyclone of name calling that she pitched forward and came awake posthaste.

Brenda Hawkins sat up. Her eyes rebelled reflexively against the morning sunshine. She felt harried by the smart-mouthed disrespect in the dream, but not perplexed. She rallied her wits and emotions, and refused to give despair a foothold. There were fundamental promises to keep and too much at stake; her son carried his father's blood in his veins, but with God being her helper, she would not allow him to become a reproduction of Ben Slaton.

She rolled off the mattress. When her feet hit the floor, a brush of movement under the bed startled her and she stopped cold. She stiffened and waited for the hodgepodge to clear from her mind, holding her breath and listening. A smile ascended her high cheekbones and made the blue of her eyes shimmer in a glittery sea. "What are you doing, Mr. Hawkins?"

The four-year-old poked his head out, innocent-eyed. "I lost my ball, Mama."

"We'll find it later, honey. Climb up here and give me some loving."

Stace momentarily pouted, then scrambled onto her lap. He didn't need her help, but rather, she had to put up a well-practiced defense to guard against his roughhouse ways. He locked his arms around her shoulders and squeezed for all he was worth. "I'm hungry."

"We'll have breakfast soon enough, but first, what's today?"

"Someday."

"Sunday, Stace. Sunday."

He puzzled over her correction, then slowly said, "Some . . . day."

She swayed side to side. "What's Sunday all about?"

"Jesus."

"Where do we go?"

"Church."

"To sing praises and be thankful."

He leaned back. "Suey? See Suey?"

She smiled brightly. "I hope so. We've been praying for her, haven't we?"

He nodded and snuggled against her. She held him tight and stroked his sandy hair. The affection between them did much to dispatch the obnoxious dream to some nether region of her soul, but fluffy residue wafted around the corners of her mind like shameless dust bunnies. She nibbled on her lip and purred words of love as a single teardrop spilled down her cheek.

The New Mexico sky was crystalline blue from horizon to horizon. A whiffing hint of a breeze graced the air as Delores Solrizo strolled along the boardwalks of Las Vegas. Dressed in royal blue finery topped off by a velvety hat trimmed by spiderweb netting around the brim, she moved purposefully toward the ringing of a church bell. There was buggy traffic on the avenues and fellow pedestrians with whom she exchanged smiles or nods in passing.

Her heart remained heavy from the staggering news that her son, Liam Greer, had returned to his killing ways. He had never strayed far from her thoughts and prayers, but rather, was permanently embedded in a craggy crevice of memory. The pain and guilt could easily slink out from under forgiveness and deliverance to distress her. Almost three decades ago, when she was a broken eighteen year old, she had miserably failed him.

The clanging of the bell plucked a buoyant chord in her and aroused the persistence to curb the hurtful recollection. Done was done; consequences endured, but the sins of the past which spawned unfixable mistakes, were washed in the blood of the Lamb to be absorbed in the unreachable depths of God's sea of forgetfulness.

Her mind drifted back to when she heeded the chiming jangle of the Sunday morning call to worship with her mother. Hand in hand they would walk through their St. Louis neighborhood in preparatory reflection. After the service their prevailing custom was to sit in a picturesque park to converse about Father Martin's homily. The bonding routine did much to instill practical application truths that in the passage of years were not wasted on the child.

The relationship and wisdom imparted was precious to Delores, but then, when she was ten years old, her mother developed an illness in her lungs and died in a gasping seizure. There was a swearing confrontation between the priest and her father, which intensified the little girl's grief. She cried day after day, until her eyes were raw and sore.

Shortly thereafter, her father's bullying behavior took a sick turn. He began by touching her private parts fully clothed while doing the same to himself; at first it was a game as he smiled and tickled her, but then, as puberty budded, he escalated the incestuous deeds with threats and blackmail, cajoling her to please her mother in heaven by seeing to his needs. He stole her virginity when she was fourteen.

She was mortified. She protested and tried to end it, but he became nastier than nasty. The nighttime encounters increased in violence as she fought and resisted. Once she attempted to gouge his eyes out, which resulted in a black and blue beating. He left her alone for more than a year, then in a drunken rage, raped her on the eve of her eighteenth birthday.

Her father's seed planted a son in her womb. She gave birth and immediately discarded the child. Now, as a veteran of murder and mayhem on the outlaw trail, Kid Greer had a hefty bounty on his head and was a nightmare that she had to relive over and over. She wept for him; she prayed for him; she assaulted heaven with petitions for his life to be redeemed.

The nuts and bolts of reality moderated her outlook, so she had no illusions or delusions about the prospects for him to make a turnaround onto salvation's pathway, but faith was the bulwark of her hope. She clung to it with a fierceness that bordered on desperation. From the well of her experience she adamantly believed that God's grace had no limitations.

Following the peals of the bell she rounded a corner to see a white clapboard church centered at the end of the block. Slow-moving clusters of people were congregated on the steps conversing as they went into the sanctuary. In the shadow of the tall steeple, a rosy-cheeked woman glanced about expectantly while a little boy kept vigil alongside her.

The lad started waving in her direction, then abruptly withdrew his hand and shook his head. Delores took note and immediately adjusted her angle to approach them. She made sure a genial expression was in place and came to a stop at the final reverberation of the bell. "Good Lord's day morning. I'm Delores Solrizo on a visit from Santa Fe."

"Brenda Hawkins," the woman replied in a distracted manner. "This scamp is my son Stace. He has the wiggles because he's anxiously waiting for our friend."

"I'm appreciative of the wave, even if it was meant for someone else," Delores said amiably. She dampened her lips as she gave them a furtive once-over. Their clothes were older and showing wear in spots, but clean and newly ironed. She gathered her skirt so she could take a knee in front of the boy. She tweaked his chin. "May I sit beside you, kind sir?"

Delores stood as he giggled and rapidly clambered up his mother as though he was climbing a tree. She had to momentarily wrestle him before he plunked onto her hip. He pressed his lips against her ear. She listened and laughed merrily. "Stace says he likes you."

"Does that mean I can accompany you, my young gentleman?"

He blushed, eyes gleaming as his head bobbed affirmation.

Delores rubbed his back. "Shall we go inside?"

"Let's do. I guess Suzy isn't coming," Brenda answered, plainly disappointed.

The doors were propped open and the steps were clear. A piano player was making its keys tinkle a medley of hymns in prelude to the service. They entered the Congregational Church and found enough room in a pew halfway down the middle aisle. In a pious reflex from the catechism of her upbringing, Delores Solrizo genuflected before taking a seat.

The Union Church in Dodge City, located on the northeast corner of First Avenue and Spruce Street, was standing room only. Butch Mackenzie had arrived early to secure a spot in the back pew on the left side. It was close to the window and he expected to take advantage of a gentle crosswind that would keep the air circulating, but that was not to be.

Nicholas B. Klaine, editor and publisher of the *Dodge City Daily Times*, effectively blocked the flow of the breeze when he positioned himself on the sill. Mackenzie, always easily irritated, bellyached a surly complaint and gave the prudish goody-goody the stink-eye, but the newspaperman paid no heed to the rotund Western Union agent.

Butch groused his characteristic grunt and returned the favor. He disregarded him and kept his attention moving around the approximately 15x50 foot sanctuary. The interior already was perfumed by a trace of sweat and there was not a single open space to accommodate another attendee, but the bell's clanking rhythm continued calling the citizenry.

Reverend Ormond Wright was in the entranceway with a grinning youngster at his side. The boy was tugging the rope that kept the toll of the bell vibrant and inviting. Wright, a Presbyterian minister raised and schooled in New Jersey, had migrated west as a zealous servant of the Lord. He arrived in Dodge City when the cowtown was so lawless and hellbent that it was rumored that even the Son of the living God wouldn't deem it safe to walk its streets.

Wright's mission to rescue the perishing and provide spiritual comfort was conducted in sleazy establishments where sin was a money-making enterprise. The rambunctious patrons of dance halls and saloons were the recipients of his compassionate ministry. A man of ardent integrity, his amenable manner garnered much respect, which allowed him to raise the necessary funds to build Union Church, the first place dedicated to worship in Dodge City.

Mackenzie had a modicum of regard for Reverend Wright, though just now he wished the cleric would instruct the half-pint junior ringing the infernal bell to stop so that the service could proceed. He thumbed a bead of perspiration from a crease above his unruly eyebrows and shifted his buttocks. His head swiveled to the right and he leaned with it.

Deputy U.S. Marshall Hamilton Bell, owner and operator of the livery, was squatting on the windowsill across the room beside the pew where Sam Beadle was sitting between Abbey Langton and Avis Lahay. Broad at the shoulder and slim at the waist, Hamilton Bell had a distinctive nose and a determined chin that defined his no-nonsense approach to all things. He was a doer and innovator who had coolness and persuasive influence in chancy situations.

Butch Mackenzie even toned down his grouchiness in his dealings with the Deputy Marshall. It wasn't a huge concession to social decorum, but if Mackenzie was chomping on the stub of a cigar when Bell entered the telegraph office on official business, he would straightway trash it regardless of whether or not the tobacco had chewable content lasting in it.

The bell ended its clarion overture in a final snappy clang. Mackenzie fished around the top pocket of his shirt and came out with the folded telegram he had received yesterday. The organ began playing the strains of *Blessed Assurance* and although the congregation got to its feet, he remained unmoved. His shoulders hunched forward and he hung his head.

Harmonious voices rose to the rafters, becoming victorious on the refrain.

> "This is my story, this is my song,
> praising my Savior all the day long;

this is my story, this is my song,
praising my Savior all the day long."

Butch Mackenzie kept his eyes lowered, his mouth clenched. The lyrics affected him, but he refused to allow those sensitive emotions to surface. He wanted to plug his ears with cotton, but instead, since no batting was available, he grit his teeth so hard that pain seized his jaw. He was obsessed with the message from the medical facility in St. Louis.

Patient not doing well. The staff reports a failure to thrive. Will
update when there is news.

The hymn concluded with a three-fold amen. Reverend Wright welcomed one and all in a robust and cheer-filled greeting, then boldly proclaimed the first verse of Psalm 122: "*I was glad when they said unto me, Let us go into the house of the Lord.*" There were a few affirmations and scattered handclaps in response. Wright's lips curled in an approving smile. "The news has been reported along grapevines and elsewhere. I am winding up my ministry in Dodge City. I have been blessed and enriched, but am weary and growing wearier.

"A return to the east beckons and a sabbatical of sorts for me to wait upon the Lord and be refreshed by his mercies. I will long remember the years of struggle and triumph we have had together. The tears, the laughter, the prayers." He drew a deep breath. "This morning, as this overflow crowd is well aware, we have a special speaker who is no stranger to us."

Deacon Coburn rushed to his feet and dashed to the podium, brusquely nudging him aside by saying, "Thank you, my friend." Never one for casual chitchat, he didn't even wait for the reverend to return to his chair on the platform before he had his Bible open. "I want to take us on a journey through the book of Hosea. Nowadays God's handling of the northern kingdom of Israel in ancient times may seem unrelated to our lives, but we can grab hold of its story of heartbreak and sorrow because it contains the promise of hope and restoration.

"The northern kingdom had been unfaithful to God, which is a common failing to each one of us. Hosea warned that idolatrous behavior had destruction as a consequence. Repentance was and is a necessity." His low-pitched voice had fortitude in its timbre. "The prophet spoke of God's everlasting mercy and righteous justice. The pages of Hosea are a living illustration that God loves sinful people. He loves sinners like you and I, and his grace is longsuffering."

Butch Mackenzie could tolerate it no more. He staunched his ears. His eyes were watery and there was a lump clogging up his throat. The hard wooden bench was suddenly extremely uncomfortable. Feelings of fear and regret were loose. He fought to get them under control, which was an unmanageable chore because he kept reading the telegram in his hand.

Patient not doing well. The staff reports a failure to thrive. Will update when there is news.

The words had the impact of an icepick stabbing at his heart to break off shavings of bitterness that floated freely. A tremulous spasm shook his shoulders and his breathing became wheezy. In an effort to put an end to the upheaval roiling through him, he folded the paper and returned it to his shirt pocket as he bit his bottom lip so hard that he tasted blood.

In a few moments he adequately subdued the disturbance so as to raise his head. His eyes darted to Abbey Langton. Curled ringlets of hair spilled from beneath a stylish sunhat to rest on her shoulders. A swell of tender affection filled him. He desired to warn her; to protect her; to keep her safe; to never allow any harm befall her. His focus riveted on her and he blanked out.

He had no indication or comprehension of how much time passed. His mouth wrenched into a grimace because a rap-rap-rapping invaded his trancelike musings. He exhaled a shuddery sigh and his head pivoted toward the front. His eyes flinched as the expression on his roundish face spread into a cynical sneer of a smile.

Deacon Coburn was using a forefinger to exuberantly tap the pulpit. "Hear me now and make no mistakes," the man from Conoy Creek said, adamancy in his tone. "Scripture is clear: God is unwilling that any should languish in eternal damnation. His intention is for his love to so overwhelm us that we willingly *choose* to spend eternity in his presence.

"Our opportunity to make that choice is here and now in the midst of the immorality of a fallen world. We are to walk in repentance day by day. And we must not be deceived. We have an urgent obligation to our fellowman. No matter Gomer's transgressions, Hosea was asked to demonstrate unconditional and unrelenting love to his wife as a metaphor for God's everlasting love. So too, we must live and care for others, especially the most wayward among us.

"God is continually in the business of redemption and no one is ever too immersed in evil to be unredeemable—all are within the reach of God's merciful kindness. We are to care for and walk alongside of others in that truth, and never yield or slacken in our efforts to be vessels of God's unfailing grace." He closed his Bible. "Agree with me in prayer, brothers and sisters."

When heads were bowed, Butch Mackenzie bolted in such haste that he almost tripped over the outstretched legs of the proprietor of the daily newspaper. He had to crunch down on his tongue to restrain swearwords, but muttered gripes as he pushed past those who were congested in the entry foyer. Outside, the fresh air smacked him like a bucket of ice water and he teetered on the steps, struggling to maintain poise and leverage in his knockdown drag-out with God.

Kid Greer cared nothing for Sunday. He wasn't even aware what day of the week it happened to be. There were serious concerns occupying his mind. He had been sporadically traveling north for over twenty-four hours, but hadn't put many miles behind him. A severe case of the backdoor trots had allowed him to be in the saddle for only short intervals.

Now, with the sun high above, a piled circle of rocks contained a smoldering fire in an untidy camp. The site was beside a trickle of a creek and beneath a leafless tree in the midst of an ocean of grassland. A pair of jackrabbits awaited skinning, but Greer was occupied elsewhere. His intestines were in an uproar. With his trousers around his ankles he hunkered on his haunches and groaned incessantly as his bowels evacuated spurts of brownish water.

He was not alone. In fact, he had an audience. Daisy, his speckled bay mare, stood at a distance munching lazily while casting observant eyes in the direction of the moaning noises. In recent months life had been especially grueling for the beast of burden, so it was grateful to have the saddle off its back and bit out of its mouth, and be leashed on a long rope. Curiosity had the horse straying closer and closer to where the man was crouching and cussing.

Greer glowered at the animal and pulled up his drawers. "What are you looking at? You ain't ever seen a dose of the flying axe-handles? My ole man got the shits all the time. Once so bad that he damn near broke his neck on the back porch. He sent rakes and shovels and such airborne getting to the crapper." He took a couple stomping steps toward his mount.

The horse whinnied and ran off to the end of its tether.

"Don't be like that, Daisy," he said sadly. "I was just messing with you." He picked at the seat of his pants as he sidled over to the firepit. He knelt beside it and removed a hunting knife from its sheaf in his right boot. He looked longingly at the mare. "I ain't got a living soul to call a friend. I've been forsaken my whole life. If you stay mad at me, then I got nobody."

Daisy whinnied again and skittishly sidestepped toward him.

"That's better. I ain't so bad, am I?" he asked, cockeyed and grinning. "You could've done worse than me, Daisy. I try my best to keep you fed and cared for, so you ought to cut me some slack." He moved off a few feet to skin and gut the jackrabbits. "You ain't gonna get any of these fine vittles, Daisy. They're mine, all mine." His head jerked around as he realized that he was chattering to a horse. He pursed his lips and muttered a blasphemy.

"What's wrong with me?" Even before the insecurity was uttered he had full knowledge of the primal truth. He was afraid—deathly afraid; petrified, even. The fires and sulfur smoke of hell haunted him; the tortuous stench of his flesh burning was inside his head—the terror was a living creature with barbwire claws that savagely scratched at the bones of his skull.

He didn't want to die. He surely didn't want to go to hell. *Obey or be devoured.* The haunting nightmare had him sleepless and sickened. A thundering headache vibrated behind his eyes and diffused its stinging throb down his spine to tingle his tailbone. His stomach was in a constant knot of cramps that periodically twisted and tightened.

He had the rabbits readied. He studied the tree for a few moments, then used the bloody knife to hack off a pair of suitable branches. He went to work preparing a makeshift spit. His eyes narrowed in pain as the freakish brute inside his noggin scraped insistently. He persevered, and in short order had his meal skewered and sizzling over a bed of coals.

When he was satisfied that the meat was slowly roasting, Liam Greer went to the edge of the brook and stripped down to his altogether. He left his dirty clothes in a heap and stepped into the shallow stream. He crouched low and gently splashed cool water on the inflamed crack of his backside. As he washed, sobs choked from his throat and tears leaked from his eyes.

Meanwhile, much of the Union Church congregation was assembled in the churchyard to enjoy the gorgeous sunshine while engaged in discussions. The discourse extended from social matters to dissections of Deacon Coburn's message. Sam Beadle was on the bottom step vaguely eavesdropping on a taletelling parley about the forthcoming Harvest Street Festival.

He soon became bored by the prattle. He cupped a hand over his eyes and assessed the potential of various conversations. He noticed the Western Union agent alone at the intersection and felt prompted to visit him. The roly-poly man was slowly pacing with his hands jammed in his pants pockets. Beadle eased past the gabbers and meandered to the street corner.

Butch tipped him a nod as he approached. "Huh."

"Are you woolgathering or thoughtfully engaged?"

"Mindful, as always. Huh."

"Lots of fodder in that sermon."

"If you say so."

Beadle smiled mildly. "It challenged me, to be sure."

"That's all well and good," Butch replied, brusque and dismissive. "I'm not one to get all weak-kneed or pigeon-hearted over a bunch of ancient words."

"Be that as it may."

"Huh. A Bible story from olden days isn't at all helpful."

"I respectfully disagree."

"I got my struggles with today."

"Sorry to hear that, Butch. Is there anything I can do?"

"Nope. Nothing nobody can do."

"I can give you a fair listen."

"Huh. A fair listen?"

"Yes. Sometimes unloading our junk can do us a world of good," Sam said, inching closer to him. "Why not put my listening skills to the test?"

Mackenzie rolled his eyes. "Are you going to be a crusty crony's confidant?"

"Just attempting to be friendly, Butch."

"Huh. Don't you have more important duties?"

"Friendship as duty?"

"It is to me," Butch answered flippantly.

"That's a dark turn of mind."

"Huh. Not really."

"Yes, it is, Butch."

"Drivel and poppycock. Huh."

"I dare-say it's a matter of perspective."

"Well, you ain't got mine, do you, Sam?"

Beadle gave him a halfway shrug. "I suppose not, but that doesn't mean I have no interest or concern. How about we have a beer together one evening this week?"

"Huh. Are you bucking for sainthood?"

"No. Are you determined to rankle me?"

Mackenzie snorted a caustic laugh. "You already got too many plates spinning, but you must figure they're unbreakable. Huh. Your wife needs care and attention, not me."

Beadle screwed his face into a mask of pure confusion. "What?" His lips pursed as he sought to keep annoyance in check. His breathing tensed. He calmed it and decisively took a different tack. "Abbey told me that you and she hashed over names for our baby."

"Damn straight."

"Did you settle on any favorites?"

"Huh. Didn't she tell you details?"

"Actually, she did, Butch," Sam replied drolly. "She also said that the two of you got to laughing so hard that tears were flowing. That's difficult for me to imagine, but obviously you have a special relationship with my wife, which is pleasing to her. And acceptable to me."

Mackenzie scowled. His jowls jiggled as a flush of color stippled his complexion. He teeter-tottered sideward and his hands clenched. For a brief and cheerless instant, he gave the impression that he was going to take a nosedive, but then, gained his balance. "Huh. You think I give a boogered up bo-peep about what you determine to be acceptable?"

Beadle was nonplussed. "I meant no affront."

"Let me tell you something, mister hotshot writer," Butch said, pressing in so close that they were almost chest to chest. "Abbey Langton is an exceptional woman and if trouble comes or anything untoward happens to her I'll be holding you to the fire." He jabbed a stubby finger under his nose and bumped up against him. "Huh. I'll not abide your lackadaisical notions any longer. She deserves much more watchfulness than you are providing."

Beadle held his ground. "You're being rude and ill-mannered."

"Am I?" Butch remarked, bristling. "Your apathy toward Abbey infuriates me. A woman in the family way requires special alertness and precautions. You think child-bearing is some risk free stroll under the stars? I'm not going to allow you to continue neglecting her."

"You best get down off that high-horse, Butch."

Mackenzie balked. "Or what?" Flecks of bluster spun in his bulging eyes. He started to raise his fists, but in startling suddenness, his expression paled. He turned his head away and his body followed. "Huh. Every morning means figuring out anew how to live long enough to get put out of the misery by nighttime and sleep," he said, then hurriedly shambled off.

Beadle watched him in befuddled amazement. His blood was hot. He could feel its heat intensifying under the tight collar of his shirt. He lurched in his footsteps when he felt a hand on his shoulder as Abbey Langton came next to him. She smiled warily. He forced a grin, but from the disquiet deepening the lines of her face he realized she was having none of it.

≈ ≈ ≈

Ten minutes later, the silence between Sam Beadle and his wife had solidified into a picket fence, which was their default relational action. They were on Second Avenue strolling hand in hand, a carefree deportment that contradicted the superficial tension riffling between them. There was no anger involved, but rather, mutual respect; each were sorting through thoughts and feelings while granting the other the privacy to do the same.

Abbey cleared her throat and adjusted the brim of her fashionable sunhat. "What was that all about back there?" she asked, slipping the query through a gap in the pointy slats.

"Nothing."

"Is that a partial truth or an outright lie, Mr. Beadle?"

He chuckled. "Thanks for the wiggle room, Miss Langton."

"You're welcome. Now how about an answer?"

"A brazen falsehood."

"I surmised as much. So what's going on?"

"I'm still trying to make sense of it, Abbey." He gave her hand a gentle squeeze. "I could use your input. What did you see? Were you ever close enough to hear us?"

Her mouth contorted and she stopped. "Whew. Our baby is kicking up a storm."

"You need to get off your feet," he said urgently. "Shall we rest for a spell?" He made a sweeping gesture to a vacant bench in front of the Wright House, a half-block south.

"I do not need to get off my feet, Sam. I am perfectly capable of walking." She raised her face skyward. A sly smile curled the corners of her mouth and her eyes twinkled. "The breeze, however, is delicious. We ought to take some time to appreciate this splendid afternoon."

"You, my dear, are an incurable tease."

"Why, whatever do you mean, Mr. Beadle?" She tugged his hand and took the lead. Her cheeks were flushed and her palms damp. He deliberately dragged his feet and kept to a snail's pace. There were other pedestrians and some buggy traffic on the thoroughfare. The scent of freshly cut alfalfa sailed on the mellow currents of the autumn zephyr.

When they were seated, she leaned back and took a considerable amount of time seeking a comfortable position. She placed her hands on the curve of her lower abdomen and focused on him. "After the service I was engaged in a give and take with Mr. Klaine. When I first glanced toward you, it appeared that a sociable conversation was in the works."

"A sociable conversation was exactly my intention," he said, "and it started polite enough, but as always, Butch had his defenses up and was gunning for an argument."

"He can be difficult, I know."

"Difficult? That's being kind, Abbey."

"Well, it is Sunday, Sam."

He bit off a smile. "As if I didn't know. I responded to the essence of the sermon and attempted to reach out to Butch by being caring and considerate, but was rebuffed."

"What agitated him?"

"He might have been born agitated."

She raised her eyebrows. "That's not at all helpful."

"The man is unstable, Abbey."

"No, that's far too harsh an evaluation."

"I think not. His mood swings are erratic."

"Eccentric and crotchety, but unstable, no," she said straightforwardly. "As I approached it was obvious that he was upset, but I never heard any of what was spoken."

"He accused me of neglecting you."

"Is that all?"

His eyes widened in disbelief. "That's rather smart-alecky, Miss Langton."

She touched his knee. "Forgive my glibness, but it's a fallacious accusation. Have you ever heard objections from me? If anything, I protest because you are too conscientious and dutiful. After all, I am not some hothouse flower who will wilt under pressure."

"You are no delicate blossom, but ofttimes, you overdo it."

"Do I?" she volleyed back, grinning impishly.

"I kid you not, Miss Langton," he replied, somewhat facetiously. "None of which diminishes my qualms concerning Butch and his unnatural attachment to you."

"Unnatural attachment? He's my friend, is all."

His face wrinkled into a defenseless expression. "Perhaps so, but regardless of your assertions to the contrary, he is emotionally unstable, which I fear cannot be resolved."

"We're not going to resolve anything sitting and slacking," she said, pushing to the edge of the bench. "Let's head down Chestnut Street. I want to stop at the newspaper office."

"No, not today, Abbey."

"Why not? There's a file I need."

"Relax, please. I have to put my foot down."

"You do and my heel will smash your toes, Mr. Beadle."

"Are you ever going to start taking it easy?"

"You can be exasperating, you know that, Sam?"

"Me? Exasperating? Really? There's a case of the pot calling the kettle black," Sam said, standing. He offered her his hand, which she accepted. He gave her a lift and did a jiffy waltz to be on her left. "Come along, Miss

Langton. Your gallant champion will escort you to the office, then home, where there'll be no quarrels; you will sit with your feet up until bedtime."

She hooked a hand in the crook of his elbow. "Of course, Mr. Beadle." A burst of unison laughter blended and stirred all around them. He gave her a moist peck on the lips. She sighed in contentment. Her fingers absently played and fluttered along his upper arm. All smiles, they moved leisurely beneath a cloud speckled sky, happiness rippling in their wake.

When a shadow was cast across the pages of his Bible, Deacon Coburn looked up into a pair of bloodshot eyes. Lines cricked rows in his brow and he suppressed the humor yanking on his lips as he made a blunt appraisal. "You look like you got a snoot-full of stinkweed, Bull."

Wallace slumped into the chair across from him. "As you know those stinkweed cocktails have no mercy," the rumpled and ragged cattle-baron said, waving a hand at the bartender. "The inside of my head feels like a bag of hammered buttholes. Midget miners are excavating for precious metal in there and I intend to flush the bums out with some hair of the dog."

"Is that wise?"

"Hell, no," Big Bull answered in a grunt. "Women and booze will likely kill me dead one day, but wisdom takes a fast train down the tracks when I get overtaken by my dual vices."

The Alhambra Saloon had a handful of early evening regulars. There were more than a few empty tables and only a pair of cowpokes lounging at the bar. The air wasn't yet a stagnant mix of sweat and tobacco smoke. Momentarily a highball of bourbon was placed in front of Big Bull Wallace; he immediately took a tiny sip, squinting painfully as he did so.

"Missed you in church this morning, Bull."

"I've never been much of a churchgoer."

"Just the same, your absence was noted."

"Does that book you got open there have anything in it about sin?" Bull asked, narrowing his eyes in a grimly serious expression. "I give in to temptation because it calls to me in the lusty charms of the ladies. I figure I'm a good-natured sinner who mostly attempts to do right, but on occasion, I fall off the wagon and indulge in excess. You need to find me a religious loophole in the Bible because I was at the China Doll until the wee hours last night."

Coburn nodded and flashed a grin. "Is that a fact? I hear tell it's a fair and fine whorehouse. I've never had reason to be inside the establishment, but more times than can be remembered working girls have sat across from me here seeking counsel and prayer, which I try to provide. Several employees of the China Doll were packed into a pew this morning."

"That's a helluva church you got."

"It ain't mine," Deacon said dryly. "And you're out of your gourd to look for loopholes. There ain't none, but the Bible promises grace and mercy aplenty for sinners like us."

"Like us? Bloody hell, you're no sinner."

"You're dead wrong if you actually believe that nonsense," Deacon pronounced, forceful and pointblank. "Like every believer, there are opposing garments woven through my heart and soul. The rags of a sinner are in constant tension with the fabric of a saint. I am well acquainted with the man in the mirror and on most days, he's more sinner than saint."

Wallace had a short pull of liquor. "I'm a know-nothing, what can I tell you?" He took off his ten gallon hat and put it on the table. "No matter. I don't have the stamina to recover from these binges as was done in my youthful gaiety. There was lots of extra sleeping today."

"Mayhap that's a cautionary lesson, old-timer."

Wallace snubbed the comment with a backhanded brushoff. He grimaced and scratched at his unshaven cheeks. "I was awakened an hour ago by a visit from the Deputy U.S. Marshall."

"What was that about?"

"We exchanged pleasantries."

Coburn eyed him suspiciously. "Do you have history with Bell?"

"Negatory," Bull answered, still picking at his gray-streaked forest of stubble. "I never met the man until he knocked on my hotel door and rolled me out of bed."

"That makes no sense."

"I agree, but as I said, I'm a know-nothing."

Coburn scrutinized him. "What ain't you telling me?"

"I'm no flimflam man, Deacon. I got no patience for such triviality."

"Why would a Deputy U.S. Marshall go out of his way to call on you?"

"Ask him," Bull snapped churlishly. "I'm a businessman and financier. I came to Dodge City to close the books on a long overdue matter." He took a gulp of bourbon. "Let's just say that as a result of our pleasantries, Hamilton Bell and I now have an understanding."

"And you tell me I'm cryptic."

Wallace roared belly-laughter, shoulders shaking. His bleary eyes watered and he grabbed hold of the sides of his head. A huge groan gurgled in his craw, sounding like wings flapping in a windstorm. When the pain and fitful breathing passed he made a hoarse attempt at levity. "One of those dwarf diggers just took a pick-axe to a rich vein of nerves."

Coburn was thoughtfully ruminating on encouraging words. He understood that the discomfort was self-inflicted, but refused to make any moral judgments. Instead he felt sorrow and empathy for his friend. Elbow on the table and chin in his hand, his lips were pursed and about to open, but a scurrying rush of movement on the boardwalk seized his attention.

A few seconds later, Avis Lahay skipped into the saloon, all bubbly and bouncy. She still wore her Sunday morning attire, a daffodil-yellow dress with a high collar and long sleeves. The folds of the skirt rustled as she hurried across the barroom. A beaming smile flared in her eyes and her cheeks were flushed as though she had been running a marathon. She scooched a chair away from the table and sat, flipping her loose and wavy auburn hair off her shoulders.

"What's chasing you, young lady?" Deacon asked wittily.

"I've had the most wonderful day," she replied in a tone fueled by giggles "For starters that was a meaningful message this morning. Thank you. Mom would have appreciated it." She was somewhat thrown off by the grizzle-faced stranger at the table. He made no detectable effort to disguise his interest. He was gape-eyed, overtly fixated on her.

"Then afterwards," she continued, "while I was jabbering with Whitey in the churchyard, Mr. Bell came over and took me aside to talk." Her hands flitted animatedly. "He told me that he was impressed by my exhaustive work in caring for Pumpkin and Gilgal. He offered me a job to groom and exercise four of his horses. He's going to pay me!"

"That's exciting news, Avis."

"I start bright and early tomorrow." She shifted in the chair and confronted the man preoccupied with her. "Why are you staring at me? Can I help you with something?"

Wallace was dry-mothed and speechless. His jaw was moving side to side.

Coburn made the introductions. "Avis Lahay meet Big Bull Wallace."

"Oh!" she exclaimed, a squeak in her voice. "That makes sense then." She got to her feet, noticeably uneasy. "I must go now. There is much for me to do." A tense smile began to form, but it slipped off. She departed in the same speedy style she had arrived.

Wallace craned his aching head around to watch until she was out the door. Queasy shock had creepy crawled up his throat. His shoulders slouched as he turned in the chair. His face was pasty white and distorted in confusion. "Holy hell, who is that girl? I must be growing into an old geezer or my brains are buggered, but she's the spitting image of Sweet Flora." He rubbed his raw-red eyes and massaged his temples. "Do you remember Sweet Flora?"

Coburn remained stoic. "Should I?"

"Land of Goshen, yes," Bull replied incredulously. "I was in partnership with Sweet Flora and it was profitable. She ran a high-class operation. On those occurrences when I was a customer she treated me like no whore before or since. You reclaimed me from her bordello more than once, as I recall. She was in Abilene last I heard, but that was years ago."

"All true enough," Deacon said, hands folded atop his Bible. He released a hiss of air and furrowed his brow. "Avis is her daughter." He let that sink in, then pressed closer, flint-eyed and coldly serious. "The woman you knew in East Texas put the whoring business behind her over a decade ago. Her name is Delores Solrizo and she's a restaurateur in Santa Fe."

Wallace had been thrown for a loop. "I'm getting cornball sentimental for long ago and far away." The memories were awash in the aftereffects of an overdose of alcohol, but a strong and flawless recollection of the vivacious woman he had known roused his loins and deepened the creases of incomprehension on his face. He alternated between muttering nonsensically and counting on his fingers. "I'm not that girl's father, am I?"

"No."

Wallace disposed of his drink in one enormous swallow. He stood and dithered some, having to grab the table's edge to get steadied. "I'm going back to bed to sleep this off." He snatched his hat, cocked it on his head and took a couple shaky steps.

"I'll accompany you to the hotel." Deacon rose and tucked his Bible under his left arm. He led the way outside, where coolness was in the air as dusk gathered the shadows of twilight into fresh sketches of pinkish gray. He kept an alert eye on his longtime employer and ally, all the while reassessing the specifics and vagaries of the multiple topics of their discourse.

Whitey Fitzgerald nearly leapt out of his skin. Jittery nervousness had him moving as erratically as a terrified hummingbird. Bug-eyed and sweating profusely, he raced past carnival games of chance and brightly colored balloons while painted clowns in floppy shoes and smeared faces clutched and grabbed at him.

Gut-rot whiskey swished in his belly; his breath stank of it. Feverish madness had twined deep roots in his psyche to hungrily suckle and grow strong. He ran as fast as he could make his legs lift up and down. He had one objective; to catch and kill Huey Butters. As of yet, his quarry was unseen, but the barber *knew* that the bunko artist was ahead of him.

The discordant pump organ noise and barkers of the midway vibrated off the bones of his skull as though his ears had become kettle drums. His arms flogged and thrashed as he furiously tried to run faster and faster. He saw where he would finally trap Huey Butters. The yawning archway maw of a funhouse beckoned him.

A gap-toothed buffoon with rouged lips and orange hair shrieked at him and pointed the way. He skidded to a shuddering stop the instant he dashed through the entrance. Silence crushed his senses; it was the noiseless hush of a burial chamber. He slowly turned round and round, eyes fluttering as the pupils became accustomed to the grayish murk.

Silver glinted in the wide corridor stretching forth in front of him. Fear squeezed his brain. He rotated to from whence he came and the pressure in his head screamed; there was no entryway, no doorway, no escape. Seconds ticked into nothingness and his heart palpitated in a galloping pitter-patter that continued increasing in intensity.

His bloated tongue, as dry as a barren desert, was stuck to the roof of his mouth. He took a shuffle-step forward, eyes catching the twinkle of silver. The sight intrigued him; more than that, the gleaming shimmer mesmerized the blood rushing to his head. His mind jumped; he became convinced that Huey Butters would be found hiding on the other side of the silver.

He burst into a sprint, legs stretching in loping strides. No matter how hard he churned to get rolling speedily, he made no headway; the distance to the hypnotizing shine never shortened. His lungs were inflamed and his heartbeat was sputtering in a mad frenzy. He skidded to a stop, gasping and full of raging fury that seared through his veins. Cusswords formed on his tongue and he spat them out encircled by a manic click-clicking.

He walked onward, eyes glued to the silvery glow that seemed to be hanging in the air. He reeled in his footsteps and listed drunkenly. The walls were alive and undulating. A mirror appeared to his left and invited him in a nefarious moan emerging from a tomb. He stared at the reflection of a homicidal lunatic with blood dripping from his hands.

The image was a ghostly replica of the swine-like ogre that resided beneath mossy rocks in some cavernous pit within. Its name was murder and it had a voracious appetite which was fed by unceasing fantasies of vengeance. Huey Butters had robbed Whitey Fitzgerald of pride and dignity—now the criminal was somewhere up ahead and it was time to end his life.

Fitzgerald pushed away from the looking glass and bolted at the fleetest possible speed. His thigh muscles were stressed and burning, but no hardship or obstacle could prevent him from finally righting a colossal wrong.

He would satisfy the ugly hunger and in doing so slaughter the rats feeding on him and silence the infuriating buzz of hornets in his head.

The farther he went into the bewitched funhouse the more and more it became a confusing network of passages; it was a labyrinthine house of mirrors in which he was given a jolt again and again. Each time he hurried past a tall or short partition of polished glass, he saw his blood-drenched hands and wildly bulging eyes.

The hallway of the maze, so broad and spacious at the beginning, was getting narrower and narrower as he progressed. The rolling walls were closing in on him. He quickened his gait even more because the glittering silver was becoming dazzling. It shimmied in the dusky gloom. A honeyed voice, emanating from the center of the brightness, called to him.

The seductive singsong cast a hex on him. He slowed and crept closer and closer until he clearly saw it. The sight thrilled and sickened him; a steely-silver pistol gyrated before him. A Remington six-shooter was whispering his name: *Whitey . . . Whitey . . . Whitey.* He plucked it out of the air and snapped the cylinder open to see that it was loaded. He flicked it closed and gave the mechanism a spin. The ticking hum of it elicited a crazy-eyed grin.

He glanced up into a misshapen mirror, in which he menacingly loomed. Now not only were his hands bloody, but spatters of gooey crimson were splashed on his face. His mouth tore open and bellowing gales of wicked laughter erupted. The roar became a fragile choking noise when, for a fleeting instant, a swish of motion materialized over his shoulder in the glass. A flash illuminated his brain—the man he was chasing was right there behind him.

Fitzgerald whirled around to find himself alone. Gun in hand he dashed forward. He repeatedly picked up his feet and put them down at full tilt. The high stepping carried him more swiftly than he had ever ran before, but regardless of his overexcited efforts, Huey Butters was nowhere to be found. The passageway kept shifting tighter and tighter, becoming a circular tube that was methodically funneling him to a particular destination.

His knees smashed together and he went sprawling face first across the floor. He couldn't breathe. He flopped around like a beached carp and after some sporadic sputtering, landed on his back. His chest heaved a gasp as his eyes popped. Standing over him was the swindler in a derby hat and twirling a brass-handled cane, smug triumph etched on his lips.

Whitey Fitzgerald immediately took aim and pinched the trigger six times. The retorts echoed in an explosion of razor-sharp splinters and fragments. His throat clamped shut and he was suffocating. He squirmed awake.

A sheet constrained his ankles and a blanket effectively smothered him; it had been matted into a hood and neck-tied over his head.

He wiggled free of the bedding and made a futile attempt to shed the nightmare. The vitality of the mirage imaginings put a wince on his face as he sorted through the absurdity and speculated as to what it all meant. He swung out of bed so hastily that a breaker of blood crested in his head and made him dizzy. The sensation released a gusher of nausea that bubbled and burped noisily. It took several minutes before calmness returned to his stomach.

He got up and lit an oil lamp. He went to a dresser drawer and moved socks aside to withdraw a nickel-plated Remington revolver. Whitey Fitzgerald grasped the white-bone handgrip and, in a reenactment from the dream, he affirmed each slot had a cartridge, then spun the cylinder. His eyes were dead and vacant, his expression vague and devoid of emotion.

September 18, 1882

Dear Diary: It's long past midnight so technically, I suppose it is a new day. I went to bed early and got a few hours of sleep, but have been wide awake staring at the ceiling for over an hour. Since I was tossing and turning I decided to get up and try to be productive. Instead of writing, however, I'm being amused by the flames on the candles.

My head and heart are full, but just now, I'm so easily infatuated by the dancing flickers. Deacon would likely tell me that procrastination is no different than anything else; it's merely an element of the human condition that requires taming because we always have the capacity to postpone or delay, even in those tasks or disciplines we find enjoyable.

I had an exciting day. After the big news from Mr. Bell, Whitey insisted that we do something special. He wouldn't take no for an answer. He didn't even allow me to return to the boarding house to change my clothes. He said that when out of the blue opportunities as the one Mr. Bell offered come around, then celebrations require spontaneity and fancy duds.

We rented a carriage from the livery and went for a ride along a trail south of the Arkansas River. It was a sunshiny afternoon. We saw a small herd of deer feeding in a meadow of tall grass. There were two bucks and a half-dozen does. The lovely sight only lasted a few moments because our presence scared them off.

Whitey and I chatted about the morning's message and wondered what it must have been like for Hosea to be faithful to

God while his wife kept running off with other men. The lesson I learned was twofold. First, God is incredible and desires for each one to receive his love. Second, I don't ever want to take God's grace for granted. I want to always live in a way that the good fortune and blessings I've received will be freely shared with others.

After we returned from our buggy-ride, Whitey had another surprise for me and once again, he wouldn't let me decline. He took me back to his apartment, where he had me sit at the table in the kitchen while he prepared a scrumptious dinner. He refused to allow me to lift a finger to help. Every time I tried he shooed me away by saying, "The guest of honor mustn't get her hands dirty, sweetie." He's a real character and so anxious to encourage me.

I haven't heard anything from Mom since her letter in July, which sort of concerns me, though perhaps that is just me borrowing trouble. She must be on the stagecoach and well on her way by now, but as to where, I have no idea. It would be nice to receive a telegram to update me, but sometimes I think she forgets how efficient and effective the telegraph system is at delivering news. It's my understanding that she intends to arrive later this month or early October.

My momentous day ended after I popped in to see Deacon and tell him about my job. He was at the Alhambra Saloon with Big Bull Wallace, so I finally met the Texas cattleman. Over the years I've heard much about him from Deacon and Mom, but up close I wasn't all that impressed. He ogled me in a not so nice way and made me feel rather miffed.

Abbey continues to do well. No news on the baby front. She's tired all the time, but that's because she stays busy and on the go. She is an inspiration to me. I am learning lots from her. She is involved in a battle with the Bureau of Indian Affairs, fighting for justice on behalf of widows and orphans displaced and suffering because of the government's relocation policies, which keeps her fiery and weighs heavy on her heart.

It is a joy running errands and assisting her as best I can. All of which is providing me with a real education. She is developing a major article for some respected and widely-read magazine back east. The research is comprehensive and the anecdotal evidence comes from her firsthand experiences. The feature will be chock-full of statistics and facts connected directly to individual stories about Lakota and Arapaho women she personally knows.

Her humanitarian efforts are truly something to be admired. She lives by a maxim which she says any journalist worth their salt ought to emulate: "A pen put to use in the defense of and quest for justice must be wielded boldly and without apology." I pray to have that sort of spunk and grit in all to which I set my heart and mind.

Abbey and Sam are so funny together. Their banter is endless. It's obvious that they're both anxious for the baby to arrive. I know Whitey and I are counting the days. This afternoon he showed me a large ragdoll he has already made, which he expects the baby to treasure. He told me of his elaborate plans to spoil the child. I just laughed and replied that when it comes to pampering and fussing, Pap Whitey will get plenty of stiff competition from Aunt Avis.

I have such an amazing family. God has been so good to me. I doubt that there will be any more sleep tonight. The anticipation of the morning and the responsibility has me too stoked and eager, but I'll give rest another try in a few minutes. I have yearned to be involved with horses and so far it has only been a hobby, BUT now it's the real deal.

Shoveling manure and cleaning stalls isn't glamorous, but I so look forward to it because it's all part of caring for horses, and honest labor is healthy and good for one's soul. I still can't believe this is happening. In my months in Dodge City tending to Pumpkin and Gilgal, I don't think Mr. Bell has said one word to me. Just nods in passing. I guess this episode proves what Mom has told me on many occasions: Hard work and diligence never goes unnoticed.

Oh, my. Back to bed I go.

Avis Lahay yawned so hugely that the hinge of her jaw cracked. She gave it a prompt rub, then hunched over and read all she had written. A satisfied smile parted her lips and swelled upward to sparkle her eyes. She closed the journal, extinguished the four candles on the desk and slipped beneath the covers. Her eyelids quivered irregularly, but scorned the whim of dropping shut. Slumber eluded her as she watched and waited for dawn to arise.

Naomi Axler was lost and afraid. All alone in a dark backwoods, she stood as still as still could be and searched through gaps in the tall trees surrounding her. Dewy dampness was in the air and serpentine ground-fog writhed around her ankles. There were puzzling lights in the sky that had her spellbound. Her heart was drawn to the streaky greenish-yellow radiance.

Her brow darkened when she realized she was wearing bedclothes; a flannel nightgown along with a fluffy cap and nothing else. Her feet were bare. None of what she was experiencing made any sense. Her soulful brown eyes, wide and wary, were secured on the ghostly light which was thrusting up and down like the rise and fall of fiery pistons.

Fear, rancid and nauseating, ratcheted up several notches; her mind manufactured new dimensions of it. She had seen those peculiar colors before, which startled a memory and sent surges of anxiety through her. It was shortly after her arrival in Abilene when the queer discoloration in the skies preceded a horrific tornado.

She began to tentatively walk forward, stepping and stopping, stepping and stopping. A prickly bed of dry evergreen needles carpeted the forest floor. The debris clung to the soles of her feet, but she advanced without regard to the distraction because she was convinced of a singular fact; her husband was somewhere in the timberland.

The mist was getting heavier and climbing higher. She waded through it, her arms extended as though she was readying to dive in and swim. A noise came out of the whiteness and took hold of her attention. Footfalls were scuffling ahead of her. She hitched in a fretful breath and held up in mid-step to listen carefully.

The footsteps were sluggish. There was no urgency evident, but rather, moving as slow as wintertime molasses. Excitement filled her and she hurriedly picked up her pace, certain that the slow-drag strolling pattern was the telltale gait of none other than Pete Axler. That conviction had the same effect on her as spurs to the haunches of a horse.

She squealed and took off running, but only for twenty yards or so, then had to abruptly halt because the circumstances were radically altered. The vaporous murk thickened and snaked above her. She thrashed against the clammy and smothering barrier, but only managed to scuff a shoulder against a tree trunk. She was stranded and unsure of how to proceed.

"Pete," she called, voice thin and feeble. There was no response except the sound of boots moseying away from her and shuffling on the layer of needles. Visibility was nonexistent. Hesitation came in fits and starts, but she persevered and felt her way along, hands seizing knobs of bark as her heartbeat sped up and anticipation tied her stomach into a knot. She sought a peek of the greenish-yellow, but the eerie lights in the sky had been concealed behind the fog.

The dense woodlot was becoming sparse. Her arms had to strain and stretch so far that pinching cramps aggravated her biceps as she hunted for a breakthrough. She had no knowledge of how far she went or how much time elapsed. She was driven by a compulsion to vigilantly inch through the soupy mist, even though the process was maddeningly slow.

The terrain was changing. She reached and reached, but there was no tree trunk for her hand to find. Wet grass was now under her feet. Her breathing accelerated. She lifted her knees high and did a faltering round-about turn. Then the fog instantaneously burned off in a chugging pulsation of the bizarre colors, which blazed and brightened the landscape. She was in a pasture and on the far side of it, her best friend and lover had his back to her.

"Pete!" she shouted, insistent and shrill. She rushed in his direction, undeterred by the long grass slapping against her shins. Her hands encircled her mouth. "Pete!"

He turned and his face crumpled into a distracted smile. She ran to him; or at least she thought she was running. Her legs functioned properly and her elbows were swinging, but she made no advances. She pressed on in the pose of a sprinter, pumping harder and harder, but despite the strenuous effort to get to him the farther he seemed to be away from her.

Pete Axler stood in the distance, silhouetted by a wedge of spectral light. He raised his right hand above his head and swayed it to and fro. Her instinct told her that it was a greeting, but iciness gripped her and she wondered if it was a farewell wave. The greenish-yellow brilliance fell all around him, then pitchy darkness gobbled him up and he was gone.

She screamed and pitched forward. A scalpel sliced at her heart to deliver pinpoints of pain. Her throat hurt and the screech of her voice pierced her ears. She woke up; shivers slinked along her spine as she loudly cried out his name. She caught her emotions and clamped a hand over her mouth. Rivulets of moisture dribbled down the back of her neck.

Shock rang through her. She was already half-sitting against the headboard. Frightened and frantic, she huffed air into her lungs and tried to pacify the frenzy of panic clamoring to be free. The promise of morning was a flush of sunlight on the floor, which brought a shred of calmness to her. She settled in more comfortably, then threw aside the blankets.

Her housecoat was bunched to the top of her thighs. Her knees came up and her bottom elevated so she could return the garment to its proper position. That done, she latched onto her husband's pillow and hugged it. She pushed her face into it and sniffed deeply. His scent lingered; loneliness coursed through her. She squished the pillow to her bosom.

"Dear God," she murmured, flinching her eyes shut. "Our Father who art in heaven, I am a weak vessel in need of all the faith thy grace can enliven in me. *Lord, I believe; help thou my unbelief.* May angels of protection be dispatched to guard Pete from all harm and troubles. Please bring him home safely. Be merciful to my petitions. Thy will be done. Amen." She sighed, low and mournful. She decisively braced her resolve and slid to the edge of the mattress.

Then, Naomi Axler mustered courage and got a start on her day.

On the prairie in western Kansas, Caleb Weitzel had ascertained that the horses in the rope-corral had spent an uneventful night. He was returning to the campsite when he suddenly stood stockstill to observe the sun rise above the horizon. The glorious array of the blazing orange and red pigments almost took his breath away.

He appreciated it for ten solid minutes. The wondrous display of God's mighty power was good for his soul. He silently prayed words of thanksgiving wrapped around a request for health and provision on behalf of Sally Twosongs—he expressed the same sentiments for their baby growing inside her. The prayers put a blush of contentment on his cheeks.

He nodded in affirmation, then as his belly growled and a smile bent his lips, he walked toward where the sizzle of bacon salted the air. "Did you see the sunrise?"

Daniel Twosongs was squatting on his heels at the campfire tending to breakfast. He glanced up from the frying pan. "I missed it, but no matter."

"It was bleeding hope across the sky."

"Hope has no meaning to me now."

Weitzel scrunched down beside him to fill a tin mug from the coffee pot. "It'll come back, Daniel. For you hope is a misplaced treasure. As you plug along and go through the grief, one day hope will find you once more." He crouched and took a seat on his saddle.

"You are so sure?"

"As a matter of fact, I am."

"Arrogance is unbecoming, Caleb."

"Certainty, not arrogance."

"Presumptuous certainty, which irks me," Daniel replied tersely. "You have always demonstrated wisdom beyond your years, but here you fail miserably. You cannot know the miles that have worn me down, or the ripped and ragged hole in my heart."

"You're correct, I cannot be inside your skin or see through your eyes," Caleb rejoined, raising a finger. "Though this I know; life has no guarantees and the living must take serious what it means to number our days. Like it or not, life goes on, Daniel."

The older man winced as though he had been mule kicked. "Tell me something I do not know." He wagged his head in regret. "Defeat and discouragement are twin villains badgering me. Consuelo is at peace and I am in turmoil. The light has gone out of my life."

"You must not give up hope, Daniel."

Twosongs used a two-pronged fork to stab the bacon and flip it over slice by slice. He performed the task several times, then stared at the spitting and hissing grease. His eyes were glazed and unfocused. When he spoke his face was marred by plowed ruts of anguish. "Hope, if it ever existed, is a foreign concept to me. There is no hope. Life is only pain and sorrow."

"A partial truth," Caleb said, taking a sip of coffee. "Pain, sorrow, heartaches, suffering are the thorns that jab each and every one of us. No one gets through life unbloodied."

"Which argues for my position."

"Not quite, Daniel."

"I don't see why not."

"The commonplace hardships are what shape us," Caleb answered somberly. "We can be crushed or sharpened, depending on the stuff within. How we respond to the pain, the sorrow, the heartaches, the suffering is what impacts our perspective and determines our character."

Twosongs shrugged contemptuously. "Character is overrated." He divided the bacon evenly and added a hardtack biscuit, then delivered a plate to his son-in-law. He picked a spot nearby and sat cross-legged on the ground. "I have walked in integrity without complaint or apology, yet darkness afflicts me. I am living proof that character is no bulwark against the monumental unfairness of life. I have done unto others and what did it get me?"

"That's too bleak, Daniel."

"It's an honest assessment."

"I think not," Caleb replied bluntly. "It's an outlook stricken by grief. I'll grant that it comes from honest feelings, but death and life are linked together. Wallowing in the muck and mire of self-pity is not a helpful response. Life is to be lived and hope is real. When we apply it, hope transcends and trumps the most devastating dilemmas that assail us."

"There you go again harping about hope," Daniel said, a ribbon of anger weaving through his voice. "I have lived in hope and it abandoned me to the darkness. The light is no more and heaven is too far away. Perhaps it would be different if today was leading somewhere, but today simply becomes tomorrow and all the tomorrows that follow go nowhere."

"Tomorrow, like today, is a gift to be cherished."

"Cherished?" Daniel scoffed, puttering around with his food. "Consuelo deserved better from God. His mercy is fickle and he can be downright capricious." He put his plate down and shook his head despondently. "My light has been replaced by darkness that has no end. I feel the darkness, I am blinded by the darkness. It is a shroud that covers me and there is no hope."

Weitzel had finished off his bacon and was munching on the biscuit. A flood of empathy muddied his eyes. He shoved his hat up his forehead and inhaled audibly. He released the air in a whistling swish. "When our families first met, there were meaningful words attributed to you. When the chips were down or times tough, my parents would quote them: *Hope is always good. Hope fixes us.* That still resonates in me, deep calling to deep, or the like."

"I was wrong."

"No. You're wrong now."

"I don't see hope fixing me, Caleb."

Weitzel pushed an optimistic smile at him. "The dirt in your heart needs cultivation, is all. Sift in some good fertilizer and give it time to do its work. Time doesn't change pain or heal loss, but when we care for our heart soil, new growth can blossom and thrive."

"There is nothing for me."

"That's an outright lie," Caleb chided, brusque and unwavering. "You have a precious daughter who loves and needs you. And a soon to be grand-child who will benefit from your guidance and philosophy. Why not give the seeds of hope a chance to grow?"

"In the darkness hope is no more."

"Jettison the darkness, Daniel. Cast it off," Caleb said, strength in his tone. "Choose to discard the darkness, then do whatever you must to make it so."

"Talk is easy, the doing hard."

"It is in the hard doing that we find true wealth and worth," Caleb opined, propping his elbows on his knees. "The weeding and gardening of your heart is indeed hard doing, but it'll bring forth a rebirth of a brand of hope that will flourish and set you free."

Twosongs disparaged the idea with a grunt and folded his arms over his chest.

Weitzel waited for several minutes, eyes lowered and legs jiggling. He swallowed the remainder of his coffee, then stood. "Enough lollygagging. We've got work to do. Let's pack up and get the herd on the trail. Fort Dodge expects these horses within a week or so."

There was no more discussion. The men busily got to the chores. Each task was done with a practiced efficiency. In less than a half-hour Caleb Weitzel and Daniel Twosongs were mounted and accompanying horses eastward. Not another word was spoken between them until the sun completed its daylight crossing and descended beneath the western skyline.

≈ ≈ ≈

An early morning slumber had Dodge City so still and quiet that it seemed strangely sinister to Sam Beadle. Front Street was almost deserted. He moved along the boardwalk, hands in his pockets and shoulders stooped against the crisp autumn chill in the air. His lips were pursed in tense reflection; eyes hooded by an abstract expression.

He was heading toward the Tonsorial Parlor for a Monday morning tradition that bordered on ritual. He would arrive around seven-thirty, before the shop was officially open for business, to get a shave and engage in verbal camaraderie with his chatterbox friend from Abilene. As he got closer he saw the former slave standing in the doorway.

"A cheery good morning, Samuel," Whitey said, taking a step back. His greeting and smile was as genuine as the purest of diamonds. "You be right on schedule as always. And I be ready and steady. Come on in and sit a spell so I can make you pretty."

Beadle chuckled as he entered. "You need to come up with a new line."

Fitzgerald click-clicked and rolled his eyes. "I don't needs no new line if'in the one I gots does me dandy." He picked up a white linen apron, shook it out and put it on. The workplace was speckless and neat as a pin. The wall-length mirror had been newly buffed and the shelf beneath it was tidily arranged with all the tools of the barbering trade.

"Inventing new lines is an essential necessity in my work." Sam took a seat in his usual chair and pushed around on the armrests before leaning back. "Last week I sent a feature article to *Harper's Magazine* and I'm afraid I could've used up all the great phrases."

"That not be happening any time soon."

Beadle shrugged noncommittally, eyebrows drooping into a frown. "Sometimes I can make myself as crazy as a loon overthinking and getting all antsy that I might run out of words. I've been up and at it since four or so, making final edits on my manuscript. Another couple weeks and it's off to the publisher in New York City."

"You ain't ever told me its story."

"It's for the reading, Whitey."

"You best not make me wait much longer."

"Why not?"

"You gots eyes, don'tcha?"

"I do."

"Canst you see that I be getting older by the minute?" Whitey asked as he spread a sheet over him. He fastened it around his neck. "My hair's whiter today than it was yesterday."

"That's bunkum. You ain't changed an iota since the day we met."

"I be awful sorry for you, Samuel."

"Why, pray tell?"

"You must have the onset of blindness."

"There's nothing wrong with my eyesight, Whitey."

Fitzgerald selected a straight-razor, then snappily slid it against the thick leather strop hanging from the side of the chair. "How long you been writing that novel?"

"Off and on since before I was a married man."

"Whew doggies!"

"Yeah. Abbey has pushed me on it lately."

"How is that sassy mother-to-be?"

"Sassier than ever, Whitey. Sassier than ever."

"That ain't a complaint I hear, is it?" Whitey asked, wrist flicking as he brushed lather up in a blue-rimmed stoneware cup. "You be the luckiest man on earth."

"You think I haven't figured that out?"

Fitzgerald had the soap foamy. "Now hush your mouth so as I can do my job." He swished the frothy suds over his cheeks and chin, smearing some on his neck. His hands were swift and sure as he took precise strokes with the blade. "Abbey be one fine woman. I remember it like it be yesterday when she come to Abilene. She took that town by storm and immediately stole your heart. You was smitten, wandering around pie-eyed and slobbery."

"I wasn't . . ."

"Don't be flapping your gums," Whitey ordered, punctuated by a pithy click-click. "You ought not be yapping, especially when your memory be led astray. I ain't no exaggerater. You was moonfaced and falling down in love. Ain't no shame in that, Samuel. You two got kissed by Cupid with a forever love. The both of you be lucky, but *you* be the luckiest."

Beadle tried to overpower a grin, but it emerged victorious. He paused for a moment, then at the last swipe of the razor, he said, "You are far more right than wrong, Whitey."

"More right than wrong? I be exactly right."

"That you be on this one," Sam agreed, holding a hand up in surrender. "I'd like to hear your view on a completely different topic. Do you think dreams have meaning?"

"Luddy mussy! Are you into monkey shines?"

"No," Sam answered tartly. "Why'd you ask?"

"I've been having some nasty dreams," Whitey answered, splashing bayberry lotion on his hands. He rubbed the creamy ointment into his customer's face and neck. "I ain't decided about dreams just yet. Is there something to them or is it all horse manure? I ain't sure."

"Me, too."

"Me, too? What . . . me, too?"

Beadle straightened up and eyed him cautiously. "I'm not sure either, Whitey. I've also been having a weird dream. Is it meaningful or has my imagination gone haywire?"

"It be too dang easy to blame my imagination," Whitey replied, eyes cracking wide in curiosity. He removed the sheet, gave it a cursory shake, then folded it and put it on the back of the chair. "Ain't it possible that the good Lord tries to tell us something in our dreams?"

"Always a possibility, I suppose."

"Ain't there lots of dreams in the Bible?"

"Of course. Joseph and Daniel were gifted interpreters of dreams."

"Well, I ain't got no Joseph or Daniel in me," Whitey said in a grumbly tone. "Mostly I just don't happen to have a hankering to learn what the Lord's trying to teach me."

Beadle laughed faintly. "I can surely relate."

Fitzgerald stood back, arms spread-out in a dramatic gesture. "What I do know for sure is that my mammy paid full attention to messages that came whilst she slept. She'd take a hard line and stick to it whether it made a lick of sense or not. Was my mammy misguided?"

"I wish I had an answer, Whitey." Sam retrieved a pricey cigar from an inside pocket of his jacket and handed it over as payment. "Take care and have a fine smoke this evening."

Fitzgerald click-clicked cheerfully. "I do my best, Samuel."

Beadle gave a nod, then strode out the door. Front Street was beginning to stir with activity. He immediately jammed his hands in the trouser pockets and headed for the Beatty & Kelley Restaurant. He assumed a quick-fire gait because he had a breakfast date with his wife, for whom promptness meant being ten minutes early, so he was already late.

For Pete Axler, the day was unfolding as a beauteous blessing of agreeable fortune. He was saddled on a favorite horse, riding a narrow mountain trail south of Gunnison. The brindle gelding, intelligent and savvy, had its ears pricked forward and was stepping lightly. He held the reins loose in a palm, allowing the animal to pick its way along the rocky ledge.

The sun was midway to the apex of a sky dotted by rolling tumbles of fluffy billows. He was relaxed and wholly at peace with recent developments. Life was spins and surprises, and just now, he had no grievances. The dice had come up sevens for him, so all was well. Three nights and a wakeup would have him returned to *WT Ranch* and at the hearth of home.

His hat was high on his creased brow and his eyes were gazing at a bald eagle soaring effortlessly. The bird seemed to be gliding circles around a shape-shifting bank of clouds, which fascinated him. After the tension of the past week, the sights and sounds of nature were sweeter than the sweetest honeycomb. He had a preposterous tale to tell his wife—the long and short of it was quirkier than trying to lasso a hurricane.

The eagle ascended and dipped on eddies and currents, and his mind drifted with the same ease and freedom, coming to rest on his family. He yearned to see them; to hug Naomi and feel her arms around his waist; to play rough-and-tumble with Jesse and Amanda, and hear their enthusiastic screeches that made his heart swell.

There had never been an expectation of having children. Even while courting Naomi in his easy-going and ofttimes slapdash fashion, he soon determined that it would only be the two of them. Offspring wouldn't be in their future because she openly told him of her heartache; her previous marriage had proven that she was unable to conceive.

He had a look at the eagle swooping in and out of the clouds, almost smirking as he remembered the astonishing turn of events. It was in the midst of their relocation to *WT Ranch* that parenthood became a real and likely possibility. The missed time of the month along with the morning sickness of the first pregnancy had made them giddy and restless; the second baby was terrific news that had caused an overabundance of tears to flow between them.

Now, as his son and daughter grew and explored the world around them, he had immense pride and the highest of hopes for them. They both demonstrated boldness around and affinity for horses, which delighted him right down to his socks. He routinely made time to take each of them riding, buoyed and upheld on his thighs to learn the reins as though they were actually in charge, when in reality he was guiding their hands on the sly.

The brindle whinnied and began side-stepping down a steep and gravelly drop. Axler transferred his weight to be aligned with the animal, but never once altered his grip on the reins. He had an inherent trust in the horse. When the sure-footed steed gained a stretch of relatively level ground, he glanced up to see that the bald eagle was still playing hide and seek amongst the puffy clouds. It was close enough for him to see its eyes.

The route entered a grove of aspens, whose branches were clothed in the brilliant yellow colors of autumn. The gelding wound its way through the tall trees, and Axler relished the shady respite, which lasted for more than a mile. As the end of the woodland approached, he noted that ahead the trail became precipitous and took a corkscrew falling-off.

The instant he emerged from beneath the leafy cover the dazzling sunshine struck and momentarily blinded him, and then, two happenings snatched leisure and goodness from the jaws of the day and put him in a life or death predicament. His eyelids were flapping like shutters when the eagle released a startling scream; a split-second later a cougar leapt off a jagged boulder onto the precarious pathway and roared at the encroachers on its territory.

The twin disruptions, occurring almost simultaneously, spooked the horse; it neighed and reared up on its hind legs, which unceremoniously dismounted Axler. He heaved over backwards and was thrown. His hat went flying and his face, with its ring of bruising around his right eye, warped into an unbelieving grimace. His arms flailed as he clutched handfuls of air. He crashed on the back of his head and his body convulsed. His neck came to rest at an awkward angle.

Blackness swallowed Pete Axler and he floundered in limbo.

Brenda Hawkins was harried and out of sorts. She had her hands full dragging a trunk with a suitcase poised atop it. Her destination was in sight, which gave her a smidgeon of relief, but her son was not cooperating. He was curious about the big adventure and far too involved in being a boy to heed instructions and stay close. He darted ahead of her and all she could do was labor away and attempt to keep her eyes peeled on him.

The sun was at high noon, which was when the stagecoach was scheduled to depart. She had twenty yards to go to the station and was getting frustrated, then help arrived. A jolly old cowboy with a limp in his giddy-up nudged her aside and hauled the luggage the remainder of the way. He even hoisted it up for the teamsters to strap it down on the roof-rack.

She thanked him profusely, then whirled about to find her four-year-old. "Stace! Get over here now." The lad looked at her from a half-block away. His innocent expression darkened in confusion, then he ran and covered the space between them speedily. She set her feet apart and braced for his charge, knowing from many past experiences, that in his final steps he would launch himself. She caught him and staggered to keep her balance.

"Mama!"

"Stace, you have to mind me, especially now," she said, swinging him onto her hip. "We are going to be in all kinds of new places and some could be dangerous." She took hold of his chin. "You can't be wandering off any more. Do you understand, Mr. Hawkins?"

"Yes'um."

"Brenda?"

She turned toward the familiar voice, which came from inside the stagecoach. Her eyes went wide, then at once narrowed as her cheekbones shot up in surprise. "Delores?"

"Are you on this stage?"

"Purchased the ticket last week."

"Really?"

"Yes. Stace and I are heading to Dodge City."

"As am I. Isn't that interesting?"

"A remarkable coincidence, I'd say," Brenda replied, walking to the conveyance. She put Stace on the floor inside, then climbed into the carriage and took a seat. She reached for her son, but was pleased when he climbed up beside the older woman across from her.

"Coincidence? I think not," Delores said, laughing pleasantly. "I have a brother of sorts in Dodge City, who I will want to introduce you to as soon as we arrive, who would say that our meeting yesterday at church and joining up for a long trip together today is no coincidence. He might even be audacious enough to refer to it as a Divine appointment."

"A Divine appointment? That's a significant concept."

One of the drivers, a ruddy-faced man with a single clumpy bush of an eyebrow, poked his head in the window. "Are all present and accounted for?" he asked in a whispery rasp of a voice as he took a quick look-over. He nodded in satisfaction, then pushed off to stroll around the vehicle. He scrambled to his roost on the shotgun side and yelled, "Tally-ho!"

Stace was beaming ear to ear as the coach creaked and rocked to a start. His head needed to be on a swivel because he kept snapping it around to one side for a moment, then the other and back again. This went on for a couple hundred rickety yards, then Delores gave him a playful tweak and stretched out an arm; he sat and snuggled under it.

"Is this your first stagecoach ride, kind sir?"

He scrunched his knees up and giggled as he bobbed his head happily.

"I hope he won't be contrary," his mother said frankly. "Or a burden."

"He'll not be any burden to me, Brenda."

"You might want to wait on that judgment," Brenda warned, taking hold of the hand grip on the wall to aid in readjusting her position. "He can be a rowdy firecracker."

"That's not new information." Delores shook her head, smiling and chuckling. She gazed at him for a long while. "He's a typical boy. Full of spit and vinegar." She noticed that he was sagging into a snooze so she tucked her arm tighter around him and held him close. "Except now. He's snuffling and purring like a pussycat. I will treasure our time together."

"He has taken a shine to you."

"That he has. He's a true blessing to me." Delores had a look at the vast openness of the passing countryside. "Is his father in the picture? Is that what takes you to Dodge City?"

"No to both questions," Brenda answered dryly.

"Forgive me for being intrusive."

"His father flew the coop the day I told him I was expecting."

"I'm sorry."

"No reason to be," Brenda said, shrugging. "I had a difficult and dreary upbringing. I made some terrible mistakes, but somewhere along the way I decided to always try to do the best I could in whatever circumstances got dealt to me."

"That's commendable."

"Perhaps, but I don't know," Brenda replied, wistfulness edging into her voice. "The day that man walked out on me, I made a vow to always do right for my child."

"You've done a fine job raising him."

"Thank you for saying so."

"You're more than welcome, Brenda."

"I can be a worrywart about whether I'm too strict or too easy on him."

"An entirely natural dilemma."

"I suppose," Brenda said, sighing tiredly. She fanned a grainy mist of dust that hovered as an ever-present reality. "Things are happening fast. I hope I'm doing the right thing. It has been a whirlwind few days. I packed up and sold off most of my belongings."

"To what purpose?"

"A new beginning, a fresh start."

Delores frowned, tense and quizzical. The expression held temporarily, then in nothing flat became a face consuming smile. "Without a doubt, this is a Divine appointment."

"What makes you say that?"

"I have much knowledge of new beginnings and fresh starts, Brenda."

"Really?"

"Not all that many years ago my life was a mess," Delores answered honestly. "I suspect I've dug out from under some of the same wreckage you're seeking to put behind you."

The younger woman nodded and pursed her lips into a bloodless line. Her beleaguered emotions and the magnitude of the choice to move on caught in her throat. She blinked tears away, then turned to survey the scenery. A large herd of pronghorns were grazing on the slope of a hill-side, which aroused in her a silent supplication for courage. By the time the antelope were out of sight, Brenda Hawkins had been strengthened by a sensation of peace and comfort.

At the Bluetick Tavern, a bucket of blood hangout on the outskirts of Little Black Water, a haze of smoke clung to the ceiling joists. Max Dawson cut quite a figure in a new outfit; denim britches, wool work shirt and a waist-length jacket the color of barnyard clay. Though the loose-fitting garb was utilitarian, it couldn't obscure her feminine charms.

The settlement on the Pecos River west of the Llano Estacado had a reputation to be rollicking, and the popular watering hole was *always* a thronged mass of locals swapping bull. Dawson was at a scarred table sipping coffee thick and stout enough to float a horseshoe, while being entertained by a blowhard holding court at the billiard table on the far side of the room. Barrel-chested and stubby necked, he looked to be a sack of bricks. He was making gimmick shots and intimidating all others, whooping boisterously at each successful stroke.

Her competitive juices were flowing. She had gleaned that he went by Bronco Bob, which hadn't been a difficult chore because on more than one occasion after he sank a ball he loudly announced, "I'm Bronco Bob and I own this frigging table." On sheer principle she had no toleration for braggarts and bullies, and Bronco Bob was getting under her skin.

Charley Jondreau, who was also attired in a fresh set of mercantile apparel, sat across from her putting eatin irons to work on a second serving of the tin plate special of the day. "Beef and biscuits are tasty, but these whistle berries ain't no picnic," he said, eyeing his partner.

"Not here nor there, Charley. Fun's a-coming."

"Let's see how the cat jumps, eh."

"You think I can't take him, Charley?"

"In pool or a gunfight?"

"Either or both, matters not to me."

Jondreau pushed his floppy-brimmed hat up his forehead and carefully studied Bronco Bob. He forked in meat and chewed thoughtfully. He washed it down with a swallow of liquor, then leaned back and smiled thin and easy. "He wears his pistol too low and it's not tied down. He's muscled up, but that's all he's got. He ain't no action, Max. Just blusteration, eh."

"All the more reason to take him down a peg, Charley."

"I'll need another whiskey if there's going to be a floor show."

While Jondreau went to the bar, Dawson removed her black Stetson and placed it on the table. She fingered the snakeskin band as if it were a talisman. Her hand dropped to her hip and she surreptitiously touched the bone handgrip of her revolver. She was grinning impishly when Jondreau returned with a bottle of hooch and took his seat.

"Bronco Bob!" Max hollered in a whiplash voice and knocked the chair over as she stood. She had the windbag's attention. His eyes bulged into a scowl that regarded her as though she was a sideshow half-wit. She strolled toward him, her reddish hair cresting in a wave on her shoulders. "You've been dancing around that table all by your lonesome for more than an hour. You want to keep diddling yourself, or does your tub of guts dare to accept my challenge?"

The crowd hushed and chairs scraped on the floorboards. All eyes turned to the budding confrontation. Bronco Bob appeared embarrassed, bopping up and down on the balls of his feet as his eyes narrowed on her, malice in them. "I ain't shooting pool against no woman."

Max hooted and clucked like a chicken, which extracted a ripple of nervous laughter from the onlookers. She chose a cue stick from the bracket on the wall. "Are you scared of a girl, Bronco Bob?" she asked snidely. Up close she saw that he was bigger than she had measured, and uglier too—he had a mouthful of crooked tombstone teeth stained to a brownish tint.

"Scared? Hells bells, I ain't scared of nothing or no one," Bronco Bob declared, hitting his stick against the edge of the table. "There ain't no upside in me whupping a sage hen."

"Are you a gambling man?"

"Depends on the wager, missy."

"A hundred bucks against a night in the sack with me."

The spectators collectively hitched in oxygen and whispers began, which soon became a rumble of derision and obscenities that called into doubt the state of Bronco Bob's manhood. His face creased into a blushing snarl. "When I whip your ass and you welch, what then?"

"I'm a woman of my word. Ask Charley over there."

Jondreau nodded. "She never lies, eh. Neither does she ever lose."

"What's wrong, Bobby-boy? You a gutless wonder?"

"The name's Bronco Bob, missy."

"Put up or shut up," Max said, eyebrows rising suggestively.

The audience in the bodega were on pins and needles; excitement had the air fraught with tingly anticipation. The forty or so patrons yelped and the voices melded into one to egg him on. He balked, but as the taunts and cheers increased, the temptation became too much for him to resist. His eyes locked on the swell of her bosom pressing against the shirt's fabric.

Max pulled the jacket open and moistened her lips by sliding the tip of her tongue side to side. "Do you like what you see? You can have firsthand experience with these stunners by taking me in one game of pyramids. My hotel room is already taken care of for tonight."

"I accept the bet," Bronco Bob said, groping in a pocket of his trousers. The gallery howled and cheered in a foot-stomping chant of cusswords. Bronco Bob dug out a crumpled fold of paper money. He counted it off, then returned a single bill to his pants. "One hundred dollars even." He sauntered over, slapped it on the bar and fisted a hand at the bartender.

"Flip a coin for break," Max suggested coolly.

"Nope. Ladies first."

"If you insist. It is, after all your hundred bucks I'll be pocketing," Max said, chalking the tip of her cue stick. "First one to pot eight balls wins. Any scratch or violation loses."

"Yes, ma'am." Bronco Bob racked fifteen red balls in the triangle, leering at her. "A win for me ain't a slam-bam poke and hasty fare-thee-well. It's an all-night roll and tumble."

"Those are the terms, Bobby-boy," Max replied, flexing her shoulders. "You understand you have to beat me, right?" She picked up the cue-ball and spotted it. The snapping crack of the break got the watchers to their feet in unison. Two balls sank. She strolled around the table, eyes intent on the arrangement of the remaining balls. She pointed confidently to a side pocket and dropped another ball; the cue ball had a superb backspin that brought it in perfect orientation for the next shot, which she executed with precision.

"She's halfway there," a looker-on said, astonished.

"Double or nothing, Bobby-boy?"

"Four ain't eight, missy."

"Right you are," Max answered, snickering. She walked all the way around the table, tapped a corner pocket and put the ball there easily. She then proceeded to whack back to back shots, which surprised the hangers-on and brought a moment of suspense; a ball jostled around its intended pocket before disappearing. She arched her back and a smirk pinched her lips as she speculated on her final shot. She lined it up and put it down with a popping flick of a wrist.

"Two out of three," Bronco Bob demanded hotly.

The cue ball was still spinning at the center of the table. She made a cavalier gesture at it. "Three out of five or four out of seven, makes no difference to me. I *own* this table."

"*You* own this table? Like hell!"

"More so than you, Mr. Braggadocio."

Bronco Bob pitched a cuss-ridden fit. The assembly of citizens were ringed around the barroom, booing and hissing. "No one likes a sore loser," the bartender shouted acidly.

Bronco Bob's eyes got buggy and the veins in his temple were full to bursting. He bulled toward her, ready to go at it hammer and tong, but Dawson would not be drawn into a fistfight when she had wiles to use. Her eyes shone and she presented a promising smile that awestruck him an arm's length from her, which was just enough for her to seize the chance.

In a flash of movement, she stabbed the butt of her pool cue between his legs; it struck paydirt squarely. He gasped spittle and crunched forward, clutching at his crotch. She followed through with a double-fisted uppercut to his chin. He wobbled backwards and went for his gun, but before his hand grabbed the grip she had her Colt Peacemaker leveled at his belly.

"One twitch and I'll make you dead," she vowed, icily low-key. "Charley, will you kindly recover my winnings. I've likely worn out our welcome at this establishment."

"Bronco Bob is the one who can vamoose," the bartender intoned, which set off murmurs of agreement from the rest of saloon. "You and your partner can stay, lady."

"Thank you, no," Charley said, tucking the windfall in a pocket of his tunic. "Recreation is over. We've got some hard miles tomorrow, eh." His eyes, keen and ever cautious, were on alert for any blowback from the blustery gasbag, but he expected none; he knew such men and also, had seen Bronco Bob skulk away and now, the big talker was making himself scarce.

Max sidled to their table, slipped on her Stetson and holstered the Colt. "You got your fill of drama, eh."

"You betcha, Charley. I'm all jacked up to hunt down Smoky Crowe."

The pards went outside into the evening coolness. Full dark had not yet fallen, but twilight was absconding. The bluish-black sky was clear except for scatters of clouds. Walking side by side, no words needed to be spoken; they had credible clues as to the whereabouts of the Ute witch, so plans were set. A second night in the feather beds of a flophouse hotel, then on the morrow, the treeless tableland of the Staked Plain awaited them.

chapter three

Deceits & Sins

"Behold, the Lord's hand is not shortened, that it cannot save; neither his ear heavy, that it cannot hear: But your iniquities have separated between you and your God, and your sins have hid his face from you, that he will not hear."

~ISAIAH~

A WEEK LATER, IN a splash of morning brightness, Deacon Coburn was a man on a mission. He hurried past the schoolhouse situated in the middle of a spacious field that sprawled from Paladora Street to Third Avenue. The longish grass was bathed in a blanket of dew. He had his hat pulled low and shoulders hunched stiffly against a late September chill.

He came to the backside of a two-story building that fronted on Third Avenue. He paused to stomp wetness off his boots, then took the steps two at a time as he scurried up the outside stairs. He hesitated on the stoop, knowing that it was almighty early in the day, but was compelled by concerns embedded in his heart. He knocked on the doorframe three times.

Soon there were padding footfalls from inside. "Who is it?"

"Deacon."

"What on earth?" The door got flung open and Abbey Langton, sleepy-eyed and hair disheveled, beheld him with an alarmed expression. "What happened? What's wrong?"

"Nothing at all, Abbey," he replied, slipping past her and heeling the door shut as he did so. "Can't a man check in on his daughter, especially when in a short and getting shorter while she'll be delivering his grandchild?" He took hold of her hand and led her into the apartment's kitchen. "Also, I knew Sam had a whole slew of commitments at Fort Dodge today."

"He told me he'd be at it from dark to dark," she said, accepting his assistance in getting seated at the table. "He'll be chronicling its closure and exploring the possibilities of Hamilton Bell's idea to transform the grounds and buildings from a military post to a soldiers' home."

Coburn hung his hat on the back of a chair. "That's a worthy endeavor." He went to the cookstove and got a sizable supply of kindling from the nearby wood box. "You're stuck with my company for a few hours so what would you like for breakfast?"

"I don't feel much like eating, but I'd take coffee if you'll fix it."

"Arbuckle's, it is." He got the fire going and stoked it, then prepared the cast-iron pot and put it on to boil. When that was completed, he sat across from her. "We've always been straight and true, so tell me without any protests or sugarcoating, how are you doing?"

"I'm more than ready for this baby to be born, Deacon."

"Are you overtaxed?"

"Sam would tell you yes, but I assure you that I am not," she answered, fluffing out the folds of her patchwork housecoat. "I have slowed down plenty. I'm not even planning on going to the office today. Avis will be here around noontime and stay until Sam gets back."

"Alright. I have to meet the ten o'clock train."

"For Mr. Wallace?"

"Yes."

"He visited the *Daily Times* the other day to be interviewed by Mr. Klaine," Abbey said, dragging a hand through her hair. "I'm unsure of when the piece will be published, though it'll certainly increase circulation because Mr. Wallace is a brash and colorful character."

Coburn chuckled cynically. "Brash and colorful are grand understatements. I've worked for the man since '65, and in my dealings he's always been readable. Until now. I have some reservations, perhaps even suspicions, because he's being considerably evasive."

"How so?"

"The whole reason he's here is problematic," he answered, hands twined together against the edge of the table. "Bull has conducted business over the wires since before the war and has brokered lucrative agreements without ever stepping an inch off the *Double B Ranch*. Why ride the rails to the *Queen of the Cowtowns* to complete a transaction with Morgan Fletcher?"

She crinkled her brow. "Morgan Fletcher?"

"That's who's arriving this morning."

"A cane-carrying popinjay?"

"That description fits."

Her eyes tensed as the pleats in her forehead deepened. "I met him in passing once at the Western Union office. He was effusive and overly familiar. He gave me the creeps."

"An intriguing perception," he said pithily. "Years ago, he and Bull were involved in a land investment enterprise in Arkansas and now some opportunity here has brought them together again. I am to escort Fletcher to the Dodge House Hotel and put him on ice."

"Why put him on ice?"

"That's a first-rate question, Abbey," he replied, smiling broadly. "I'll do so because I'm a reliable employee following the instructions of my boss. Bull has other pressing matters, which if the rumors are accurate, includes deer hunting with the *Double B* crew still in town."

"Sounds fishy to me."

Coburn raised his eyebrows and nodded assent. "There's definitely ambiguity here. For reasons unknown, Big Bull wants to send a message to Fletcher that he will get to him when he's good and ready, and I'm to be the conduit to convey it." He stood and got a dishtowel to use as a potholder. He carefully poured two mugs of coffee and served her.

"Thank you," she said, a glut of tears thickening her voice. She held a hand up in dismissal when she recognized the mixed up uncertainty showing on his face. "There are no worries. I'm fine, Deacon. My emotions are just so high-strung and unmanageable. I got to thinking about how grateful I am to have you in my life and the blubbering started."

"That's a two-way avenue, Abbey."

She used a thumb and forefinger to smudge the dampness away. "You do know that at the Harvest Street Festival tomorrow night, when the Dodge City Cowboy Band is set up in front of the Longbranch Saloon playing jigs and such, I expect my father to ask me for a dance."

"As it was last year, it will be my supreme pleasure," he said, settling on his chair. "I'll be sure to pick a tarrying tune. We can't be hoofing it or you'll go into labor there and then."

"Very funny."

Coburn shrugged in a self-deprecating manner. He had his mug at his lips, eyeing her fondly over its rim. He took a breathy sip, then put it down, never modifying his focus. "You are a treasure to me." His vocal cords were overwrought; the words muffled and quivery.

"What is it, Deacon?"

He exhaled in a noisy rush. "I've been thinking about your mother a lot lately."

"As have I."

"There are so many regrets in me, Abbey."

"Seems I'm not the only one with out of kilter emotions."

"I reckon not," he conceded sadly. He began picking at the overgrown brush of his moustache. "Getting older means remembering bits and pieces of shame or guilt. I know it's my fault. Things should've been different between her and me. We could've . . ."

"No!" she cut in, sharp and firm. She skewered him with a withering look. "You can't go down the should've could've road, Deacon. I've heard you explain that truth to others."

Coburn sat back and smiled wearily. His eyes were doused in sorrow. "I can help others, but much more often than I willingly admit, I am useless in helping myself."

"Your secret is safe with me."

His lips puckered as he struggled with fervent feelings. "I stand validated on my previous disclosure; you are a treasure to me," he said, reaching over to softly caress her cheek. "I am so proud of you, but that pride is outshone by your mother beaming from the shores of heaven."

She shivered in a breath and let out a quaking sob, which he echoed. Their hands joined together and tenderness passed wordlessly between them. Time ticked away. The coffee cooled as the shared heat of sincerity sealed the bonds that connected them as father and daughter.

Avis Lahay was the wind. Every muscle in her body was in accord with the strawberry roan beneath her. She had the bead of the chinstrap on her skimmer pulled tight against her jawline and was leaning forward with her knees pulled up. An enraptured smile spilled over her face. Her heart was racing and she had her cheek pressed against the animal's sweaty neck.

The horse was galloping flat-out, a half-mile south of Dodge City and directly toward the rising sun. Its eyes were lively and animated, its snout transfixed in an excited grin. The clip-clop tempo of its hoofbeats matched her pounding heartbeat. Thrills were pulsing through her veins; it was as though she was one with the mare.

She murmured its name and relaxed her thighs. The horse responded by immediately beginning to gradually decrease its speed. She straightened in the saddle. Over the course of a hundred yards or so, the strawberry roan progressively slowed until it was walking. She gave a slight tug on the reins and it came to a full halt.

The sun blazed above the horizon, burning off the dewiness of dawn. She slipped to the ground and began stroking its hindquarters. "That was an impressive workout, girl."

Pumpkin snorted and wagged its head in agreement.

She laughed giddily. "You don't have any conceit, do you?"

The horse neighed and attempted to nuzzle her shoulder.

"We got no time to play, Pumpkin."

The train whistle blew, long and loud. She looked to the west and saw chugs of smoke from the approaching locomotive. A frown stitched her eyes into slits; she wondered if the train was early or if she was late. She thought that through and decided there was no chance she could be off schedule because she had blocked out her day precisely.

She had been up since before first light and the chores at Bell's Livery were completed soon thereafter. The interval to take her horse for a free-spirited run was all part of her time allotment. She figured she would return to the livery and give each of the horses under her care rubdowns and still fulfill her noonday commitment to Abbey Langton.

"Come along, Pumpkin," she said, smoothing out a crease in one of the calfskin gloves. She took hold of the reins and led the mare north, her eyes vaguely watching the smoky puffs moving eastward. The whistle hooted once again. A stiff breeze riffled past, which caused her to shiver. She began to hurry at the bridge spanning the Arkansas River.

The clip-clops on the planks reverberated noisily. Once on the other side, she doubled back to take the horse on a well-worn pathway to the edge of Hog Creek, a winding watershed tributary of the main channel. While Pumpkin quenched its thirst, she loosened the chinstrap and removed her skimmer. She tossed her hair, briefly finger combed it, then put the hat on so that the leather thongs rested on the nape of her neck.

In the shadows cast by a row of tall trees, she had a prudent glance around to be sure there were no witnesses. Persuaded as to being unseen, she released three buttons of her black and red checkered shirt. The heavy flannel and flimsy camisole were sticky with perspiration. She fluttered the material for several seconds, then refastened the buttons to the collar.

She waggled her arms and legs as she waited patiently. When the strawberry roan had its fill, she led it onto Second Avenue and looked ahead to Front Street. The direction from which the diminishing black smoke of the locomotive came told her that the train had reached its destination. She spoke encouragement to Pumpkin and redoubled her speed.

≈ ≈ ≈

Though it was just past nine-thirty, Morgan Fletcher was already tipsy drunk. The constant clack-clack rocking of the train on the rails had worn him down. Bored by the stark desolation of the endless prairie rolling past the window, he had popped the cork on a bottle of bourbon an hour ago and took swigs from it for the final leg of the journey. When he returned it to his carpetbag there was a mere slosh of an inch or two remaining.

He stood in the bright sunshine on the platform of the Atchison, Topeka & Santa Fe Depot, surveying the activity on Front Street while dawdling about waiting for Deacon Coburn. Two leather suitcases, along with the flower-patterned carpetbag, were near his feet. His legs were wobbly, but he had much proficiency in masking intoxication.

A tall and slinky clotheshorse, he had a strikingly handsome countenance; deep-set gray eyes that just now were bleary and overtired. Usually clean-shaven, he had two days growth of stubble and therefore was anxious for the services of a barber. He was dressed in a classy manner; pinstriped pants and a double-breasted black frock coat. He carried a brass-handled cane and wore a felt derby hat; both of which could be used for flairs of showmanship.

The boredom that had driven him to drink was lurking to overcome him again. There was not enough interesting diversions on the thoroughfare to keep his attention occupied. He twirled the cane from one hand to the other, but his coordination was too fuddled to complete the transfer. The walking stick fell and clattered about, and he went to a knee to retrieve it.

From that position, he spotted a shapely woman leading a horse and coming toward him. Even attired in the clothes of a ranch-hand, she was exquisitely attractive. His breath caught in his throat and he reveled in a pleasurable carnal stirring. He stood, and his eyes roamed from her head to her hips and back again before coming to rest on her fetching bustline.

His blood was rising at a breakneck rate. Lewd images swamped his mind; the woman disrobing and smiling innocently at him. The fantasy had his libido all atingle. He possessed the knowledge of the impropriety and risk involved, but couldn't help himself; due to the influx of alcohol his governing controls weren't functioning at optimal levels.

He looked to the right; he looked to the left—he repeated the process twice more, then decided that the coast was clear. His concentration zeroed in on the woman in the skimmer who was moving at an invigorating jiggle, which elevated the craving in his loins. If he didn't act swiftly, the prospect of making a play for her would be gone.

"Excuse me, ma'am," he called, hastening into the street to intercept her. He doffed his bowler and bowed at the waist. When he terminated the formality he peered into her eyes. "Sorry to barge in on you, my good woman. I am not a student of horseflesh, but I must tell you that your mount is so impressive that I required a closer look. What a marvelous color."

"Thank you, mister."

"Morgan Fletcher, at your service, ma'am."

"Nice to make your acquaintance."

"And you are?"

"The owner of Pumpkin."

He noted her refusal to complete the introductions, but was undeterred. "What an absolutely perfect name for such a superb animal." He reached out to give its neck a pat, but the horse shook its head and shied away. He retreated in a draggy backward step. "I apologize for my bumptiousness. Apparently Pumpkin doesn't cotton to strangers."

"I'd not take it personal."

"Nor shall I," he said confidently. "I will, however, be crushed to the core if I cannot know your name. You are a vision of loveliness, my dear. I wish to engage you in some delightful conversation and I humbly offer you the friendship of a gentleman."

"I'm not in the market for that sort of friendship, sir."

He pressed in closer. "A woman of your bearing *needs* a man."

Her teeth clenched against the smell of liquor coming off him as her cheeks blushed at the earthiness of his implication. "You are brash and impertinent, sir. A man of your obvious ilk needs to be given rudimentary lessons in courtesy and honor."

"My offense was unintentional."

"I'm not stupid, mister."

"I made no such suggestion."

"Your crass advances *were* intentional and inappropriate."

"Forgive me, my dear lady."

"I do not wish to be rude, but your tasteless flirtations are holding me up. Please depart and quit blocking my way," she said strongly. "I have several obligations to get to this morning, so I would appreciate you giving me the roadway because our conversation is over."

"Grant me a small indulgence of your time."

"Thirty seconds, mister."

Fletcher nodded and smiled, bold and lecherous. He tapped his cane against the toe of her right boot. "I'd enjoy having dinner with you this evening, ma'am." He allowed his eyes to take a close-up tour of her body; he thought he was being clandestine, but the bourbon mixed with venting hormones falsified his perception. In reality, he was demonstrably enthralled by her topside. "If you would be so kind as to join me for a meal and companionship."

"You are no gentleman, sir. Your blatant indecency sickens me. Put your eyes back in your head or you'll be sorry," she told him, bristly and outraged. "A dinner date with me is not a remote possibility. You are a vulgar and disgusting guttersnipe. Now give me the roadway."

His face was crimson; his expression lusty with arousal. He grabbed her wrist and gave it a hefty twist as he tried to jerk her close. Pumpkin objected by whinnying angrily; Avis Lahay's reaction was direct and unrestrained. Her right hand lashed out—it started as an open palm, but when it connected between his nose and chin it was a fiercely balled fist.

A trickle of red emerged from his bottom lip. "You bitch!" he exclaimed, lifting a hand to strike back. It was then, grimacing and hotheaded, that he saw the tree-branch shouldered agent for the *Double B Ranch* approaching. Morgan Fletcher blanched and came to his senses. He moved aside so she could pass and when she did, he scuttled onto the platform. He was fearfully afraid that his cover as an upstanding businessman had been blown. His head throbbed and he leaned heavily on the cane; otherwise he would have swooned and fallen.

Silent and steaming, Deacon Coburn watched Avis Lahay lead the strawberry roan away. There was heat simmering in him that he was making no effort to stamp down. He stood on the same side of the street, a mere ten yards from where the confrontation occurred. He had seen enough to deduce the dishonorable underbelly of the man in cahoots with his boss.

He put his eyes on Morgan Fletcher, who was attempting nonchalance, a multihued carpetbag in one hand while clutching the cane as though it was an extension of his right arm. His face was mottled and pasty, eyes veiled and dull. Coburn stepped past him and without so much as a head bob greeting, picked up the two leather suitcases

"That was not what it appeared to be," Morgan said, sputtering and excitable. "It took me by complete surprise and I'm unsure of its meaning. It was an unfortunate misunderstanding."

Coburn was poker-faced. He carried the luggage across Front Street.

Fletcher tagged along, filling the air with a ramble of words. "I was minding my own affairs when that woman stopped her horse and began chatting with me. She did so in the manner of a strumpet. She was coy and flirty, but I resisted and merely admired the animal. She came on stronger and stronger. I maintained tact and decorum, and as best I could, attempted to extricate myself from her trap. She took offense. I question that woman's stability."

Coburn entered the Dodge House Hotel and halted in the middle of the lobby, which had only one occupant; a clerk with a knobby Adam's apple. Coburn paid him no mind. He put down the suitcases and turned on the man following him. "*That* woman is a friend of mine."

Fletcher swallowed hard. "It was an ill-fated encounter, Mr. Coburn."

Coburn muscled in close, eyes hot and snapping like tongues of fire. He crowded even closer, and in a scratchy and passionate barfly rasp he said, "I have endeavored to put violence behind me, but if you ever touch that young lady again, it will be more than your lip that gets bloodied. I will personally castrate you and be sure to use a dull and rusty knife."

"Is that a threat, Mr. Coburn?"

"I don't make threats, Mr. Fletcher."

"If it wags its tail and barks, it's a dog."

"True enough."

"So you *did* threaten me."

"No, but be certain that I am a man of my word, Mr. Fletcher."

"Seems that you're splitting hairs."

"Giving you fair notice, is all."

"I repudiate your forewarning, Mr. Coburn."

"Your repudiation is meaningless."

"Castration?" Morgan asked, contemptuous and sarcastic. His eyes were scornful and brimming with taunting laughter. "That's extreme for a minor faux pas."

Smiling, Coburn quoted the wisdom of Solomon. "*Can a man take fire in his bosom, and his clothes not be burned? Can one go upon hot coals, and his feet not be burned?*" The smile became as rigid as granite. "There'll be no place for you to hide from the consequences. If you ever touch that young lady again I will hunt you down and keep my word."

"Is there no milk of human kindness in you, sir?"

"Your actions caused it to curdle," Deacon replied tautly. His mind took an easy leap to a passage of truth written by Paul of Tarsus. "*Be not deceived; God is not mocked: for whatsoever a man soweth, that shall he also reap. For he that soweth to his flesh shall of the flesh reap corruption; but he that soweth to the Spirit shall of the Spirit reap life everlasting.*"

Fletcher gave him a puzzled look, then sloughed it off. "I tried to explain, but you're not listening." He backed up a step and held his hands at half-mast surrender. "It was nothing more than an unfortunate misunderstanding and an ill-fated encounter."

"An unfortunate misunderstanding? An ill-fated encounter? A minor faux pas?" Deacon queried rhetorically. The seething surge of anger in him was still bucking and kicking, but he had ensnared it and gotten it under control on a short leash. "I see it much differently because innocence is to be protected and justice is important to God."

"You have my sincere apologies."

"For what?"

Fletcher sighed in exasperation. His eyebrows sagged and his forehead furrowed as he glanced away for a moment, then he shifted and fixed his attention directly on his adversary. "I am sorry that you're bent out of shape and got your hackles up over nonsense."

"A nice non-apology apology, Mr. Fletcher. You ain't repentant for that which you are responsible," Deacon said, calm and understated. "Besides, I don't bend out of shape and my hackles ain't up yet. When I put that rusty blade to work is when my hackles will be up."

"Is that charitable or Christian, sir?"

Coburn laughed heartily. His face wrinkled into an expression of mockery. "And you're the paragon of virtue who will lecture me about charity and Christian character?"

Fletcher shrugged uncaringly. "My virtue, whatever its shortfalls, is self-made and has served me well." His expression took on all the attributes of a prideful peacock. "I don't use the Bible or religion as a crutch as is your example. I do what I must to survive and get ahead. Your faith is drivel because God, if he exists at all, doesn't give a damn about any of this crap."

"You're so sure about the Almighty's priorities?"

Fletcher grimaced, scorn and disrespect smoldering in his eyes. "Your hypocrisy makes me want to puke. Your reputation as a holy man is proved to be a lie by your threats to make me a capon, for what? For conversing with a spicy angelica on a public boulevard? Your high and pious ways will be your downfall and I will be there to applaud your disgrace."

"Innocence is to be protected and justice is important to God," Deacon repeated, grinning nonchalantly. "I'm positive sure that when my time of dying comes and I'm standing in front of the Judgment Seat of God, you ain't going to be the one sitting on the throne. And, when my days are no more, the opinion of the One sitting on that throne is all that'll matter to me."

"To hell with you, Mr. Coburn," Morgan said smartly.

"Stay clear of that young lady," Deacon replied in a stony voice that conjured images of death. He took several steps toward the door, then stopped and turned back to him. "Bull will be engaged in other involvements for a day or so. According to his orders, you are to sit tight. When he's ready to do business he'll come here and he better have no problem finding you."

"That's intolerable. Am I to be confined to my quarters?"

"I'm just the messenger, Mr. Fletcher," Deacon answered, eyes hard and flinty. "Big Bull Wallace is a man who expects his biddings to carry weight and be adhered to, so you'd be wise to heed his counsel, but make whatever choice your self-made virtue thinks best. Be sure to sign the register. A room has been reserved and paid for through your time in Dodge City."

Fletcher was grim-faced as he shuffled sideward toward the front desk where the clerk awaited. He cleared his throat. "Are you going to tell Big Bull about my misbehavior?"

Coburn chuckled derisively. "What are you, twelve years old?" He cocked a forefinger at him as though it were a pistol. "Stay clear of that young lady," he reiterated, then was gone. On the boardwalk he didn't pause, but rather, made a beeline to Bell's Livery. His singular intention was to check in on his silver-dappled buckskin as a pretext to converse with Avis Lahay.

Whitey Fitzgerald was in a mucked up bind of an impasse. His emotions were unraveling as his brain sent urgent dispatches that had to do with a coldblooded assassination. He could hardly breathe and his throat hurt. His complexion was as milky pale as was possible given the natural pigmentation of his African forebears.

He acted as though he had seen a ghost and perhaps from his skewed perspective, that was true. His mind was spinning and his head ached; his blood pressure soared so high that there was an incessant buzz behind his eyes that was akin to an angry swarm of hornets. He sat as stiff as a board on a bench in front of the Beatty & Kelley Restaurant, where he had been since shortly before the ten o'clock train arrived a half-hour early.

The breakfast—taters, eggs, toast and coffee—served by a smiley-faced waitress, had been scrumptious and filling, but was now souring his stomach as though it was nothing more than a ball of grease. Upon exiting the eatery, he made a spur of the moment choice to wait for Avis Lahay because he expected her to be along soon enough.

Then the train came smoking into the station. From his vantage point, fifty-odd yards west of the depot, he had a clear line of sight. He settled in for a serious bout of people watching, but shock was about to smack him senseless because amongst a smattering of disembarking passengers was the man Whitey Fitzgerald knew as Huey Butters.

What transpired next put the pint-sized black man in the darkest of places and the foulest of moods. Chaos exploded inside his head. He instinctively shrank into the surroundings. All the nasty memories of being taken to the cleaners came back in cascading madness; the blood and aggression rampant in his nightmares burgeoned into vexing realism in his mind.

Frozen and gape-eyed, he was crippled by an immobilizing helplessness. He had watched the happenstance between Avis Lahay and Huey Butters from beginning to end, but could not hear any of their interchange. He also saw Deacon Coburn arrive and wanted to shout his name, but not a peep came from his mouth; not even a click-click.

Rats were loose and gnawing at the tissue of his soul; the unforeseen emergence of the perverse rodents scandalized and horrified him. He cringed and attempted to fight against the squirming sensation roiling around his inner parts, but it was a futile battle. The desire to kill Huey Butters was an all-consuming hunger growling and itching to be fed.

His breathing was shallow and erratic. His hands were knotted and thumping against his thighs. When Deacon Coburn and Huey Butters entered the Dodge House Hotel, Fitzgerald came out of his stunned stupor. He shillyshallied to his feet and swayed crookedly as he forced the heels of his hands against the sides of his head—agony shot through the roof of his skull as though he had rapidly swallowed ice and the result was an excruciating brain freeze.

He recovered, then moving like a wooden-legged marionette, he hobbled on the boardwalk and felt his way by palming the walls or grasping windowsills of storefronts. His lips were moving as though he was sipping or sampling a full-flavored beverage. Passersby nodded or spoke to him, but he was blank-eyed and nonresponsive, resembling a rubby-dub street drunk weaving and wobbling in the throes of a severe attack of a trembling delirium.

He came to the Alhambra Saloon and there was not a moment's hesitation. He huffed in air and straightened his posture in an effort to saunter into the barroom, though there was nothing casual or routine in his demeanor. He bellied up to the bar. The place was empty except for the balding mixologist on duty and a pair of regulars at a table yammering; old-timers who spent mornings telling lies about their lives while quaffing mug after mug of coffee.

"Pot of tea, Whitey?" the bartender asked cheerfully.

"No. Whiskey."

"Whiskey?"

"Yeah. Whiskey."

"For who?"

Fitzgerald thumbed his chest. "Whiskey. Now."

"Is this a joke? Are you testing me?"

"No. Whiskey."

"Are you crazy, Whitey?"

"Crazy? No. Whiskey."

"How 'bout I put the water on for tea?"

"Whiskey, damn it!"

The barkeep made his neck disappear in a greatly exaggerated shrug of his shoulders. He poured an ounce of Kansas Sheep Dip. "I hope the hell you know what you're doing, Whitey."

Fitzgerald grimaced. "The bottle stays and leave me be."

The bartender, a gregarious and sociable man who often engaged in philosophical chatter with the barber, shook his head in distress and complied with his patron's request. He went to the far end of the bar, sat on a stool and fidgeted as he kept eyes on the white-haired customer.

Whitey Fitzgerald could taste the liquid in the shot glass. His nostrils flared and his tongue kept darting over his lips. He was parched drier than a popcorn fart. He lifted the drink to eye level and stared longingly at it; lovingly, even. He sniffed it and breathed in its essence. His eyes were glazed. He put the shooter down and ran a finger around the rim; again and again he did so. He raised the whiskey to his mouth and shuddering gooseflesh passed over him.

The certainty of doubt had Whitey Fitzgerald unnerved and thirsty.

Naomi Axler was on the verge of tears. Lately that had become the customary and normal state of her emotions. It didn't matter that the sun was shining and the skies were blue; or that her children were on the porch with her, babbling as they built a wooden block tower. Her eyes were reddened and the focus unclear; her attention encumbered by a heap of worry.

She was tired. Her nocturnal slumber had been disrupted by merciless nightmares which gave rise to wrestling matches against sleeplessness. Night after night insomnia triumphed to rob her of rest. Her joints ached as though she had been tortured on a rack, but those pains were minuscule in comparison to the heartache clutching at her.

Her husband was more than a week overdue. That fact tore at her sensibilities and slashed away at the bedrock underpinning of her faith. She despised being fretful and distrustful, and fought against those sneaky feelings by affirming Scriptural truth and reciting verses, either silently or aloud depending on the nuance of the moment.

She kept returning to a passage from Isaiah for reassurance. Again and again, she turned the words over in her mind as though the promise was fecund soil being cultivated to sprout buds of hope. *Thou wilt keep him in perfect peace, whose mind is stayed on thee: because he trusteth in thee. Trust ye in the Lord forever: for in the Lord Jehovah is everlasting strength.*

The rocker she sat in was old and scarred, but despite its creakiness offered comfort and security. She stared vacantly, her head angled to the northwest, which was from where she anticipated seeing her unhurried hubby arrive. He would be upright and relaxed in the saddle of a brindle gelding plodding along at a gait that copied the moseying amble of its owner.

The aspens on the wall of mountains that surrounded *WT Ranch* resembled festive bunting in magnificent shades of yellow, which usually stimulated awe and wonder in her, but presently, the beauty of nature didn't even register on her brain. Terrible thoughts and scenarios dominated her thinker. She couldn't dismiss or flee from the premonition and misgivings. An expectation of danger had formed in her, which resulted in one over-shadowing question; what could be delaying Pete's return? Her focus was getting progressively blurrier.

"Mommy's crying," Amanda said, soft and shy.

"Shush," her brother whispered in an insistent tone.

"Why's Mommy crying?"

"She misses Daddy," Jesse explained simply.

"I do, too."

Naomi shivered a breath. She backhanded the wetness off her cheeks. "Mommy's just being silly," she said, pursing her lips. She looked apprehensively at her son and daughter. The almost seven-year-old had a hand on the shoulder of his four-year-old sister, his face rutted by a frown reminiscent of his father. She opened her arms and reached out to them. "Climb up on my lap and we'll rock the squeaks out of this cranky old chair."

Jesse and Amanda were soon snuggled in place. They wasted no time in getting the chair pitching in an energetic motion. The wood groaned complaints that set-off a chorus of giggles as an amusing counterpoint. Naomi had to smile; it was strained by tension, but for a wee hiatus it chased disquiet off her face. She held them close and tight, and was encouraged by the tenderness, but then, a powerful undercurrent of agonizing anxiety besieged her.

Her legs stiffened, which despite the children's continued efforts, stopped the rocker. She inhaled sharply and stewed over the cruel ebb and flow harassing her mind. What if the awful and unspeakable had occurred? What if Pete had been maimed or killed? What if she had to raise Jesse and Amanda to adulthood without Pete at her side—the ideas panicked her. She embraced her children forcefully. They squirmed and wiggled until she relaxed her hold.

"When's Daddy coming home," Jesse asked, pensive and timid.

Naomi flinched and thought it over for such a long while that his little boy impatience got the better of him so he asserted the query again. She sighed and made a gesture in the direction from which she figured he would come. "I expect one of these mornings or afternoons your Daddy will come riding out of those trees and when he does we'll throw a party."

"Why?" Amanda wondered, her voice rising.

"So that man of mine knows how much we missed him."

"Mommy," Jesse said, slow and unsure.

"Yes, honey."

"I don't like it when you cry."

"It's alright, Jesse," Naomi said, attempting to dispel his concern by patting his back. She kissed his brow. "Tears aren't always bad. Sometimes we cry happy tears."

"Are you crying happy tears?"

Naomi puckered her mouth. Her first inclination was to stonewall her son and that notion troubled her. A fresh batch of teardrops welled up and glistened. Her brown eyes were sorrowful. She briefly considered lying but dismissed that as an unacceptable possibility. Instead, she chose to exercise her ability to divert and deflect. "Do you want to be a part of a big surprise?"

"For Daddy?"

"Yes, later for Daddy," she replied, an inflection of cheer in her voice. "But on this bright day, I suspect Hank likely misses shepherding you two urchins. Why don't we pay a visit on Sally Twosongs? We can see if that baby is getting ready to meet the world yet."

The affirmative reply came in the form of a unison shriek of delight.

Naomi hugged them as they speedily slid to their feet. "Put the blocks in the basket and take it to the play-box in the living room. When that's all done we'll go for a nice walk."

Brother and sister did as they were told. When they were in the house, she rubbed her eyes hard and voiced the verses from the prophet Isaiah. "*Thou wilt keep him in perfect peace, whose mind is stayed on thee: because he trusteth in thee. Trust ye in the Lord forever: for in the Lord Jehovah is everlasting strength.*" She then summoned the courage to boldly pray. "Our Father who art in heaven, make your word alive and free in my heart and mind. Amen."

She stood and in an urgency of determination, clung to faith and hope.

～ ～ ～

"Caleb! Caleb Weitzel!"

The rancher from Colorado tugged on the reins and maneuvered his horse around. His face cracked in a wide grin. "Sam Beadle." Shadrach whinnied and became as still as a statue when Weitzel dismounted. "I didn't anticipate seeing you until I reached Dodge City."

"Here I be."

Weitzel covered twenty yards in a stiff-shouldered trot. Beadle bolted off the broad veranda and down the stairs of a sturdy stone building. The men met on the hard-packed street and clasped hands, exchanging what amounted to verbalized grunts, which were accepted as amiable greetings. They stepped back, squinting at each other in the bright sunshine.

It was midday. Beadle glanced around. "Did you ride in alone?"

"No. My father-in-law trailed the horses with me. We arrived and camped west of here late yesterday afternoon, but he wandered off before dawn. I have no idea where he is, which has been the inevitable outcome lately," Caleb said, frustration worming into his voice.

"You need any help?"

"No, I concluded my business an hour ago," Caleb reported flatly. "I had to haggle with a skinflint Sergeant acting as the quartermaster who pretended he had never heard of *WT Ranch* and feigned ignorance about the deal. I produced the documentation. He groused and cussed some, but finally took delivery of the horses and I got the agreed upon price."

"Glad to hear it. Did I have a hand in any of that stock?"

Weitzel ruminated on it for a short spell, then raised an eyebrow and nodded pleasantly. "I hadn't thought much about that, but as a matter of fact, yes. Three of the stallions and a mare were birthed when you and Abbey were with us in the spring of '79."

"That was a well-spent year for us at *WT Ranch*."

"Yeah, it was," Caleb agreed, smiling. "When are you two coming back?"

"A fair question, but whenever it is, there'll be three of us."

"We've got plenty of room," Caleb said, removing his hat. He rubbed his forehead with the heel of a hand and surveyed the area. "This place looks and feels like a ghost town."

"It sure enough does," Sam replied cheerlessly. "Time marches on, as they say, but it's difficult to believe that an essential fortification on the western frontier is being abandoned by the U.S. Army. Fort Dodge has been the buttress against Indian attacks at this intersection of the dry and wet route of the Santa Fe Trail since '65. Many a Kiowa and Comanche died of lead poisoning because of the troops stationed at this outpost on the plains."

"Are there contingency plans to protect the citizenry?"

"Who knows with military bureaucrats?" Sam answered, shaking his head in disgust. "It came as a surprise when the fort was closed in June. There are folks in Dodge City still shocked and up in arms over it, but there's nothing to be done. In a week Old Glory will be lowered for the final time and the last soldiers will transfer southward to Fort Supply."

"What's going to happen to these buildings?"

Beadle shrugged, eyes enthused and arms outstretched. "Who knows? All the structures are solid and mostly in good repair." He gestured toward the one he had been in when he'd seen the distinctive steeldust through a window. "This functional dwelling here used to be the Officer Quarters. General George Armstrong Custer himself was once housed here."

Weitzel retuned his hat to his head, then took several side-steps and had a thoughtful look at the property. "To discard this stronghold is folly and a waste of serviceable resources."

"No argument," Sam said succinctly. "A custodial arrangement is being put in place for now until the powers that be come up with an alternative use for the facility. Some of us residents of Dodge City are kicking around ideas and we won't quietly disappear."

"That's heartening. Push the administrators hard, Sam."

"If I slacken an inch, Abbey will certainly prod me onward."

"Hey, before I forget," Caleb said, then turned slightly and gave a hiss of a whistle. "Shadrach, come." The muscular stallion lifted its head and immediately juked briskly to him. He flipped open a flap on his saddlebags and rearranged some of the contents to acquire a thick manila envelope. "Please take this to your wife from my wife. I promised Sally Twosongs that I would pass it along the moment I saw you or Abbey. It's now your responsibility."

Beadle accepted the correspondence and tucked it in an inside breast pocket of his jacket. "I have several more tasks and claims on my time to keep me busy for a few more hours, but bet your bottom dollar that Abbey will receive this letter the instant I arrive home."

Weitzel sprang into the saddle. "I want to grab a room at a hotel and get a tub of hot water. I mean to be in town for a few days. Let's make plans to visit and catch up."

"Definitely."

"Where will I find Deacon?"

"The Alhambra Saloon is his usual office," Sam replied, chuckling slyly. "In fact, I can likely meet you there some time this evening, soon after I check in with Abbey."

"That's fine by me."

"Then I have to rattle my hocks, Caleb."

Weitzel touched the brim of his hat and nudged Shadrach with his knees. The horse bobbed its head and pranced sprightly, as though it was cavorting and showing off in a parade. He pinched off a smile and pointed his mount onto a northeasterly road that had worn down grooves from years of excessive wagon traffic. The steeldust established a stately canter.

Alone and scared witless, Whitey Fitzgerald was stark raving mad. A maniacal dementia had taken over his faculties. He was wild-eyed and entirely intractable. He stood outside of himself, dizzy and weak in the knees as he watched a slobbering lunatic sitting on a chair hypnotized by the spinning cylinder of a nickel-plated Remington revolver.

The walls of his apartment seemed to be getting tighter and confining him. And there were voices inside his head—lots of crackbrained voices screaming, shrieking, screeching a deranged mantra; *kill, kill, kill, kill.* He paced in circles, never grasping the realities of what was happening. The crazed absurdity had him frenzied and out of his gourd.

He saw the man with the gun put the barrel in his mouth. His teeth clamped around the steel as his finger toyed with the trigger. He was moaning and helplessly grappling to seize a reason not to put an end to it all. The chanting noise bouncing around the chamber of his skull was pulsating louder and louder; pounding, pounding, pounding.

His heartbeat drummed at his temples. A bellow swelled in his throat, rising like a titanic tidal wave, but when its foam washed over the beach of his lips it was a breathless whimper. The thwacking blast of a gunshot rang out and jangled the windowpanes. He gasped and recoiled in his footsteps. His eyes popped wide and protruded from the sockets. Where was the blood? Where was the release of death and the sweet cessation of madness?

Another gunshot. And another; but no. His ears were deceiving him. He staggered and came close to falling, but reeled about and found a semblance of balance. *Whitey.* He craned his neck and tilted his head. He clearly heard his name; someone was calling to him. The familiar voice sliced through the swirling incantation singing inside his head.

There was gunfire along with the grating and grinding sound of wood being strained to its breaking point. He removed the weapon from his mouth and gawked dumbstruck down the black hole of the muzzle. He swayed and tottered in the spinning trembles of a drunkard. The door crashed open as fragments and splinters flew, and Deacon Coburn hustled into the room.

In a flickering blink of sheer lucidity Whitey Fitzgerald understood; the banging wasn't the reports of a firearm, but rather, the fist of his friend knocking harder and harder on the door, then slamming against it until the lock shattered loose from the doorframe. The handgun dropped to the floor and he collapsed like a lifeless ragdoll into Coburn's arms.

Fitzgerald sobbed in helter-skelter heaving that threatened to shake bones loose from tendons and cartilage. He convulsed in an agitation of hysterics and gulped breaths as best he could in the anguish of the unrelenting spasms. His feet weren't anywhere near the floor; legs dangling and flopping as Coburn supported him in a fierce bear hug.

Coburn elevated him even higher and took a thrashing knee to the midsection. He winced and leveraged his stability and composure to lug him to a chair. There was nothing easy about the task of getting him sat down; it was a flailing elbows fight, but when it was achieved, he knelt in front of him and continued to vigorously hold on.

Almost ten minutes passed before calmness eased over Fitzgerald. His eyes, wet and raw, were out-of-focus. He cupped a hand over his mouth to wipe away runners of sticky drool. He slumped his shoulders and click-clicked as he glanced around as though he was reconnecting with the surroundings. "No," he murmured shakily. "I ain't gonna kill him."

"Kill who?" Deacon asked, bewildered.

Fitzgerald eyed him warily. "Deacon? What are you doing here?"

"I stopped in at the Alhambra. You ordered whiskey."

"I never drank a drop. I swear."

"I know," Deacon said, eyes crimping in encouragement. "The bartender told me that you gave it several good sniffs and did everything with the glass except tip it back."

"I blacked out or something, Deacon."

 "Want to talk about it, my friend?"

"There's nothing to say," Whitey replied, click-clicking weakly. "I stared at that shot of whiskey for I have no idea how long. I don't even remember leaving the barroom."

"What made you thirst for whiskey?"

"Ain't no matter."

"I ain't buying that poppycock."

Fitzgerald jerked back and palmed his mouth again. "Was Avis harmed?"

Coburn smiled wryly. He rose, sidled to a straight-backed chair and turned it around to straddle it. Discernment showed in his eyes. "Why would you ask such a question?"

"I saw that brute hassle her on Front Street."

"Avis is fine. Morgan Fletcher, however, has a fat lip."

"That weren't no Morgan Fletcher."

"Yeah, it was, Whitey. In the flesh."

"No. His name is Huey Butters."

"What?"

"Do you recall when I became a boozer?"

"That's forgotten and forgiven, Whitey."

"Forgiven, I suppose," Whitey said, hands clenching together. "Forgotten? Not by me. Huey Butters used a woman to rob me of my dignity and my life savings." He had the shakes and was white-knuckled. "The man you hooked up with at the train depot *is* Huey Butters."

"Are you sure?"

"Positive."

Coburn puckered his mouth inward and outward several times, causing his moustache to waggle. "That rips it apart, doesn't it? My gut has tried to tell me there was something unseemly about that strutting show-off, but I chalked it up as wrong because he was in business with Big Bull." He scratched at his chin. "Now my skepticism and mistrust of what my employer might have up his sleeve has really got me overburdened with guesswork."

"What are *we* going to do?" Whitey wondered, relaxing some.

"No guff, Whitey. Are you alright?"

"Do you believe me about Huey Butters?"

"Mr. Butters will be held to account. I promise."

"Then I be better than alright."

"Leave it to me," Deacon said earnestly. "I'll have a plainspoken discussion with Bull." He stood, went over and snagged the Remington off the floor. He flicked the cylinder open, removed the six cartridges and pocketed them. "You still have any need for this pistol?"

"Why don't you sell it for me, Deacon?"

"After I fix your door."

Fitzgerald took a quick glance at it and laughed heartily. "Since you be the one to bust it, I'd say that's only fair." He got up and stretched. "I'll get us some grub while you do so."

The deal was clinched by a mutual nod. Whitey Fitzgerald got busy with pots and pans, while Deacon Coburn went to Zimmermann's Hardware & Lumber to borrow tools and purchase the materials necessary to repair the lock and doorknob. After the job was completed, the old companions spent the remainder of the afternoon reminiscing and making plans for the future. Night had fallen by the time Deacon Coburn made tracks to the Great Western Hotel.

≈ ≈ ≈

More than a dozen candles and oil lamps were arranged on the counter and tabletop to make the kitchen bright and cheery. Abbey Langton had a penchant for utilizing lots of tapers and nightlights to chase away the darkness—she had inherited that trait from her mother. Her eyes were moist from a mix of remembrance and sorrow. She had finished reading the letter from Sally Twosongs and was considering its contents when her houseguest spoke up.

"I have the chesterfield fitted for sleeping, so I'm staying."

"That's not necessary, Avis."

"I will be gone before sunup."

"Sam shouldn't be with Caleb just now."

Avis angled her head and frowned in surprise. The expression dimmed her eyes as she took a seat across the table from her. "Well, he is, and that means I'm here at the ready."

"This baby's not going to drop on a moment's notice," Abbey said, frustration woven into her voice. There was strain on her face, which was flushed and puffy, especially around the eyes. Her posture was awkward and she appeared to be extremely uncomfortable. "I am not without instincts and intelligence. There will be signs and stages. If I am here alone when the contractions start or my water breaks I can bang on the floor and holler for help."

"Are you tired of my company?" Avis asked, teasing and snappy.

"Of course not," Abbey replied firmly. "I'm just plain old fashioned tired and I do not want to put you out or take advantage." With pronounced effort she modified her position. "I don't mean to be difficult, but you might have noticed that I have a willful streak. Sam claims that Missouri mules could learn a lesson or two about stubbornness from me."

Avis snickered. "Maybe so."

"Don't be too quick to agree with my husband. He's not *always* correct," Abbey said, laughing as she picked up her mail. "You've never met Sally Twosongs, have you?"

"No. Deacon has mentioned her once or twice."

"Let me share her letter. She is such a unique person." Abbey thumbed the creases in the heavy parchment paper. "She and I discovered a genuine kinship in our brief time together. We have been corresponding for a couple years." She cleared her throat and read in a strong and expressive voice, enunciating each word as though she was in the spotlight on stage.

August 1882
WT Ranch, Colorado

My Dearest Abbey, greetings. I was delighted by the wonderful news in your last letter, which I received in June. It is stunning and somewhat spiritual that we are both expecting a child. The fact that we have similar due dates truly excites me. I cannot help but wonder if the Creator has some grand design for our children. Isn't that a lovely thought?

The days ahead are never certain, but that doesn't prevent me from daydreaming about positive possibilities. I haven't been sleeping properly for several months, which means I have had plenty of peaceful times to pray and meditate. Being alone beneath starry skies draws me close to creation and gives me insights that warm me from the inside out.

Two nights ago, while the quietness of the third watch bathed the valley, I sat on the porch swing spilling out my petitions on my flute. The notes were soft and pliable. I could feel each one as it was released from my heart. I had the sensation that my spirit was rising higher and higher until it was as though I was in the midst of the heavens. The scintillating colors were too much to behold and impossible to describe or explain.

A soothing voice counseled me. I was told that distresses were coming, but I was not to ever be disturbed or discouraged. The adversity, deprivation, mourning, or whatever would be arriving on the turns of tomorrow could never alter the wondrous truth encased in the miracle of each sunrise. I was overwhelmed by how precious life is in this sweet old world.

No matter how often the silent darkness of harshness encroaches on us, to breathe air and experience the simple and exquisite marvels present all around us has an energizing force we disregard at our peril. No day should ever be taken for granted. Life itself is more valuable than all the riches accumulated by all the kingdoms down through the ages. I am currently attempting to discipline my mind to apply that revelation with vigor and consistency.

How is your writing? I so appreciate every article you send me. Please continue to do so, though I must issue a tiny complaint. I miss talking the ideas over with you, which means that I would be negligent if I didn't ask when you and Sam will be returning for an extended stay. As I have mentioned many times, there is a standing invitation that will always be open.

Ranch life has been productive, though lately it seems that horses are secondary. I have become the center of attention. My pregnancy has brought the guardian or fusspot to surface in everyone here. Between Hank, Caleb's parents and your Aunt Naomi, I am hardly ever alone during daylight hours. Even your little cousins get in on seeing to my needs.

To be loved and cared for is truly a godsend that is valued deep within, but on the superficial level my abiding independence chaffs at the much ado being made over me. I do my best to be polite because I am no ingrate. I surely understand. The outpouring of affection and love humbles me. I receive every deed of compassion and concern with graciousness.

Write soon. Be encouraged. Know that my heart holds you close.

Love and Prayers,
Sally Twosongs

P.S. Father arrived yesterday with news that Mother passed from time to eternity. I am saddened, but take solace and inspiration in the assurance that she is at peace in the presence of Jesus, which is the mystery and majesty that awaits on the other side.

Abbey put the missive down, sighing heavily. "So sad. She has a God-given epiphany, then shortly thereafter, likely as she was still processing all that she had seen and heard, she learns that her mother is dead." Her lips pinched as she steadily shook her head. "The only guarantee life has is that heartaches come as sure as seasons change the weather."

"Ofttimes life is unfair."

"Which is why we have to be grateful for each day," Abbey said enthusiastically. "The highs and lows; the ups and downs; the joys and disappointments; the dreams and disasters." Her face tensed as she shifted her bottom. "Life is a crate of memories, good and bad. We spend our days unpacking and sorting through them, and all the while praying that we get things right."

"You sound like Deacon."

"I hope so," Abbey replied, nodding. "My mother, too. Her example of serenity and perseverance against difficulties and obstacles resonates with me even now. She buried her husband in the morning and I was born in the afternoon. She could have shriveled into a bitter old prune, but instead, she went forward in dignity and raised me to have grit and pride."

"Wow," Avis murmured, tears reflecting on her cheeks. "I have so many positive influences in my life. Mom, Deacon, Whitey, you and Sam.

Sometimes I feel guilty. What did I ever do to deserve all these blessings God has given me? And what can I do with them?"

"We are blessed so that we can bless others," Abbey answered matter-of-factly. "Which can sometimes be hard, but is always worth it." She stiffly pushed to her feet and began snuffing candles. "I'm going to bed. We'll leave a couple oil lamps burning low for Sam."

"That'll work. I'm plumb tuckered out."

"Goodnight, Avis. Thank you for being here."

"You're welcome." Avis took a skip-hop step to get in front of her. She gently put her hands on the pregnant woman's shoulders. "Thanks for adopting me as your sister."

Abbey felt a wellspring of emotion spout through her, which caused a breath to catch in her throat. Her already ruddy complexion blushed into a deeper shade of scarlet. The ladies hugged and leaned against each other. Teardrops and loving kindness mixed like a mystic balm that drew them closer together. The lengthy demonstration of tenderness delayed bedtime, but when it came, there were no hindrances for either woman to slip into satisfying slumber.

In a suite at the Great Western Hotel, Deacon Coburn sat in a wing-back chair with his right leg crossed over his left. The lamplight was pale and the windows were open. His hat rested in the crook of his knee and his hands were folded over his beltline. His voice was dispassionate as he related the revelatory details that the day had brought to the forefront.

Big Bull Wallace stood across the room, listening without interruption. He had a tumbler of bourbon in hand and was puffing on a cigar. When the tale came to an end, he placed the twist of smoldering tobacco in a copper ashtray on an armoire desk, turned its chair sideward and put his buttocks on it. He emptied his glass in a wincing swallow, then asked, "Is Whitey sure?"

"There's no doubt in him, Bull."

"Then it's settled."

"What's that mean?"

"The freight is all unloaded."

"Tell me straight-up, Bull. What game are you running?"

"Did Morgan Fletcher get my message?"

Coburn nodded tersely. "He was told to stay-put in clear-cut terms."

"Will he do so, is the question?"

"Intuiting that is above my pay grade."

Wallace methodically cracked each knuckle on both hands, smiling ambiguously. "How high do I have to raise your wages to get the answer I want to hear?"

"I'll not tell what I don't know for any amount of money."

"It was a wisecrack, Deacon. Cut me some slack."

Coburn thumbed aside his moustache. "Perhaps if I wasn't in the dark regarding your reasons for being in Dodge City, I'd be more inclined to perceive your humor."

"All I'm doing is finalizing a business transaction."

"Ah-huh. Something has a bad odor here."

"Whatever occurred between us for you not to trust me?" Bull asked sharply. "I've been fair and level with you for coming up on twenty years, yet since arriving in Dodge City, I'd have to be deaf and dumb not to sense wariness in you directed at me. State your issue."

Coburn held his hands apart and shrugged. "Morgan Fletcher or Huey Butters or whatever other alias he goes by isn't legitimate. You, a man of integrity, ought not to be in partnership with him." His eyebrows lowered as he latched his fingers around his knee. "Even before the events of the day I had plenty of uncertainties about the man's character."

"My plans are set, Deacon."

"Doesn't new information demand a reevaluation of those plans?"

"That horse doesn't ride in this rodeo."

"Whitey deserves better from you."

Bull grunted disdainfully. His face was marred by an ugly sneer when he said, "I'm not responsible for what happened to Whitey. And I cannot change those circumstances."

"*We* can do something in nothing flat."

"How so?"

"We confront Fletcher immediately."

"Confront him?"

"Of course. We go together now."

"Nope," Bull said adamantly. "I have a transaction to complete with Mr. Fletcher that will be worthwhile on many different levels." He picked up the cigar and examined it, then poked the burnt out end at him. "You make yourself scarce, you hear me?"

"I think not, Bull."

"You need to back down, Deacon."

"Can't do it, Bull. I gave Whitey my word."

"What if I make it an order?"

"I'd tender my resignation," Deacon replied, abrupt and unflinching. "I was looking for a job when I came to the *Double B Ranch*. I haven't forgotten how to find paying work, but that's not the way this gets resolved." He rose to his feet and put his hat on. "I told you he assaulted Avis Lahay in broad daylight. That's crime enough to swear out a complaint and launch an investigation. I'll use the clout of my influence to dig up Morgan Fletcher's past."

"Hold on there, Deacon."

"Give me a reason."

"Twenty-four hours is all I'm asking." Bull said, eyes wide and persuasive. "If I can't broker this arrangement with Fletcher and be done with it by tomorrow evening, then I'll be the one to back down. I will step out of the way and you can handle Morgan Fletcher in whatsoever way you see fit." He returned the cheroot to the ashtray. "And you have *my* word, if at all possible I will factor Whitey's tribulations into the wherewithal of the balance sheet."

Coburn mulled the proposition over. "Alright. You've got as far as sundown tomorrow. I'll see to it that Whitey keeps a low profile until the Harvest Street Festival gets started."

"Is that necessary?"

Coburn nodded quickly. "Whitey may be just a nameless chump to Fletcher or Butters or whoever he is, but we shouldn't take the chance of the man recognizing him."

"Yeah, makes sense. It's a dicey state of affairs."

Coburn strode to the door and stopped with his hand on its knob. "Whitey better not get hung out to dry, or else you and I are going to have a serious problem." He gave a half wave, then was in the corridor. He moved rapidly down the stairs and across the lobby. Outside, though it was exceedingly late for him, he headed for the Alhambra Saloon. His nightly custom was to check in and gather any tidbits of information that might be floating around the barroom.

The poorly ventilated room above the stables of the overnight way-station was dank and musty. Delores Solrizo, wearing a full-length nightgown and cotton housecoat, sat on the edge of a ramshackle four-poster bed waiting for her newfound friend to return from washing up. A single oil lamp's weak flame cast dull light from its position atop a pedestal table.

Her taut smile had sadness woven through it, but not because of the inadequate and grungy accommodations. She was listening to delicate snoring; each mellow note of the little boy snoozing incited complex feelings in her. She admired his innocence, but also, self-reproach and remorse had been revived. Long ago and faraway, she had given birth to two babies, but due to the sin-befouled condition of her soul, she had not raised either son or daughter.

The abandonment of her children never strayed far from her mind. She prayed for them daily by name and exerted much emotional sweat to keep the guilt and shame detained within a citadel of grace and mercy, but when exhaustion depleted her strength, the haunting could slip from under multiple layers of God's forgiveness to slice her heart into ribbons.

She went to the pallet on the floor and knelt. She swept strands of hair off his forehead. "You are beautiful, Stace," she whispered, fluffing the covers around him. "So much promise. I pray you will always be surrounded by those who nurture hope in you." She returned to the bed and turned down the blankets. She noted that though the mattress was hard and lumpy, at least the linens were clean. She sighed and sat so she could lean against the headboard.

There were footsteps on the creaking stairs, then Brenda Hawkins entered, and swiftly closed and barred the door behind her. "All I can say about that well water is that it's wet."

"It has a peculiar odor, doesn't it?"

"Yes," Brenda replied, perching on the only chair in the room, which wobbled badly. "It smells like rotten eggs or worse." She began to give her thick ginger hair a meticulous brushing. "This place doesn't qualify as much more than a slummy hovel. Someone has tried to decorate and pretty it up with patchy splashes of whitewash, but a painted pigsty is still a pigsty."

"We'll survive the sleaze, then we only have to endure the nuisances of two more nights on the road," Delores said optimistically. "The stew and biscuits for supper was delicious."

"For which I am grateful. Stace enjoyed way too much."

"Two helpings and he wanted another bowlful."

Brenda smiled and shook her head. "He's growing so fast. I'm afraid that on whatever meager income I can scratch out, his appetite alone will keep us in the poorhouse."

"What do you want to find in Dodge City, Brenda?"

"I honestly don't know. A clean slate, I hope."

"What work did you do in Las Vegas?"

"At the mercantile, organizing shelves and tracking inventory. I itemized each day's receipts and did some of the bookwork," Brenda answered, satisfaction in her voice.

"Bookwork? You mean finances?"

"Yes. I had a steady job there since soon after discovering I was expecting Stace. I proved myself trustworthy and was given more training and responsibility," Brenda replied, then flipped her hair forward and back. "Before that I had no reason to take pride in anything I did."

"You mean trading sexual favors for money?"

Brenda stiffened in surprise. "How'd you know?"

"An educated guess derived from experience," Delores said in an offhand manner. "I've walked in those shoes and I assure you that it can all be put behind you."

"I'm trying hard to do so."

"With time and distance it gets easier, Brenda."

"Oh, I guess so, I think."

"It does, believe me."

Brenda absently tinkered with the brush's bristles. "After I got pregnant I had a fanciful idea that Stace's father and I could have a chance to build a life together, but that dream turned sour mighty fast. I hung around Las Vegas for years hoping against hope that he would return and claim Stace as his own, but being Ben Slaton, I should've known that'd never happen."

"Ben Slaton? He's Stace's father?" Delores asked in a gasp.

"He was until Kid Greer killed him."

Delores grimaced, disbelief and shock quivering in her eyes. Her complexion blanched and her mouth twitched as her hands obsessively clamped together. She sat up straight and put her feet on the floor. "Ben Slaton was the gambler Liam Greer shot a week or so ago?"

"Shot him dead."

"I heard about the shooting, but not the victim's name," Delores said, doubt and worry in her voice. "There truly is something significant in us meeting up, Brenda. I knew Ben Slaton. In the winter of '78 he was laid up at my place in Santa Fe nursing a broken leg."

Brenda frowned, eyes narrowed. "He came back to me using a crutch."

"Then he abandoned you and your unborn child."

"Yes, but he got his digs in first."

"Mean-spirited, was he?"

"He told me I was nothing more than a whore slut."

"That's a boldfaced lie from the pit of hell," Delores said passionately. "Don't you dare give any credence to that foolish hooey. I was a whore once. In fact, I was worse than a whore. I turned young girls out and destroyed lives, but I repented and by God's grace forgiveness found me and keeps on finding me." Tears shined like gold dust on her cheeks. "I am living testimony to the truth that there is hope and new life on the other side of sin and brokenness."

Brenda nodded, sniffing and wiping her eyes. "Thank you."

"Let's pray together." Delores Solrizo bowed her head and took a calming breath. She assailed heaven with blunt requests for protection and guidance based on promises lifted from Scripture, which she appropriated by faith. At crucial junctures Brenda Hawkins murmured agreement. When the final amen came, both women were crying and smiling serenely.

A peace and presence had fallen over the dingy room.

Sam Beadle was running faster than he ever had in his life. The pulse-points at his temples were rising and falling in a fanning flutter. Sweat seeped from every pore and his muscles ached as though he had been in flight for hours. Panic was crawling around inside him and doing nauseating things to his intestines.

Something or someone was chasing him, though he had yet to see whoever or whatever it was that had him in its crosshairs. He had tried and tried; his head recurrently swiveled to the left and right while his eyes, enlarged and manic, kept bending over a shoulder in an effort to catch a glimpse, but no such luck. The fury of the racing footfalls were closing in, which produced an inflamed discharge of briny bile that rifled up his throat.

The dusty streets of the town were familiar, though indistinct and grotesquely different somehow. His brain rebelled as it processed what his senses took in. Off in the distance, the hoofbeats of horses and longhorns thickened the manure-scented air with grainy grime that made it difficult to breathe. It was noisy and boisterous, but all the commercial establishments were empty and deserted. There was no wagon or pedestrian traffic at all.

He was scared and alone; alone that is except for his relentless pursuer. He forced his legs to carry him faster and faster. His lungs were getting clogged by puffy swirls of gritty particles, which aggravated the flaming secretion erupting up his esophagus. He choked and coughed, but refused to slow down because the person or creature following had sped up.

The shrill hoots of mockery raked his ears. He ran and ran, and used the fiery muscular pain that accompanied each bone-jarring stride as motivation to press on. The chase continued unabated, but then in wild suddenness, the sprinting footsteps behind him were now in front of him. The man or beast had passed by unseen. Confusion reigned in him.

He pumped harder than humanly possible and in doing so, careened over the edge of control. He slipped and flew forward in an awkward and disjointed belly-flop. His chin bounced on the roadway and shards of dirt collected in his eyes as he frantically sprawled and flailed. He skidded to a stop with his face in a pile of steaming dung. He spat and got onto his knees.

While he picked gunk and crap out of his eyes and nostrils, he realized he was on a main thoroughfare of Abilene. His body convulsed as an obscene sight stabbed his eyes; the vulgarity of it released explosive agony that reverberated in his skull. His arms involuntarily stretched out with palms upward as though he was attempting to ward off the spectacle.

There could be no denying what he saw; it was as though the couple was in love and posing for a family portrait. There, on the steps of Drovers Cottage, slouch-eyed Liam Greer stood hand in hand with Abbey Langton, who was leaning firmly against his shoulder. He had a newborn baby cradled in the nook of his arm and triumph etched on his face. Flamboyant shrieks of laughter broke free from Greer's mouth, screaming to the sky.

Sam Beadle sat upright, awake and stupefied. "That's impossible."

"What's impossible?" his wife queried softly.

Beadle jumped as though he had been poked by a cattle prod. His chest was heaving, eyes bugged out and hands moving spasmodically. He was bathed in perspiration. He squinted and began to adjust to the darkness. He turned to his right where Abbey Langton was laying cocooned beneath the blankets. "Nothing. Just a hairball nightmare."

"What's impossible?" she asked again.

"I don't know. It's all fragmented and gone," he lied, dropping back onto the pillow. He blinked as though his eyelids had become erasers that could eliminate the offensive image. He increased his efforts to make it go away by inhaling several even breaths, but to no avail. The profane picture of Liam Greer holding a swaddled babe with Abbey Langton smiling beside him remained stitched inside his head. He groaned downheartedly.

"What is it, Sam?"

"Nothing, Abbey. Really."

"Sam, talk to me."

"It was a bizarre and meaningless dream. I'd like to let the spooky rubbish disappear," he replied passively. He cuddled her and placed a hand on her tummy. "How's our baby?"

"Still and sound asleep."

"Sorry if I woke you."

"I was staring at the ceiling when you started whipping from pillar to post." She gave his hand a squeeze. "At first you were quite entertaining, but then, it was disturbing."

"It's all aces now."

"You're just saying that so the pregnant lady won't worry."

"The pregnant lady needs to get another forty winks."

"We agree on that, Mr. Beadle."

He reached out for her. There was some repositioning and tousling with the bedspreads, then they came to rest face to face. He kissed her forehead and she responded with a smiling sigh as her eyes flittered shut. He watched her. His mind wouldn't closedown. When sleep overtook him an hour later, the nightmare's nonsensical finale prevailed vividly in his imagination.

Liam Greer ran like a monstrous roadrunner, legs high-stepping and neck thrust forward. His efforts were futile; he was getting nowhere fast. He was the main attraction in some primeval amphitheater. An enclosure formed by thundering clouds of fire and copious spires of smoke hemmed him in, but that didn't prevent him from circling in a terrified rush.

Encompassing the rolling flames and pulsating columns of soot were a series of tall standing stones—black obelisks that towered against a combustible sky. Each monolith had a saw-toothed gargoyle crouched on its peak shouting directives in the language of insults and blasphemies; legions of imps and goblins, armed with daggers or spears, executed every order, screeching and marching around the perimeter of the showground.

The red-skinned devil, pointy ears and horns and a goatee, sat upon a glassy gemstone throne and orchestrated the action. A conspicuous grin dominated his triangular face; his forked tongue was a lewd tiny dancer flickering hungrily over his lips. "Obey or be devoured," he roared, raising a pitchfork high over his head.

Obey or be devoured. The edict blazed through Liam Greer. His stomach did a plunging somersault and he faltered in his running, but managed to stay upright for a dozen or so more strides. Then his legs were rubbery. The terrain was molten gravel that detonated into pieces with each step. He listed and flailed, stumbling in a head-over-heels fall.

He came to a halt sprawled akimbo. He was horrified and benumbed, unable to move a muscle despite panicked exertions. All his energy and efforts dissipated in a surging subtraction from his body. Any attempt to move was utterly useless. His mouth was wrenched into a warped contortion that hurt the hinges of his jaw. The agonized wails and gnashing of teeth from the throng of lost souls trapped in the brimstone kingdom mocked his predicament.

Greer lay in petrified stillness, naked and on fire, but his blackened flesh didn't burn. The emperor of the netherworld came off the throne, which called forth a yodeling snarl of an anthem from the gargoyles. The song soared and voices harmonized, growing louder and louder as their supreme commander pranced to the rhythm established by the swaying of his arrowhead tail.

The liar and father of lies capered forward. As the canticle of the beastly choir became deafening, he hopped and leapt in a whirligig around the desperado. The skipping promenade increased in speed until it was a reddish-black blur, then it snappishly stopped. Satan glanced upward at his adoring audience as he poked Greer with the three-pronged implement.

Kid Greer cringed and tried to squirm away but had no vigor to do so. Spurts of blood erupted all over his body. The archfiend loomed over him howling hideous laughter. His tail crackled like a horsewhip, which got his legs moving in a fluid two-step hop. Round and round he went, thrusting the trident pitchfork skyward to stimulate impassioned pleas from his minions. He then granted their appeals by violently jabbing the prongs into his victim.

The melody of the gargoyles became a chanting drumbeat to which the devil gyrated and whirled in a slow motion pirouette that was frightful and mesmerizing in its depravity. His feet were swift and nimble as little by little the booming momentum grew to a feverish pitch. He stomped and spun, and in a seamless instant a diabolical transformation engulfed him.

Greer's eyes, so huge and bulgy that the sockets were straining to prevent them from exploding outward like miniature cannonballs, were fixated on the metamorphosis. The evil prince of darkness mutated into a great serpent that had powerful forelegs and gigantic talons. It hunkered on its heavy haunches and clawed the air.

There was silence and awe in the inferno of hell. The imps and gargoyles bowed in worship of the fire-breathing dragon. It thumped its tree-trunk of a tail once. A squad of goblins, heads misshapen and ears nothing more than stubby protrusions, bristled to attention. Three were dispatched by bellowing curses from the barbaric creatures atop the monumental pylons.

The trio of vile foot soldiers raced into attack formation and lickety-split had Greer prostrate and subdued in a spread-eagle position. He was held in place by daggers used as spikes that nailed him to the incinerated ground. Terror seized Liam Greer. He was shrieking and bawling at the top of his lungs, but all that emerged was soundless whimpering.

The ancient serpent, who in the eons of antiquity had dwelt in the glorious palaces of the heavenly realm and served the Most High God, now was salivating and savoring the delights of its delicious meal. It moved with a halting intentionality. A longish tongue slithered and darted over its human feast as its nostrils puckered and sniffed ravenously.

Its baleful eyes were slits of smoldering coals and its teeth were an abomination. The dragon spoke in an otherworldly graveyard voice. "Obey or be devoured." It crouched low and chomped its glistening choppers as a prelude to feeding on him whilst he was still alive.

Liam Greer's shrill screams echoed across the emptiness of the prairie. He was up and on his feet punching riotously before comprehension grasped his brain. Wakefulness came over him slowly. He flopped onto the tangle of his bedroll, sobbing and retching. He clutched at his belly for that was where the dragon had taken the first bite; suffice it to say that its loathsome teeth were razor-edged horrors that would torment Greer's memory until his dying day.

"Please, Jesus," he said in sheer desperation, then a litany poured out of his soul, "I don't want to burn in hell. I don't want to burn in hell. I don't want to burn in hell." He gasped several times and backhanded slobber off his straggly chin-whiskers. He sat and stared into spaces of the starlit night until his breathing was restored to natural patterns.

An iffy calmness came over him, but the past encroached upon it. He went to his saddlebags and pulled out a handkerchief. He unfolded it to examine the withered souvenir of Ben Slaton's ear. *Obey or be devoured.* He cowered, knowing that to be obedient meant doing to Sam Beadle and Charley Jondreau what had already been done to Ben Slaton. He remembered the instructions of Smoky Crowe: "*Take an ear from each kill. After all are dead, bring the trophies back to me. I will make you a medicine bag and you will be invincible.*"

Liam Greer squatted on the grass, hugged himself and wept.

Midnight, the witching hour, had passed. Morgan Fletcher was fuzzy-eyed and exhausted, and also, three sheets to the wind. He had been chain-smoking and swilling bourbon since Deacon Coburn left him in the lobby of the Dodge House Hotel. He was tediously afraid that all was lost; that due to his ungentlemanly conduct with the young lady on Front Street, he had blown a favorable and long prepared for opportunity to reap a bonanza payday.

His corner room was on the second floor on the backside of the building. It had two windows, both of which were open a foot or so to provide a moderate crosswind. There were three oil lamps lit on the roughhewn desk that had patchy scuffs and splinters rippled on its surface. He sat brooding and engaging in plans for damage control.

A fastidiously rolled quirley between his lips had burned down to an inadequate fragment. He pinched it into an overflowing tin ashtray and reached for his gold-plated case. He fingered the MF monogram, then popped it open and mumbled a curse because there were no cigarettes remaining; he had smoked an entire day's supply and then some.

He glanced around to find the drawstring bag that held the paper and tobacco fixings, but was distracted by a flicker of firelight reflecting off a bottle of Kentucky's finest, which was the third one to be delivered by management and put on his tab. He tipped it back and took two large swallows, wincing slightly as the liquor scorched down his throat into his empty belly. It had been more than twenty-four hours since he had bothered to eat.

He tilted the chair back on two legs, wavered to the brink of toppling over, then plunked forward and decided to return to a chore that had occupied him earlier. His hands, shaky and hesitant, cleared a workspace on the desktop and in doing so almost spilled the contents of the ashtray. He slurred a swearword and unsteadily gained his feet.

Fletcher scratched his unshaven cheeks and tried to recollect his most recent actions. The fog hovering through his head turned thinking into a rigorous exercise. He took a number of wobbly steps then abruptly turned and smiled as though a lightning bolt of brilliance had filled his groggy mind. He now saw that the whetstone and straight blade knife with a curved brass handle were on the windowsill exactly where he had placed them.

He retrieved the items and sat down. His head was already spinning, yet before getting started on the task, he took another whopping swig of whiskey. He bent forward and squinted to pick through the discarded butts in hopes of finding a salvageable ciggy, then gave up and uttered another profanity as he fumbled to palm the sharpening stone.

There was persistent ringing in his ears, which he did his best to ignore, but even so, its high notes grated on his nerves. His teeth were gritted against the annoying noise. He began honing the blade in slow circular motions while he schemed about how he could redeem or rescue the proposition that he expected would set him up for the rest of his life.

The uneasiness in him was substantial, but dwarfed by self-assurance that customarily had contemptuous scorn for others. He had yet to meet with Big Bull Wallace, so he was stewing and a bit disturbed. He had notions that all had been scuttled because Coburn blabbed to the Texas cattleman about his misadventures while waiting at the train station.

Those paranoid concerns were beat down when his ego ascended to its apex. His mouth tightened in determination. If his reputation as an upstanding squire of commerce had been cheapened, he was certain he could make allowances or amends and apologies to excuse his behavior. He took great pride in his ability to fix glitches and smooth ruffled feathers.

What others mistook for oily brashness and cockiness he recognized as a special gift for daring and repairing breaches. If Coburn had ratted him out, Fletcher would do whatever was necessary to soothe Big Bull Wallace and proceed with the big con. After all, Fletcher had previously earned Wallace an equitable percentage in Arkansas, and thereby stirred enough interest in the wealthy rancher to keep him on the hook for several years.

The noise in his ears swelled through his skull, but he refused to allow it to hinder what he was doing. His hands moved in measurable and methodical strokes. When he was satisfied as to the blade's keen edge he went looking for its sheath and found it leaning against the desk. He picked up the scabbard, which did double duty as the shaft of his cane, and slammed the blade in until he heard the compelling snap of it being secured.

Morgan Fletcher drank from the bottle several more times, then blinking in confusion, realized that the bourbon had been entirely consumed. He whiffed out the oil lamps, removed his shoes and crawled beneath the covers fully clothed. The mattress coddled him and he groaned. In the bat of an eye he became stiffer than a cadaver and sank into a stupor of sleep.

The man moved like a peg-legged scarecrow, weaving circuitously through thickets of sagebrush and hedges of creosote bush. He was half-mad and feverish; death nipped at his heels. His heartbeat, fragile and thready, struck his eardrums in erratic throbs. He was hatless and his skull was on fire. Hunger and thirst amplified an agony of delirium in his bones.

His ordeal beneath the blazing sun had him parched dryer than dry; desiccated, even. He had endured torture and escaped a renegade band of Utes led by a boom-voiced leader, and now, with blood matted on his forearms he staggered, hollow-eyed and nearly ready to drop in his tracks. Grimness motivated him onward. A refusal to die raged in his veins.

"Lawrence . . ." The air was as still as the deadness inside of catacombs, but he heard a breeze singing out in a sweet alto voice that riveted him. "Lawrence . . ." His head cocked in curiosity, then sudden-like, he was no longer scratching to survive on the high desert. He was dressed in wintertime clothes and standing in a doorway of a warm and cozy home.

His eyes were full of wonder and confusion as he gazed at a slender woman sleeping softly beneath a load of blankets against the February cold—a woman who an hour earlier had been in his arms as they cried out together and finished in a passionate and blissful exchange of tears. He was outside himself and grappling with an all-consuming conflict.

He wanted to strip off the garments he had just put on and crawl back into her bed and stay forever, but the underside of that desire was a compulsion beyond him; an irresistible force within that liberated guilt, shame, unworthiness and undiluted fear. Bewilderment was a twister slashing across the pockmarked and battle-scarred panorama of his psyche. The inner storm lacerated unhealed wounds; he had no comprehension of it, but his soul was bleeding.

The woman rolled over onto her back. Her auburn hair pooled around her head to frame a countenance that shone in the darkness. She pushed up, baring her shoulders as she used her elbows for support. Their focus riveted in a penetrating fashion; their concentration was heated and extreme, the connection between them so much greater than mere affection.

Her smile melted him. "Where are you going, Lawrence?"

"Everywhere . . . nowhere."

"I will wait for you."

"I should stay."

"Yes. If only you would stay."

"I'm a mess, Angela."

"I will look for and find you. I'll help you, Lawrence."

"I should come back to bed."

"Yes. If only you would come back to bed."

"I'm a mess, Angela."

"We're all a mess, Lawrence."

"I'm afraid I'll fail you."

"There will be dismal days when I'll need a friend."

"I'm sorry."

Her eyes sparkled and her lips compressed. "If you leave and abandon me there'll be so many lonely nights when the lamp burns low and I reach out to hold you to be tender."

"I'm sorry, Angela."

"You will miss out on a good life."

He hung his head. "We should be married."

"Yes. If only we would share a wedding day."

He paled and crunched forward as though he'd taken a punch in the solar plexus. The interior combatant pummeled him and gained an upper hand. He reeled in his footsteps and felt the strangling weight of defeat knock him off stride. Psychologically crippled by war and the wholesale slaughter of innocence, he slumped to his knees in no holds barred capitulation to the chaotic montage of bloody thoughts that unendingly battered his fragile sensibilities.

His eyes squashed shut to eliminate the gruesome imagery, but the self-defense reflex was feckless; he would never remember how to forget the gore of the past. He had done duty as an abolitionist soldier fueled by zeal; a sharpshooter attached to the Army of the Potomac. While clad in blue, how many husbands and fathers in gray had his skills hastened to an early grave? The death of hundreds of men desecrated his conscience.

She coughed and cleared her throat. "Please stay, Lawrence. We love each other, we need each other, we are helpmates to each other," she said, voice weakening to become a hiss.

His eyelids slid open to shimmering brightness. The room, where his lover and he had been entwined, was aglow with candlelight, but there was no joy present. The woman in bed was the same, but profoundly different; her face embodied lonesome sadness. Her unadorned beauty had been annihilated; she was a straggly and haggard shadow, eyes glazed and empty.

The ridges of her cheekbones jutted against bunched up wrinkles of papery skin. She was emaciated and jaundiced. Her jumble of hair was stringy and had lost its luster. Her upper body was propped up on a stack of pillows. She had a letter clutched to her breast as she breathed laboriously. A cistern of sickly fluid in her lungs created a mist with each rattling gasp.

He stood numb-eyed inside a silent scream that tore him apart. The broadness of his shoulders diminished and sagged as he watched her die, helpless and morose. Deacon Coburn was weeping when he woke up. Sloppy sobs heaved out of him. He turned onto his back. Longing glistened in his eyes as he stared at nighttime's variable shades.

"Angela," he whispered hoarsely. He reminisced about their life-altering sojourn together. Her love had found him when he was a lost and damaged refugee from the battlefields of the Civil War. She gave him the name Lawrence because shell-shocked trauma had robbed him of any clue as to his true identity. Now, as he yearned for daybreak, Deacon Coburn chose to harness King Solomon's admonition to be wise and abide in the house of mourning.

Avis Lahay rushed into her room and gave the door a one-legged mule-kick to close it. She acted as though someone had hounded her to the boarding house, but not so. She was simply running behind on her self-imposed timetable and on those rare occasions when that occurred she had a tendency to get flustered. Her face was streaked with sweat and grime.

A hurried sigh murmured over her lips. She removed her skimmer and calfskin gloves, and untucked the checkered flannel shirt. She began releasing the buttons top to bottom, then paused to assess her feelings. The hard-backed chair and pedestal-legged desk in front of a window gained her attention. She went to it and sat, nodding in affirmation of her choice.

She traced a finger over the engraved butterflies, then flipped the leather-bound notebook open to the first page of clean paper. She had failed to make an entry the previous day and knew that if she did not get to it now, another would be missed. Her diverse thoughts jingled together as she primed the pen in the ink well. She disciplined her mind and began writing.

September 27, 1882

Dear Diary: It has been a busy couple days. I feel like I haven't stopped since before sunup yesterday. The job of caring for horses keeps me hopping and makes some muscles ache, but I wouldn't trade it for anything. This morning Mr. Bell gave me wonderful encouragement. He said that he much appreciated my attention to detail and work ethic. Of course I thanked him, but kept my smile under wraps until he returned to the office.

Now it's past noon and all I want to do is get out of these grungy clothes, soak in a hot tub, then get all gussied up for the Harvest Street Festival. From all reports of past affairs, I expect it to be a frolicking shindig, but for me to enjoy the evening's merry-making to the hilt, I have to first unload a headful of ugly feelings here.

I had a run-in with a stranger yesterday that still irritates me. He accosted me on the street while I was leading Pumpkin back to the livery. Presumably he wanted to admire the horse close up, but he was rummy-eyed drunk and there was no mistaking his intentions. He leered at me and made an off-color remark that made me sick. As if that wasn't enough, he clutched hold of my left wrist, which resulted in me punching him in the mouth.

He then called me a repulsive name, but at least got out of my way. I didn't realize it at the time, but thankfully, Deacon was not at all far behind me and saw the whole incident. A short while later, he visited when I happened to be grooming Gilgal. It was a nice surprise and sort of funny because he started to pretend that he was just peeking in on his gelding, but by his protective manner it soon became apparent that he had concern for me.

We talked things through and he assured me that the boorish man wouldn't bother me ever again. I expressed unease about tonight. Deacon chuckled in his stern way and told me that if the reprobate had the gall to show up at the street dance, the invitation to one and all would be revoked for him without qualms or hesitation. Even so, I am worried that he will attend and make a nuisance of himself. The man's unwanted advances deeply upset me.

Why are some men such letches? I was tending to my own business, with nothing on my agenda except getting the undertakings finished so that I could spend the afternoon and evening with Abbey. He came off the platform of the depot and blocked my way. I was polite and reserved. I didn't do anything to give him ideas that I had an interest in conversation.

I refused to even properly introduce myself, so where did he get off thinking it was fair and acceptable for me to be ogled like a piece of meat by a starving wolf? He was foul and crude, which raised heated anger in me. I felt dirty inside and it shouldn't be that way. I didn't do anything wrong, but I feel like I brought this on myself. Why is that?

If I had an answer, then I wouldn't be frittering around with words. In the end I suppose it doesn't matter, so I hereby put the unpleasantness behind me to go forward. There is soap and hot water in my immediate future, then fixing my hair just right. Whitey says we're going to have us a hog killing time. I'm not sure what that even means, but he made it sound like a ton of fun.

Avis Lahay closed the journal. A smile bloomed and its petals filled her eyes.

It was mid-afternoon when Big Bull Wallace lumbered into the Dodge House Hotel. His ten gallon hat rested high on his forehead and his hands were flexing as his arms swung like hulking cudgels. There could be no misinterpreting the indomitable set of his jaw, or the pace of his heavy foot-steps. He accelerated across the lobby and up the stairs without as much as a nod of acknowledgement to the knob-throated clerk loitering at the desk.

On the second floor he went directly to the back corner room and rapped ever so gently on the doorjamb. He waited for over a minute before repeating the knock-knock with a much stronger emphasis. Another minute passed. He heard no voice or stir of movement from inside. He fisted a hand and started pounding so hard that it seemed to shake the whole building; the pulsating percussion vibrated along the hallway.

The door was flung open with a snarly curse that got bitten off and swallowed when the occupant saw the flesh and blood mountain making the ruckus. Morgan Fletcher shrank back and almost tripped, gape-mouthed and rheumy-eyed. He was unshaven and unkempt, appearing as though he had just awakened and rolled out of bed, which was exactly the circumstance.

"Mr. Fletcher, we have business to conclude," Big Bull said drolly.

"My apologies, Mr. Wallace," Morgan replied, hanging onto the door-knob for support. His pinstriped pants and black frock coat were badly wrinkled. "Could we arrange for another time? I have come down with a stomach virus and am sicker than that proverbial dog."

"An overindulgence in bourbon usually has that result," Big Bull answered, then true to his nickname bulled him backwards and shut the door with an authoritative thud. "That clerk downstairs is in my employ. A half-hour ago I received a full and fair rendering of your activities since arriving at this fine establishment." He took him by the shoulder and led him to the bed. "You don't actually expect me to foot the room service bill, do you?"

"Of course not, sir."

"That's mighty peachy of you, Mr. Fletcher." Wallace patted him on the back in a friendly manner. "You probably want to sit so we can get down to business."

Fletcher plopped onto the mattress and the bedsprings squeaked. He bent forward, elbows on his knees. His heels were angled upward; his legs started jiggling and jumping. He stared at the cattleman as though his blurry eyes were lying. "What are you doing here, sir?"

Wallace dragged the chair away from the desk and placed it beside the bed, then planted his husky rump on it in such a way as to overcrowd him. A deathly cold smile tilted his mouth and slinked up the slabs of his cheeks. "You have to answer for that Arkansas deal."

Fletcher sucked in an audible breath. "Excuse me?"

"You think that farce you played in Little Rock could fool me for long?"

"I am uncertain as to your meaning."

Wallace's expression darkened. "You used my good name in Arkansas. You got your backers and finances together based on me vouching for you. Then you swindled the lot of them. All except me. You made sure I made just enough profit to keep me satisfied."

"That's unadulterated mendacity, sir."

"Big words from a small man," Bull said, laughing frigidly. "It took me six months to sort through all the gobbledygook nonsense and get reports from those you fleeced."

"You were misled, Mr. Wallace."

"I put out feelers for you, but you disappeared like smoke," Bull continued as though the man had not even spoken. "I bided my time. When you contacted me on this proposal, I knew that God was in heaven and all would be made right in my little corner of the world."

"Give me an opportunity to explain. You are mistaken, sir."

Wallace raised a beefy finger and jabbed it under his nose. "You sullied my reputation and cost me plenty. I made restitution on every cent you stole, so you owe me money and one way or another I intend to collect it. I'll extract it from your veins if necessary."

"You are being unreasonable, Mr. Wallace."

"Six of my men are around town," Bull said colorlessly. "I give the word and they will take you for your last ride. No one will ever find your body. Or, since I am flawed by generosity, we can take a stroll to visit Deputy U.S. Marshal Hamilton Bell. He and I had a chat awhile back, so he anticipates making your acquaintance. What would be to your liking, Mr. Fletcher?"

"I am at a severe disadvantage, sir."

"Mulish stupidity isn't an option," Big Bull replied, grim eyes fixed on him. "My crew can take you for a tour of the countryside before giving you a necktie farewell. Or you can turn yourself in at the jail and take your chances with the legal system. There's likely enough paper on you to put you away for a long while, Mr. Fletcher. Or is it Mr. Butters?"

"What? Who?" Morgan blustered, paler than pale.

"Ah, yes. You have to answer for Whitey Fitzgerald."

"Who?"

"A friend of mine whom you defrauded some years back."

Fletcher exhaled and nodded, somewhat flippantly. "Shall we go have a conversation with the Deputy Marshall, so all this can be straightened out prim and proper?" He started to stand, but wavered and wind-milled his arms as he returned to his backside. "Would you be kind enough to hand me my cane, sir? My legs are giving me a mite of difficulty."

"Happy to oblige." Wallace pushed to his full six-six, kneed the chair aside and went to the desk where the walking stick rested beside a whet-stone. He made an evaluation in a heartbeat and picked the cane up to slyly examine the detailed handicraft under the guise of admiring the grain of the wood. "That's a nice piece of workmanship," he said, running a hand along the length of the shaft. "Age takes its toll, so I may soon need one of these."

Fletcher smirked coyly. The drowsy sluggishness in his eyes receded. "When all this disharmony is behind us I will make arrangements with the craftsman on your behalf."

Wallace grinned, laidback and agreeable. "You're a real peach." He made an elaborate gesture, gripped the brass handle and feigned passing the cane to him, then flicked his wrist and withdrew the knife. "Were you presuming to use this toad-sticker on me? You take me for a hillbilly yokel or what?" He hauled off and viciously walloped him upside the head.

Fletcher grunted a guttural cry as his neck whiplashed and he crumpled spinelessly onto the bed. He waved his arms in protest. "I can explain, sir. I swear by all that's holy . . ."

"You lying sack of shit." Wallace cuffed him again and again. He proceeded to smack him around until blood flowed from his mouth and nostrils. "If you have half a brain you'd stay down," Bull said fiercely. "Otherwise I'll use this blade of yours to carve out your gizzard."

While Morgan Fletcher a.k.a. Huey Butters quivered and bled all over the mussed up sheets, Big Bull Wallace conducted a thorough search of his luggage—two leather suitcases and a flower-patterned carpetbag. He discovered a stash of greenbacks, which he riffled and made an estimated count. He then casually pocketed the cash. Appeased and lighthearted, he manhandled the charlatan to his feet and roughly escorted him to the local constabulary.

The afternoon had dwindled down to the beginning of twilight; the sun sat on the western horizon and gray fingers stretched out to cast shadows across the streets. There was restlessness in the air as workman put the final preparations together and musicians tuned their instruments. Townspeople were gathering in gossip circles to wait for the party to get started.

At the Alhambra Saloon, there was a steady influx of patrons coming and going. Deacon Coburn paid no heed to the turnover. He had sorrow sketched on his face, which was rising up from the overflow of his heart. His eyes were teeming with compassion and empathy. He was at his predictable table listening to an old companion bare his soul.

Daniel Twosongs, croaky-voiced and coal-black eyes lowered, spoke in a whispery tone that conjured sadness. When he concluded the specifics of his wife's passing and touched upon the grief that plagued him, he removed his flat-brimmed hat and placed it on a vacant chair. He sighed forcefully. "I cannot shed the discouragement. Neither do I care anymore."

"You have my sympathy and support," Deacon said sincerely. "However, I promised to castrate a man yesterday so I ain't sure counsel or insights from me are worth much."

Twosongs stared at him, doubtful and suspicious. A tiny hint of a smile crested on his lips for a momentary instant. "That's likely a story worth hearing, preacher."

"Not just now, my friend. Let's talk some life and death philosophy."

"Life and death. That's always the crux, isn't it?"

"We live, we die," Deacon replied dourly. "It's the choices we put into practice in that crooked and unfair parcel of time between birth and death that makes all the difference."

"And when doubt triumphs over faith?"

"Faith is not the absence of doubt," Deacon said, smiling gently. "Faith is fighting against and rising above the disappointment, disillusionment, discouragement and doubt of life."

"Do you ever get tired of punching?"

Coburn had a sip of coffee. "Certainly. Your current crisis is every man's brawl at one time or another. The Psalmist wrestled with the agony of doubt. *As with a sword in my bones, mine enemies reproach me; while they say daily unto me, where is thy God? Why art thou cast down, O my soul? and why art thou disquieted within me? hope thou in God: for I shall yet praise him, who is the health of my countenance, and my God.*"

"I'm no king of Israel, preacher."

"Neither am I," Deacon countered, rumbling laughter. "But I breathe air and bleed and skirmish against all the same dynamics of life and death that he had to come to terms with as he put forth efforts to walk upright and be a man who sought to be a reliable witness to what he said he believed. He knew pain and loss; he knew the bitter tears of defeats and betrayals; he knew what it meant to proclaim faith in the day by day slugging and grinding."

Twosongs stared at nothing in particular. "It's the daily boxing match against all the foibles of human nature that threatens to put me down for the count. The struggle to stay the course is too much for me to reconcile my grief. There are forlorn hours when the impulse to hold my hands up in surrender and say no more, no more is formidable in me."

"You ain't no quitter, Daniel."

"It's like I'm in prison."

"You don't have to be in prison to be imprisoned," Deacon said dryly. "Our weaknesses and failures, our sins and temptations, our skin and bones, plus so much more about our flesh are the bars and stonewalls that keep our soul incarcerated. We are spiritual beings trapped inside physical shells for whatever number of days the Almighty has written for us."

"Knowing is not doing, preacher. My emotions deceive me."

Coburn squinted expressively. "Feelings are liars, which is why while in the midst of doubt is the time to be anchored in an excavation of God's Word. Exploring doubt in the light of Scripture produces greater dedication and understanding, and a stronger devotion."

"Forgive me, but digging only makes the pit in me deeper."

"What has changed?" Deacon challenged, eyeing him tenaciously.

Twosongs scowled, guarded and skeptical. "I don't follow."

"Therein is revealed the root of the issue," Deacon answered, hunkering forward. "Do you think it's just a roll of some cosmic dice that you exist?

Is it merely a tumbling twist of Divine luck that you are a traveler through the beauty and hardness of this world?"

Twosongs fidgeted and grunted a negative reply.

"So did God's character undergo a surgical makeover?" Deacon asked sharply. "Before and after Consuelo's passing, what has changed about the character of God, Daniel?" Then in a demanding and rapid fire approach he unloaded on his comrade; his tone was confrontational. "Is God still all-powerful? Is God still supreme and peerless? Does God still know the beginning from the end? Is God still intimately acquainted with all your ways?"

Twosongs hung his head. His fingers twined together and kept wriggling.

Coburn pressed in on him even harder. "Has anything occurred that took God by surprise, or does the Creator of the universe remain all-seeing and all-knowing?"

Twosongs slouched his shoulders. "Foolishness blinded me. Shamed me."

"You have been human, my friend."

"I must dwell in the stronghold of the Almighty." Twosongs abruptly got to his feet. "I will trust in the Lord for he is my fortress and refuge. He will rescue me from the snare of pestilence. I need to be on the trail alone with my Maker. I have healing to receive."

Coburn stood, tentative and watchful. "Wait until morning."

"No. Nighttime riding is best for reflection," Daniel said, gathering long strands of shiny hair up under his gray hat. "Remember the evening we first met? We rode until dawn."

"And that was Nebraska in December."

Twosongs smiled and nodded pensively. "Tell Caleb not to worry on me. As God leads my heart will find its way back to that place where hope is always good. The Lord willing, I'll return to *WT Ranch* to hold and bless my grandchild before Christmastime."

"I'll convey the message," Deacon said, emotional thickness creeping into his voice. He took a large breath. "*Vaya con Dios*, my good friend. Take these words credited to Moses and enfold them in your heart as assurance from the Most High: *He shall call upon me, and I will answer him: I will be with him in trouble; I will deliver him, and honor him.*"

"Thank you, preacher." Moisture gleamed in his eyes. "Our paths will cross again." Their right hands clasped in a firm shake accompanied by puckered lips and head bobs. When it broke off, Twosongs spun around and exited the barroom in a bow-legged amble. Deacon Coburn, sad and sober, waited several minutes before departing to attend the Harvest Street Festival.

The moon, full and bright, was the centerpiece jewel in a diamond studded sky. Front Street, bathed in torchlight and abuzz with activity, had been swept spic and span. Businesses were decorated by festoons of red and white bunting. The Dodge City Cowboy Band was on a raised platform in front of the Longbranch Saloon, and currently performing a waltz.

Butch Mackenzie paced back and forth beside a stool he had carried from the Western Union office. He had a half-smoked cigar clenched at a corner of his mouth. He was jittery and anxious, hands jammed into the pockets of his baggy pants as he kept his attention riveted on a woman laughing and smiling as she danced with her father.

When the slow song ended, the ensemble immediately launched into an up-tempo jig that featured dueling fiddles. Mackenzie hopped onto his toes as though his derriere had been goosed. His fleshy jowls reddened and fretfulness skyrocketed in him. He did a waddling skip off the boardwalk and rushed onto the makeshift ballroom of the thoroughfare to assist Deacon Coburn in ushering Abbey Langton to the seat he had brought specifically for her.

"Thank you, Deacon. That was lovely."

"My pleasure, Abbey."

"And thank you, Butch," she said, still holding the crook of his arm. "Your kindness and thoughtfulness on my behalf is so sweet. You are my special gentleman knight."

"Huh. Someone has to protect you from your antics."

"Truly spoken," Deacon said, grinning roguishly.

"Are you two ganging up on me?"

Coburn shook his head. "You are in expert care with Mr. Mackenzie." He bent over to buss her brow. "I'll be within earshot, young lady. Call if you need me and I'll come a running." He touched her cheek, then headed off to make rounds through the crowd.

"Huh. Where's Sam?"

"He'll be along soon enough."

Mackenzie rolled his eyes in disgust. "Something could happen anytime." He stuck the burnt out cigar in his shirt pocket. "He should never leave your side, Miss Abbey."

"You and I are not going to discuss such matters."

"Huh."

"I wish only to enjoy the music and your company, Butch."

"Huh. My company?"

"Of course."

Mackenzie smiled proudly. He peered at her over the top of his bifo-cals, which appeared ready to slide off the precarious perch at the end of his nose. "That's fine by me because the only reason I'm attending this bother-some hubbub is to be close to you, Miss Abbey. Huh. If I had my druthers I'd be stretched out alone on my bed reading or snoozing."

"Why is it that we connect, Butch?" she asked cheerily. She shifted and fluffed out the pleats of her tent-like dress. "We have from the moment we met. Do you remember?"

"I surely do," he replied, wheezing a chuckle. "It was ten years ago. I had been in town for all of a week and was still setting up the telegraph ap-paratus when you breezed in wanting information about boarding houses. I explained my situation, sleeping in the office and such. You introduced yourself and told me that we newcomers had to stick together. Huh. Two days later you returned with news about a room available for me. I still live there, Miss Abbey."

"Sam and I had been married for only a month or so at the time."

"You treated me kindly from the beginning."

"As have you to me, Butch."

"Your spunk and gumption reminded me of someone I used to know," he said fondly. "And now that you're with child those same attributes have got me worried to a frazzle."

"I'm finer than fine, Butch."

"Huh. I hope you never again leave Dodge City."

"Never is not a likely possibility."

Mackenzie opened his mouth prepared to protest and provide reasons why making Dodge City her permanent residence would be best for raising a child, but was interrupted by a shout. His plumpish torso turned in the direction from whence it came and he spotted her husband rushing toward them. Butch stammered a grunt and his lips pursed into a hard line.

"There you are, Abbey," Sam said, halting at her side. "Sorry I'm late. Got to talking to Caleb at the Great Western Hotel. He bailed out, wanting to make it an early night."

"I will need to visit with him tomorrow," Abbey rejoined, fingers in-tertwined over the jutting mound of her midsection. "I must find out when he's planning to head back to *WT Ranch*. I intend to write a letter to Sally Twosongs, which he can deliver."

"That won't be a problem," Sam answered confidently. He started switching weight from foot to foot when the band lit into a moderately metered tune that showcased the trombones. He draped an arm around her shoulder. "Are you ready to gently cut the rug, Miss Langton?"

"I am indeed, Mr. Beadle."

"Huh. Go easy, Miss Abbey. Please."

"I will. I promise."

Beadle gave him a good-natured nudge. "I'll hold her close and safe, Butch."

"Huh." His clumpy eyebrows dipped into a belligerent scowl as the couple walked hand in hand to the middle of the street and began to sway together in a comfortable pattern. Butch Mackenzie glared worriedly and fetched the stub of rolled tobacco from his shirt pocket. He stuck it between his teeth and obsessively chewed it from one side to the other.

Big Bull Wallace had fences to mend. While the Dodge City Cowboy Band took a pause for refreshments he sidled around clusters of partygoers, oblivious to the merriment. He would not be distracted until all breaches were repaired. He kept to the fringes of activity, figuring that'd be the territory where he would find the end of trail agent for the *Double B Ranch*.

His search was soon rewarded. Deacon Coburn sat off by himself balanced on the edge of a water trough. Wallace came alongside him and said, "Morgan Fletcher is in jail."

"So I heard."

Wallace viewed him with surprise. He removed his ten gallon hat and dragged a hand over his close-cropped hair. He spat a glob of saliva, then returned the headgear so it rested high on his forehead, which was plowed by massive furrows. "How so?"

Coburn shrugged. "Small town, to which I'm plugged in," he answered, and shifted sideward to give him a steady look. "The only question is will I ever know the full story."

Wallace proceeded to explain every detail. He spoke short sentences in a reserved monotone that had threads of fatigue contracting its inflection. He concluded by saying, "I kept you and my whole outfit in the dark because frankly I was embarrassed and ashamed that I had been hoodwinked by such a lowlife scam artist. A man of my standing and position could not allow the news to spread that I'd been conned. Period. End of discussion."

"Big Bull Wallace got taken? That should be written in a book."

"A helluva book, but on the last page I righted the wrong, Deacon."

"Yeah, you did."

Wallace persistently regarded him. "I sincerely regret that my use of duplicity to nail Fletcher's hide to a wall raised strife between us. I value your friendship and respect."

"Enough said and backatcha, Bull."

"Thanks. Now I need to chat with Whitey."

"You'll have to wait, Bull." Deacon stood and pointed to the center of the dance floor. Whitey Fitzgerald and Avis Lahay were in the middle of a circle of clappers. The musicians had returned to the stage. Spectators were calling out song requests and stomping their feet. The leader did a showy countdown, then the band launched into a rollicking reel.

As the drum aced a boisterous bass-line, a squeeze-box and fiddle engaged in a note for note dialog that soared to the cloudless sky. The couple in the spotlight didn't disappoint. Whitey led with panache and conviction; Avis responded in a flair of poise that had her maintaining perfect symmetry and rhythm. They never slowed or broke stride, whirling and kicking up a storm as onlookers hollered and cheered them on.

When the song ended the hoots and shouts were gleeful. Whitey took a bow and Avis did a wee-curtsy, which caused a fresh chorus of uplifting whoops. Big Bull Wallace had inched close to the throng encircling the dancers. He was applauding and yelling the barber's name. Whitey heard him, broke free of the swarm and went over with Avis beside him.

"Didn't know you were a dance critic, Big Bull," Whitey said, click-clicking.

"I require a few moments of your time," Bull replied directly. "Both of you." He gave a gruff gesture to those closeby, effectively shooing them. He strode down the street; Whitey and Avis followed him past the last two torches. "Miss Lahay, may I have a private word with Mr. Fitzgerald. If you could wait over there a ways. I would like to talk to you in a bit."

Avis frowned in reluctance, but acquiesced to his request. Wallace tarried until he was sure she was out of hearing range. "Huey Butters is under arrest, Whitey," he said, satisfied and observably amused. He pulled out a handkerchief folded around the bundle of money he had recouped from Morgan Fletcher. "How much did that scum take off you?"

"Close to three thousand dollars."

"Here's five thousand he had in a suitcase. Call it interest."

Fitzgerald balked. "I don't want it. I'd just waste it."

"Be smart, Whitey. Make an investment for the future."

"No," Whitey said, curt and inflexible. His gaze inclined to his dance partner. "You make an investment, but not for me. You do it for her. She deserves that and a whole lot more."

Wallace glowered, curious and prying. "Why? Why her?"

"I was a drunken souse, Bull."

"We all got sludge in our yesteryears, Whitey."

Fitzgerald click-clicked a pitiful few notes. "That be factual, but I was drowning in a bottle and readying to lay down and die. That sweet child showed me compassion and kindness. Her insistent friendship reclaimed me from a dung heap. I owe her much, so if this here gravy from heaven can provide her an opportunity, then I has got to take advantage of it."

"I see. An easy decision."

"I be happy to hear that," Whitey said, hands fidgeting. "Make it hush-hush and secret. I don't want her to ever know I had anything to do with it. You be able to do that, Big Bull?"

Wallace returned the plentiful bankroll to an inside jacket pocket. "I pay my lawyers enough that they can and will do whatever I order them to do. Consider it done, Whitey."

"Avis can never know."

"I'll make it so, young fella. I swear."

Fitzgerald grinned. "I be glad I be your friend, Big Bull."

Wallace flinched a smile, then took long steps over to Avis. "Would you be kind enough to make an old man's heart happy and go for a stroll in the moonlight with me?"

She retained an arm's length distance, but kept pace. He noted her caution, and strictly honored it. "I haven't seen your mother in many years. Except of what I see of her in you."

"So I figured when we first met."

"I used to be in business with her."

"I know. The whoring business."

The Texas cattle-baron blushed beet-red. "Well, that's true enough. I'm surprised by your knowledge of that offbeat aspect of times past. You ought not to hold any of it against her."

"Oh, I don't, Mr. Wallace. I am proud of my mother."

"As you should be. Deacon tells me she's on her way here."

"I had hoped she would've arrived by now."

Wallace heard her disappointment. He wanted to give her an encouraging embrace, but contained his gusto. Silence settled between them. He didn't understand the extreme protective feelings loose within him, but chose not to fight the emotions zipping around his heart. Big Bull Wallace realized there and then that making relational repairs invigorated him.

≈ ≈ ≈

Between Gunnison and Wagon Wheel Gap, Pete Axler rode careful and stress-free, eyes mostly straight ahead, but periodically he gawked at the big white moon illuminating the pathway. The splendor had him awestricken by matters too wonderful for him to grasp; speculating on what went on in the heavenlies put him in an intensely introspective mood.

He marveled at the vast clearness of the sky. Each quadrant he chose to focus on had clusters of stars which appeared to be winking at him. The exquisite magnificence swelled hope and gratitude in the chambers of his heart. He was homeward bound and it was as though the shining white rock, surrounded by twinkling jewels, was leading him onward.

He stopped the gelding to allow it a few minutes to rest after coming up a steep slope. He yawned and stretched, arching his back. A few kinks released, but just as many tightened. He had already been in the saddle for sixteen hours or so, but there were no plans to quit; respites would be fleeting breathers and come on the fly. The anxious desire for home sweet home had him doggedly resolved to prevail over the soreness and vicissitudes of the trail.

By his reckoning he expected to reach his destination shortly after daybreak, which meant several more hours on horseback. He imagined his homecoming. Hugging his wife, throwing his children up in the air, hearing their laughter and squeals. Looking into Naomi's big brown eyes and seeing nothing but tenderness mirrored at him. Family life was precious and he meant to make sure his loved ones understood how important they were to him.

The horse whinnied as though it was bored standing still. He ruffled its mane, then stretched again and almost knocked his hat off; it sat at an odd angle because thick strips of linen were wrapped around his forehead. The make-do bandages were grubby and soiled—blood had soaked through the right side, and was now dried and crusty hard. The wound beneath it was itchy, but he refused to even acknowledge the discomfort or irritation.

"We'll be home soon," he said in a barely audible murmur as he tickled the brindle between its ears. He took a long gander at the well-lit surroundings and appreciated the moon all the more. He made a slight adjustment to the brim of his hat, then gave the horse a prod and it sprightly cantered forward. He rubbed its neck and uttered soothing words.

The horse responded by snorting loudly; the sound disturbed the stillness of the mountains and its echo cascaded across the canyon. Somewhere, many miles away, a lone wolf yapped a howl as a petulant comeback. Axler chuckled blithely. His face, lined by a seemingly permanent frown, had a beaming smile that mimicked the brilliance of the moon.

He felt good and at peace, and fundamentally amazed by the recent turns of events that had befallen him. Nothing much ever ruffled him. He had a way of rolling through the shocks and surprises that came his way without much deliberation. Just now, however, it was impossible to deny or gloss over that he could've been dead; not once, but two times.

Instead, here he was on a savvy and spry mount not at all far from *WT Ranch* and the bosom of his family. His joints ached and his belly growled for food, but tiredness had no sway over him because determination surged through his veins. The weather was perfect so he would ride through the night, which was emblazoned by light from above.

He turned his head side to side several times. His eyes glinted in satisfaction when a crick in his neck was freed; *his neck*. The large smile expanded—he could've been killed; twice. Pete Axler was not a man to take good fortune for granted. In fact, as he rode at a draggy gait, he pondered the notion that destiny or inevitability had given him an extra anointing of luck.

In northwestern Texas, south of the Canadian River, moonbeams were enlightening the Llano Estacado. The yellowish glimmer cast an aura across the mesa commonly known as the Staked Plains. Longtime partners Charley Jondreau and Max Dawson, riding parallel to each other, were spooked by the weird glow that fringed the farthest reaches of their sightlines.

An odor of death was a stagnant miasma contaminating their nostrils. It was foul and abhorrent, almost pulsing in the air like some malicious heartbeat. The stench made Dawson's eyes water and she had a bandana tied over her mouth and nose. Twenty yards separated them and they kept a close watch on each other. Their horses were skittish and the pack-mule was ornery stubborn, halting fast and firm every so often.

"Crowe is close," Max said in a whisper.

"Or, he *was* close, eh."

"*Is* close."

Jondreau turned up the collar of his jacket and hunched his shoulders against the chill of autumn. His hands were together on the saddle horn, reins held loosely between his fingers as he unconsciously twiddled his thumbs. The stallion's ears were twitchy. He implicitly trusted the dapple gray's instincts and intelligence, so he pressed forward. His eyelids stretched wide, then fluttered as something littering the ground ahead caught his attention.

He stood in the stirrups and strained to see, but could not distinguish any specifics. He ran a finger along his jawline and his teeth locked into a clench; his chin and lips took on the appearance of a bulldog. A menacing foreboding began squirming around his belly—when it squiggled up the back of his throat he paid it heed. He dismounted. She followed suit.

Their communication was without words, but entirely comprehensible. Picket lines were set for each of the animals. She withdrew a Winchester from its scabbard, then double-checked the loads in her revolver. He didn't wait, prowling forward in catlike footsteps. She had to scurry to get even with him and when she did, lobbed him a scrunch-eyed glare, which he ignored.

The radiant moonlight, with its spectral queerness girdling the borders of their vision, was constant. A shiver passed between them. The sensation caused their eyes to connect for a transitory instant of affirmation; the temperature was dropping perceptively. They cautiously closed in on what was strewn across a widespread swath of scrub grass.

Evil was alive and afoot; they could smell and taste its coppery thickness as it clogged up their breathing and put flaming pressure on their lungs—the hair-raising *feel* of evil was slimy maggots slithering over their skin. A clamor of revulsion roared through them when realization buffeted their hearts; they had come upon a graveyard of corpses.

The skeletal remains of crows and coyotes covered a sweeping piece of real estate. Death was a haunting omnipresence that relentlessly assaulted their senses. They stared at the carcasses and attempted to assess the sick aberration displayed before them. The number of sacrifices were uncountable; each had been skinned and the flesh was in various degrees of rot.

"My God, Charley."

"No Deity is in this debauchery, eh."

"It's an open-air burial ground," Max said, side-stepping to its edge. "My father told me of such rituals." She visibly trembled and put a hand against the neckerchief knotted around her lower face. "Crowe tortured and killed them to make powerful medicine in preparation for some prime slaughterhouse brutality. He *was* close, but now he's gone."

Jondreau hunkered on his haunches. His hands were clasped as he rocked on the balls of his feet. A spasm of clairvoyant force abducted him and refused to let him go. His frame constricted in an outrageous seizure. His eyes rolled back in his head. He fell on top of a coyote's bones and blundered around for despicable seconds, then stiffened into a near unconscious state.

"Oh, crappola, not now," Max muttered, grimacing helplessly. She knelt next to him, unable to do anything aside from remaining vigilant. She had witnessed the manifestations of his precognition many times, and in his own closed way, he had told her of the spiritual vitality over which he could exercise no control. She laid her hands on his chest. His heart was racing so robustly that she illogically worried it might bust free of his ribcage.

The smell of the skunk was overwhelmingly on him. In his mind's eye, the scene was as transparent as noonday: Smoky Crowe, bow in hand and arrow in its string, was stalking Liam Greer across a desert landscape bereft of sagebrush, but dominated by massive and bizarrely shaped colonnades of rock. The renegade's milky left eye seeped gummy juices.

Greer was running and scared, akin to a lost little boy set loose on a battleground that completely deceived him. His eyes were saucers; his head rotated hither and thither in frantic tremors. Tears and whimpers gushed out of him. There were no options or routes leading to a dodgy breakout, which mattered not because his will and energy were no more.

Crowe toyed with him, yelling at him in mocking arrogance. He screeched a war whoop and in the sputtering blink of an eye became a scaly-skinned dragon. Fire and smoke haloed its head, and ghastly laughter squawked from its throat. The outlaw stumbled and sprawled gawkily, and the dragon pounced, its tongue flickering over the sobbing victim.

Jondreau called the dragon by its ancient name, which snatched Greer from its salivating jaws. The dragon whirled from its prey, snarling and snapping. Eyeball to eyeball, neither the creature nor the warrior gave an inch. Jondreau made a defiant move, went for his knife and hurled it in a precise motion; in the same flashing second the beastly serpent lurched at him and poison spewed from its maw. Charley Jondreau convulsed in agony and in that juddering jolt, was released from the foreknowledge. A fragment of a smile animated his face.

Max Dawson crouched over him and cocked her head to an inquiring tilt. Undisguised fear crumpled her pretty countenance into a disfigured contortion. "What did you see?"

"I will kill the dragon, eh."

chapter four

Tempest & Tears

"That day is a day of wrath, a day of trouble and distress, a day of wasteness and desolation, a day of darkness and gloominess, a day of clouds and thick darkness . . ."

~ZEPHANIAH~

THE DAY BEGAN EARLY for Deacon Coburn. Insomnia had its hooks dug in deep. The bed had been given every opportunity to take him to dreamland, but that was not to be. It became impossible for slumber to overthrow the blockades of a mind that increasingly refused to shut down. The sleeplessness was exacerbated by a troublesome ache behind his eyes.

Dawn was still hours away. He strolled the length of Front Street, which was deserted except for debris and clutter leftover from the Harvest Street Festival. He went from one end to the other and back again, hands tucked in his pockets, head lowered and hat jammed down on his brow. While the town slept off the effects of its full-blown celebration, he was a solitary watchman thinking through and mulling over the laments clattering in him.

He was commencing his seventh reconnoitering of the avenue when he heard his name in a murmur. He turned to see a form coming out of the darkness. His eyes wrinkled into a squint as his lips curled in recognition. He watched the man approach, and as he did, recalled the teenager who had rescued him when death stalked him beneath a blistering New Mexico sun.

"What are you doing out and about, Caleb?"

"It's purely accidental bumping into you."

"Accidents don't happen."

"I suppose not, Deacon. I couldn't sleep."

"You're missing Sally Twosongs."

Weitzel shrugged stiffly. "That'd be as straight as it gets."

"Worrying on Daniel, too, I suspect."

"He's in a bad way."

"Daniel is fine," Deacon said emphatically. "He has penance to do, but we remedied his outlook and navigated our way through some crucial stuff. He's on the trail setting things right with the Almighty. He intends to be at *WT Ranch* to spend Christmas with his grandchild."

"That's welcome news."

They fell in side by side, wordlessly walking and appreciating each other's company. For a hundred or more yards the only sound was their quiet footfalls on the hard-packed dirt. The vivid clarity of the moon, yellowish and low in the sky, was waning. At the platform where the band had played Coburn made a gesture with his thumb and they angled onto the boardwalk near the Longbranch Saloon. They settled on a bench in front of Rath General Store.

"What's got under your skin, Caleb?" Deacon asked, elbows resting on knees.

Weitzel exhaled a rush. "I don't want to talk about it, but I'm glad you asked." His lips pressed into a scarcely discernible grin. "I need to process and figure out some junk in my head. I'm wandering around at this hour because I got scared awake by a horrid nightmare."

"There's a lot of that going around, I hear."

Weitzel frowned and pushed his hat up his forehead. "I've had almost the identical one at least twice and it makes little or no sense, but it's chucking some fear into me."

Coburn pondered that for a spell. He leaned back and put his right ankle on his left knee, then spoke in a confident tone. "It is written in Scripture that *there is no fear in love; but perfect love casteth out fear: because fear hath torment. He that feareth is not made perfect in love.*"

"I've been reminded of that by Sally Twosongs."

"She would be one to know," Deacon said, direct and sincere. He folded his hands in his lap and gave the young man a probing look. "With the Apostle John's truth about fear and love as a framework, we ought to hash all this out and see if we can get some enlightenment."

Weitzel nodded in agreement. "In the dream I'm a little boy at our home in Gettysburg. The battle is booming and spreading carnage across the countryside. Blood and gore. Piles of amputated arms and legs. Cannon fire and smoke. Screams of pain, soldiers weeping. My father loading the dead onto flatbed wagons." He paused to catch a deep breath. "My mother with her hands inside a mutilated man's belly. Our sitting room a blood-stained operating theater."

"Your parents told me bits and pieces of those abysmal days."

"I was nine years old when the war came to our farm," Caleb said candidly. "None of it ever wormed its way to the surface to trouble my consciousness until recently."

"Memories can be troublesome."

"Does the dream mean anything?"

"Hard to say what, but surely dreams ain't insignificant," Deacon replied, shoulders huddling upward. "I know from experience that memories can't be constrained forever. Sooner or later the past sheds denial or the rubble of years to confront us and demand attention."

"Could the nightmare be a warning?"

"A warning? About what?"

"I have no clue, Deacon. That's why I'm asking."

Coburn smiled thinly. "A warning? Maybe, but just as likely, maybe not. How can we really know? Who can determine with authority the meaning or purpose of our dreams? Perhaps in hindsight we may see it all clearly, but there's danger in making it a guessing game. We can be driven batty trying to decipher the nuances of memory shanghaied by imagination."

"That's sensible counsel."

"At a tender age you were an eyewitness to bloodletting," Deacon said, removing his hat. He massaged a pain-induced gnarl from above the bridge of his nose. "All of which is ominous because it stole your innocence and there's no getting back what was lost. Your life, including all the bygone days, is what it is, but take heart and be assured, you are not alone."

"Implying what?"

"That war destroyed more lives than can be known," Deacon answered grimly. "The dead and wounded; the walking dead and wounded. Folks whose minds and spirits couldn't resolve or live through the futility and horrors of bloodshed and loss. Calling killing moral or virtuous, and the godforsaken bloodbaths nearly cost me my sanity. I was closely acquainted with madness and there are still times when I am forced to sort through the butchery in my mind."

"That's where your wisdom comes from."

Coburn flipped his hat onto his head. "If so, it was a helluva price to pay, Caleb. War changes us. We cannot know the traumas it slashes on our hearts and souls."

"Those are essentials to heed."

"We won't though," Deacon opined in a pitiless voice. "Wars and ru-mors of wars will be a scourge on humankind until kingdom come." He sighed and stooped forward, elbows returning to his knees. The footprints of age around his eyes hardened into a workaday expression. Silence now domineered the space between them as the discourse was internalized by both men.

The hint of daybreak was a pinkish line drawn on the eastern horizon.

Birth pangs were heavy on Sally Twosongs. Pain made the small of her back feel like it was being squeezed by a viselike contraption. The pressure squashed through her abdomen in spasmodic bolts that were excruciating. Her hands were fisted and sweat dripped from every pore. Her long and glossy hair was a loose and disheveled mat of tangles.

A breeze streamed through the open window; the air had a brittle and frigid quality. Her voice was stuck in her throat. With each new fiery jab her clenched jaw wrenched to cry out for help, but the only sounds to emerge were hisses of breath. She was all alone; alone that is except for the swarm of pale-skinned demons shrieking hideously at her.

The fiends were clustered together at the foot of the bed. She was on her knees in the middle of the mattress, cringing and thrusting an arm outward each time one of the hellions darted at her. The evil spirits were excited and overjoyed; as they danced and leered, their mouths droned a triumphant song that hummed like a symphony of mandolins.

A jagged wire of panic threaded its way through her. From the tips of her toes to the top of her head, terrorized fear stabbed deep sutures that tore the fabric of her strength and resolve. Her flannel nightgown was hitched up over her hips. Contractions were constant; the baby was coming. She could feel the pressing bulge moving downward. Her hands clutched together over her privates in a desperately useless effort to prevent the inevitable.

High-pitched screeches of ecstasy sprang off the lips of the horde of demons. A brute with an extremely malformed head hovered close to her. Its yellow eyes blazed as brightly as beacons and its nostrils were reeking cesspools. The inmate of hell grinned as it maliciously blew a rancid blast of breath in her face. "Your newborn will die. We will devour it."

She could no longer withstand the force of what was happening. The bones of her pelvic girdle were strained and in tension; it felt as though her insides were ripping apart. She guided the head and shoulders free of the birth canal—the baby didn't move or make a peep. She fell backwards in a shuddering convulsion of weakness and exhaustion. Somewhere closeby a dog was barking, which didn't prevent a devilish fiend from seizing the stillborn child.

Sally Twosongs gasped and sat up, hands held possessively over the swollen protrusion of her abdomen. "No. That will not happen. In the name of Jesus, that *will not* happen." She blinked and her head jerked around to see that she was safe and secure in her bedroom. The trepidation that held sway over her in the nightmare was now entirely gone.

Smidgeons of dull morning daylight were scattered across the room. Hank, wide-eyed and tongue dribbling, was standing over her on the bed. Her mother-in-law sat stiff and still, staring at her. "What will not happen, Sally Twosongs?" Eliza asked anxiously.

"Evil will not triumph over me. Not now, not ever," Sally Twosongs replied, shifting her bottom. "Nor will it harm my baby because Jesus is good medicine." She grabbed the collie by the scruff of the neck and gave it a playful tug. "Thank you for your protection, but it would be wise for you to jump off this bed or else Caleb will have your hide. I'm fine, Hank."

The tricolor dog tilted its head doubtfully. Its eyes were expressive as it whined and growled in protest. She gave it a persuasive shove, which caused it to grudgingly obey. It turned a circle and its toenails clacked on the hardwood floor, then it laid down and watched her.

"Anything to report in terms of cramps or such?"

"I wish it were so, Eliza," Sally Twosongs answered, and slowly put her head on the pillow. "I am wondering if this baby is ever going to decide to be born."

"God's timing is all that matters."

"Until then are you going to sit at my bedside every night?"

"I only came in a few minutes before you woke up," Eliza told her, shrugging. "I heard you making all kinds of troublesome sounds, but couldn't understand any words."

"Really? I was talking?"

"Not exactly talking. Grunts and yelps."

Sally Twosongs sighed tiredly. "My voice was silenced in the dream."

"You yelled loud enough to awaken me."

"That's surprising."

"Sally Twosongs?"

The Navajo woman frowned darkly. "Yes."

"Are you positive there are no problems?"

"All is well."

Eliza stood reluctantly. Concern and apprehension were gloomy clouds on her face. "I'll put the coffee on and get breakfast started. You best stay where you are and rest."

"I'd like to, but I have to go potty. My bladder is about to burst," Sally Twosongs said, smiling girlishly. She heaved up and placed her feet on the floor. There was muddled hesitancy in her movements, as though her brain had a bothersome fog which required her to think through each action before being able to do it. She pulled a housecoat on over her nightclothes and slipped into moccasin slippers. "Hank will happily be my companion to the outhouse."

"That's certainly true," Eliza said, grinning.

Sally Twosongs yawned and stretched. The bushy-haired collie attentively brushed against her legs. She patted its head and murmured soothing words, then went outside with her four-legged guardian on her heels. The fortress of mountains cast deep shadows on the valley of *WT Ranch*, but the gray tinted sky had promising hues of blue. She strolled slothfully on the pathway, enjoying the mercies and newness that came upon the arrival of each dawn.

Abbey Langton was in distress. Labor pains were coming fast and furious. The amniotic sac had broken while she was still on the boardwalk; the result was a flooding gusher of water that splattered all over the place. She could hear much activity around her, but embarrassment had her eyes slammed shut. She was flat on her back, knees pulled up and dress hiked over her thighs. Her petticoat and bloomers, bloody and soaked, had been removed.

Whitey Fitzgerald was chattering instructions and click-clicking in rapid-fire spurts. The fulltime barber sometime dentist was coaching a scraggly-faced man whom she couldn't identify because she'd only caught a glimpse of him when she was carried inside. He was now crouched low and coaxing the baby out by telling her how to breathe and when to push. His hands were clammy—every time he touched her exposed skin, she gritted her teeth and shivered.

She had a sense that she would fall because she was precariously balanced on a narrow table. Her body felt as if it was at war with itself. The opposing factions were exchanging blows and unleashing fiery bombs of pain. Whenever she thought the stringent discomfort could not possibly become more severe, it intensified to an unimaginable level. She was crying, but attempting not to; the gurgles coming forth were akin to strangled wheezes.

The man charged with the task of birthing her baby began to chuckle in a manner that startled her. It wasn't a hopeful throat-clearing to encourage her; neither was it a knowledgeable chortle signifying that all was proceeding according to nature. The noise surfacing from beneath the bunched folds of her garment was infantile giggling.

Her eyes popped open and she lifted her head and shoulders, and strained to see what was so funny, but the rounded hillock of her tummy obstructed her view. The back of his hands were against her inner thighs, and the odd merriment leaping off his tongue increased in volume. Icy coldness released a hot spring of sourness that festered up her throat to choke her. A seething frenzy of incessant quivering shook her from the inside out.

Amid mumbles of silly snickering, he ordered her to push harder and harder. Her face clenched against the agony as she forced every ounce of potency to comply. A shrill squeal came rushing from her as she gave the final full effort. The baby immediately cried loudly. Her eyes gaped wide in elated anticipation, but then, waves of shock smashed over her.

Liam Greer, slouch-eyed and slump-shouldered, stood proudly between her legs. He cradled her newborn in the crook of his arm, glowering hatefully at her as he cackled like an escapee from a madhouse. The maniacal laughter was pounding against her eardrums when she broke free of the arms of Morpheus—the god of dreams—sobbing and shaking.

"Abbey! Breathe, Abbey!"

"Oh, sweet Jesus," she exclaimed in a gasp. Her eyes broadened into huge circles, then flinched because the bedroom was awash in sunshine. Her husband was kneeling over her, his face a disconcerted mask. She hugged his neck. "Hold me, Sam. Hold me close."

Beadle helped her to turn on her side. He scrunched down and protectively wrapped his arms around her. He nuzzled her neck and kissed her earlobe. "What is it, Abbey?"

"I feel so dirty. Violated."

"Dirty? Violated? What?"

"Liam Greer delivered our baby," she replied in a deadened tone. Her lungs were still panting as if she had been running fast. "His hands . . ." She paused, gulping audibly. "His hands were down there." She was cold and goosepimply. "I need to take a bath."

His jaw tightened. "It was a nightmare."

"*Just* a nightmare?" she asked, voice trembling. "I pray so."

"You were overtired from dancing and the late night, Abbey."

"I pray so," she said again.

"Your brain and your body conspired in rebellion."

"You think?"

"I know," Sam answered staunchly. He placed a hand on her belly as gently as the caress of a feather. "The sun's up and daylight is burning, Miss

Langton. Whenever we're roused and ready to get on the go, it would be my supreme pleasure to take you out for breakfast."

"I'll not be the one to deprive you of that pleasure, Mr. Beadle," Abbey said, hiding a smile against the pillow. "Afterwards you can drop me at the Western Union office. I need to send another telegram to those malingerers at the Bureau of Indian Affairs in Washington."

"If you insist."

"I do," she replied, varying the position of her shoulders and hips. "I also want to visit Butch for a little while. Then I'm sure he'll escort me to wherever I will find Caleb."

"The Alhambra. We made plans to meet up there."

"Sounds perfect." She continued to make adjustments to be comfy. He did what he could to assist her, which mostly meant waiting for her to stop stirring. When she settled in, he fluffed a pillow and snuggled against her backside. His strong arms held her intimately, hands cupped in tenderness around her bosom. They exchanged whispered expressions of love, then lay beneath the covers listening to each other breathe as sunrays frolicked on the floorboards.

The sun was not yet cresting above a craggy pinnacle in the east when Pete Axler rode out of the aspens onto the acreage of *WT Ranch*. He was a half-mile from his house. His bones ached, his stomach growled and his eyes were groggy so it was good that his mount, still sturdy and full of stamina, plodded onward without direction or prompting from him.

He leaned back in the saddle and tilted his head. The grayish splotches in the sky were being cloaked by vibrant brushstrokes of cornflower blue. He enjoyed the simple beauty. When the first slice of sunshine slashed over the lofty mountaintop, relaxation swelled in him. He filled his lungs as though the air of home tasted sweeter than elsewhere.

While he was still a far way off, he heard his name screamed in a piercing pitch. The downy hair at the nape of his neck prickled. He looked and saw the one true love of his life bolting off the porch of the ponderosa pine dwelling. A thrill went through him, and his heart leapt so high and hard that for several moments he had difficulty breathing.

Naomi Axler appeared to be a woman caught up in the anguish of hysteria. She had her skirt clutched over her thighs and was racing toward him. Even from a distance he could discern wetness glistening on her cheeks. A loop of emotion entwined around his Adam's apple, almost gagging him. He was consciously preoccupied by his bride, who was prettier than beautiful, but then, a scurry of movement grabbed his attention and caused a smile to consume his face.

His son and daughter were scampering as swift as their little legs could carry them. Pride thickened in his throat and got mixed in with a desperate need to protect them. His jawline tensed. Arms thrashing wildly, they were yammering for her to slow down, but despite their impressive efforts, were falling farther and farther behind.

As she got close enough for her big brown eyes to make his heart beat as robustly as hummingbird wings, he dismounted. She sped up and covered the final ten yards in an energetic surge. He set his feet apart to be braced, but even so, she crashed into him with such an impact that he reeled off balance—the horse prevented them from tumbling to the ground; his upper body thumped against and was supported by the brindle gelding.

She clung to him, crying and saying his name over and over. Jesse and Amanda arrived, all elbows and knees as they climbed him as though he was a knotty old tree. It was then, as his wife squeezed the stuffing out of him and his children loved him to crazy that Pete Axler knew beyond all doubt that he was indeed the luckiest man on the face of the earth.

Thirty minutes later, Naomi Axler had snipped the sinew stitches away from the wound on the right side of his forehead, cleansed the four-inch scabby gash and plastered herbal ointment on it along with a fresh gauze bandage. She threw the blood encrusted dressing in the garbage, then put the scissors and tweezers away in the first-aid kit.

"I'll make you a ham sandwich and pour another Arbuckle's, then I want to hear details of what happened to you," Naomi said, rinsing her hands under the pump's spout. She dried them on a terrycloth towel. "No shortcuts and don't make me pry particulars from you."

"No, ma'am. I'll be straight and thorough," Pete answered plainly.

The aroma of coffee, strong and stout, filled the kitchen. Wherever she went in the room, she kept her concentration affixed on her lanky husband. A queer expression rumpled Axler's face; he was markedly ill at ease because of all the fuss being made over him. He sat in his chair at one end of the table, while the children were cross-legged on the floor on either side of him, messing around with wooden blocks and watching him, wide-eyed and grinning.

"By the way," Pete said, reaching into an inside pocket of his cowhide vest. "This letter had just gotten to the postal station on my way north." He placed it on the table.

"I have no interest in any correspondence at this time," Naomi replied, filling his mug with steaming coffee. "Whoever it's from and whatever it's about, it can wait." She served him a sandwich, then sat across from him. "I want to hear what delayed you."

"It was the damnest thing . . ."

"Language, Mr. Axler," she cut in, eyebrows raised. "Ears in the cornfield."

He nodded and scratched at his whiskery chin. "The yearlings were no problem. Not a single issue on the trip to Gunnison. I delivered the string of horses to the rancher. He was more than satisfied with the stock. I got paid in cash money. The succession of troubles started shortly thereafter." He bit off a huge chunk of ham and bread, and chewed methodically.

Her brow knit into a frustrated frown. She waited and waited for him to swallow. When he finally did so, he lifted the sandwich to chomp off another portion of it. She gently touched his forearm. "Smaller mouthfuls, please. I am anxious to know what happened."

He took a nibble of crust. "I was riding into Gunnison to put the currency on deposit at the bank when a liquored up gang of miners with clubs and crowbars jumped me. I was knocked off my horse. I put up a fair defense for a few minutes, but there were too many of them. They were riled up and began beating me senseless. And then it got real ugly."

"Uglier than getting bushwhacked for no reason?"

"Yep. Uglier than that," he replied, taking a sip of coffee. "When one of them uncovered the money in my saddlebags, I got busted in the belly and chops so many times I thought I was going to die." He had another swig of the black nectar. "A rope came into play and a lynching party was in the works. I was being dragged to a tree when shouts and several gunshots ended the mob's plans. A pair of lawmen came to my rescue, then I passed out."

"Dear Lord, Pete. It makes no sense."

"I ain't sure my brain has it figured yet."

"What then?"

"I came to in jail, bruised and bloody," he answered, resignation in his voice. "I was conscious for five minutes or so before I was hauled into a courtroom and in front of a judge who listened to one witness after another swear that I was a thief and stone-cold killer." He pressed the palms of his hands around his mug. "The judge gave me the opportunity to say a handful of words, then rolled up his sleeves and pounded the gavel. I was sentenced to hang."

"For what?"

"That's what I asked, Naomi," he said, eyes narrowed. "Turned out that while I was ten miles north of Gunnison completing the transaction, a mining operation had its payroll stolen and a clerk was shot dead. I fit the description of the lone gunman, plus I had a load of cash."

"How's all that even possible, Pete?"

"Mistaken identity, wrong place wrong time, is all," Pete said, shrugging wearily. "The circumstances done me in. I foresaw getting my neck stretched because the gallows were being built in the courtyard outside my barred window. The judge sent a couple badges to check my alibi, then the rancher came into town and verified my not guilty status."

"Thank God, Pete. I prayed and prayed."

"That's not the end of it, Naomi." He exhaled a sigh and took a tiny bite. He washed it down with a gulp of coffee, tipped a wink at his son and daughter, then resumed. "When I was set free, I went to the bank to take care of business. After that I skedaddled southward. I was in an introspective mood and riding along a ridgeline trail observing an eagle when a cougar came out of nowhere and panicked the gelding." His lips split apart in a short-lived smile.

"The brindle? That horse is tried and true."

"Don't I know it," he stated bluntly. "It was a freak incident. The eagle screamed and that big cat was right on top of us. I was dusted and flying on a lick and a promise. I cracked my skull on a rock, which is how I got this laceration. I was out cold for I don't know how long. When I had my wits about me, I was on a bearskin beside a warm campfire in a Ute lodge."

"Jehovah Jireh, our provider."

He eyed her, serious and resolved. "I'd not argue against that notion, Naomi. At first, my eyesight was blurry and my brains so scrambled that I thought the woman was an angel."

"Perhaps you were tended to by angels unawares."

"I ain't disagreeing." He finished his coffee and picked apart the sandwich. "Nice family. Man, wife and two children, a boy and girl, about the same ages as our youngsters. They nursed me and saw to my care and recovery. We communicated fairly well. I discovered I had more sign language in my noggin than I ever realized. When I left them, I made sure they understood that if they *ever* needed *anything* they had lifelong friends at *WT Ranch*."

"I can tell you this, Pete Axler," Naomi said, holding his hand. "You are not leaving this ranch to go anywhere anytime soon. When we're finished here, I'm filling the tub with hot soapy water and you are going to soak until your skin is as wrinkled as a baked apple."

"You'll get no resistance from me, Naomi."

"Daddy," Jesse piped up, bright-eyed and squirmy with curiosity. "How come you were getting your neck stretched? Ain't your head in the right place no more?"

Axler squinted and let loose a horselaugh, eyes shuttering and shoulders bobbing up and down. He shoved his chair away from the table and gathered his children onto his lap. His arms locked around them. "My head and whole body is in the right place just now." He leaned back and gave them a bronco-buster ride on his knees, which produced squiggles and squeals.

Naomi Axler beamed cheerily. Her eyes were pools of happy tears.

Butch Mackenzie was weeping. Huge sobs crunched out of him. He sat alone at his desk, elbows propped on its edge. His head was bowed and held up by his hands, which were locked together over the top of his cranium. Blood pulsated hard and fast against his palms. He was fearful that vessels were popping loose and splattering inside his brain.

The Western Union office felt like a torture chamber; it was as though its plank walls had turned to stone and were inextricably closing in on him, dank and crawling with a slippery sheen of mossy mold. He wanted to scream; he wanted to thrash against and eradicate the scathing pain raging within; he wanted to choke every doctor and nurse he had ever known; he wanted to damn the entire medical profession to the deepest recesses of hell.

Instead, he simply wept uncontrollably as tragic events from the past battered him with appalling memories that were cruel and ruthless. Huge rivulets of snot dripped over his lips, and his eyes were raw and sore. He slumped backward in the barrel-like swivel chair and heaved in a gust of breath. He enunciated curses that became a rhapsody of blasphemies; the sacrilegious profanities smashed at God, ferociously calling into question his love and mercy.

All the niceties and Bible words woven into sermons that Mackenzie had endured hearing were empty banalities; nothing more than silver-tongued malarkey that provided false hope in the Almighty's loving-kindness which, in his reckoning, was gibberish bathed in hogwash. He had no incentive to renounce or modify his assessment. Providence had been weighed in the balance of Butch Mackenzie's scales of fairness and deemed to be fraudulent.

A movement from the boardwalk passed in front of the window and altered the sunlight to cast a shadow on the floor. He nearly leapt to his feet, and in doing so, stumbled to a knee. He grunted and got his stubby legs under him, then trudged over and pulled the blinds down to the windowsill. He also closed the shade on the door as he secured its lock.

He swabbed wetness off his cheeks, then rubbed the heels of his hands roughly against his eyes. He fell onto the chair and mishandled his bifocals. Finally getting them wedged on his nose, he picked up a crumpled telegram from the medical facility in St. Louis, which had come over the wires an hour ago; the final nail in the coffin of a fifteen year old living nightmare had been driven home. In the dimness, he read it again and shed another abundance of tears.

> *It is with sorrow that we inform you of your wife's passing.*
> *Arrangements have been made according to your instructions*
> *on file.*

≈ ≈ ≈

The woman was on Texas Street in Abilene. A film of perspiration glistened on her face as she strolled with no particular place to go. She wore a colorful sunbonnet for protection on a steamy and sticky summer day, and had just eased past McInerny's Boot & Saddle Shop when she turned around and saw her son a half block away coming in her direction.

Her heart did a panicky jump and her lungs burned. The temptation to flee was an urgent prompting in her, but rather than succumbing to its enticement, she straightforwardly approached him and stood strong to block his path. "May we visit, Liam?"

"We ain't got nothing to say to each other."

"Indulge me. Please, Liam."

"I got shopping to do."

"Liam, please. There are some things I need to tell you."

"I ain't interested in anything you have to say to me."

"I'm not the monster you think I am."

"I don't think you're a monster. I know you're a whore."

"Yes, I was a whore," she replied earnestly. "I cannot deny any of what is behind me. I have no excuses. And I do not expect you to forgive me any time soon, but I want you to know that I am sorry for all the wrong I inflicted on you. It was a mistake for me to leave you."

"Why did you?"

"I was lost, Liam."

"What's that mean?"

"I was messed up and confused. It was a dark, dark place to be. In a way I did to you what was done to me by another," she told him, honest and vulnerable. "You deserved better than me. Jack Greer was also much worthier of better than I had to offer."

His deeply tanned baby-face softened and his eyes narrowed on her. "Until not so many years ago I thought you were dead. Pa told me you died when I was born."

"Perhaps the lie should've been true."

"Maybe that would've been best for all concerned."

"I've thought the same more than once," she acknowledged, forthrightly peering into his eyes. "I floundered in a chaotic maze for a long time. I was lost and afraid, Liam."

"I know what that's like, I think."

She smiled sympathetically. "My feelings were jumbled, my perspective and outlook jangled. I couldn't find my way back to who I was and took so many wrong turns."

"I suppose that's something, but it don't help me at all."

"I am sorry, Liam," she said openly. "I own all the poor choices and errors in my life. I live with the consequences of them every day. I am ashamed of so much."

"Thanks for saying so, I guess."

She inched closer, and in an impulsive and tremulous motion, gently placed a hand on his shoulder. "I haven't changed all I would like to yet, but I know I'm not the same."

"You ain't accountable for the sins done to you."

"What?" she asked, mystified.

"The sins of your father. You ain't answerable for them." His lips curled into a cockeyed smirk as his shoulders perfunctorily stooped in acceptance. "He's my father too, right?"

"Yes," she whispered in a sputter.

"I ain't responsible for his sins either. Nor do I carry any blame for yours," he said, a friendly inflection in his voice. "The sins of your father bent me, but I had chances for a different life. I could've rode a noble trail instead of being decoyed by the allure of evil. My choices were mine." He took hold of her hand. "I forgive you, Ma. You remember that, always."

Dolores Solrizo gasped and faltered sideways. At that moment the stagecoach was in the middle of a turn when it struck a rut that shook the conveyance mightily. She woke up clutching handfuls of air in an effort not to fall off the bench-seat. A deluge flowed on her flushed cheeks as though her tear ducts were sponges being wrung out by brawny hands.

"Are you alright?" Brenda asked, watching her warily. She sat across from her with Stace snoozing, stretched out and using her lap for a pillow. "You were sleeping restlessly."

Delores steadied her breathing. "I had a visitation from days gone by."

"Good or bad?"

"Good, I presume," Delores answered, blinking rapidly. It took several seconds for her eyes to focus properly. "The dream was almost exactly how it happened ten years ago, but then, it had a peculiarly hopeful ending, which was a far cry from what was truly said and done."

"Hopeful is good."

"Mostly, yes," Delores agreed, unmistakably distracted. She reflexively swayed to the cadence of the rocking carriage and clacking wheels. She fanned puffs of dust, then looked at the countryside. There was nothing but billows of grass for as far as she could see; the grassland and blue skies seemed to blend into each other. "Liam Greer is my son," she said, eyes absorbed by the vast horizon. "My subconscious just replayed the last time I saw him."

"Kid Greer?"

"Yes, Liam is my son. I abandoned him."

"How? When?"

"I was raped," Delores replied dispassionately. "I was young and a frantic nervous wreck, but there can be no evasion or song and dance regarding my guilt. He is flesh of my flesh, bone of my bone, and I willfully discarded him immediately after giving birth. There's never been a reason for me to share the starkness of the whole truth with my own beloved daughter."

Brenda swallowed thickly. "I cannot imagine the burden your heart carries."

"The tender mercies of God sustain me through my darkest hours."

"I can truly relate."

"I imagine so," Delores said, smiling delicately. She pivoted to scrutinize her directly. "I apologize for not being forthcoming when you told me that he had killed Ben Slaton."

"No apology is necessary."

"Perhaps not, but there it is, Miss Hawkins." The subtle expression on her lips expanded to fill her eyes with compassion. "You do understand that if things don't work out for you in Dodge City, you and Stace will always be welcome in Santa Fe at the Suncurl Café."

"As you have said, Delores. The possibility intrigues me."

"Wonderful. We can discuss it afresh when you meet my daughter." She maneuvered her backside around, then when she achieved a modicum of comfort, she brushed gritty grime from the folds of her skirt. Her gaze came to rest on the little boy softly snoring. Emotion swelled in her veins. Her eyes squeezed shut and her mouth pinched in determination as she silently held the child before the throne of grace and prayed blessings for his peace and protection.

The stagecoach rumbled onward, a haze of dust swirling in its wake.

September 28, 1882

Dear Diary: I am exhausted, but not tired. Does that make any sense? After the fun and excitement of the Harvest Street Festival I couldn't fall asleep. I was giddy. The bed had no chance to contain me. I was up humming or singing songs under my breath. The band's music was in my head all night long. I may have gotten a couple hours of sleep, but that's all.

It was full dark when I went to work and now, it's not yet ten o'clock and all my chores at the livery are completed until tomorrow. I have a slew of freedom ahead of me. Pumpkin is at the hitching rail outside waiting for me. The weather is warm and impressive. Not a cloud to be seen in the blue sky. I intend to explore north of the city and ride the afternoon away, then if nothing happens beforehand, spend the evening on the lookout for birth pangs with Abbey.

A highlight from the wingding merrymaking took me somewhat by surprise, but as I had opportunity to process it while sweating and shoveling this morning, I have concluded that Big Bull Wallace is truly a nice man. He initiated a one on one with me, which was significant and enlightening. The conversation was timid and unsure at the beginning, but we found our stride and the result was that we covered a far-reaching range of topics.

He insisted that I call him Bull, claiming that he would be extremely insulted if he ever heard me say Mr. Wallace. The funny thing is that he always addressed me as Miss Lahay, and did so in such a respectful way that I felt honored. We spent a half-hour or more strolling and chatting in the shine of moonlight. It's obvious that he harbors special fondness for Mom. He informed me that she was the most astute entrepreneur he had ever known.

Just before we went our separate ways he said something mysterious. It didn't register that way at first, but as I have reconsidered the exchange, it strikes me as strange. He told me that I had nothing to worry about because he would take care of matters on my behalf. Those were his words. I smiled at the vague reference, but am at a loss to understand it.

No matter. A day on horseback awaits, so I am out of here.

Avis Lahay closed the butterfly engraved notebook and returned it to a corner of the pedestal-legged desk. She screwed the top on the ink well, then noisily bounced the hard-backed chair sideward and was giggling about it as she stood. She peeked in the mirror and was pleased by her reflection. She flipped her golden skimmer on and adjusted it to a rakish tilt.

A few minutes later, she was in the saddle chatting to her mare. The sunrays felt nice on her face as she leaned her head back to search the immeasurable heavens above. She murmured in contentment. Little did she know that she was embarking on her final ride on the strawberry roan. By nightfall, her world would be in a tempest of tragedy and vengeance.

While her husband soaked and catnapped in the tub, and her children played outside on the porch, Naomi Axler pondered a long ago departure. She sat at the kitchen table turning an unopened envelope over in her hands. The contents were unknown, but nevertheless, the letter had her worried. Her heart was anxious, her mind racing with questions and memories.

The name above the return address disclosed that it was from her sister. It'd been a decade since they were together or had any contact with each other. Their parting had been contentious—in a haughty burst of acrimony Martha Hochstetler declared that their sibling relationship was over and slammed the door to accentuate the termination.

Naomi shuddered and hissed in a breath as she recalled the ugliness of the scene, the enmity of her attitude and the malice of those words: *Then I no longer have a sister*. She tapped the envelope against her palm and tore off an end of it. Her hands had a slight tremble as she removed a single cream-colored sheet. She noted the heavy determination of the handwriting. Tears, unbidden and unwanted, blurred her vision as she read the message.

> *July 14, 1882*
> *Lancaster, Pennsylvania*
>
> *Dear Naomi: It has been dry and blistery here at home. Even so, the grass is green and lush, the crops all doing well. Our orchard promises to provide a lavish bounty, which means caldrons of apple butter and cider, and a busy harvest season. We are richly blessed because of all our hard work and faithfulness. You have missed so much.*
>
> *The family gathered yesterday. It was on short notice, but we managed to pull together a farewell service. We buried Mother. Her death came suddenly. She passed in her sleep. I found her dead in bed on Tuesday morning. Of late, she had complained*

*of heartburn and bouts of digestive troubles. I thought you would
want to know.*

*I understand from the source that you have been correspond-
ing with Anna, which doesn't surprise me since you are both
cut from the same rebellious cloth. My daughter writes me on a
monthly basis, but my life is always too involved with church, family, mission and farm work to find the time to respond to her. I
expect you to convey the news of her grandmother's death.*

*Also, I have no knowledge as to where to reach your brother
Deacon via the mail system, so you will be required to enlighten
him as to the end result of willful disobedience. Mother died
from a heart broken by the defiant and sinful ways of you two
transgressors.*

> *Sincerely,*
> *Martha*

Naomi's mouth was clenched, her complexion ashen—it wasn't anger
that tightened her jaw and discolored her face, but sorrow; seething sorrow
coursed through her. The profoundly intense mourning did not come from
the fact that her dear mother had claimed her eternal reward, but rather, it
was due to the prideful self-righteousness dripping off the page.

The immense sadness for her sister's viewpoint began to slink toward
resentment and judgment, but then, the opening verses of Matthew chapter
seven leapt to mind. She gave the creeping bitterness a swift kick by saying
them aloud: "*Judge not, that ye be not judged. For with what judgment ye
judge, ye shall be judged: and with what measure ye mete, it shall be measured
to you again.*" She repeated the passage to underpin its positive impact on
her.

She peacefully prayed hard for Martha Hochstetler. The phrases were
framed within the context of Scripture. Afterwards, she checked on her husband and children, then purposefully indulged in good remembrances of
her mother. As she did so, she went to her box of letters and filed the latest
one in the back. There was nothing to be gained for her to ever read it again.

≈ ≈ ≈

On the boardwalk in front of Western Union, Abbey Langton gave her
husband a kiss on the chin, then watched him rush off to complete tasks
before lunchtime. Warm affection curled like tendrils around her heart, but
were plucked away by a startling chill that passed over her. Frowning darkly,
she put her hand on the doorknob, only to discover the office locked. She

stepped back and noted the blinds drawn down. She shook her head and knocked.

"We're closed. Huh."

"Butch? It's Abbey."

"Huh. Give me a minute."

"Sure." She waited for much longer than requested, shifting weight from foot to foot and striving for even a hint of comfort. Her ankles were swollen and aching. There was stress in her lower abdomen and the small of her back hurt. "Hurry up, Butch. I need to sit down."

The door instantly flew open. "Sorry, Miss Abbey." He offered an arm, which she took hold of as he led her to the stool he had taken to the street dance. When she was settled on it, he returned and fastened the lock on the door. "Is there anything else I can do for you? Huh."

"I'm fine now," she replied, squinting against the half-light. It took many seconds for her eyes to adjust to the contrast between the brightness outside and dull gloom inside. "Actually, there is, Butch. Could you please put up the blinds and let in some sunshine?"

"No. Huh. No business today."

It was then that she really saw him. Surprise caught in her throat. His eyes were bloodshot and raw; the long ago scars of acne on his cheeks were beet-red and blotchy, raised up like angry welts that dotted his roundish face. Her brow creased in concern. "What's wrong?"

"Nothing."

"Butch? Please tell me what's going on."

"Huh. You're frazzled," he said sharply. "You *must* take it easy."

"I do my best, Butch." She had her hands clasped daintily on her tummy. "There's *always* too much to be done. Sitting on my fanny and doing nothing is an impossibility."

"I can't . . ." Emotion strangulated his voice. A twist of pain squeezed his eyes. He paced in front of the desk, head wagging and arms swinging. He stopped in a haste and stared blearily at her. "Bad stuff happens, Miss Abbey. I can't live if something terrible goes wrong."

Shock hit her and she recoiled. "Butch? What is it?"

"I was a grandfather for two hours once. Huh."

Her eyes spread wide. Her mouth moved soundlessly. Understanding filtered through her mind in a blindingly clear flash. She winced and swallowed dryly. "Dear Lord. I am so sorry."

He rejected her expression of regret with a grunt and a surly wave. He dropped onto the barrel-chair and turned toward her. "A girl with a fringe of blondish hair and wrinkly skin."

She was speechless. She got to her feet and moved the stool close enough to put a hand on his shoulder. The moisture of empathy glistened in her eyes. Her heart was overwhelmed by waves of compassion. She attempted to encourage him with a head bob and feeble smile.

He patted her hand and let out a mournful noise. "The doctor told us everything was normal. No problems or complications. Huh." He raked fingers over his grayish whiskers and pulled at his jowls. "Even when labor started in an unexpected and distressful manner the nurse assured us that all was well. My wife Madge believed every word and put her faith in the experts. I, on the other hand, had no confidence whatsoever in their misleading assertions."

His eyes were narrow slits aimed over her head and focused on a spot in the timbers of the ceiling. "Our daughter's name was Becky, a glittering jewel in my miserable life. She had your spunk and grit. As headstrong as a block of granite." His mouth twitched involuntarily. "And also just like you, she had a tenderness of heart. She could not abide unfairness."

She eyed him sympathetically. "That tender heart came from her Daddy."

"Huh." He shook his head and his lips pursed as if he had just been forced to swallow a glassful of pickle juice. "Becky suffered for better than two days. It wasn't until the last few hours that the medical staff acknowledged that there were serious difficulties. Madge prayed. As did I, on my knees with my hands pressed together in supplication. I bargained and pleaded, but either the words went nowhere or the mean-spirited bastard refused to listen to me."

His teeth and fists were clenched, his voice coarse and gravelly. "Becky hemorrhaged to death in childbirth. She never even got to hold her daughter. Madge and I had brief moments with the baby. She was chubby and beautiful, the spitting image of her mother. We named her Roseanne. Five minutes later our newborn angel died in Madge's arms.

"About then Becky's husband Freddie arrived. He was a salesman and had been on the road drumming up business. I punched him out and rained curses down on him. He cowered and slobbered all over the place. Hours later, while we were distraught and in the midst of trying to make funeral arrangements, Freddie took the coward's way out. He went to a back alley and put a pistol under his chin. His body was discovered by a couple pipsqueaks."

Mackenzie slumped back. "Huh. Madge was always fragile. She became hysterical at the graveside and had a mental breakdown. She screamed and threw herself over the coffin that held our daughter and granddaughter. Something broke inside her head and it couldn't be fixed. She's been heavily medicated in an asylum in St. Louis for over fifteen years." He grabbed the cable and gave it a sneering once-over, then pushed it at her. "I got this news around dawn."

Abbey Langton was crying unashamedly. She took hold of the telegram and thumbed tears aside as she read it in a shaky voice. "*It is with sorrow that we inform you of your wife's passing. Arrangements have been made according to your instructions on file.*"

"Huh. Don't tell me not to care or worry about you, Miss Abbey," he said, eyelids and lips quivering. "Bad stuff happens and I'm of a mind that God doesn't give a damn."

She exhaled a whispery sigh. "That's pain talking, Butch."

"Pain is all I know just now, Miss Abbey."

"Not so. You have my care and affection. Always." She caressed his shoulder in a circular rhythm. "In my heart you are my lovable uncle. Our relationship is extremely important to me and I don't ever want to harm it or cause you worry." She stood and leaned over to press her lips against his forehead. "I promise to heed your counsel and take it easy."

He carefully put his arms around her and rested his head against her chest. Then, in a convulsive outpouring, Butch Mackenzie came apart at the seams. He retched and coughed and wheezed gulping sobs as his flesh quaked and quivered in merciless spasms of grief. She held on as best she could, weepy and blubbering supportive phrases meant to console him. The turbulent upsurge of repressed grieving was an untidy mess that steadfastly bonded them together.

There were a smattering of noontime customers at the Alhambra Saloon. Among them were Caleb Weitzel and Sam Beadle seated at the table that was generally deemed to belong to their mutual friend Deacon Coburn. The Colorado rancher and jack-of-all-trades writer were having a few beers, while immersed in a good-natured gabfest.

"Then what did you do?" Caleb asked, grinning.

"I scarfed down the slop and won the prize," Sam replied nonchalantly. "I fought the gag reflex on every spoonful, but toughed it out and gained a fifty dollar gold coin, plus cashed in on a couple side-bets. That barroom had never been so entertained, scoffing and hooting cheers while laying odds. My mouth was in flames and sweat was gushing out of me."

Weitzel was smirking and chuckling, eyes lit up like candles. "You are a reasonable and intelligent fellow, Sam. Whatever possessed you to take on that challenge?"

"A thin wallet motivated me."

"Are you serious, Sam?"

"I was still wet behind the ears, Caleb. Greener than green."

"There had to be another way to earn cash."

Beadle shrugged and had a swallow of foamy suds. "I was an adventurous greenhorn on my wanders westward and needed an influx of funds. The sign in the window read *Hellfire Stew Fifty Dollars*. It peaked my curiosity. Who'd pay fifty dollars for stew?"

"Where was this?"

"Some gambling den hangout in Baton Rouge," Sam said, twining his fingers around the dewy mug. "I went inside and discovered that it was a longstanding contest that had never been won. Eat one bowlful of Hellfire Stew and receive fifty dollars. Seemed easy enough."

"What were the ingredients?"

"I didn't ask until the bowl was empty, which was just as well," Sam answered, making a sourpuss face. "Seeds and spices I'd never heard of before or since, okra, a dozen different kinds of peppers and alligator meat, which was, by the way, as rubbery as all get out."

"I'd not partake of alligator for the riches of a king," Caleb declared, head shaking and lips pursed. "Nothing more than overgrown lizards with powerful jaws and lethal fangs."

"I might've declined had I known, but maybe not. I needed to get flush," Sam said flatly. "I paid an ugly price for the cash. The next morning the after-effects were excruciating. A severe case of unstoppable cramps and loose bowels. I had fiery water running out of me for more hours than I can remember. The one-eyed wonder of my backside was inflamed for a week."

Weitzel was laughing effortlessly. "Hellfire Stew? What did you expect?"

"Did I mention the fifty dollars and the side-bets?"

"A puckered arse for money?"

"What can I tell you, Caleb?" Sam asked, struggling not to give in to laughter. "I was perilously close to penniless and wasn't about to borrow any money. Shakespeare isn't gospel, but he penned the fine point. *Neither a borrower nor a lender be, for loan oft loses both itself and friend, and borrowing dulls the edge of husbandry. This above all: to thine own self be true, and it must follow, as the night the day, thou canst not then be false to any man.*"

"Polonius from Hamlet, Act I."

"You a fan of Shakespeare?"

"Not exactly," Caleb replied, taking a sip of amber brew. "In the home I grew up in, when it came to my book learning education, Shakespeare played a close second fiddle to the Bible. My mother made me memorize and recite key passages from both sources."

"I had a teacher in Souderton who used the same technique."

"Souderton? Souderton, Pennsylvania?"

Beadle frowned at the surprise in his voice. "Yes."

"My mother was born and raised in Souderton," Caleb said dryly. "She was a teacher in a one-room schoolhouse there before she married my father and moved to Gettysburg."

"Miss Pringle? Beth Pringle?"

"Yes. Everyone called her Beth. Everyone that is except Pa."

Beadle sat up straight and tall, as though he was a schoolboy and had just been reprimanded. "Beth Pringle is your mother? Whoever said it was a small world had it right. I remember much about her. She instilled a love for words and learning in me. I also recall that her departure was almost scandalous. One day she was our teacher and all was well, then a member of the school board came in and told us she was relieved of her duties."

"Almost scandalous?" Caleb tapped the table and chuckled easily. "My parents never told me that part of their story." He shoved his hat up his forehead. "Now you and Abbey must return to *WT Ranch*. Ma and Pa relocated from New Mexico in the summer of '80. We built a cozy log cabin in a secluded little clearing on the hillside between the two large houses."

"This is truly an amazing discovery."

"It is that and more, Sam."

"Makes me think about the currents of time and history. How is it possible for the years and miles to turn in such a way as to connect us?" Sam asked, then polished off his drink.

"Life, destiny, chance, fate? The hand of God?"

Beadle glanced around. "We still got awhile to discuss the likelihoods. Abbey is going to meet us here. She should be along shortly. She may enjoy exploring all these dynamics and have something to contribute to the philosophizing. I'll get us a couple more beers."

Caleb Weitzel agreed and watched while his friend went to the bar. He sat back and relaxed for a mere moment, then his face became rigid and he sat bolt upright as an icy sensation crawled up his spine and cast whitecaps of coldness over him. He had no understanding of the bad feeling, but soon enough, comprehension would be too horrendous to be real.

At *WT Ranch*, Hans Weitzel and Pete Axler were sitting on the front steps of Caleb Weitzel's house, minding Jesse and Amanda as they ran and played. Between periods of silence the men chatted about this and that as they waited for news that nature had taken its course. Hank was behind them on the porch, pressed against the door and whining almost continuously.

"That collie doesn't recognize that it's a dog," Pete said, shaking his head.

Weitzel grunted, eyebrows raised. "Caleb gave Hank orders to protect Sally Twosongs. I've never seen or known anyone who trains and commands animals the way my son does."

"Me neither."

Weitzel glanced upward and squinted at the sun, which was at two o'clock. That meant they had been on watch for over an hour. He shook his head, shifted his buttocks and clasped his hands together. "I despise this part of it. Squatting here as useless as a pair of eunuchs."

"Sally Twosongs is in good hands."

"Anything can go wrong, Pete."

"Naomi and Eliza are fine midwives."

"Maybe so, but no one has any real control on those doings," Hans said, grimness in his voice and etched on his face. "Believe me when I tell you that anything can go wrong."

Axler rubbed the smoothness of his newly shaven chin. He turned in such a way as to rest his back against a column of the porch. "Seems to me that you're borrowing trouble, Hans."

"Remembering bad times, Pete."

"The past ain't always a harbinger for the present."

"We can't escape memories, Pete. No matter how hard we try."

"Memories do have a way of floating to the top."

"Especially the nasty ones."

Axler nodded. His perpetual frown deepened. "I ain't one to nose into a man's business, but I also ain't one to leave a friend swinging in the wind if a listening ear can help."

"I appreciate your steadiness, Pete."

"So have at it."

"Two women on different continents separated by an ocean," Hans said, vaguely staring at the children practicing somersaults on the grass. "In Germany my first wife died in childbirth and the baby survived for less than an hour. I immigrated to America and fortune shone its light on me when I met Eliza. All was on form with her pregnancy until crunch time, then it was a long and frightening crisis delivery. She had too close an encounter with death."

"That's a burdensome millstone to drag around, Hans."

"No varnish on it."

"Best let it go. Piddling with it serves no purpose."

Weitzel flexed his hands into fists then bumped them together. "I am aware of that and mostly adhere to it, but in tensions such as this, my head gets full of crazy doubts and questions. When Sally Twosongs was a young girl she had some unnatural difficulties. She's already lost one baby for certain and I get to worrying that her plumbing may be permanently damaged."

"You keep that all inside you, don'tcha?"

"Until now."

"Best let it go," Pete said once more, low and persuasive.

Hans Weitzel abruptly stood, jammed his hands in his trouser pockets and strolled to a corner of the house. A wiry thread of anxiety stitched its way across his shoulders. He looked around as though he expected to see someone wielding a darning needle. A lump shot up his throat and a sensation in his gut convinced him that troubles were an imminent danger.

Three miles north of Dodge City, Avis Lahay had her muscles in accord with the animal beneath her and it felt good. Her knees were pulled up and she was bent low to nimbly rise and fall in exquisite ease. She was giving Pumpkin a thorough workout; alternating racing as fast as possible for fifty yards or so, then slowing to a walk for approximately the same distance. The exercise was a favorite; both horse and rider were grinning.

A breeze blew hard enough to cause the tall grass covering the gently rolling terrain to appear to be undulating waves that never crested. She enjoyed being alone on the plains. The emptiness of it stirred secret places in her soul; her imagination came alive when she was on horseback in the wide open spaces and she wanted times such as these to go on forever.

When the mare came to the end of a route, she gave the reins a slight tug and whispered a command, then dismounted. She removed her skimmer and fanned her face with it. The sheen of perspiration dried almost instantly. She tucked her hair under the hat and tightened the bead to her chin. "What do you say, Pumpkin? A few more sprints, then homeward bound?"

The strawberry roan snorted and reared up on its hind legs in assent. She waited for it to get over the exuberance, then patted its neck and sprung into the saddle. "To the top of that knoll yonder," she said, pointing to the west. "Then back here nice and easy." She made a click-click sound and the horse twitched its ears; before she gave it a nudging order to run, she burst out laughing as she realized she had inadvertently mimicked Whitey.

Her smile was enormous, eyes sparkly and bright. She whooped loudly, which was all the encouragement her mount required. Pumpkin leapt forward and in four loping strides the mare was at full speed, its reddish coat gleaming in the sunshine. Avis rode poetically. Wind rushed past and she found it entirely glorious. Thrills tingled across her thighs and up her spine.

At a juncture where acres of level land began its ascent to slope into a hillock, a colony of prairie dogs had built a thriving village. The small mounds of the entrance and exit burrows were concealed by bunches of lush meadow, and the rodents lived in peace and comfort. The resourceful mammals had no inkling that calamity was inescapably approaching.

Avis spotted the hazard a split-second too late. Pumpkin's right foreleg struck a hidden tunnel at such angle that its hoof went straight down. What transpired next was horrid. The yelping yap-yaps of a coterie of startled prairie dogs accompanied the screaming screech of the strawberry roan and shouted exclamation of Avis Lahay, who was soaring through the air like some crazed predator bird, arms flapping and legs splayed awkwardly.

A kaleidoscope of images mingled in her mind. The workhouse of her childhood and Peaches threatening her; the Suncurl Café of her adolescence and the relationships forged within its walls. The matron berating her; the hag becoming the nightmare face of the woman who bore her. Then, in a flicker, the truly compassionate face of her mother—that's what Avis Lahay saw when she hit the ground headfirst. Her body crumpled freakishly. Blackness encompassed her.

Liam Greer, notorious as Kid Greer, casually crossed the bridge spanning the Arkansas River and cut eastward down to Hog Creek. He slid off the saddle and led Daisy to the water's edge. While the speckled bay mare drank its fill, he knelt and dipped his battered old hat into the stream. He relished the refreshing coolness when he dumped it over his head.

He stood and shook like a dog, then yanked the hat low on his forehead. He wiped and finger combed the residue of sweat and dust from the untamed patch of stringy whiskers that obscured his features as effectively as a bandana. He stretched and waggled his legs as he had a brief look around. He withdrew the Smith & Wesson and checked the loads.

The sun was midway across the western sky, which was cloudless and as satiny blue as a fine-spun silk blouse. He holstered the pistol and mounted. He had another look-see as he reined Daisy to take an easterly option, following the winding turns of Hog Creek for a few hundred yards. He rode at a lazy gait, which belied the singularly strong resolve simmering in him.

Revenge and the prospect of shedding blood had him edgy with excitement. No worries or concerns troubled his mind because his trigger finger was itchy. The paralyzing fear of burning in hell was a measly undercurrent submerged in the visceral anticipation that exhilarated him whenever mayhem was nearby. He was zeroed in on the task of vengeance and before much longer expected to pocket a second ear as a souvenir.

His left hand jerked on the reins. The worn down old horse dutifully turned and plodded northward across a barren field of scrub grass. He meandered over the railroad tracks and came onto Front Street a block or so east of the Atchison, Topeka & Santa Fe Depot. Surveying the main thoroughfare of Dodge City, he wasn't at all impressed.

Kid Greer, a hunted fugitive with a five thousand dollar bounty on his head, slouched on his flea-bitten horse as cool and calm as a riverboat gambler with an ace up his sleeve. He stuck a chaw of tobacco in his mouth and chewed it around until it was soft and gooey, then adeptly using his tongue, formed it into a ball and slotted it between cheek and gum.

There was no hurry in him. He savored these moments when murder was in the air and he was the one in control. It was as though all else ceased to exist—it was just him on the prowl to provide fodder for newspapermen to write another batch of tales that would add to the lore of his legendary outlaw exploits which had already been publicized far and wide.

A simpering leer lifted the corners of his mouth and caused his eyes to become glassy and impassive. He pulled his hat even lower on his forehead and spat a streamer of brown juice that splatted on the compressed dirt of the street. He placed his hands on the saddle horn and waited, concentration narrowed and alert for any movement or clue. He was in his killing zone.

Avis Lahay had no idea how long she resided in the realm of unconsciousness. When she swam out of it her head was a spinning throb that made her nauseous and dizzy. Pain, a whirling knife blade between her ears, seemed to slash downward and stab at her right shoulder. She made every effort to focus, but all her surroundings were fuzzy and elongated.

A sickening clamor arrested her attention. She couldn't identify the source. She sat up much too swiftly; the result was piercing agony and a mouthful of sour vomit, which she spewed out in a choking sputter. A brush of breeze riffled her hair. She groaned as gasps attempted to fill her lungs. She squeezed her eyes shut and forced herself to breathe evenly.

Another spurt of acidic bile erupted up her throat. She discharged it. The squealing hiss of panting kept filling her ears. She wobbled to her feet and swerved drunkenly. Her eyesight had made a slight improvement; everything was still lengthened and distorted, but the blurriness was receding. She took several tentative steps in the direction from which the sound originated.

Her heart thumped wildly. Her brain, scattered and hardly functioning against the slices of razor-sharp torment, finally ascertained the appalling noise. The strawberry roan was laying helplessly on its side, huffing and whinnying in tortured shrieks. She cried out its name. Tears spilled down her cheeks to mix with the blood flowing from a gash in her skull.

It was then that she saw the skimmer clutched in her right hand. She found it odd that it was there, crushed and blood-covered. Her interest riveted on it. Her hand was claw-like and dug into the torn straw. Her forearm was cramping; electric darts radiated from her head all the way to the tips of her fingers. Her eyes went up her arm to see a grotesque sight; the shoulder was dislocated. The humerus bone protruded from the joint and bulged against her shirt.

Avis Lahay staggered backwards, then passed out in a grassy thicket.

When Sam Beadle exited the Alhambra Saloon into the afternoon sunshine he had an immediate destination in mind—the community privy. His kidneys had processed one too many mugs of beer without being tapped. He intended to deliver his wife to the City Drug Store, then while she was inside shopping he'd dash over and relieve the internal pressure. He was holding her hand as they strolled on the boardwalk, with Caleb Weitzel alongside them.

"Maybe next summer, Sam?" Abbey said, giving him a hopeful smile.

"What, next summer?"

"Visit *WT Ranch*, silly. We were just talking about it."

"I suppose it's a possibility."

"What do you think, Caleb?"

Weitzel nodded. "We'll plan on it, Abbey."

"As shall we."

"Glad that's all decided," Sam said, grinning. A crampy stab went through his groin area, which made him want to hurry, but then in surprising suddenness, the nape of his neck felt icy and prickly. He slowed to glance over a shoulder and became intrigued by a crowbait speckled bay, hoofs dragging and head hanging. There was a familiarity about the stoop-shouldered man in the saddle that bothered him. The rider picked his way along Front Street, swiveling his head side to side in an obvious search for something or someone in particular.

"We're here, Sam." Abbey roughly bumped into him, giggling in a musical tone. "We're here. Unless you're planning to come inside with me, you'll need to let go of my hand."

Beadle didn't respond at all. His attention was distracted and faraway.

"Hit him harder," Caleb suggested, standing beside him.

Just then, the City Drug Store door opened and a bell tinkled. Whitey Fitzgerald came outside, tucking several cigars in his shirt pocket. "Whew doggies," he said, eyes twinkling. "I be mighty pleased to see you folks." He click-clicked and reached over to gently grip the pregnant woman's wrist. "Any doings down below, Miss Abbey?"

"Do you have to be so uncouth, Whitey?" she asked, laughing.

"I just be concerned, ma'am."

"I know, Whitey. No difference from yesterday to today."

Sam Beadle had sirens blaring in his head. The straggly-faced man on the bag of bones horse was close enough for him to see deathly-cold eyes beneath the lowered brim of his hat. In a moment of recognition, Sam Beadle had no need to go to the bathroom. His tongue swelled, his scrotum puckered and all the fluids in him dried up. He knew he was a dead man.

Kid Greer pulled to a stop in front of the City Drug Store. The plug of tobacco made his cheek puff out like he had some disease. He leaned to the side and spat a dribbling burst, then took a backhanded swipe across his mouth. He shouted in a snarky voice, rocked back in the saddle, drew the Smith & Wesson, and in a flash two gunshots rang out atop each other.

Chaos rapidly became pandemonium. A thunder of running footsteps swirled up dust as bystanders descended on the uproar; there were cusses and cries for help. The first bullet hit Sam Beadle smack between the eyes and exited in a spray of brains, blood and bone. He would never see or hold his child; he would never again embrace the woman who changed his life; he would never see his novel published. He was dead before his body thudded on the boardwalk.

The second bullet slammed into Caleb Weitzel and spun him to his knees. Blood misted the air and he automatically clutched at the wound. In that frozen second before the gunslinger pulled his pistol, he had taken a challenging step toward the desperado. His teeth were now gritted into a grimace as he tended to the ragged hole in his left shoulder.

Whitey Fitzgerald was aghast, but leapt into action, click-clicking in sporadic bursts. He made an instantaneous decision that skewered him with remorse. Sam Beadle was dead; nothing could be done to help his old-time friend. The white-haired barber went to Caleb Weitzel and crouched beside him, endeavoring to curtail the bleeding with his hands.

Greer withdrew a knife to acquire the trophy he had been ordered to obtain. His face was cracked in a smirking grin and he was in the throes of demented laughter, which was muffled by the screams of Abbey Langton. He went rigid and smacked his lips. She stared at the delinquent ruffian—their eyes locked for a heartbeat. Her unfettered wails increased in volume. Gunky goo drooled from his mouth as he squirmed in the saddle, entirely unnerved by her presence.

A lineup of gawkers were grouped together behind Daisy. Kid Greer viciously spurred his mount and twisted the reins. The speckled bay bucked wildly as it screeched and snorted, then whirled around in the midst of infuriated hollers. Greer had no ear in hand; he was pissed off, but headed southward, hunched over the mare's neck to make a galloping getaway.

Abbey Langton was screaming at a fevered pitch when her water broke. The gushing rush happened as bloody gore from her husband spurted over her—fragments of bone and ooze were embedded in her hair. The shrillness of her frenzied outburst reverberated along the avenue. There were onlookers and much activity around her, but she couldn't fathom any of it.

"Get the doctor!" she shrieked angrily. She was on her knees beside the only man she had ever loved, having no memory of when or how she had gotten into that position. Most of the top of his head was missing, but in her rabid denial, his face was intact and smiling. Her hands were busy undoing the collar and front of his shirt, fingers fumbling with each button. "Everything is going to be fine, Sam. We'll get the doctor here and he'll take care of you."

A contraction went through the top of her belly. She ignored it. "I've already got the plans in place for where we'll go after being at *WT Ranch* next summer. We must return to the Dakota Territory. Put some flowers on Old Blue's grave. Visit our Lakota Sioux friends." Her eyes were glazed over and dilated, her expression almost childlike. "Yes, let's do."

"Abbey."

"Go away. Can't you see this is a private conversation?"

"Abbey." Deacon Coburn hunkered low and placed his hands on her shoulders. As gently as possible he lifted her up and hugged her. She twisted around and glared at him, then threw a roundhouse punch that hit squarely on his chin. Even though it was undisguised, he did nothing to block it; his head jerked back, but he held on tight. She flailed against him, fists pounding his chest. He allowed her to vent, took the beating and never said word.

Another contraction struck her. She gasped and winced. Her assault petered out and she buried her face against him. She sobbed, then shaky and trembling, leaned back and looked him full in the face, tears flooding down her pale and blotchy cheeks. She glanced down at the corpse of her husband. Her brow furrowed in sheer certainty. "My God, Liam Greer killed Sam," she said, harried and breathless. She convulsed against him. "And our baby is coming."

Meanwhile, at *WT Ranch* there were no concerns or any sense of urgency. Everything was proceeding slowly and naturally; perhaps too slowly. Sally Twosongs had her shoulders propped on pillows against the head of the bed. Twenty minutes ago, labor pains had been intense and getting closer together, but now were stalled to a standstill.

"I'm sorry."

"For what?"

Sally Twosongs looked at her mother-in-law and shrugged in discouragement. "It was all going along so well, then nothing. It seems this baby is never going to be born."

"Don't be silly." Eliza Weitzel stood and went to the window to draw the curtain all the way open. The bright rays of the afternoon would soon fade to gray as the sun dipped below the mountaintop. A supply of candles and oil lamps were assembled in readiness at strategic places around the room. She returned to the chair beside the bed and sat, hands folded on her lap.

"Was it this way for you?" Sally Twosongs asked softly.

Eliza frowned, head tilting. "That was a long time ago."

"Longer than your memory?"

"Of course not."

"Did you have false starts?"

"I suppose at the beginning it was hit and miss," Eliza replied, eyebrows rising. "What I remember most is the anticipation and excitement, then the waiting and waiting and waiting. The actual labor turned difficult and chancy. I had a real hard go of it, Sally Twosongs."

"Will I?"

"I think not, sweetheart."

"It's all in the Creator's hands, however it goes."

"Faith is all about having confidence that whatever will be will be, and by God's grace we have the hope that he sustains and supports us no matter what," Eliza said assertively.

Sally Twosongs smiled, thin and apprehensive. "That stance is what keeps me level and centered, but I must be honest. Just now I am missing Mother so much that my heart hurts."

"And you think that's not appropriate?" Eliza asked, brow furled. "Standing strong on faith never means that we must suppress normal human emotions, since doing so is ridiculously impossible. You would have to possess an awfully cold heart if you weren't missing Consuelo. And your heart, dear daughter, happens to be among the warmest I've ever known."

"Mother told me I was her miracle. An answer to prayers."

"For different reasons, I suspect my son would say the same."

"I should've never insisted that he honor the contract with the army," Sally Twosongs said, regret in her tone and on her face. "After the news about Mother, he wanted to cancel it via a telegram, but I was adamant that he follow-through on it. I wish he was here."

"I'm sure that you have been on his heart the whole while."

"As he has been on mine."

Naomi Axler breezed into the room. "Any changes happening here?"

"Just girl talk."

"And me playing a second guessing game," Sally Twosongs added chirpily.

"So I'll settle in for the long haul," Naomi said, taking a seat. "I went onto the porch for some fresh air and I can tell you that you've got quite a vocal cheering section. Pete and Hans have requested updates in twenty minute intervals, which I did not agree to provide. Jesse and Amanda, on the other hand, just want to know whether the baby is a boy or a girl."

"That fact may be unknown until tomorrow or later."

"I think not, Sally Twosongs," Eliza chided, shaking her head. "My guess is that the next time the contractions begin, which could be at any moment, it will be a quick delivery."

"That'd certainly be a welcome scenario."

Naomi nodded pleasantly. "Stay positive, Sally Twosongs."

"I am trying. What was your labor like, Naomi?"

"The first time, exactly how Eliza just described," Naomi replied, crossing her legs and swishing out her skirt. "I had a round of contractions in the early evening, which lasted ten minutes or so. About an hour later there was a flurry of pressure and discomfort, then whoosh, a few big pushes, and our son was on my tummy while Pete cut and tied the umbilical cord."

"Pete delivered Jesse?" Eliza asked, eyes widened in surprise.

"Amanda, too. He insisted and wouldn't hear otherwise." Naomi chuckled and glanced over her shoulder. She leaned forward and in a secretive voice said, "His reasoning was that because we made them together we would birth them together and raise them together."

"Hard to argue with him, I suppose."

"True enough as far as it goes, Eliza," Naomi said, almost glibly. "Pete's a most difficult man to quarrel with on any subject or circumstance." She stood and took a few steps. "I just had a thought. If I were to go and brew a fresh pot of Arbuckle's, my suspicion is perhaps the baby will seize the chance to interrupt me and begin some serious squirming to get out here."

Sally Twosongs forced a bit of taut laughter. "It's a good plan, Naomi." She watched her depart, then adjusted forward to fluff and scrunch a pillow. She moved around some, but the awkwardness of it frustrated her. Try as she might, no position could be found to achieve even the slightest comfort. Her eyelids shuttered shut and the tiniest of smiles touched her lips. In her mind, prayers were sent heavenward in the delicate notes of a flute.

Kid Greer was riding like a maniac. After the initial southward dash, in which he drew attention by howling as he crossed the bridge, he utilized a ploy meant to convince the posse that he continued in that direction, but in fact, he had darted east and followed the Arkansas River for a few miles. After fording at a shallow point, he was now riding northwest.

So far Daisy had been steady and strong, but he could feel the mare flagging beneath him. The strenuous exertions had its coat sweated and its lungs straining like leaky bellows. He eased it to a walking pace, not so much to give it a rest, but rather, so he could sit back in the saddle to take time to ruminate and consider laying low or disappearing in wild country.

The speckled bay responded with a grateful whinny. He turned in the saddle. A smirk bent his lips as he checked his back-trail and slow-dragged his eyes across the countryside. All was as it should be. He was confident that his ruse had worked—miles away, a cloud of dust stirred up by a large detachment of riders, was moving southerly.

He relaxed and allowed the horse to take an even more leisurely gait. The animal blew and bobbed its head. Its breathing was rasping, but as it strode unhurriedly, the raggedness began to subside. Greer yawned and slobber leaked over his chin. He spat out the hunk of tobacco. Gummy juice dribbled through his whiskers and he didn't bother swiping it away.

"Abbey is pregnant," he muttered in awe. "That should be my baby."

His shoulders slouched lazily. He remembered an incident from the night he met her. He had escorted her to her room at Drovers Cottage in Abilene. In his recollection, she didn't resist his advances, smash a knee into his crotch, or pull a derringer on him. She received him with a moist kiss and led him inside. She took him to bed where he put his brand on her.

The carnal imaginings mixed with the exhilaration of the kill to make his blood rise. It was an enjoyable sensation that distracted and entertained him for a few hundred yards, but then, a noise or movement or something jarred him out of his delightful reverie. His eyes were wide and he was on alert. He searched near and far, and listened intently. There was nothing to see or hear on the plains except the breeze sporadically rippling through the grass.

He sloughed it off and tried to recreate the bliss that had heated him from the inside out. He wanted to recapture the detached ecstasy that overcame him whenever murder flamed from the barrel of his gun, and have that rapture blend in with the surge of arousal, but alas, those feelings were gone. All that remained in the wake was shame and guilt.

Greer cursed under his breath, cringing against the humiliation rising in his craw; it coupled with an intense detonation of raw fear, which unraveled him. He was undone and in an oddly real daze. His flesh burned and the putrid stench of perdition seethed in his nostrils. *Obey or be devoured.* His fists clenched and tightened on the reins so tensely that Daisy halted.

Eternal torment pranced before his eyes, while tongues of flames hungrily gobbled at him. Sulfur and brimstone desolation was everywhere. He yearned to run away, but his feet were trapped on the molten terrain. He was choking and cussing in the netherworld of agonized souls where bonfires blazed from the sky and there was no relief from asphyxiating soot and noxious gases. Many other tortured prisoners were writhing and bawling all around him.

The red-skinned devil—pointy ears, horns and a goatee—clip-clopped toward him on cloven hooves. His pitchfork was thrust forward in a fuming rage. He grinned, triumphant and proud. His forked tongue slithered over the glistening daggers of his teeth. Greer buried his face in his hands and wanted to escape, but the occult affliction held him captive.

The fright in him had powerful jaws clamped around his intestines. Legions of imps and goblins encircled him, screeching and salivating. The clamor of their voices stridently shredded his eardrums. Then, in a brutal fit of pulsating shakes, he was released from the apocalyptic phenomenon, crying and perspiring profusely. He trembled and listed in the saddle.

"Please, Jesus," he murmured hastily. "I don't want to burn in hell." He was baffled and indecisive as to his whereabouts. "I don't want to burn in hell, dear Jesus." He blinked repeatedly so as to accelerate the evaporation of tears, but the ducts were still producing a flow. He lifted his hat and dragged a hand over his brow and through his hair, sighing despairingly.

He grit his teeth and outlasted the inexplicable disorientation, then scouted the area. His vision was bleary, but he had the ability to determine that the landscape surrounding him was grassland prairie, yet the imps and goblins of hell were still shrieking. His head cocked to a weird tilt. He pushed up in the stirrups, eyes narrowing and face flinching.

Realization gripped him. The sound he heard wasn't residual echoes from the waking nightmare, but rather, it came from the base of a gradual slope in the distance. He gave Daisy's rump a slap, and the mare jumped to a trot. Greer was extremely wary. His pushed his hat up his forehead and stretched his eyes to investigate nooks and crannies in every direction.

When he saw what was raising the ruckus, he pulled up and slipped to the ground. A strawberry roan was bleating in anguish, its right foreleg stuck upward at a ninety degree angle. The poor beast incited pity in him. He cautiously approached it, withdrew his knife and knelt. He placed a hand over its bulging eye and slit its throat to put it out of its misery. Blood squirted on his shirt and pants as he weighted it down until its struggle for life was no more.

A lone prairie dog poked its head up, irately yapped at him for thirty seconds or so, then returned to its burrow. He sheathed the knife as he stood. He had a look around for the dead horse's rider. In doing so, he admired the ingenuity of the rodents for having entrenched the colony's mounds in tufts of meadow. He turned around, eyes searching and probing until he came upon an unconscious woman in a small gully hedged by tall grass.

He sped to her and hunkered low, and was slam-bang flabbergasted. She had a familiarity that stunned him. He was forcibly drawn to her. That numbing realization knotted his stomach as a shiver passed over him. He gingerly touched her cheek. "Who are you?"

He removed a crumpled skimmer from her tenacious grip and tossed it aside. There was blood clotted in her hair along with continuing seepage from a jagged wound almost dead center at the top of her head. She wore the no-frills trappings of a ranch-hand, but even sickly pale and injured, her beauty could not be denied. He studied her and asked again, "Who are you?"

Her right shoulder was an ugly mess. A shard of pain dug in behind his eyes. He put a finger under her nostrils and felt faint breathing. He pressed an ear against her chest and heard a thready heartbeat. Squatting on his heels, he bopped forward on the balls of his feet and racked his brain. He concluded that she reminded him of a photograph he had seen, but in his current dilemma, couldn't figure why he sensed a sort of kinship. "Who are you, woman?"

He pressed his hands together and in an instant of clear-eyed sober-ness, came to a decision and it was one of the risky kind. He sucked in a lungful and braced himself, then got his arms under her to hoist her up. His feet had to be quick and agile to prevent toppling over. He carried her to his horse, tottering in a wobbly gait. It took prodigious effort for him to heave into the saddle with her balanced in front of him, but somehow, he accomplished the task.

"Go Daisy," he said in a grunt. His intention was to do whatever was necessary to get the woman medical assistance in Dodge City. To that goal, he guided the speckled bay south, urging it with heels to its haunches. The old mare snorted and took off at an audacious clip. It still had the guts and courage for such runs, but age and miles had stolen its stamina and durabil-ity. In defiance, Kid Greer pushed the horse faster and faster.

And even faster.

At the City Drug Store, Abbey Langton was in duress. She had been carried inside and was now flat on her back on a narrow table, which was just wide enough for her backside. Her shoes, stockings and undergarments were in a heap on the floor. Her knees were pulled up and her dress hitched over them like a tent. She thought it peculiar that her bare feet were cold.

There were three men in the room with her; Deacon Coburn, Whitey Fitzgerald, and the bug-eyed pharmacist. Discomfort pressed down on her abdomen, but she was weathering it. She bit the inside of her bottom lip against the goosepimply embarrassment of her exposed privates. Her vocal cords were frayed and sore from the ferocious screams that came when her husband's brains were blown out. When she spoke her voice was a grating croak.

Coburn was at the front of the store, ever watchful. Word had been sent and he was awaiting news as to the doctor's arrival. He had Butch Mackenzie in sight. The bespectacled town grump was on the street duck-waddling toward him as fast as his stubby legs could go. His cheeks were ruddy, his expression pinched tighter than a moneygrubber's purse strings.

Coburn cracked the door open. "What is it, Butch?"

"Huh. The doc ain't going to make it. He's on rounds in the country."

Coburn's mouth twitched, grimness gathering in the wrinkles of his brow. He shouldered the door shut and guardedly made eye contact with the diminutive barber. "You heard?"

"I got this," Whitey said with a nod, click-clicking confidently.

Coburn strolled over and took a knee behind his daughter. His head was level with hers. He put his hands on her upper arms. "Stay strong, Abbey. Everything will work out fine."

"Why? Why'd this happen? Why was Sam killed?"

"I can't say."

"Can't say?"

"There ain't no explanation for evil, Abbey."

"Liam Greer needs to hang."

"Sooner or later he'll likely dance at the end of a rope."

She tensed in pain. "I can't do this, Deacon."

"Yes, you can."

"No, you don't understand. I can't. Not without Sam."

"You have no choice, Abbey."

She swallowed, which caused her lips to clamp shut because of the inflammation in her throat. Her hands were fidgety and restlessly on the move. She fingered hair off her forehead and felt dried blood and gunk that a short while ago was enclosed inside her husband's head. Curdled nausea spurted upward and her face cramped into a grimace.

She was scared and she didn't know what to do with the overwhelming nature of the fear. The unconstrained thoroughness of it shocked her—she rationally understood that her anatomy was perfectly formed for the natural function of childbirth, but the horrifying idea that all her innards would spill out with the baby was an exaggerated riptide troubling her mind.

A twinge went through her pelvis. She tried shifting, but quit when taking a fall off the table seemed quite plausible. She listened to Whitey's erratic click-clicks, but couldn't see him because he was crouched low behind the barrier of her dress. The rail-thin pharmacist, however, stood in plain view holding towels and staring at her lady parts. She wondered why he was there—he was a nice enough man, but appeared inept and hopelessly out of place.

Her eyes closed as a contraction roiled her midsection. Air hissed through clenched teeth. The downward force arched her back and ignited eager anticipation. Her tongue felt thick and gluey, and her first inclination was to push, but an inner admonition compelled her to resist the impulse. Instinct made her know that it was not yet the fullness of time.

At *WT Ranch*, contractions were being timed at three minutes apart. The afternoon was growing old; frail colors of twilight were casting longish shadows on the floorboards. All the candles and oil lamps had been lit, which created a cheery aura that glowed like a bubble against the ceiling. Sally Twosongs remained with her shoulders on pillows; Eliza Weitzel and Naomi Axler were on either side of the bed musing over recent happenings while waiting.

"Forgive me," Eliza said, laughing lightheartedly. "The idea of Pete being accused of robbery and thrown in jail is incredible. Talk about silliness. How badly was he hurt?"

Naomi shrugged. "He's plenty bruised, but will recuperate sure enough."

"Life certainly can be quirky."

"Ouch." Sally Twosongs flinched and fisted her hands until the spasm passed. She rolled with each labor pain and prepared for the exact moment to get into the kneeling position.

"Incrementally closer," Naomi reported calmly. She had no timepiece, but her acumen and intuition was dead-eyed accurate. "It's slow going, though that could be for the best."

"It'll be soon now," Sally Twosongs said, eyebrows crinkling.

"What's different? What are you feeling?" Eliza asked keenly.

"Nothing different, really. I just know."

Eliza smiled, gentle and shrewd. "No worries now?"

"No. Some anxiousness, but mostly, I'm at peace."

"As you should be, Sally Twosongs." Naomi placed a hand on her shoulder and patted caringly as she bent to plant a supportive kiss on her forehead. "I have a word from Isaiah for you: *Fear thou not; for I am with thee: be not dismayed; for I am thy God: I will strengthen thee; yea, I will help thee; yea, I will uphold thee with the right hand of my righteousness.*"

"Thank you. I receive it and believe it."

"Yes, thank you, Naomi. An excellent reminder at this hour," Eliza said, sitting forward. The faint lines of age around her eyes were puckered and especially noticeable. "Fear, especially the unreasonable or irrational variety, can be a severe detriment in times such as these."

"Fear is frequently a useless emotion," Sally Twosongs stated bluntly. "Caleb and I have often discussed the nature and ramifications of fear. On more occasions than can be counted, we've encouraged each other with this verse: *There is no fear in love; but perfect love casteth out fear: because fear hath torment. He that feareth is not made perfect in love.*"

Eliza nodded agreeably. "That is indeed a rare piece of truth."

"One that sustains me whenever doubt strives for the upper hand," Sally Twosongs said firmly. Another contraction came, having about the same vigor as the past two. She sat up and gulped several shallow breaths, then exhaled in a whistle. When the pang ended, she relaxed contentedly on the pillows, secure in the knowledge that soon she would be a mother.

In front of the City Drug Store, Butch Mackenzie sat on the edge of the boardwalk, his legs sticking out straight. He was a nervous bundle of anxiety and anger, on the verge of tears and unable to cope or channel his emotions in any constructive way. A stump of a cigar was being chewed from one corner of his mouth to the other and back again.

A few stragglers were milling around replaying the news about what Kid Greer had done, and gossiping about proceedings within the retail establishment, but no one ventured close to the Western Union agent. He was entirely alone inside the panic-stricken ravings of an imagination deformed by year upon year of harrowing sorrow.

All Mackenzie could think of was tragedy and death—his dead wife, dead daughter, dead granddaughter. And a son-in-law who had found an instant solution to the conundrum of loss and agony. As the slobbery chub of tobacco went back and forth, Mackenzie pondered the basic mechanics of suicide and concluded that it would be ever so simple and swift.

Darkness, blacker than the deepest pit of despair, dragged him down into its abyss. He felt its oppressive weight close off his lungs; he heard its whispery promise of freedom from struggle; he tasted its sweetness on his tongue like honey; he saw the all-encompassing gloom of oblivion and succumbed to its embrace. He knew what needed to be done.

There was a handgun in a lower drawer of his desk at the office. He would get it and put it to good use. He teetered to his feet and took a few shaky steps, then pain the size of his chest cut through his torso like lightning. He gasped and in doing so almost swallowed the cigar. He spat and sputtered it out as he doubled over and plunged into the street.

Dust filled his mouth and nostrils. The darkness purred to him, drawing him deeper into its cavernous sphere. He was floating and floating, and it was warm and soothing. He wanted the sensation to last until time was no more, but then, all of that changed instantaneously. He was frigid and no longer floating; he was in a full-blown freefall with the ground rushing at him.

Clarity flickered in the whirlwind of blackness, and his arms and legs pumped crazily in resistance to gravity—it wasn't the ground that would break his fall, but rather, the grim reaper of death awaited him. He cried out in guttural grunts as a vivid realization that life was precious diverted him. The smiling face of Abbey Langton pressed on his mind. He stopped cold.

Something was clogging up his throat and he was having difficulty breathing. He came to in a blinking fit of choking to find himself face down in the thoroughfare with a mouthful of dirt on his tongue. He used his fingers to scoop it away, then rolled over and lay on his back, eyes staring skyward. The cloudless blue tinged by the gray of dusk mesmerized him.

"Huh." He had been unconscious for an indeterminable interval. His head was foggy and eyes watery, his breathing so ragged and wheezy that the noise of it rang in his ears. He remained still while attempting to gain his senses. A disconcerting ache had taken up residence behind his breastbone; the throb tingled and radiated through his back and across his left shoulder.

He got on his hands and knees. A prickly numbness originating in the roof of his mouth stung like a wasp behind his eyes as he crawled to the boardwalk. It took strenuous effort for him to push to his feet. He stuttered in an unsteady circle and looked around to see that Front Street was all but deserted. He scratched at his whiskery chin and scowled in utter confusion.

Then he remembered. "Huh." He moved as though a jolt had shocked his posterior. He scrabbled to the window of the City Drug Store and pressed his face against it. He tried to settle his huffing and puffing so as to not steam the glass, but had no success. Even straining his eyes as hard as possible, all he could see was the back and broad shoulders of Deacon Coburn.

Off in the distance he heard the thudding of hoofbeats.

The Alhambra Saloon had become a center of activity. The body of Sam Beadle was stretched out on the bar with a raggedy old blanket wrapped over it. Frightened townspeople were huddled on the backside of the bar-room, murmuring and chattering. The gregarious bartender stood on guard near the door with a short-barreled shotgun cradled in his arm.

Big Bull Wallace had used whiskey to cleanse Caleb Weitzel's shoulder and was now packing the hole with cotton. "Muscle damage, but no bone splinters that I could see."

"The bullet went through. I was lucky."

"I doubt that," Bull said, taping a gauze dressing in place. "Greer put both bullets just where he intended. Yours was a simple warning to mind your own business." He had a gander at his handiwork. "As soon as it's do-able you need to have a real doctor patch that up. He'll likely sew in a couple stitches and use some ointment to see that it doesn't look to infect."

Weitzel tilted his head sideward. "Your doctoring will be sufficient."

"That'd be an unsafe call, young man," Bull replied, slumping into a seat across from him. "Let a sawbones with at a mite of schooling under his belt take a peek." He set aside his ten gallon hat and sighed loudly. "Unbelievable. Greer gunned down an unarmed man in the shank of the day. That was an assassination. You have any ideas as to what it was all about?"

"Not a clue. You?"

Wallace shook his head. "At least a dozen men saddled up to ride with Deputy Marshall Bell. He won't suffer fools gladly or put up with slackers, but I'll tell you this; there's not a tree tall enough or a rope short enough to give Greer what he's got coming to him."

"That's a more than fair assessment."

Wallace gruffly waved him off and took a swig from the bottle he had used for medicinal purposes, eyes glinting roguishly. "I'm just a cattleman from Texas. What do I know?" He had another drink of whiskey, then jostled his chair around so he had a clear view of the doorway. Doing nothing was not in his nature, but in short order, he would be in the thick of the action.

Twilight shades of pink and orange were painted along the western horizon when Kid Greer pounded off the prairie onto Paladora Street. His left arm was numb and cramping from the shoulder to the wrist. Keeping the encumbering deadweight of the unconscious woman securely perched on his lap was no small feat, which was accomplished only because his determination to do so prevailed over all other considerations.

Daisy also demonstrated perseverance beyond all measure. Its eyes were bulging as though a bloody explosion was imminent. The horse had nothing left in its tank a mile ago, yet against all odds, it faithfully kept galloping in mindless surges of energy. Its lungs were heaving, its mouth and nostrils frothy with a mixture of mucus and saliva.

Greer was puzzled and perplexed; mystified, even. His brain was praying that the woman would live, which had an absurdity to it that was senseless to him; *prayers for a rank stranger?* He had no idea who she was or how she had come to be on the path of his escape route, but was overwhelmingly fascinated by her, and as a fresh flow of blood seeped from her head wound and trickled down his whiskery cheek he pressed on ever harder and more single-minded.

His decision to rescue her had been made in spontaneity, but his motivation had no roots in any conceivable logic. His prayers for her swirled from that same bottomless unknown that provoked him onward. In transitory flashes he had the sensation that his instincts were straight and true, despite the fact that his defiant efforts were incomprehensible.

The speckled bay listed and almost tumbled when it made a turn onto Front Street. Its forelegs bent weirdly as its hindquarters careened in a lopsided lurch. Greer tipped dangerously and nearly lost hold of the woman, but reacted quick enough to gain a clutch-grip on her. He used all his strength and knowhow to will the steed into an upright gait.

Daisy gasped forward, its hoofbeats thundering. Blood vessels were popping inside its skull; the foamy lather amassed in its mouth and nostrils was dripping crimson. In a meteoric burst reminiscent of an Arabian thoroughbred sprinting for the finish line, the crowbait mare covered the final half-furlong racing faster than it had since it was a yearling.

Greer yanked on the reins as he came to the City Drug Store. "God . . . Jesus," he said in utter desperation. His feet hit the ground and he went to his knees, wildly clinging to the woman. She moaned, which was the first sound he had heard from her. She convulsed, and he scrambled to get his legs under him, but before he could hobble and hop to do so, his mount's heart ripped to smithereens as it collapsed in a panting mountain of horseflesh.

He froze, glaring in disbelief at the dying mare. "Jesus . . . God," he muttered as the corners of his mouth drooped in understanding. There was no viable way out of town—Dodge City would be his last stand. He stared at the woman's face and once more, wondered. He hurried onto the boardwalk and made crazed eye contact with a roly-poly red-faced man, then went inside. The bell tinkled and the door slammed shut. Kid Greer skidded in his footsteps and put the woman on the floor, while outside, a gravelly shriek tore the evening apart.

"Kid Greer is back! Kid Greer is back! Avis is hurt! Avis is hurt!"

"Kid Greer is back! Kid Greer is back! Avis is hurt! Avis is hurt!"

Butch Mackenzie was in a frenzied state of agitation. He ran on the boardwalk in one direction, then turned and went an equal distance the other way. He spun around in a circle and lumbered into the street waggling his arms and lifting his knees in a frantic high-stepping dance as the rattling wheeze of his voice continued to blare a pleading alarm at the top of his lungs.

In the Alhambra Saloon, Big Bull Wallace knocked his chair over and was across the barroom in giant strides. He grabbed the shotgun away from the bartender and hit the boardwalk. What he saw first filled his face with a confused smile. He sidled to the middle of Front Street to watch the portly Western Union agent seemingly caught up in a seizure of insanity.

"Kid Greer is back! Kid Greer is back! Avis is hurt! Avis is hurt!" Butch kept repeating the mantra whilst prancing and bounding about like an overgrown three-year-old. He was hoarse and winded; neither of which slowed or hushed him. His graceless demonstration was gathering a crowd; folks were poking heads out and emerging from where they had gone into hiding.

Wallace cuffed him on the cheek to secure his attention. "Where?"

"Huh." Butch's eyes were glassy and blank. He sputtered and wagged his head so rapidly that his jowls jiggled. He groaned and glanced around as though he was lost. "Where what?"

Wallace slapped him again. "Where is Kid Greer? Where is Avis?"

"Huh." Butch Mackenzie dropped to his knees, hands clutching at his face. He started squealing sobs, chest heaving. "Oh, my God! That murderous cur is in with Miss Abbey!"

"Kid Greer is in the City Drug Store?"

"Huh."

Wallace spun on his heels and strode down the center of the street. He broke the breach of the gun open and was pleased to see that both barrels were loaded. He took up a spot directly aligned with the entrance of the City Drug Store. While he readied for a shootout, more and more excitable spectators were coming together in huddles at various locales on Front Street.

Butch Mackenzie was on the move. He hitch-hopped on rubbery legs, arms stretching in front of him as though he was swimming. He fell, picked himself up and hastily carried on to his destination, which was the plateglass window of the City Drug Store. He flattened his face against it, huffing and puffing in anxiety as his bloodshot eyes tensed.

The door swung open and Deacon Coburn filled the frame. "I got Mr. Greer here and we're coming out. He's under my protection, so there'll be no gunplay." He took a step onto the boardwalk and surveyed the scene. "I'm walking him to the jail and expect no trouble."

"You're too trusting a soul, Deacon," Bull said roughly.

Mackenzie grabbed at Coburn. "Miss Abbey? Huh."

"No baby yet, Butch. She's good and strong."

"Avis?" Bull asked, wary-eyed.

"She's in a bad state, but Greer had no part of it."

"The hell you say!"

"Take it down a notch, Bull," Deacon demanded, eyes pulled tight.

"You want to mollycoddle a coldblooded killer?"

"The law, Bull. Ain't you a law and order man?"

Wallace paused, mouth puckering into a sneer. "I can bide my time." He targeted the gun at the heavens above and was as good as his word; until that is, Kid Greer came outside. Then, the cattle-baron went ballistic. "What the Sam Hill? You didn't disarm the maggot?"

"He's not a trusting soul, Bull," Deacon said, grim humor in his voice. "The street is full of those who wish him ill will. He insisted on keeping the pistol. He'll give it up at the jail."

"You accept his say-so?"

"I do, Bull."

"You can't save him, Deacon. He's blackhearted."

"Maybe so, but no one is unredeemable."

Wallace studied the outlaw. "You gutless yellowbelly scum!"

Greer grinned thinly. "Are you addressing me, you old fart?"

"Is there another yellowbelly scum here just now?"

Greer had his hands held at half-mast. He ducked his head and had a long look at the dead horse that he had stolen from a sodbuster in the territory of New Mexico. The mare had been a reliable mount for several years; it had carried him on many forays in and out of trouble. He licked his lips and fearlessly eyeballed the cattleman. "You want to pull on me?"

"An easy peasy proposition, punk."

Greer smirked and angled his head to the west to regard the sunset, then slouched a few steps toward him, hands still level with his chest. "You ready to die, old man?"

"I got a scattergun on you at short range, arsehole."

"I'll kill you before your trigger finger can tremble."

"Back-down, Liam. It's the end of the trail," Deacon said snappily.

Greer was all smarmy laughter, relaxed and freewheeling. "Leave it alone. Otherwise all bets are off, Coburn. I'll drop you and three others before my jig is up."

"Don't do this, Liam."

"Why the hell not?" Kid Greer asked coolly. "The old-timer with the shogun challenged me. One more killing ain't going to make no difference. I can only hang once."

Wallace was unmoved. "Come get it, you lily-livered bushwhacker."

"Put a cork in it, Bull!"

"Not a chance, Deacon."

Kid Greer set his legs apart. He scowled down the barrels of the scattergun aimed at him. His hands hadn't changed position. Time ticked slowly and the air became dense and heavy. The gunman leisurely leaned back on his heels, then began reaching for the sky, palms held upward, but in the split-second before he did so, the fingers of his right hand twitched downward.

It was the briefest and most miniscule of movements, but enough to elicit a reaction from Big Bull Wallace. He squeezed the triggers and gave him the loads from both barrels—the blast of buckshot struck Kid Greer square in the chest and hurled him into a backpedalling whirl that ended when he fell dead and came to rest slumped on the corpse of the speckled bay mare.

"Go to hell, arsehole," Big Bull said, lips curled in satisfaction.

Deacon Coburn's expression embodied sorrow. Moisture misted his eyes as a bedlam of shouts erupted from cloistered clusters all along the thoroughfare. There were an abundance of heartfelt utterances and mournful prayers accompanied by oodles of shocked exclamations in language that would never be heard in a Sunday morning meetinghouse.

In the afterclaps there was much discussion about whether or not Kid Greer intended to surrender, or was the raising of his arms just a gimmick to lure the cattleman into lowering his guard. Some said that Greer had blood in his eyes and wanted to partake in a glorious killing spree, while others were equally adamant that he had seen the light and willingly capitulated. A few even had the unmitigated gall to suggest that there was heroism involved in his death.

Truth is, only God knows for sure.

"Push, Miss Abbey."

Abbey Langton, with the roar of the shotgun still in her ears, clenched her teeth and fists to comply with the instruction. Her calf muscles knotted into rolling cramps. The small of her back arched upwards and her backside lifted off the table. Little yelps escaped her throat and her face scrunched as the intense constricting heaviness pressured her pelvis.

"Easy, easy, easy," Whitey said, click-clicking and chuckling around an enormous smile. "Almost there, Miss Abbey. On the next pain give it all you got and you be a mammy."

"I don't think I have another push in me."

"Sure thing you do. Just one more."

She tried to relax her breathing, but had no success. She was panting like Old Blue used to on hot summer days. Her head was tilted back and her eyes were focused on the ceiling. There were desolate and lamentable places her brain wanted to go, but she absolutely refused to give it access to any pathway that distracted her from the urgency of the moment.

She waited. Each second felt like a minute or more. Her eyelids squeezed shut and she filled her lungs in anticipation of the oncoming contraction. When it started her forearms jerked and she pressed down with every ounce of strength she could muster. Her husky voice peaked on a high note that pealed long and loud, then took a veering descent into a drawn out groaning sigh that gave way to crying giggles as she heard the vigorous wailings of a newborn.

"A healthy and hale boy," Whitey said, holding the squirming bundle high. "Ten fingers, ten toes, and all the other parts in the right spots. You done good, Miss Abbey."

"He's beautiful," she murmured, choking on a flare-up of emotion.

"Of course he be beautiful. He come from beautiful people."

"When can I hold him?"

"Give me a minute, ma'am." He knelt and busied himself doing all the necessary functions, chattering and clicking to himself all the while. The bug-eyed apothecary handed him two towels, then squatted out of her view. Whitey put one to use to clean her up, then folded the other into a swaddling blanket. "Here be your baby. I done my best for you, Miss Abbey, but the doc ought to give you a once-over when he's available. Now I has to see to Avis."

She cradled the sloppy and wet infant in the crook of her arm. His face, albeit squished and wrinkly, was a perfect replica of his father. "Oh, dear God, thank you." She held him close to her bosom, and through a film of saltwater and in a tone that was swollen and scratchy, told him, "Life is all quandaries and quagmires, my son. Quandaries and quagmires."

A strangled sob punctuated her words. She steadied her breathing and gently laid a hand upon his cheek. "You come from sturdy stock, Langton Coburn Beadle. Three surnames which you must carry well. I will see to it." Then, projecting a smile past an overabundance of tears, she added, "And you better learn right now; I do not tolerate any shenanigans."

It was then that the bell above the door rang, and Deacon Coburn returned. He moved stealthily through the room, eyes reddened and squelched into thin slits. His attention took in the situation with Avis Lahay, who was stretched out on the floor being cared for by the pharmacist and Whitey Fitzgerald, then he came to his daughter's side. "You are glowing, Abbey."

"Mom would be proud," she said, crying.

"As am I."

"Want to hold your grandson, Papa?"

"I do." He enfolded the babe in a vigilant hug.

"Is Liam Greer dead?"

"Yes," he answered as his jawline stiffened in distress.

"That seems fair and apropos."

Coburn pursed his lips and produced an unenthusiastic nod. "At the dawn of life there is death," he said, reverence in his demeanor. He studied the child's tiny features. His moustache lifted and his countenance got rosy in awe. He swayed on the balls of his feet and cooed under his breath. As he did so, his eyes glistened and huge teardrops burned down his cheeks.

At *WT Ranch*, Sally Twosongs came off the pillows. "The time has come," she announced, complexion fervent and shiny. There was no panic or fear in her, but instead, she had certainty and control. She moved with fortitude and purpose to the middle of the bed, where she got into the kneeling position and hiked her flannel nightgown over her hips.

No sashbelt had been strung from the rafters to assist her at the crucial contraction, so Naomi Axler supported her elbow and shoulder on the left, while Eliza Weitzel took charge of the same task on the right. The two women exchanged raised eyebrows and held their breath in unison, which reflected skepticism and caution because this was their initial experience in birthing a child using elements of the traditional Navajo way.

The bedroom was a place of peace and blessing, where calmness was to prevail in the midst of the miraculous. Cedar smoke wafted from an abalone shell on the dresser which gave the air a sweet and serene scent. The smudge had been lit by Eliza less than five minutes ago as she carefully followed the sacred protocols given by her daughter-in-law.

Sally Twosongs felt an enormous discomfort pressing down. Her head bobbed vigorously as she clamped onto her helpers and gently pushed. The pain thickened in her womb and lasted for so long that for an instant fear nipped at her, but she decreed it to be gone. There was tearing of tissue and sharpness in her groin. She gave a final exuberant effort and uttered a guttural exclamation that was a prayerful plea for the Creator's sustaining protection.

Naomi rapidly responded to the goings-on. She cupped a hand over the child's crown and guided a dark-haired, plump-cheeked girl to a soft landing on the mattress. "Oh, my!"

"Lord, have mercy!" Eliza said, eyes misty and excited.

Sally Twosongs beamed. Her eyelids were blinking away tears and droplets of sweat. She slumped back as the placenta was discharged, then in a harmonious soliloquy, offered petitions of thanksgiving and honor in the vernacular of her tribal ancestry. Her voice kept rising and falling until the ladies completed all the tying and cleansing that needed to be done.

Eliza, now a watery-eyed grandmother, worked quickly and tenderly, then swaddled the newborn in a quilt stitched special for this purpose. "Here, dear daughter, is your child."

"Thank you, Beth," Sally Twosongs said, smiling.

Eliza recoiled and a crease tented on her brow. "What?"

Sally Twosongs peeled back the edges of the rainbow blanket so she could peer into the baby's dark eyes, which were wide open. "You are Beth-suelo Twosongs Weitzel, the offspring of strong and noble bloodlines. A treasured gift from the One who does all things well."

"Lord, have mercy," Eliza whispered through quivering lips. "I am humbled."

"Miss Weitzel is a chub-chub, isn't she?" Naomi said happily. "So pretty."

"Yes," Sally Twosongs agreed, fingering the downy swirl of black curls. She stared off in space for several moments and recalled prophetic words spoken to her years ago, and repeated them aloud: "*Unto you a daughter will be born and it will be well with your soul.*"

Eliza frowned. "What? Who?"

"Charley Jondreau." Sally Twosongs had a faraway twinkle in her eyes. Her cheeks were flushed. "He told me that on the day I met him, which was just after I lost our first baby."

"He has an old soul," Naomi said, "and his foretelling was correct."

Sally Twosongs nodded thoughtfully. She pushed her bottom lip out. "The afterbirth must be buried. Direct Hans and Pete to do so near the storage shed in the grove of aspens."

"By all means." Eliza gave a wee shrug. "We'll leave you alone for a spell. After the men return from the digging chore, you'll have their company, along with Jesse and Amanda."

"I will be ready for visitors." When the door closed behind them, Beth-suelo Twosongs Weitzel wiggled and let out a gurgling cry. Sally Twosongs immediately shifted back against the head of the bed and bared her bosom. She removed the quilt and made a few more adjustments so as to engage in breastfeeding. The naked child latched on and suckled contentedly.

Midway through the sunshiny brightness of the next day, the stagecoach carrying Delores Solrizo and Brenda Hawkins arrived in Dodge City. Stace, exhausted and grungy dirty, was fast asleep on the older woman's lap and had to be jostled awake when the carriage came to a rocking stop across the way from the Atchison, Topeka & Santa Fe Depot.

Upon disembarking, Delores gave the teamsters a generous gratuity with instructions to deliver all the baggage to the Dodge House Hotel, then turned to her traveling companion and said, "Get a suite or a couple rooms, whatever is available. While you settle in I'll go find my daughter, then come back and we can all sit down and have a nice meal together."

Brenda shaded her eyes against the sun. "Thank you, Delores. You're too kind."

"Kindness ought to have no boundaries, Brenda."

"My resistance about returning to Santa Fe is wearing thin."

Delores laughed easily. "I certainly hope so."

Brenda held her drowsy son on her hip. "I'm going to soak Stace in a tub." She squinted and pointed off to the west where a photographer was making modifications to his equipment, and a boisterous crowd formed a half-circle that extended into the street. "What's going on?"

"Looks like a party or revelry," Delores replied, touching the brim of her sunbonnet. She gave a nod, then strolled in the direction of the hoopla. She was tired and thirsty, and anxious to give her daughter a stout hug and receive one from her. She didn't bother to use the boardwalk, but simply strolled along Front Street, which was not a problem because, except for whatever was happening in the distance, there was no traffic or activity on the avenue.

Her eyes never quit moving. She saw that the hubbub was in the vicinity of the Longbranch Saloon. She angled toward it, then as she approached, glanced past the assembled swarm to see the broad and straight shoulders of a valued friend. He was at least fifty yards away and his hat shadowed his face, but she could identify his distinct bearing anywhere.

A smile flooded her eyes; a joyful enchantment that was destined to be transient. She kept her pace, curious to investigate what had gathered such a rambunctious throng. She pushed past a ring of yammering folks, then stopped cold. Her heartbeat sped up as her eyes bulged. She gasped. Pain soared through her soul. Her legs weakened and she nearly fell over.

An open coffin leaned against the hitching rail. Inside the burial-box was Liam Greer; a crudely painted sign had been attached to a rope necklace and centered on his chest: *Kid Greer, Thieving Murderer*. People, as individuals or in rowdy groups, were posing alongside the casket to have their pictures taken, with the Longbranch Saloon for a backdrop. The photographer, a bulb-nosed man grinning toothily, was stage-managing the ugliness.

She stood gaping in disbelief, riveted to the detestable display. Her brain couldn't process the hideous circus atmosphere. It sickened her; a boiling tide of bile swelled up her gullet into her mouth. She spat nastily. Her head was spinning with shame and guilt; hurtful musings assaulted her and then, from within the inner maelstrom, she heard her son's words spoken in a dream: "*My choices were mine. I forgive you, Ma. You remember that, always.*"

The sentiment ignited a fuse in her that set-off an explosion. Delores Solrizo charged at the tripod that supported the bulky box camera and sent the apparatus flying, while in the same battering motion plowed a fist into the owner's most prominent facial feature. Blood was spurting from both nostrils before he even landed on the seat of his pants.

Surprised shouts of protest were suffocated by the undiluted fierceness that erupted out of her. She heatedly shoved would-be recipients of pictures away from the coffin. She kicked and scratched like an insane woman cut loose from a straitjacket. "This man is not an animal," she yelled, her expression beginning to twist and distort. "He was a baby once. He *is* a mother's son!" Her face became a disfigured mask of wrath.

Deacon Coburn burst into a run and hastily raced past those she was chastising. A gleam of shock showed in his eyes because he recognized the contortion profaning her appearance. He had been mugged by the deforming glower shortly after its description was provided by Delores Solrizo's daughter in hopes that it would no longer haunt her sleep.

"He *is my* son!" she shrieked, and the confession was still searing the air when she was encompassed by bleak unconsciousness. She hit the street in a thud and drifted through the past darkly. It was the eve of her eighteenth birthday and her father, mean and drunk, had her pinned down on the mattress; she was beating his chest, biting and clawing at him, but he finished the dreadful deed. Then, her legs were spread to give birth to a scrawny baby boy in disgrace.

The shiv of memory ceased slicing and stabbing at her, and her sensibilities came back in bleary impressions. Her body was motionless at the base of the pine-box. Her eyes flittered open to be dumbfounded once more. Coburn was kneeling at her side, and from the olden days of a life long gone, Big Bull Wallace was hunkered over him. Both were staring sadly at her.

She whimpered nonsensically and passed out again.

≈ ≈ ≈

Twenty minutes later, Delores Solrizo had recovered. Smelling salts were used to revive her, then she was given a shot of whiskey and a tall glass of cool water. There were other somber events and circumstances that she needed to hear about, and when Deacon Coburn elaborated on the details, she poured herself a second boost of liquor and drank it in a jerky swallow.

Now, hands locked together and stomach knotted, she struggled to maintain composure against worries that threatened to unravel her emotions. Disparate thoughts zipped through her mind like fireflies and there was no way to connect any of the darting dots. She sat vigil at her daughter's bedside in a teeny rectangle of a room above the City Drug Store. The window overlooking Front Street was pushed up, allowing an influx of fresh air.

Avis Lahay slept heavily, on her back and oriented upward by a series of pillows. Her head was wrapped in a thick turban of bandages. Her right shoulder was strapped in a crisscross pattern of tape, and the forearm secured tightly across her chest. Her breathing was slow and shallow. Dark circles below her eyes accentuated the paleness of her complexion.

Delores prayed, or at least she made every effort to fashion pleading phrases together to send heavenward, but there was too much confusion and disorder in her head; the lighting bug contemplations kept flying furiously. Her eyes were closed, her lips pursed. She shifted on the hard-backed chair, and vaguely wished for one of her bentwood rockers.

"Mom?" Avis murmured weakly.

Delores scuffled on the seat as if it had become a bed of hot coals. "What are you doing here, young lady?" she asked, putting on a brave face. "You scared me half to death, Avis."

"Myself, too."

"How are you?"

"My head aches all the way down to my bellybutton," Avis answered, trying on a grin that slipped away and stressed into a grimace. "The doctor says that I have a concussion."

"What do you remember?"

"Not much, Mom. They tell me the outlaw Kid Greer saved my life."

Delores, overcome by the tension and turmoil, unsuccessfully stifled sobs. "Thank God for Liam Greer," she whispered, tearfully grateful. "Yes, thank God for Liam Greer."

Avis wrinkled her nose. "What?"

"We'll talk after you convalesce," Delores said, mouth puckering shut. She moved over and sat on the edge of the bed to hold her precious patient's free hand. A chill shivered between them. Delores Solrizo felt lightheaded— she had knowledge of such a grand paradox that she almost swooned: The nightmares of terror that her son had scorched across the western frontier came to an end when, in a praiseworthy act, he sacrificed his life to rescue her daughter.

$\approx \approx \approx$

When the twilight strains of dusk were creeping across the Llano Estacado, Charley Jondreau and Max Dawson were on their bellies crawling, and had been at it for over a mile. The barren landscape of scrub grass and sagebrush provided little cover, so the going was slow as they used every trick and tactic; their faces were streaked and dirty, their clothes decorated with pieces of shrubbery and brush. They inched forward, all but invisible.

 The desert was quiet and still, and the evening had tingling coolness in it. Their senses were on edge; they had been tracking their quarry since picking up his trail at dawn. An hour ago, while riding along a ridge, Jondreau had locked onto Smoky Crowe in the binoculars. The Ute butcher was alone, settling into a natural encampment on the backside of a ravine.

They picketed the horses and mule in a hollow, then went about the task of gathering bits of camouflage and attaching it in a convincing manner. Now, close enough to smell the creosote scent of Crowe's campfire mixed in with substantial whiffs of tobacco smoke, determination coursed between them like some primeval breed of living current.

The moon was on the rise and stars were beginning to wink awake in the bluish roof of the world. Dawson had her Winchester at the ready, while Jondreau was confident of his prowess with his weapons of choice; six-shooter holstered high on his right hip and a superbly balanced throwing knife in a leather sheaf hooked on the same belt on the left side.

A boom-voiced chant disturbed the sounds of silence. Jondreau and Dawson pressed tighter against the sandy soil and eyed each other, communicating instantly and instinctively. Their wordless interaction lasted less than ten seconds, then they simultaneously went into action, wriggling as rapidly as possible while the song ascended louder and louder.

The partners had the same objective, and together, arrived at the craggy cliff that fringed the ravine and put eyes on Smoky Crowe, exhilarated and frightened all at the same time. The thrill came because the renegade marauder was twenty-five yards below them; the fear was the result of a malevolent presence of iciness that restricted them.

Unable to move or even breathe normally, Jondreau and Dawson observed the obscene rites of Smoky Crowe worshipping the Evil One. He sang a mantra incantation as he slit the throat of a goat and smeared its blood on his face and chest. He raised his arms and howled in a high pitch, then traced fingers through the stringy strands of his hair. He put his curved blade back to work splaying the animal and stretching it wide as its guts sloshed out.

The witch had prepared the counterfeit of a holy symbol and he used it with an ease that made Jondreau and Dawson comprehend that it was a well-practiced ritual. He impaled the goat on the sharpened points of the crossbeam of an inverted cross, which was planted in the ground and supported by a pyramid of rocks. He took a knee and reverently bowed his head.

When Smoky Crowe stood he had a leering grin of triumph plastered on his face. He tossed a smug glance in the direction of the watchers, then began stoking the fire. He piled sticks and deadwood on until the flames licked and lapped skyward. He proceeded to caper in a fluid hop-skip around the bonfire, dancing like a man possessed. He intoned warbling wizardry; the hex built note upon note until the crescendo became a bellow that blackened the badlands.

When the bawling roar climaxed, the power that imprisoned the pards dispersed. Dawson put Smoky Crowe in the sights of the Winchester—an easy shot. His head craned to a rightward slant and the milky sickness of his left eye pulsed unswervingly at her. She pulled the trigger and in that precise instant, Crowe turned sideways and disappeared through a portal in the air.

Max Dawson leapt to her feet and blanketed the campsite with lead, but every bullet from the rifle's magazine merely sparked on rocks or kicked up dusty silt, and the gunshots resounded as contemptible laughter. She grit her teeth and hissed huffily. "Did you see that, Charley?"

"No matter, eh. I will kill the dragon."

≈ ≈ ≈

~THE END~

www.ingramcontent.com/pod-product-compliance
Lightning Source LLC
Chambersburg PA
CBHW070838030726
47504CB00005B/1143